Breakfast in Bed

Eleanor Moran

sphere

SPHERE

First published as a paperback original in Great Britain in 2011 by Sphere
Reprinted 2011 (twice)

A CIP catalogue record for this book
is available from the British Library.

ISBN 978-0-7515-4549-4

Typeset in Sabon by M Rules
Printed and bound in Great Britain by
Clays Ltd, St Ives plc

Papers used by Sphere are from well-managed forests
and other responsible sources.

MIX
Paper from
responsible sources
FSC® C104740

Sphere
An imprint of
Little, Brown Book Group
100 Victoria Embankment
London EC4Y 0DY

An Hachette UK Company
www.hachette.co.uk

www.littlebrown.co.uk

For Kate, with huge love and huge congratulations.

Chapter 1

Waking up is the worst; those first fragmented seconds of consciousness where I try to glue the pieces back together, remember where I am. I don't just mean physically – the move from a skanky marital home on the outer reaches of the Central line to a posh pad in Shoreditch has its compensations. It's more about where *I* am with a capital I (and yes, I do realise it's always got a capital I). I've gone from smugly oblivious wife to shell-shocked single in nine gruesome months and I'm not remotely acclimatised. It's like I've been banished to a galaxy far, far away, without enough warning to pack so much as a spare pair of knickers and a toothbrush.

Enough. One thing I'm fast learning is that self-pity is fatal and on today of all days, there's no time for it. I propel myself out of bed, right foot squashing down on a half-melted Kit Kat I vaguely remember wolfing down when I got back from work in the wee small hours. I peer at the carpet, but not too hard, fervently hoping it's not an antique. It's floral and musty, and could either be a five-pound bargain from a junk shop or lovingly imported from a palace in seventeenth-century Siam. The thing about living with Milly is that you never quite know if you've got an heirloom on your hands.

I've got the interview of interviews today, a shot at a job that might provide some comfort for my personal life gaily nose-diving off a cliff. If I could win a place in Oscar Retford's kitchen, it'd make the years of dicing carrots and disembowelling poultry all worthwhile. I childishly cross my fingers as I stand under the shower, trying to resist the expensive unguents that Milly's left in there and stick to my carbolic own-brand skin stripper. I don't know much, but what I do know is that I want this job more than anyone else has ever wanted a job in the whole history of job-seeking.

I deliberate hard about my outfit, even though I've got another four hours to perfect it. I've only been here a few weeks, and my bedroom already looks like a junk shop, piled high with half a house worth's of possessions. I yank a mirror out from behind a leaning tower of boxes and critically examine my first attempt. I wish I knew if it was Oscar himself who'd be giving me the once-over. I'm not a total ho (if I were, I'd be a very, very unsuccessful one, having slept with the grand total of one man in a decade) but there's no escaping the fact that making myself pleasing to the eye would be no bad thing. Whereas if it's some spiteful female sous chef who's eaten her own body weight in pastry, she's not going to be impressed by the *Mad Men*-esque black shift I've just yanked on. Or maybe she would, I think, grabbing the stray saddlebag of flesh that's sneakily welded itself to my left buttock. Surely misery's meant to turn you waif thin? I've never been a beanpole, but the fact I've become an even bigger fan of the midnight feast than the Famous Five is wreaking a terrible revenge on my arse.

2

But is it just my behind that's on the slide? I stare critically at my face, wondering if it still actually looks like my face. You know how some women have those amazing cat-like eyes, all seductive and slitty? I fear that what I've got are dog's eyes, cocker spaniel ones to be more specific. They're dark brown and hooded, almost black. I'm happy to say that I don't have a wet nose and wagging tail to match. Instead, I've got one of those buttony ones – nothing elegant, but it's not one of those enormous hooters that leave some people's faces looking like Stonehenge. I'm not a ravishing Vivien Leigh-style beauty, but I guess being married left me feeling appreciated enough not to worry too much. Now that I'm alone, my face feels like a question that's constantly being posed to me. Is this a face that will inspire love again? If Dom met me now, would he feel the same traffic-stopping pull he did the first time round, or would I be nothing more than a face in a crowd? It's when I'm squashing it right up to the mirror in an attempt to establish if my forehead's got train tracks bisecting it, that Milly appears, elegantly clad in a pair of rose-pink pyjamas. They appear to have a corsage pinned to them, like she was expecting some-one to invite her to a tea dance at 3 a.m.

'What in heaven's name are you doing?' she asks, quite reasonably.

'If you didn't know how old I was, what'd you say? If we were on *10 Years Younger*?'

'What's *10 Years Younger*?'

Milly grew up being shipped around the globe following her father's naval postings, an upbringing that's oddly left her more unworldly than worldly. Many of her expressions are gleaned from the black-and-white films that her mother would watch,

3

mournfully nostalgic for England, and her knowledge of popular culture is riddled with glaring omissions. Our mums were school friends and every now and then Milly and her mother would escape to England and come to stay with us. I used to look forward to it for weeks, making charts of how many sleeps were left until Milly arrived and I'd have a fellow girl to square up to my two older brothers with. Her parents have since retired to some far-flung corner of Scotland, having made sure to set Milly up with this amazing flat to make up for their extended absence. I want to resent her trustafarian status, but she's so generous and lacking in grandeur that I couldn't begin to. Besides, a lack of financial necessity always strikes me as a mixed blessing: it must imbue work with a certain pointlessness, however much you slog. Milly's a case in point: she's as bright as a shooting star, but she's never found her mojo, professionally speaking. She's been interning at a series of charities for the last couple of years, but never seems to get past teamaking and on to something more permanent and rewarding.

'It's not on TV any more,' I say, peeling my sweaty cranium off the mirror. 'It was about people with yellow, tombstone teeth getting a new life. Now, what d'you think of this as an interview outfit?' I ask, striking a pose. 'Close but no cigar?'

'No, it's nice,' she says, head cocked quizzically, blonde curls bouncing pneumatically around her pretty round face like a cloud of bubbles. They add to that sense that she's floating, ungrounded – like a sudden gust of wind might snatch her up and take her away. Before I lived here and I'd come to visit, she sometimes felt to me like a dice, rattling around this cavernous space never quite rolling her way to a six.

'Is it too much?' I ask, yanking up the saddle bag and letting

4

it drop. I wonder how much it weighs. Perhaps it'll develop a mind of its own and start directing operations from below my left hip. 'I just thought womanly might be the way to go if it's Oscar in the hot seat. They always pick a bloke, so I've got to work any angle I can come up with.'

'The dress looks great, it's just . . . you don't look very comfortable in it. It's a bit like it's wearing you.'

I demonstrate the lift and drop action again, but Milly waves a dismissive hand.

'You can most definitely carry it off, there's no worries on that score,' she continues. 'It's more that you look like you're wearing a costume.'

I look again, observing myself from a critical distance. Sometimes my whole life feels like a costume I'm wearing, like I'm stranded at a creepy Halloween party with a load of swingers and no one will call me a taxi. But it doesn't end, this party, there's no going home.

Stop it, I tell myself sharply, there's nothing creepy about being with Milly. Dear Milly, I'm eternally grateful she's taken me in, that I've got her to come home to. Not in a muff-tastic lesbian way, you understand, more that if you work the kind of hours I do, it's hard to nourish your friendships. Trying to rattle through the last three months in three hours and three glasses of wine is more like a party game than a meaningful social interaction, so having the day-to-day contact with Milly is vital in making me feel there's a life beyond work. Without that, now there's no Dom, I'm not sure how I'd remember what intimacy tastes like.

'Now, can we have a moment for Oscar Retford?' Milly asks. 'He's criminally manly, is he not?'

'They're all *manly*,' I say cynically, thinking of the raft of megalomaniacs running kitchens the world over. Like the Park Lane hotel I cooked in, where the coked-up drunkard in charge would think nothing of aiming a skillet at any poor unfortunate who crossed him. Or the Michelin-star pretender who branded an underling with a hot knife in a fit of pique about a curdled hollandaise sauce (or a fish soup – whatever it was it was definitely less important than world peace).

'No, but he's seriously handsome. I'm sure there's a thing about him in a *Harper's Bazaar* I've got. Research can only be good.'

'You're right, but I know all the important stuff. Like the fact that he pretty much got Violet their second star single-handed.'

'I thought it was an Angus Torrence restaurant?'

'Yeah it was, but it was all down to Oscar.'

Oscar broke away from his media-whore mentor a year or so ago, a man whose cooking has been dwarfed by his multiple endorsements and television appearances. Torrence wasn't up for being dumped, not when he'd set Oscar up as the star attraction in his latest high-profile opening, so a bitter court battle kicked off, with Oscar eventually winning his freedom. The net result is Ghusto, which he opened a matter of weeks ago. Right now I'm a sous chef (second-in-command with a fleet of junior chefs to do my bidding) in a charming, terminally unadventurous bistro in leafy Richmond. Getting in at the ground level on a new opening as hot as this could really move me up to the big league. I'm so determined that I'm going up for a chef de partie post, a lowly job I haven't done for a good three years.

'There's no harm in knowing the goss too,' says Milly.

'You're right, you're right, I know you're right,' I say, quoting *When Harry Met Sally*, my all-time favourite film.

'I'll go and dig it out,' she says, then pauses, eyeing the chaos that is my bedroom. 'Darling, do you want a hand with all of this? If we blitz it, it'll be vaguely habitable in no time.'

'Oh, don't worry,' I mutter, ashamed of the squalor. It's not like me at all: my cooking station is like a laboratory, oils and spices lined up with scientific precision. I need to start accepting that this is where I live now. 'I'll do it, I promise.'

'I'm not being critical.'

'No, no, I know you're not.'

She gives me a sympathetic smile, then heads off to find the magazine. I hope it's going to be OK going from best friends to landlady and tenant. It's not her fault, it's not like she's suddenly metamorphosed into Rigsby from *Rising Damp*, it's more my own paranoia. I cast a guilty look at the scene of the Kit Kat crime, and then turn my attention to the boxes. 'Living room' says one, and I take a reluctant step in its direction. As luck would have it, the first thing I pull out is a five-year-old holiday photo of Dom and me in an orange pedalo, grinning our stupid, naive heads off. It feels as spiky as a porcupine and I drop it back in the box so hard that the picture underneath shatters (my dad in a chef's hat, brandishing a chicken breast on a skewer), splinters of glass flying off in all directions.

'Oh, fuck it!' I shout, way more furious than I should be. Milly comes rushing back in.

'Darling, what is it?'

I point into the box, trying not to cry, and she gives me the kind of all-enveloping hug that only a best friend can administer.

'I'm sorry to be such a grumpy self-obsessed old cow,' I say into her shoulder.

'Don't apologise, you're not made of Teflon! Anyone would be feeling this way right now.'

'I hate him, Milly.'

'Do you *actually* hate him though?'

'Mostly,' I say, 'but not as much as I hate her.'

'Oh God, we all hate her. I wish it was olden times and we could put her in the stocks and throw rotten tomatoes at her.'

'Tomatoes are way too good for her, think of the vitamins. Eggs, rotten eggs.'

'Mmm, lovely,' giggles Milly. 'They'd stick to those God-awful highlights.'

I force myself to smile, to pretend it's just a momentary blip. I know she loves me and that's why I want to protect her from the full force of my woe. Milly's never even had a live-in boyfriend, let alone a husband, and I don't want to scare her with the knowledge of quite how hazardous loving deeply can prove to be. That however much you think you know someone, the sky can still turn from bright blue to pitch black without any kind of extreme weather warning.

'Forget about her. Look what I found,' says Milly, producing *Harper's Bazaar* with a flourish. 'And it's far, far more revealing than we could've dreamed of.'

'Show me,' I say, grabbing it off her, eager for distraction. I've only seen a few grainy internet images of Oscar up to now.

'Admit it, he's hot,' says Milly.

'I guess,' I say, scrutinising the image.

Oscar's been photographed in his kitchen, clad in his chef's whites, arms folded. His gaze is direct, a challenge and a threat –

he wants you to know that he's lord of all he surveys. Those piercing eyes are an intense blue, screwed right down deep in his face, an unexpected contrast with the shock of chestnut hair that springs from his scalp. He doesn't look much more than forty, and yet his hair is shot through with a couple of lightning bolts of grey, like he's standing tall right in the eye of the storm. His face is angular and sharp, every line of it definitive. This is not a face that wants to pose any kind of question. As a package it definitely works, and yet it almost repels me. Even flat on the page I feel like he wants to dominate and control.

'And there he is *en famille*,' adds Milly, pointing to a paparazzi shot of Oscar at what looks like a garden party. He's flanked by an impossibly groomed blonde of indeterminate age, plus her teenaged mini-me, who's brandishing an enormous Chloé handbag like it's a deadly weapon.

'Ooh, actually it's way more complicated than that. Listen.' Milly begins reading aloud. '"His surprise separation two years ago from his coolly elegant wife of twenty years caused shock waves throughout their close-knit group of culinary movers and shakers. Not only were the couple said to have one of the most envied relationships in London, but their domestic partnership extended into the kitchen, with Lydia running front of house for her multi-starred husband. Her move to Ghusto alongside her estranged spouse only goes to prove the depth of their connection. Some whispers suggest a reunion is something of an inevitability, not least for the sake of their mutually adored daughter, Tallulah."'

'How does *anyone* do that?' I ask, utterly nonplussed. 'How can they possibly stand being around each other? They've got to being doing a Burton and Taylor, haven't they?'

'Maybe they really do just still get on, just not in that way.'

A shudder runs through me as I imagine having to see Dom every day. I'm dreading the thought of laying eyes on him again, even though the idea of never laying eyes on him again feels equally wrong (a usefully unsquarable circle, I'm sure you'll agree). We've finally got a buyer for our shoebox zoo of a flat, and we're supposedly only weeks from exchange. Once that's gone through, there'll be nothing left to bind us, no trace of the last ten years bar a few photo albums and the odd present that I haven't been able to purge. Like the original 1950s food mixer Dom gave me for our third Christmas together. He always came up with a genius gift, thoughtful and specific, while I seemed to find myself running round the only shop left open on Christmas Eve at midnight, having got stranded at work. 'Merry Christmas, darling. I know there's nothing you long for more than a bejewelled festive waistcoat from Shepherd's Bush market.'

'But they must've been crazy about each other once,' I say. 'Surely having some horrible, cheap, knock-off version of what they once had must be gruesome? Every time you saw the other person, you'd be reminded of what you'd lost.' My voice has gone all high-pitched and screechy, and I grab my make-up bag to give myself something to do.

'Of course you still miss him,' says Milly quietly.

'I don't want to miss him, not after what he did,' I say, defensive. 'But you're right, I do.' I perch unsteadily on a box, brandishing a lipstick like a deadly weapon. 'I miss such stupid, pathetic things . . .'

'Like what?'

'How he'd make me breakfast in bed on Sundays, with proper tea you need a strainer for. Or how he covers Topsy's ears when people say Labradors only live for ten years, like she gets it.'

'Topsy?'

'His mum's dog. Ignore me, it's all nonsense. I'll be fine. I'm sure Robert Pattinson's getting bored of that girl's neck; it's only a matter of time before he turns up.' I give myself a mental shake, force myself to putty my puffy face with foundation. No one's giving a cry baby a job in a top-class kitchen, that's for sure.

'Amber, feel free to tell me I'm a blithering idiot, but are you sure, are you absolutely sure, it's dead and buried?'

I refuse to tear my eyes from the mirror, trowelling determinedly instead.

'Yes,' I tell her (and me) firmly. 'How can you ever come back from an affair? Every time ... every time he touched me I'd be thinking about him touching her. Every time he left his phone out I'd be sneaking a look. Once the trust's gone ... Look at my parents.'

'But they're still together!'

'Yeah, but they had three kids to factor in. And Dad's a bloody saint.'

I look fondly at the smashed up photo, smiling to myself at Dad's awful eighties hair. I think it must've been taken at a barbecue for my brother Ralph's twelfth birthday. I can vaguely remember begging him to let me have a go on the grill, even though I was barely big enough to see over the top. Dad should've been the chef, not me, but he stayed at home looking after us kids so that Mum could conquer the world (or at least conquer NatWest's human resources department).

'Mils, let's talk about something else. Honestly, I'm boring myself. Are you going on another date with the vet with the dodgy brown moccasins?'

Three dates have been had so far, and Milly is trying to work out if her antipathy is a knee-jerk response to the shoes, or evidence of a deeper incompatibility. But before the cost-benefit analysis can begin in earnest, my phone shrills out, an unfamiliar number flashing up on the screen.

'Hello?'

'Is that Amber Price?' says a clipped female voice.

'It is,' I agree, but she's carried on talking over me.

'You're due to see us at two p.m., but something's come up. Can you get here as soon as is physically possible?'

What would be physically impossible? Flying, I suppose.

'Um, yes, sure, of course. I'm only twenty minutes away if I scoot ... I've actually got a scooter,' I add stupidly, in case she thinks I'm using it as a verb. Not that it matters. Oh God, this interview's already a disaster and it hasn't even begun. I mime leaving to Milly, spraying a haze of perfume at myself and making myself cough.

'We look forward to it,' she replies, briskly replacing the receiver.

I take a last look at my ill-judged dress and jam my helmet on my head, trying not to worry about the potential for looking like the sixth member of the Jackson Five.

It takes me ages to find a parking spot, so I arrive even more hot and bothered than I started out. I afford myself a five-second pause, taking a peek through the glass frontage at the restaurant within. It's like looking onto a stage, the brightly lit cream room offset by a zinc bar that sweeps across the back wall. The walls are punctuated by the kind of modern art that is either absurd or genius, depending on your point of view (I'm from Stockport, so take a wild guess which way I'm leaning), and the glass tables look like they've been stolen from a 1920s Parisian salon. My cheap as chips dress feels like it might disintegrate the second it enters such a temple of chic, but nevertheless I force myself over the threshold. I feel like I've entered a war zone. Waiters are tearing around setting up lunch tables, chefs are hurrying in and out through the double doors of the kitchen and a cleaner is randomly mopping, threatening to upend the lot of them with every stroke. Of course it's frantic, but there's something more I'm picking up. There's a top note of fear, a mania about the way they're working. I approach a grim-faced waiter and tentatively put a hand on his arm as he races past.

'I've got an interview?'

As he turns towards me, I hear that same cut-glass voice behind me.

'And you must be Amber.'

Lydia's every bit as picture perfect as she looked on the page. She's no natural blonde, but her dye job's so good that you instantly forgive it. She's got that hard-bodied look which screams bi-weekly private Pilates instructor, and is wearing the kind of ostentatiously bright flowery dress that you can only get away with if there's nothing to hide (e.g. she has no worries about looking like a two-seater on discount at DFS). She's hard to age (late thirties, early forties?), neutrally beautiful in

13

a way that makes her face seem almost mask-like. I get the sense that she's got giving nothing away down to an art form.

'I am, yes,' I say, thrusting out my hand, praying it's not too sticky. She looks towards the kitchen, using her turn back to cast a sweeping look right across me. An illogical spike of shame hits me, a feeling that she can see into my deepest darkest recesses. How ridiculous is that, particularly because if we're starting with divorce, it's a stain we share.

'I'll go and retrieve Oscar,' she says, leaving me marooned in the maelstrom. But before she's halfway across the floor, he comes barrelling through the swing doors, whites doused in blood. Maybe they moved up my appointment because he murdered his 11.30? Lydia puts a hand up to stop him, but he ploughs on.

'Yeah, I can see she's here,' he says over his shoulder, extending a calloused hand in my direction. 'Come on then,' he says, jerking his head towards the bar. 'I haven't got long.'

He cuts right through the chaos of the restaurant, seemingly oblivious. I try not to scuttle, determined not to seem cringing and intimidated. You have to have way bigger balls than any man to survive in a place like this. I watch his retreating back as I speed after him. He's shorter than his picture implied, compact and muscular. There's something animalistic about the way he moves across the space, a jungle confidence that makes sense of the fear I'm smelling around me. I don't think I like him very much.

Oscar effortlessly swings himself up onto a bar stool and I try to do the same. Unfortunately I miss, boomeranging off the side, before sheepishly pulling myself onto it. I would make the world's worst cowboy.

'Drink?' he asks.

'Um, water would be lovely.'

'Really pushing the boat out there . . .' he looks down at the CV he's holding, 'Amber,' he finishes, giving me an unexpected half-smile.

'Can't see you hiring me if I ask for a tequila shot,' I say, immediately wondering why I've been so cheeky.

'Tequila I could forgive; bottle of 1974 Petrus and you'd be out on your ear,' he shoots back, turning those intense blue eyes on me. And no, I don't fancy him. I like goofy and shambolic – the kind of men who don't know they're sexy. Marmite men, basically. I feel a little pang, momentarily pricked by the thought of Dom's tight springy curls. It's a Jew-fro, there's no getting away from it, and it's not like he's got an epically handsome face to compensate. I think his gangly awkwardness has propelled him through life, it's what made him such a great maître d'. He's had to use raw charm to get everything he's got, me included, and he's got high from the challenge. Maybe Rachel came along when he needed a fix.

'At least I know what not to ask for on round two.'

'It's lunch service, so you can forget about a second round,' he says, all twinkle extinguished. 'So tell me about,' he looks down again, 'Byron's,' tone nose-diving at the very prospect of my response.

'It's one of the best places in Richmond,' I say, and he looks at me like it's an oxymoron. 'I've been there a couple of years now, and I like to think that I've shaken up the kitchen quite a bit.' Forget the oxymorons, I'm the only moron around here. He's actually looking round the room, he's so bored. 'I've radicalised the rota of suppliers we use, focused on getting the best of the best—'

'Genius,' he says. 'So apart from kicking the supermarkets into touch, what else have you done? What do you actually cook? Actually scrub that,' he says, waving a dismissive hand. 'You probably cook risotto primavera for twats in four-by-fours.' He leans in, intense. 'What would you *like* to cook? If I turned over my kitchen, what would you do? And by the way, I'm not going to,' he adds, glaring at me.

I look around the room feeling faintly desperate. I so want to unlock him, to prove to him that I'm the person he needs. Why, I don't know, considering what an obnoxious arse he is. Still, I can't bear to be defeated, not ever, but certainly not now. If only my brain wasn't pickled in aspic.

'Um,' I start, rather brilliantly. He's staring at me, hawk-like. 'The thing is, that's the last thing I'd want you to do.' He shakes his head in disbelief, but I plunge on. 'And I'll tell you why: the whole reason I'm here is to try and get the chance to learn from you. What you've done with all those off-plan cuts of meat is incredible. That pig's blood ice cream you've got in your book, it should be disgusting, but it's amazing. You've turned offal into an art form. Me and my ...' I breathe in. 'I saved up to take my friend to Violet for ... her ... birthday and it was honestly the best meal I've ever eaten. So if you tried to leave the kitchen, I'd hold on to your ankles and beg you to stay.'

'Lovely image.'

'I try.'

He tilts his face and considers me. 'You're either a complete bullshit artist or my number-one fan. Not planning on nailing my feet to the kitchen floor to keep me there, are you?'

'You're not a goose!'

'Sorry?'

'Isn't that what they do for foie gras?' Shut up, Amber.

Lydia sails up before he's had a chance to form a response to my idiotic remark. I'm going to be sautéing scallops in the suburbs for the rest of my natural life, I just know it.

'You need to wrap this up,' she says, quietly authoritative. 'The next candidate's here.'

'What I *need* is to get back to the kitchen,' he replies churlishly.

'Then you shouldn't have over-run,' replies Lydia tartly, casting me a look that makes it abundantly clear who's to blame.

My eyes flick back and forth, analysing the verbal ping pong. How fascinating is the dynamic between other couples? Human beings are fundamentally competitive, whatever we pretend, and I'm ashamed to say I'm more competitive than most. It's no wonder we pore over celebrity divorces with such morbid fascination, quietly enjoying the revelation that the galling, shiny *Hello!* version of the relationship was a sham, that our own imperfect unions aren't so bad after all. There have been points since the divorce where I've felt like some kind of exotic reptile, intriguing and repellent in equal measure. People long to know why, but they want to stand far enough back not to catch 'it', whatever 'it' is. PDS, perhaps: Precocious Divorcee Status. It summons up a complicated cocktail, even with close friends (bar Milly). I know their sympathy is genuine, but there's judgement there too. They want to know where I went wrong so they can guard against making the same mistakes, make sure they're not making them

17

right now. But the truth is that I can't reassure them, even if I wanted to. I know in my heart it takes two to tango, two people to break a relationship in half, but I'm not yet ready to look at my part in the two-step full in the face.

'Sounds like we're done,' says Oscar, admitting defeat. I don't know why, but I can't drop the eye contact. That tiny window I've got from watching him and Lydia has piqued my interest. Some mad part of me wants to understand the man behind the über-macho chef shtick, even momentarily, but there's no chance of Lydia letting that happen. She stands there, sentry-like, waiting for me to vamoose.

'Thank you for seeing me,' I say awkwardly, sticking out a rigid hand, like a prefect sucking up to the headmaster.

'My pleasure,' says Oscar, softer than he's been and maybe, just maybe, holding my hand a second longer than is strictly necessary. Lydia looks pointedly at the keen-as-mustard chef who's hanging around the front desk. She sets off to get him, and I say a quick goodbye, before beating a retreat.

'Hold up,' calls Oscar. 'You never answered the question.'

'Question?' I say, turning back.

'What would you cook, right now, if you wanted to impress me?'

Lydia's already greeting Keen Boy, leaving me next to no time to think. 'Coq au vin,' I say hastily. 'With tiny roast potatoes.' Oscar looks totally baffled, which is unsurprising considering I've come up with a dish that Mrs Beeton would dismiss for being too retro.

'I know it sounds ridiculous but the reason, the reason I cook is because of my dad. He's never been remotely cordon bleu or fancy, but everything he cooks tastes utterly ... truthful.' I blunder on, trying too hard to overcome Oscar's obvious contempt. 'Which sounds totally stupid, but what I mean is that he makes all his amazing ingredients sing up at you, right off the plate. He cooks with total integrity ... and I can't help thinking that's a little bit how you cook.'

'Trust me, you won't catch me dishing up coq au vin any time soon,' says Oscar coldly.

'That's not what I meant ...' I say, but before I can dig myself an even bigger grave, I'm interrupted by the arrival of Lydia, with Keen Boy positively skipping behind her. 'Bye,' I mutter, but Oscar can't hear me over the sound of her declaiming the highlights from his no doubt earth-shattering CV.

I get out as fast as I can, muttering expletives to myself like a mad old tramp. How could I have been so naive? It's all very well knowing what exact model of Chloé handbag his offspring totes, but it was never going to be his starter for ten. I feel a sharp pang from the knowledge that Dom would never have let me leave the house without a cast-iron answer to that most obvious of questions. Love Milly as I do, there's so much she doesn't know about me, about the world I exist in. When, oh when, will all roads stop leading back to this most pointless of destinations?

I'm such an ungrateful wretch. Milly's amazing, sluicing wine down my throat like there's a grape famine and doggedly assuring me that there are plenty more jobs in the sea, or something. It helps, it definitely does, but now I'm out the other side, I'm suddenly aware of how much I've built this job up. It's a bit like being asked out by the hottest boy in the Upper Sixth, before getting unceremoniously dumped on

19

Sunday night. Right, I'm boring myself now. I top up Milly's glass to the brim and ask her what the current state of play is with the brown-hooved vet.

'We must stop talking about him in terms of his shoes,' says Milly admonishingly. 'I'm determined to give him a proper shot.'

'Don't say that to him, he'll probably think you're going to tranquilise him. What is his name again? Neil? Neil the vet?'

'Don't say it like that,' says Milly, laughing. 'Hi,' she says, looking deep into my eyes. 'I'm Neil and I'm here to stifle your hamster.'

'Don't worry, a body this tiny can only feel a tiny amount of pain,' I add in my best Dr Crippen voice.

'Stop it,' says Milly, convulsing. 'Seriously, I'm going to afford him a Friday and see if there's proper sparkle when we don't have to worry about work in the morning.'

A mean bit of me wonders how much stress seven hours of tea-making can really deliver, but it's only because I'm dreading tomorrow's sixteen-hour double-shift spent cooking risotto primavera for twats in four-by-fours.

'I'm sure you're right to do that, but don't . . .' I struggle for the right words, desperate not to sound patronising. 'Don't force yourself. If it isn't right, it isn't right.'

Milly turns to me, blue eyes baleful, and I'm hit by a sudden wave of compassion. I don't mean that previously described bogus version that's equal parts self-satisfied condescension, I mean genuine compassion for the fact she's never felt true love, never known what romantic certainty tastes like. She had the obligatory three-year university boyfriend, whom she organically and politely shed after graduation, but no one

20

who's made her feel like she's got some exotic illness that makes you stick pencils up your nose and see the world in Technicolor. It's no wonder she's always trying so hard to scientifically prove if someone's right or wrong. There's no emotional litmus paper that allows her to simply know.

As I think it through, I start to wonder if that's better or worse. I'm no less single than her, but now that I know what the good stuff tastes like, I'm pretty sure I couldn't settle for the dodgy non-organic version from an Eastern European supermarket chain. Or am I a fool? If my darkest suspicion is right, that true love only happens once in a lifetime, maybe I should settle for something else while there's still time; mildly dishonest love, where you get the companionship and the chance of children without the same level of risk.

I'm pulled from my navel gazing reverie by a shrill peal from my phone. I peer at it suspiciously, wondering what unknown number is calling me at gone midnight. Gone midnight? I'm looking at a maximum of five hours before I've got to be up and dressed.

'Hello?' I say cautiously.

'Amber?' says an unfamiliar male voice.

'Yes.'

'I don't have long. Do you want the job or not?'

Now I know who it is: the rudest, most abrupt man in England.

'Of course I want the job. I wouldn't have come for the interview if I didn't want the job.' Now that was rude. 'Sorry, yes, I would love the job. Thank you very much for offering it to me.'

'You got lucky, the rest of them were a bunch of total

fucking numpties. I need you to start immediately, we're up to our necks.'

'I'll have to give notice,' I say, giving a thumbs-up to a delighted-looking Milly. 'I reckon if I really plead, I can start in two weeks.'

'One week or I'll find someone else.'

'Ten days.'

'A week. And you're on fish, so you better warn your boyfriend about the smell.'

'Um, I don't actually have one.' Why did I say that? It's a) completely irrelevant, and b) none of his business.

'Suits me, you can marry the job. Sort it and I'll see you on the twelfth.'

And with that he smartly hangs up, leaving nothing but a dial tone.

Let's just hope I'm good enough for the hottest sixth-former on the block ...

Chapter 2

So, it's week two at Ghusto and the hottest sixth-former on the block has so far uttered seven words to me: 'Fish Girl, move it with the haddock,' to be precise. He might've preceded it with 'Oi', giving me a grand total of eight, but it doesn't change the fact that as a chef de partie, I am officially small fry. His second-in-command is sous chef Mike, a sadistic Scouser with a heart of darkness. Right now, we're in the midst of Saturday night service, the busiest shift of the week, and he's pacing the stations baying for blood. Senior chef de partie is Maya, a fearsome Aussie who rules meat and sauces with a rod of iron. There's also pastry, overseen by an embittered French drunkard, Jean-Paul, and vegetables, the lowest of the low. Here resides Tomasz, a Polish commis chef who's been nothing but sweet to me since I arrived. He and Michelle, my commis on fish, are the ones keeping me sane. What's keeping me interested is a whole other story. Oscar's eyes are scanning the room, intuitively aware of how every cog in the wheel is turning. He's a ball of energy, a force of nature, and just for a second I can't quite pull my gaze away from him.

He's holding a slab of beef, slamming it down on the counter, demonstrating exactly how he wants it cut. I can't hear the words, but I can almost smell the cocktail of brilliance and bullying that he uses to try and drag us all up to his standard. He knows exactly what he wants, and woe betide anyone who can't deliver it. I'm still repelled by the brutishness of him, by his sheer arrogance, but it also keeps me rapt. It's probably a good thing I've only earned eight words: I know I'm fumbling things, failing on tasks I can do with my eyes shut, just from sheer nerves. Everything still feels so unfamiliar.

'Earth to Amber!' yells Mike, waving his sweaty hands in my face. 'Where the fuck is the bream? You catching it yourself?'

I've been gutting like an automaton these last two hours, but I know better than to answer back. 'It's right here,' I say, making sure it's perfectly prepped for his pan. Contrary to popular belief, it's not the head chef who cooks in these places: Oscar wouldn't dream of approaching a pan on a Saturday night shift. He's the gatekeeper, standing at the pass, inspecting every dish before it goes out. Right now he's on to a plate of lamb's kidneys, peering at them suspiciously like an antique dealer who's been offered a hooky Ming vase.

'What's wrong with them?' he demands of Joe, the unfortunate chef de partie who's offered them up.

I can see Joe's eyes flicking over them desperately as he tries to come up with a reply. Of course if he knew, he never would've brought the plate out, but that's so not the right answer. Oscar's gaze sweeps over him, blue eyes so cold and deadly that they look scorched. His taut body quivers with

24

pent-up tension. It's almost palpable, a shimmering heat haze that perpetually surrounds him.

'Are you just having an off night or are you a little bit retarded?' shouts Oscar, unimpressed by the silence. 'Look at that fucking parsley! It's like a tornado blew through.' He bangs the plate down on the counter so hard I'm surprised it doesn't crack. 'We're not in Kansas any more, Joe-Joe, get *back* to your station and start again. I'm not having that monstrosity going out with my name on it.'

'Yes, Chef. Sorry, Chef,' mutters Joe, backing away pathetically. You can almost guarantee that his station will be paying for his humiliation for at least a week. I risk exchanging a quick eye roll with Michelle, before we quickly turn our attention back to the oily mountain of fish.

'Table three have ordered the trout special three times. Get a wriggle on!' shouts Maya.

'There's only two left,' I shout back, crossing the kitchen to search maniacally through the other fish in case one's gone astray.

'Why the *hell* didn't you warn me?' she snarls.

'I told Mike, he was meant to tell front of house.'

Tactical error to sound like I'm passing the buck, but I really did pass the vital info on. 'Fuck's sake!' snaps Maya, storming off as I carry on my fruitless search for a rogue fish. As I'm crouching by the fridge, the swing doors almost knock me unconscious with the sheer velocity of one of the waiters barrelling through. I stand up, momentarily dazed, getting a rare glance of front of house. Is it, could it be?

Oh my God, it's Tristram Fawcett. A restaurant critic with a sharp quill and an exacting palate, he's recently been poached

25

from the *Independent* (well respected, small circulation) by the *Sunday Times* (monster circulation, bad review equals a weapon of mass destruction), and no one's noticed he's sitting right there on table three. Lydia would surely have caught it, but she's taken an unheard of weekend off (kitchen gossip suggests it's of the dirty variety). I only know it's Fawcett because he was a regular at my old joint in Richmond: he loved the simple, unpretentious cooking that defined it. I bet he'll loathe Oscar's belief that he can reinvent the wheel, and our inability to provide him with the trumpeted daily special is the perfect opener for a coruscating assassination.

I can hear raised voices behind me and just for a second I slip back to childhood, into my long-forgotten fantasy that if I can't see it, it doesn't exist. But as the volume peaks I force myself to turn around, locking eyes with Oscar for the first time since my interview. Jesus, I wish I hadn't. His gaze is like sniper fire, molten anger radiating straight out of him. He's incandescent, grimly hanging on to his station with his powerful hands.

'So you're meant to be in charge of fish, you do realise that?'

'Yes, Chef,' I reply as humbly as I can.

'Not much of a fish girl if you can't even add up a *fucking special*!' he shouts, hammering the station for emphasis. There's something genuinely frightening about him, that animalistic quality I spotted the first time we met. It's as though every emotion runs through his sinewy form as fast as it runs through his brain. I will not be intimidated. I refuse to be intimidated. Am I a mouse or a man? A chef or a Chihuahua? Sod it, I'm going for broke.

'All I ask for is back up,' he continues. 'If you can't even manage that ...' Before he has time to fire me, I jump in.

'I want to, I want to back you up and that's why you need to listen to me.' I can see a new wave of fury hit the shore as I interrupt him, but he lets me continue. 'Table three's not just any old table, it's Tristram Fawcett's table.'

'Fawcett's here?' he croaks. He's white now, and I'm sure I can detect fear coming off him, not just rage. It's less than six months since he broke away from Angus Torrence, and his own reputation isn't yet sufficiently established to withstand the kind of brickbats that might be coming his way next Sunday. I use the tiny window of shock to blunder on. I might be walking through fire en route to getting fired, but I'm not going down without a fight.

'Chef, I will get you trout. Please trust me, even if I have to scoop a fish out of the canal with my bare hands.' Where did that come from? Note to self: brain before mouth. 'Well, you know what I mean. I'll get it, if you can keep him happy for half an hour. Which of course you—'

'Christ, will you please shut the fuck up? Do your worst,' he says, waving a dismissive hand. 'Go on, get on with it. We'll spin out the starters and hope for a miracle.'

He turns back round to talk to the sous chefs, leaving me to grab my bike helmet from my locker and race out the door. I'm shaking, keyed up, determined to prove him wrong. I don't rate my chances either, but I can't bear looking like an idiot. He may have torn a strip off me, but I deserved every word. Or at least Mike did. I can't believe he had the barefaced cheek to let me take the rap. He's staring at me as I race to the door, most likely amazed I haven't dropped him in it. I can't face wasting time on 'he said, she said': the flesh is willing, but the plan is weak.

I jump on my moped, jamming the helmet on and zooming off across Clerkenwell. First stop is Pelligrino, an upscale Italian deep in the heart of the city. My friend Bruce is the head sous chef, and I know he's a big fan of fish. I've tried calling, but no one's going to be picking up the phone in the midst of Saturday night service. I arrive on the back steps, sweaty and helmet-headed. I've made it in four minutes flat. If Oscar can spin out the starters, this situation might just be salvageable. Bruce is nose-deep in a hare, the basis for a Roman special he's particularly proud of, and he's not too thrilled to see me.

'Bruce, I'm sorry, I know this is a total imposition but if I don't get trout I'm gonna be out of a job. Have you ...'

He embeds his cleaver in the hare's flank, barely pausing for breath. 'What do you think you're doing here? It's not bloody Tesco!' He softens, taking in my obvious distress. 'Let me call Jerry, they're all fish. He might be able to help.'

Jerry's news to me, but good news nevertheless. He runs a branch of a chain of mid-range fish restaurants back over in Islington. There's a heart-stopping moment as he puts down the phone to search his fridge, but the promise of a fifty-pound bung secures me my precious trophy. It's fifty quid that I really don't have, but I'll just have to eat Rice Krispies for the rest of the month. I virtually snog Bruce with joy (gay, so not gratified) and text Maya that the fish is on its way.

I speed down Upper Street, skidding through a couple of red lights before I screech to a halt outside Jerry's joint. He's an obese chain smoker, who insists on puffing his way through one and a half fags before he'll hand over the booty. 'Take a chill pill,' he smirks, knowing full well that this is an emergency.

'Can I go and get it myself?' I ask in desperation, before he reluctantly peels himself off the step and waddles inside.

'Thank you kindly,' he says, as I hand over my hard-earned cash.

How did I forget to bring a rucksack? Tucking the well-wrapped fish inside my cleavage, I leap back on the bike and floor it. It soon becomes clear that acceleration and fish wrangling are not a good match. It judders horribly, constantly threatening to make a bid for freedom, particularly when I slam the brakes at the sight of a police car. Let's hope that if it ever does make it to Tristram Fawcett's plate, he never finds out what a roundabout route it took to get there. Oscar's USP is all about provenance. I can see it now: 'We guarantee that all mains will have been lovingly nestled in a breast crevice no more than two miles from your plate before they're served.'

I park up and run in, pulling the fish from its comely resting place as I tear through the door. Oscar's darkly pacing around the stations, sticking a spoon into the various pans and considering the contents. He looks the exact opposite of a happy bunny. A suicidal hare perhaps.

'Trout,' I pant, skidding to a halt beside him, narrowly avoiding knocking Mike's skillet from the hob. He stares at me, taking in my red, sweaty visage.

'Sorry?'

'Trout, Chef.'

'Trout, Chef,' he repeats, the ghost of a smile playing around his lips. 'Don't even tell me where it came from. What exactly are you waiting for, Fish Girl? Gut the fucker!'

'I'm gutting, I'm gutting!' I shout, scooting back across the kitchen to start surgery. I've never worked so fast, adrenalin coursing through my veins as I cut in. I take it back over and he grabs it from me, barely turning to so much as look at me. Mike's poised and ready, but Oscar grabs the pan himself. I pause for a forbidden minute to watch, fearsome concentration etched into his features as, like me, he does everything in his power to make sure that last, lone fish delivers. He follows it out of the kitchen like a doting father sending his only son off to war, stopping to talk Fawcett through what it is that he's set to eat. I only catch a glimpse, but the chummy laughter that erupts from his table convinces me he'll be benevolent. Let's just hope the same can be said of Oscar.

I stay deep into the night, trawling through the fridge and freezer to ensure I know what's in stock, right down to the very last gill. Mike clocks me as he's leaving and skids to a halt.

'Practising your adding up?' he says, voice pitched like a primary school teacher. I grit my teeth, knowing I can't afford to be arsy.

'Just wanna be sure it's all in order. It is *my responsibility* after all.'

'Glad to see you're learning,' he says, grinning, face more slappable than you'd believe possible.

After he's made his exit, my rage gradually subsides. It's gladiatorial here, no question, but what I saw in Oscar tonight has made me all the more sure I made the right move. He cares about it, not just about the potential for stars and plaudits, he cares about every last drop of sauce and scale of fish. No one looks at a trout that way if they're just in it for the glory. He might still think I'm a total waste of space, but I'm determined to prove him wrong.

I jump out of my skin when, deep in the cold store, I hear a sudden clatter of pans. Surely I'm the last one here? As Ghusto is all about fresh produce, the best weapon the freezer offers up is a bag of peas and I'm not sure they'll provide much protection. I cautiously edge out of the darkness, peas clenched in my fist, only to find Oscar sizzling butter in an enormous pan. He turns, stares at me, then turns his gaze to the peas.

'It's the artist formerly known as Fish Girl. Remind me what you're called out of hours.'

'Amber, Amber Price. I'm sorry, I thought you'd gone. I was just finishing up . . .'

He cocks his head upwards. 'Flat's upstairs, did no one tell you that? Fuck it, I'll get you a glass. Can't sleep, could do with the company. That is, if you can bear to abandon the peas.'

'Definitely, I shouldn't be two-timing the fish.'

'No, you shouldn't, you really shouldn't.'

'And I *really* don't want you calling me Pea Girl.' I can feel myself blushing crimson at my own idiocy.

'Consider yourself spared,' he says, smirking.

He lopes across the kitchen in search of another glass. He pours some wine into it, coming close to hand it to me, chinking his own glass against it as he does so. Just for a mad second, I imagine him kissing me, imagine it's us chinking against each other. It's the first time even a trace of desire has passed through me since Dom left. I'd started to worry that a switch inside of me had been flicked off. I savour the tremor for the briefest of seconds, then stamp down hard on it.

31

'So what is it you're making here?' I ask brightly.

'Trying stuff out, saffron, lemongrass. Experimenting with some starter ideas. Even fuckwits will take a risk when it's a starter.' I wish I had a swear box I could tie round his neck like a nosebag. I'd be a millionaire by Tuesday.

'I loved that beetroot and goat's cheese soufflé you did earlier this week.'

'Glad someone did. Lydia told me off, said I'd land up with a load of neurotics convinced they had bowel cancer.'

There's an awkward pause as I wonder if he's heard the scurrilous gossip about her taking off to Paris with a toy boy and, if he has, whether it hurts him like it hurts me to think of Dominic ripping that floozy's knickers off with his teeth (fish gutting leaves far too much spare brain space available for lurid fantasy). My worst nightmare suddenly bores its way into my brain – Dom and Rachel having post-coital coffee in Lapaine, our favourite place in the whole wide world – and before I know it, I'm confiding.

'I'm divorced too,' I say quietly.

Being embarrassingly young to be in possession of a decree nisi, it's rare that I get the chance to ask anyone else how it was for them. It's not just that though. It's also that cocktail of repulsion and fascination working its way through me. I want to know him, I want the light to overwhelm the dark in my eyes, and in order to do that, I need to find out what's underneath.

'Bully for you,' says Oscar, a hardness in his voice that immediately tells me I've overstepped the mark. I should've known better, and not only because he's my boss. I'm not proud of the amount of people I don't know well enough

32

who've tried, and failed, to tactfully enquire about my divorce and ended up with their bloody heads rolling across the carpet.

Oscar has turned his attention back to the pan, hurling prawns into it at great velocity, seemingly oblivious to the hot fat that's spitting up at his face.

'Sorry, I—'

'Forget it,' he says, scraping his wooden spoon around the recesses of the pan like a sadistic dentist. I watch him, still compelled, embarrassed to realise that it's not just me wanting to know him, it's me wanting him to want to know me. As the silence yawns on and on, I work on my exit strategy, discreetly trying to glug back the rest of my wine so as not to appear rude. Just as I'm about to make my excuses, Oscar thrusts the spoon at me.

'Here, taste this,' he says gruffly. 'Grace me with your opinion.'

It's absolutely boiling. I try and swallow without revealing the fact that the top of my mouth's been incinerated, somewhat delaying my reply.

'Yeah, it's great.'

'Don't be a kiss arse. What do you really think?'

I'm busted, the catch in my voice clearly audible. 'I guess I might just put a bit less chilli in there, it kind of overpowers the lemongrass. And ... oh, nothing.'

'What? If anyone's going to know about prawns, it's you, Fish Girl.'

'I just thought a creamy avocado salsa might be nice with it, that's all. To balance out the fieriness.'

He smiles. 'Good call, you can stay,' he says, chinking glasses. What does that mean? I don't want him to think I'm offering myself up to him on a bed of rocket (so 90s). I tip back the dregs of my glass.

'I should go.'

'OK,' he says, unconcerned. 'I've got Mimi to keep me entertained.'

There's no Mimi here. Is he brazen enough to have a call girl on speed dial? Kitchens are hotbeds of lust, no question, but that's pushing it. Suddenly an aria rings out across the kitchen at top volume.

'*La Bohème*,' he says. 'Just listen.'

I stop in my tracks, taking a moment to soak up the beauty of the music.

'It's Puccini, isn't it? It's lovely.'

'He's the man,' says Oscar. 'He pisses on those other chancers like Handel.'

'Pah, Handel. And as for Berlioz, what a dork.'

He gives a half-smile, then turns his attention back to the fridge. I assume I'm dismissed and head to the staff room to dig out my coat and helmet, only to find him in the doorway as I come back through.

'Allow me,' he says, taking the coat from my hands and holding it up for me.

'Thanks,' I say, struggling to thread my arms through the holes like I'm a mentalist being forced into a straitjacket.

'My pleasure,' he says, waiting patiently without comment.

Once I'm in, he leaves his hands lightly resting on my shoulders. He's only slightly taller than me, way shorter than Dom, but his lack of stature doesn't remotely emasculate him.

'Well done,' he says quietly as I step backwards. 'You did all right.'

'What? Trout-gate or the thing with my arms?'

Oscar laughs. 'Trout-gate. You might not be able to add up, but you've got something rattling around up there.'

'Thanks,' I say. 'And thanks for not firing me. I really, really wanted to work for you. Now I really am being a kiss arse, but honestly . . .'

'Nightie night, Fish Girl,' he says, crossing to unlock the door. I half expect him to kiss me, at least on the cheek, but he lets me go without another word. I look back at him through the glass door, but he's returned to the pan, intent on tasting the contents, probably thinking what a bumptious little madam I am for making suggestions. Is it all about the food for him, or are there other things keeping him awake until the wee small hours?

Chapter 3

The next day is Sunday, heralding my first free day in almost two weeks. Actually, free is a slight exaggeration, I've got an 'emergency' brunch with my friend Marsha but after that, it's a yawning chasm of relaxation. Marsha was at school with me and while we were never the best of friends, we've somehow stayed firmly embedded in each other's lives. It's a peculiar bond: deep and significant, but faintly medicinal. If there was a nuclear attack or a flood, I would absolutely want Marsha on my team – she'd make herself into a human dam to save me from drowning, share the last of her rations with me – her loyalty is absolutely bottomless. She's a proper thinker too. I like how she'll drag me off to an exhibition that would never have occurred to me or take me to a film that sends my spongy brain into spasms of deep thought. But if I want a really fun night out, drinking overpriced pink drinks on a roof, Marsha is the last person on my speed dial. She'd turn up in some kind of bottle-green corduroy pinafore, tut at the high prices and then leave unfeasibly early to get the last bus. I always feel a tiny bit disapproved of, even though I know she loves me up, down, and through the middle. I've got no idea what the emergency can possibly be – Marsha's not the kind of person who'd normally countenance something as suspiciously Transatlantic as brunch – but I'm intrigued to find out.

It's a testament to Marsha's doggedness that we've stayed friends so long. The truth is, and I'm not very proud of this fact, that I developed the worst case of 'Muff before Mates' ever recorded after I met Dom. College was in London, and it was a heady year of drinking and snogging and flambéeing in roughly that order of importance, but my first placement brought me down to earth with a resounding bump.

I was sent off to Poole, to a skanky hotel on the seafront, where I was to prep vegetables for a volcanic Czech chef with breath as fierce as his temper. I was gutted; it felt like there was so much less to learn from him than from the brilliant, impassioned teachers I'd had in London, and I'd lost my tight-knit gang of friends. For the first time in my life, I felt isolated. Although I'd often bitched about the fighting, football and farting that characterised growing up with two older brothers I'd never felt alone, and college had been relentlessly social. Now, here I was in a totally unfamiliar environment, struggling to break into the fear-ridden clique that peopled Vlad's kitchen.

It was Dom who took pity on me. He was waiting tables out front, and was the one who always cleaned up on tips and phone numbers. He was a gangly streak of energy, so skinny you'd think he'd been fashioned out of pipe cleaners, and always on the move. His hair was as wild and boundless as the rest of him, an untameable mop of springy curls. Everything

37

about him was fast, from his rapid diction to his ability to survey a packed restaurant and know immediately what's needed. He felt like nothing more than a mate at first, a much needed partner in crime.

He would come out back to sling me the orders and, without fail, make me wet myself laughing. It'd be some pitch perfect impression of the anorexic Chelsea refugee asking for an egg-white omelette cooked in water, or the dowager duchess who'd promised to leave him a rogue castle in her will. But when Dom talks to you, he's got an uncanny knack of making it feel like you're the only person who exists for him, and soon I realised how much I was longing for him to explode through those double doors. He wasn't remotely my type, but it had stopped mattering. I wanted him, properly wanted him, but I didn't know if he was charming the pants off half the staff. There's no greater love rat than a geek reborn (just ask Woody Allen) and I wasn't up for emotional target practice.

Two weeks in, Dom invited me down to the beach, displaying a heart squidging nervousness I'd never seen before. It was a nightly occurrence for the front of house crew, a chance to get stoned and swill beer until the stress of a titanically long shift was a fuzzy memory. We peeled away, snuggling close on a bench, and finally he kissed me. It was a toothy kiss, a messy collision of mouths, but it was utterly meant. There was no pretension, no barriers, just uncalculated connection.

He seemed to decide, with absolute clarity, that this was serious from the first morning we woke up together (the very next day, to my great chagrin) and secretly I agreed, even though I wasn't going to tell him straight off the bat. I found out fast that Dom was more complicated than that easy charm suggested. His dad had died the year before, taken after a long fight with cancer, and Dom had deferred his history degree (for ever, as it turned out) to stay close to his mum. I would ask him about it, but he'd always keep it general.

'I want to help you,' I'd plead, 'I want to understand.'

'I don't want you to understand,' he'd say, kissing my head. 'You don't need to know yet, not when your parents are still young. I'm keeping you safe. If you love someone you want to keep them safe.'

I worried that he knew more of me than I knew of him. I was compelled to tell him everything, turn myself inside out and know that every single part of me was seen, was accepted. I didn't want secrets; there'd been too many secrets in my life. He heard it all. It was as though that quick mercurial brain of his had added up every bit of me and approved the sum. But did I even know my own magic number? We think we know who we are at twenty-one, but we're amoeba-like, jellies being shaped and morphed by the tides of life. He was my tide, the shaping force of my existence, but perhaps I wasn't his.

I'm shaking the last of the cornflakes out of the box when Milly finally emerges from the shower, yawning.

'Ooh, I'd forgotten you had a day off! Do you fancy doing something jolly like the cinema?'

'Quite possibly, but it'll have to be post-Marsha.'

Milly pulls a face and I give her an admonishing look, even though I'm secretly a little bit gratified by their tug of love. Marsha thinks Milly's a flighty wisp of a person who ought to buckle down to a career (she's a partner in a dental practice, deep in the 'burbs) while Milly . . .

'Man hands,' mutters Milly, casually dropping a slice of bread in the toaster.

'Don't be mean!' I say without much conviction. I guess I like the fact they're so different; it feeds separate aspects of me. That said, I well and truly got my comeuppance when I asked both of them to be bridesmaids. Cue the hen night. Of course Marsha would think an authentic eight-course Elizabethan banquet, eaten in full period costume, would be the ultimate culinary treat – tasty and educational! But it wasn't, particularly once I was left trying to digest an entire side of beef at the pole dancing class that Milly had scheduled directly after.

The landline starts to ring, a sound so unfamiliar that we both stare at the phone like it's some kind of alien life form. It's either a cold call or a parent: in this case, it's mine. Milly hands me the phone. 'It's your dad,' she mouths, and I wander off to my room with the phone clamped to my ear.

'Hi,' I say guiltily, painfully aware of how incommunicado I've been since I landed at Ghusto. Or maybe longer, truth be told. 'What are you up to?'

'Hello sweetheart!' I love the way he always sounds so thrilled to hear the sound of my voice. 'I've got my hand halfway up a goose's derrière, since you ask.'

'Sounds messy.'

'Too right. It's like having a newborn baby, the amount of love and attention it needs.'

'Hopefully you never put any of us in the oven.'

'Not to my knowledge, no,' he laughs. 'But honestly, love, every half hour I'm syringing out the fat, basting the little bugger. Don't know what possessed me.'

'Was it the sides?' I know my dad, he loves a culinary challenge.

'You're like Columbo, you are. Yes, pickled pears. Quite a departure. When you going to come home so I can demonstrate my prowess?'

'Um, I don't know. Soon. It's hard ... you know what it's like with a new job.'

There's a pause, a pause in which I start to feel like the worst daughter ever. But then Dad lets me off the hook.

'So give me the scoop on this Retford fella. I've been Internet searching him.'

'People tend to say Googling, Dad,' I say, loving him even more than normal.

'Do they? Well, clever clogs, I've got Yahoo.'

He stays on the line until the goose needs its next bout of intensive care. He's about to go off to fetch Mum when he comes back to me.

'Sweetheart?'

'Yes?'

'Are you all right? I mean ...' Dad's not too good at this kind of thing. 'Feelings-wise.' I feel myself choking up, grateful for the clumsily expressed concern.

'Better every day, Dad. Better every day.'

'That's my girl.'

Then he's off to get Mum and I wait, fingernails lightly digging into my palms.

'Hello, darling,' she says, voice clipped. 'Dad tells me you're still not able to find time for a visit.'

Why let a whole sentence go by dig-free?

'I will, Mum, but it's only my first month. I want to have a few days and—'

'Yes, it's completely understandable,' she says in a tone that conveys the absolute opposite. 'Have you finished off all that horrible paperwork?'

The hideous divorce papers, how I hated them. The reason we'd parted writ large, made real and legal.

'Yes, Mum. The decree nisi arrived a couple of weeks ago. Adultery.' There's an edge to my tone, but she either chooses not to take the bait or fails to notice.

'Good girl. Best to get it out of the way. Now we've just got the absolute to go. Did you do the financial statement like you promised?'

'No, Mum. Dom's never going to come after me for my money. Besides, he knows perfectly well I don't have any.' It's true. However much I might malign him, I can't see him taking me to court for three skillets and an aluminium saucepan.

'You've got the proceeds from the house sale.'

'We bought at the top of the market. I've got about enough to cover my overdraft and my credit card bills.'

'I can't help but wish you'd gone for something that offered a bit more security. Look at Ralph. He worked his guts out to get that medical degree but now he's got that lovely house in Acton and proper savings. You just slave away without so much as a nest egg.'

'I'm not a chaffinch!' I snap, exasperated. It's always like this: Mum calmly chipping away at me until I lose my cool and all my power with it.

'Do simmer down, Amber. We just worry about you, that's all.'

I breathe in, trying to work out why I'm incapable of letting it wash over me. She's my mum, for God's sake. I should appreciate her.

42

'Did you get that leaflet I sent you about setting up a pension?'

Oh my God, I want to kill her. However, I've already played the stroppy card for this phone call so I keep it bland and sweet, catching up on the family gossip and telling her what Milly's been up to.

'So you'll make sure they give you a night off for Ralph's birthday, won't you?' she asks as I'm winding up the call.

Ralph's birthday, now a mere week away. I love my brother dearly, but I'm dreading the dinner like it's an execution. It'll be a couple factory: couple after couple lined up like battery hens, pecking at my ringless finger and looking at me, beady-eyed, like I'm the world's biggest failure. And perhaps I am, but who knew the rules were this complicated?

Dom's a maître d' at Marquess, one of the West End's top restaurants, a place that drips with old-fashioned glamour. Despite the air of laid-back chic, every last penny is accounted for. It's owned by a team of hard-nosed backers who want to wring out every ounce of profit they can. When management heard their key lawyer was changing, they were horrified. A new person inevitably tries to score as many fringe benefits as possible: it's all about the last-minute tables and off-menu ordering. There's no better way to prove your status than lording it up at the hottest joint in town, and it's the maître d' who's got to make it happen. What a relief when the new kid on the block turned out to be a friendly, self-deprecating girl rather than a sharp-suited tosspot with testicles. Dom shared the happy news as soon as he met her, then mentioned that she'd come straight back in again the following week with a gang of friends in tow.

'You must've shown her a really good time,' I said, a whisper of anxiety running through me. How stupid, I thought, flinging it off me like a speck of dust. Infidelity had never been an issue with us, despite the thrum of opportunity that beats out like a tattoo in any catering job. Of course I'd been attracted to the odd waiter, the odd busboy with a cheeky smile, but I'd never done anything about it. I suppose I assumed that Dom had the odd meaningless flirtation, a harmless flex of his charm muscles, but I was sure the same was true for him. Perhaps I should've asked. Forewarned is forearmed and all that. How naive we were, marrying at twenty-five without any big conversations, but with just blind faith that we had our love to keep us warm.

She didn't come up again, not even when the backers organised a fancy Friday night dinner to celebrate the restaurant's achievements. I thought about asking if she was there, but something stopped me. I told myself it was because I didn't want to sound paranoid, but it was more than that. As soon as the spectre of suspicion had been raised, that blind trust would be gone for ever. We would be entering a new era of marriage, a time in which our love for each other was no longer the full stop, the trump card, the incontrovertible truth. He was late back that night, very late. But what right did I have to complain, considering the hours I was working? I'd just been made sous chef and all I seemed to do was cook or sleep. I couldn't deny I was taking him for granted, but I hoped we had enough in the bank for me to be able to afford a few months' grace, just until I got myself established. It's always *like that, this job. You always think it'll only be this hard for a little time longer, then you turn round and find a decade has snuck past on the sly.*

Silences had started to open up between us, silences I was too tired to fill. One evening, as I pounded on a chicken breast, I realised it was our anniversary. Not our wedding anniversary, neither of us would be quite thick-headed enough to miss that one, but the anniversary of the night we shared that first joint on the beach. Enough, I thought to myself, and miraculously inveigled myself an early pass out. I went to surprise him, arriving while he was still dealing with evening service (Marquess is one of those places that serves the post-theatre crowd until they drop).

I watched him for a few minutes, quiet as a mouse. He was gliding between tables, using his perfect recall to greet regulars like old friends, sending drinks to tables that faced a wait – he was brilliant, and he was mine. I took that image and retreated to the alcove bar, thinking I'd get someone to alert him to my presence when it was less frantic. There was another woman sitting alone, nursing a drink, and I wondered if her boyfriend was pulling a late shift too. She looked a bit too polished to be arm candy for a catering monkey, and I idly speculated that some banker had stood her up. I grabbed Julie, a waitress Dom had poached from his last post, when she came in to get a drinks order.

'Hey,' I said, giving her a quick kiss, 'can you tell that husband of mine that he's got company?'

'Hi!' she said, her voice too high. 'Yeah, yeah, of course.'

'I know what Dom's like. If you don't, he'll be out there until every last customer's tucked up in bed.'

And as I said his name, I saw her head swivel. It was involuntary, she tried to correct it, but it was too late. Her eyes flicked over me, assessing the competition, before she looked down into her wine glass with fierce concentration. An icy calm descended over me as I went into ninja mode. I hopped off my stool and approached her.

'You must be Rachel,' I said, sticking out a shaking hand. 'I'm Dom's wife.'

'Hi,' she said, all nasal and posh. She gave me a confident, toothy smile, brazening it out. But we both knew.

I hit myself lightly on the head, trying to remind my stupid brain that it's got to stop ordering all events in relation to my ex-husband like a demented mental game of Snap.

'Mum, of course I'll be at Ralph's dinner. What kind of sister do you think I am?'

I'm about to say my goodbyes but she beats me to it.

'I'll have to ring off now, darling. That fatty beast your dad's been dallying with is ready for eating. Speak soon.'

'Bye, Mum,' I say, suddenly wanting to say more, say something that means something. It's too late though, there's nothing but a dial tone.

The one thing I unpacked when I got here was my box of recipe books. They're all lined up on the shelf, and I grab my musty old copy of Elizabeth David's *I'll Be with You in the Squeezing of a Lemon*, feeling instantly comforted by it. I leaf through the dusty pages, loving the starkly beautiful line drawings that punctuate it. They perfectly represent her pared down simplicity, her understanding that, as cooks, we should respect and celebrate the best ingredients rather than bastardise their flavours by being over-clever. I love Oscar's audaciousness, but you have to know the rules backwards in order to break them. Oscar – what was going on last night? Was he actually flirting with me, or am I flattering myself? I give up trying to work it out, absorbing myself in a hard-backed Nigel Slater, pages intermittently stuck together with butter. I hope he'd take it as a compliment. Before I know it, I'm mapping out ideas for menus and thinking about potential recipes. Days off are a bit of a contradiction in terms for me.

Luckily, the hour of brunch has arrived, saving me from my terrible workaholic tendencies. I'm late, as ever, scooting through traffic like I'm in *CHiPs*. Marsha's chosen the Marylebone branch of Giraffe as our venue, which strikes me as a very strange place for a state of emergency. As I hurry towards it, I focus properly for the first time on what the emergency could be. Am I being glib? Marsha's so stolid and practical that she honestly might think nothing of announcing she's got terminal cancer over a Hippy Hippy Shake tropical smoothie. I jog up the street, panicked. I find her at a large table at the back, sipping a tap water and reading the foreign news section of the *Guardian*.

'I'm so sorry I'm late!' I say, collapsing on to the bench, breathless. She waves a dismissive hand, a gesture that makes it clear she'd expect nothing less. 'It was just that my parents rang, and I hadn't spoken to them for ages and ... Anyway, forget all that. What's happened? Tell me.'

At which point Marsha extends her admittedly rather large left hand, to display a modest diamond solitaire. 'Peter popped the question,' she says, sounding about as excited as she might about receiving a parking ticket. Marsha doesn't really go in for over-excitement.

'Wow, that's great!' I exclaim as though I've inhaled a burst of helium. 'I'm so happy for you.' And I am, I really am, but I can't help also feeling acutely, painfully aware how closely life resembles a game of snakes and ladders. 'How long's it been now? It feels like it's only a few weeks since you met him!'

'No, no, it's over a year. It probably seems that way to you because you've only met him a couple of times.'

It's true. She met Peter (never Pete, as far as I'm aware) at some kind of transglobal meeting about molars just as my suspicions about Dom were starting to hit. I made a fleeting visit to her birthday drinks a couple of months later, and was briefly introduced. Terrible though it is to admit, he barely made an impression. He was squarish – in build and in spirit – with hearty good manners. I made a dumb joke about grown men wearing dental braces, and was pleased to see how attentive he was to my friend. I met him one more time at a dinner party, but my post-break-up moments with Marsha have all been *à deux*. Looking back, I realise she probably avoided telling me how well it was going so as not to rub salt into the wound.

'Well, that's great, Marsha. I didn't even realise you were living together.'

'We're not as yet. We're looking for something large and monstrous we can gut. Hopefully we'll need room for kiddy-winks and such like.'

'So it doesn't feel too soon? You're definitely ready . . .'

'Trust me, Amber. If it did, I'd have sent him packing. A year feels like a decent amount of time to get the measure of a person, and I ...' Her face suddenly lights up with a rosy, beaming smile that tells me how much she loves him. 'I know without a shadow of a doubt that we'll make an excellent team.' Ah, the romance: in the World According to Marsha, that's the equivalent of taking deadly nightshade and lying in a tomb.

'That's fantastic,' I say, smiling back at her and reaching across to feel the ring. 'How exactly did he pop the question?'

'He took me off to the Highlands for a walking holiday, and on the last night he left the ring on my pillow.'

'Were you staying in some haunted windswept castle?'

'Oh no, it was a youth hostel. Very lovely one though.'

'A youth hostel?! We're thirty-one!'

'You can join the Youth Hostelling Association at any age. You'd be surprised by the quality of the accommodation outside London.'

'Right ... So did he get down on one knee? The whole works?'

Dom proposed to me constantly, from about three months into our relationship. 'Marry me,' he'd say as we snaffled chips on the Dorset seafront. 'Will you do me the honour of being my wife?' he'd ask, pulling a packet of loo roll off a supermarket shelf and presenting it to me with a flourish. 'Let's get hitched,' he'd declare, off the cuff, as he effortlessly reversed our crappy Citroën AX into a tiny space. But the fact we still had a Citroën AX was why I laughed him off. We were too young, no rush, no pressure. But by the grand old age of twenty-five, with four years of relationship history under our collective belts, there seemed no good reason not to. He took me back to Dorset for my birthday, and we went to dinner at a beach café that, for me, had far more charm than the fanciest restaurant in London, and proposed properly. We toasted each other with good-ish sauvignon blanc and agreed to make it official. Maybe it wasn't enough of a novelty, too much of a continuation of a life we were already living. I know Marsha secretly worried it wouldn't happen for her and now it has, she'll guard and protect it like a piece of treasure she's retrieved from the ends of the earth. I hope I didn't treat my treasure like I'd retrieved it from the end of the Northern line.

'Absolutely,' continues Marsha. 'It was a bit cramped, but at least there was a bed!' Ew. I'm not sure I like thinking of Marsha in an erotic context. 'So that's my news.'

'It's fantastic news! But, Marsha, why did you say it was an emergency? This is the exact opposite of an emergency. I was really worried.'

'Wanted to make sure there'd be no last-minute cancellations,' she replies matter-of-factly. I'm about to protest but truth be told, she's got a point. 'And I wanted to tell you face-to-face so I could ask ...' Oh God, I know what's coming, '... if you'd be my bridesmaid.' She holds up a commanding hand before I can speak. 'I'm no fool, Amber. I'm aware that it might feel like a Herculean task so soon after your divorce. I'll quite understand if you can't face it, but I couldn't imagine not asking you. Have you heard from him at all?' she adds gently. 'Do you know if it's still going on?'

I pause for a second, choked. 'No, we haven't spoken in, I dunno, five months?'

Rachel was understandably twitchy once I'd guessed who she was. 'How did you know?' she asked, faux-friendly.

'Just a hunch,' I replied, my eyes raking over her for clues. After all these years, what was it about her that had turned Dom's head? My evidence was still scant, but I knew there was something between them. It radiated off her, and yet I couldn't obviously see what would have drawn him to her.

She was fair, like me, but unnaturally so. You could see she spent a lot of time in the salon tapping out messages on her BlackBerry with a perfectly manicured hand while Guido did his worst. Her outfit was perfectly put together but looked terminally false, like she'd seen it in Vogue and bought every single item straight off the peg. She wasn't fat, but she had that broad-in-the-beam hockey player look beloved of the boarding school massive. I hated her on sight.

She claimed she'd been in with a gang of friends and had stayed behind to ask Dom a work question, but that smelled like so much bullshit to me. He knocked off work soon after, entering the bar with a hangdog expression that confirmed my worst suspicions. Her confidence was breathtaking as she spun out a question about projected Christmas turnover, but his reaction told me there was more to it. Gone was the easy, affectionate Dom who would always squeeze me against him like we couldn't be close enough. Yes, he kissed me, but it was a dry peck. He was stiff, awkward, and incapable of sustaining eye contact with either of us. My heart sank like a stone as he suddenly felt like a stranger, just another person with a shoal of secrets that I wasn't party to. Of course every relationship has its pockets of mystery. If you had to expose everything you ever did or thought, it would be too eviscerating, but this was a colder, darker version of personal space.

When we left, I stalked right off, forcing him to run down

Piccadilly after me. He told me I was being ridiculous in a hundred different ways, veering between contrition at the fact I'd felt uncomfortable, and fury at the way I was maligning him. Whichever way he swung, he insisted that there was nothing going on. I wanted to believe him, oh God, I wanted to believe him, but I could tell from the timbre of his voice that there was something to uncover. I turned my back on him in bed that night, and didn't tell him I loved him for the first time in nine years. We'd always vowed we wouldn't go to sleep angry, but my hurt was too great. And it stayed that way. I had no proof, I didn't really want proof, and yet I couldn't purge the suspicion from my system.

I changed, no question. I put on a good show, but I'd turned into a pre-menopausal Miss Marple, sniffing his clothes for perfume and checking his phone at any opportunity. It was hard for me to track his movements, the hours we worked, but I did spring a couple more impromptu visits on him. We had more sex, not less, but it was all wrong. It was technically accomplished, but it had a nasty edge to it, like it had become a competitive sport. Which for me, perhaps it had.

A word to the wise: don't snoop unless you're tough enough to deal with the fallout ...

I look into Marsha's kind, open face and force myself to engage with what's at stake. They say you're never more beautiful than on your wedding day, but somehow with Marsha I know that won't be true. She's big-boned and cheerful, with the kind of solid bosom that's more like a sideboard than a cleavage. She's got the kind of glowing natural skin that you can't get in a bottle, and yet it doesn't make her youthful. She's always been old before her time. I suspect it's only now, in her thirties, that she'll finally grow into herself. Make-up never looks quite right on her, it works against the simplicity of what and who she is. A full-on meringue is going to look like a tent, billowing off those breasts like a canopy, and blow-drying her mouse-coloured hair will make its wispiness all the more apparent. I can't leave her to the mercy of a tribe of bridezillas-in-waiting. It's more than that though: it's about who she wants standing alongside her. She's never abandoned me, despite the fact that I've been consistent only in my flakiness, and I can't abandon her.

'Yes. Yes, I will be your bridesmaid,' I say, as fervently as if I was accepting a proposal.

'Excellent,' says Marsha, 'I felt ninety per cent sure you'd say that, which is why I took the liberty of inviting Lisa. She'll be your partner in crime.' Lisa's another school friend of ours, whom I'm incredibly fond of, but hardly ever see. In fact, I've probably only seen her a couple of times since Dom and I separated.

'Great,' I say yet again, the reality of dress fittings and hen nights hitting me hard. Just then my phone rings, and I turn away to answer it, glad of the distraction. Lisa's timing is perfect. I slip away from the table, waving hello, as she slides past me and into the booth.

'Is that Mrs Newby?' says an oily, ingratiating voice. I know exactly who this is.

'No, it's Amber Price,' I snap back. 'I've told you repeatedly, *Steve*, that that's not my name. It wasn't even my name when I was married, but now I'm not, it most definitely isn't my name.' I try and control my heart rate, well aware I'm making a prize chump of myself. Why, oh why, did we choose this hateful bunch of tossers to sell our flat (you know the ones – stupid little 'classic' cars, more Brylcreem than brain cells). I know exactly why: they promised us the highest price and we were too greedy/desperate to turn it down. They didn't get it, of course, and even if they had, it wouldn't have made up for how infuriating and patronising they are. I hope they're driving Dom equally mad.

'I'm sorry to say I'm calling with bad news,' says Steve, not sounding remotely sorry. 'I took the purchasers back round to the property this morning to measure up, and it seems there's a leak from the toilet.'

Oh no, now they're going to think they're buying The House that Jack Built. I can't bear it if they pull out, and it's not like plumbing's my strong suit.

'Have you called my hus ... have you called my ex-husband?'

'Mr Newby doesn't appear to have his phone on.' Of course he doesn't. He probably pulled a double shift yesterday like I did. I'm suddenly struck by a pathetic longing for my dad. He'd sort this all out in a heartbeat.

'OK, I'll get over there as soon as I can and get a plumber out.'

'Thank you Mrs ... Amber, I think that would be advisable. Now you have a nice day!'

How likely is it that I'll have a nice day, if the most pressing part of it involves crossing London to submerge my hand in a toilet cistern?

'You too, Steve,' I say, through gritted teeth. I return to the table, briefly précising the headlines of the call.

'Poor you,' chime the girls sympathetically, and I chastise

myself for how rare it is that I make the effort to spend any time with them.

'Isn't this exciting?' says Lisa, clapping her hands at the sheer thrill of it. 'Not the cistern, of course!' she adds, and we all laugh.

'It's brilliant news,' I agree.

And it is. It's just that I can't help wondering, now that I'm back at the bottom of the board, how I'm ever going to find my way to the top again. When I got married, I was a novelty bride, the first to go over the cliff. Our wedding was riddled with horny twenty-something singletons, rendered all the more up for it by the gushing torrent of free booze. Dom and I presided over it all like two of the wise monkeys, tutting indulgently at their excess. Something tells me that now, six years later, Marsha's news represents the beginning of an onslaught: wedding fever will surely hit like a deadly virus. I've seen it among Ralph's friends. Suddenly, every summer weekend will require a chintzy dress and a beatific smile as I'm squeezed onto a table with the only available thirty-something man, a 'confirmed bachelor' who's more interested in checking out the groom's arse than making small talk with me.

'Is the first thing planning the engagement party?' I ask Marsha. 'You've got to have drinks at the very least. In fact, should we have some champagne now? It's two o'clock, which surely counts as wine o'clock in these parts.'

'Not for me,' says Lisa, smiling coyly, and just for a minute the world appears to stop.

'You're not—'

'I am!' she positively shrieks. 'Only two months, so I'm not meant to say, but obviously I can't not tell you.'

'Con-grat-u-lations,' I say, iron tongue refusing to peel itself off the bottom of my cavernous mouth. 'But you and Jed aren't even married yet!'

Lisa snorts with laughter. 'Yeah, but it's not Victorian times. We've been together six years now!'

'Yes, of course. You don't have to be ... that's great.'

'It's terrific, isn't it?' agrees Marsha. She gives me a small, sympathetic smile and I give her little look back to tell her that it's OK. Even though it's not. Why can't I be more like the Dalai Lama? Not so much the orange robes and glasses, more the deep spiritual perspective. If I'm going to spend the foreseeable future taking everyone else's joys as a personal slight, then I'm doomed.

'Surely half a glass won't hurt?' I say, forcing a bright smile. 'We've got two bits of news to celebrate now!'

'You're probably right but ... I don't want to take any chances,' she says, patting her tummy almost unconsciously, perfectly tuned in to the life growing inside her.

Suddenly the background noise feels like it's been turned up, and all I can hear is hordes of children squealing and shouting as they gobble down their lunch and scribble on their menus with the abundant supply of crayons. There's a serious looking little boy on a scooter, circling round and round with a face filled with fierce concentration. And me in the midst of it, stranded on an island partly of my own making. Not yet at the stage of a Tibetan deity, I find myself unexpectedly grateful for that leaking cistern. We chink fresh mint teas, and I promise to think about potential venues for engagement drinks.

'And any thoughts on the hen night?' I ask Marsha, putting on my coat.

'Oh, surprise me!' she says, and I try not to grimace. How

am I going to work out what's fun in Marsha Land? I'll probably book pedicures and afternoon tea, then find out she'd have preferred to go potholing in sub-arctic temperatures, before cooking lentils for ten on a primus stove.

'Maybe Lisa should take the lead,' I say hastily. 'This was so great!' I add, giving them each a kiss. 'Congratulations again!' I seem to be physically incapable of uttering a sentence that doesn't require an exclamation mark. I beat a retreat, trying to navigate the mix of happy and sad that's bubbling away inside me.

I am pleased for Marsha, genuinely pleased. She was miserably single when I got married, and I have to admit that I didn't hold out much hope. She's lovely, but she's not the kind of girl men flock to and she never has been. Is there some terrible part of me that feels resentful that the roles got reversed when I wasn't watching? It was pretty easy to sit there saying the perfect man was round the corner, knowing that mine was safely in the bag. Now that it's me out in the cold, I can't deny the tinge of jealousy that's polluting my pleasure at her good fortune. A tiny bit of me is pleased that Peter's pudgy face is vaguely akin to a potato: it'd be too much if she'd scored a perfect ten on all counts. And I hadn't even started contemplating the arrival of babies. Lisa's radiating nuclear-strength happiness, her glow so blatant that she could've stepped right out of the pages of a pregnancy manual. Dom and I hadn't really talked about children; they were a hypothetical given for a far-off time when we'd stopped relishing our work-hard, play-hard lifestyle. It's not like I crave motherhood. In fact, I'd go so far as to say I find it more than a little bit frightening, but the idea that it might not even be an option is more frightening still.

I haven't been to the flat since the removal van rolled away six weeks ago, and I'd hoped to let the sale proceed without ever needing to come back. I don't believe in ghosts, but I can't help wondering if houses hold on to a trace of what's gone on between their four walls.

I feel way less spiritual once I'm in front of the aforementioned cistern. The bathroom is a perfect expression of why this flat's taken six months to sell. Both of our families constantly told us that we had to get on the ladder, that the airy flat in Holloway we were renting was not enough, so we bought what we could afford, right at the top of the market. Here we have the loo, snuggled up so close to the shower that you virtually have to stand on it to wash your hair. I always longed for a bath, but the amount of space it would have required was roughly akin to the dimensions of the second bedroom. It's the perfect home – for a family of midgets.

I gingerly peer around the outer limits of the loo, swiftly finding a pool of dubious-looking water that's seeping into the lino. I optimistically pull up the top of the cistern, as if the angel Gabriel might have blessed me with plumbing skills in much the same way he blessed Mary with the son of God. None are forthcoming and I retreat to the empty living room to search for my mobile. The nakedness of it feels shocking, almost obscene. I need to get out of here as fast as I can. I'm hanging on for 118 118, ready to settle for any old cowboy they can offer up, when I hear a key turning in the lock. I freeze, heart racing. Stupid, surely it must be oily Steve?

'Hello?' shouts out a familiar voice.

But it's not. It's Dom.

Chapter 4

So here's how it happened. Here's how my marriage went up in flames.

Gary Holland, the head chef at Marquess, has a country out-post in the Cotswolds. It's an über-posh restaurant with rooms, a place for overworked bankers to indulge their over-spent wives. Every year the team would go there for an overnight stay, take some time out to work on their strategy for world domination. When it came around again, I couldn't object and nor could I trigger World War Three by demanding to know if Rachel was going. My phone snooping reached whole new levels in the days leading up to it. There didn't seem to be much to see, though his inbox was suspiciously bare. Still, I had permanent butterflies in my stomach. It wasn't just the creeping dread, it was also the sense of what I'd become. I wanted to stop with the nosing around and the watchful distance, but it seemed to be beyond my control.

I was down for a double shift on the Friday that Dom was going away. I brought him a coffee in bed, looked at him

sleeping, thought for a moment about telling him how des-
perately insecure I felt. Then I remembered how adamant he'd
been that night, three months before, and decided it would
simply mean we'd part angry. I woke him up, wished him a
good trip, left the house, got to the end of the road and span
the bike straight round like a novice hell's angel. I kissed him
like I meant it for the first time in weeks, holding on to him
tightly enough to have his smell with me all day. He kissed me
back, seemingly perplexed by why I'd risked a bollocking for
a kiss from his morning-breath mouth. Or maybe he was pre-
tending to be perplexed. Either way, I didn't tell him. I simply
clung to him as tightly as I had to my dad the day he left me
at school for the very first time.

I worked too hard that weekend, fraught and adrenalised.
When Dom called me at lunchtime on Sunday to say that he
was home, I didn't have time to think about what it meant,
even though both of us were too kitchen-savvy to ever call
mid-service. I just carried on knocking out plates of bloody
beef to hordes of customers, getting home past midnight. I
found him nursing a brandy like a bucolic old colonel, nose
deep in our wedding album. I saw the tears rolling down his
cheeks as soon as he turned his face upwards to look at me. I
collapsed backwards into a chair, the blood draining from
me.

'What is it?' I demanded. 'Just tell me.'

All he could say, again and again, was 'I'm so sorry' and all
I heard in my head was 'It's over.'

'I need you to know that it wasn't ... it hadn't gone too far
until a couple of weeks ago.' He tried to come forward to put
his arms around me but I pushed him straight off.

'I knew it. You made me feel as though I was going mad, but I knew it. How could you, how could you let me feel like that?'

'Nothing had happened when you asked me. I swear to you.'

'So how long? How long has it been going on?' It turns out that it's impossible to talk about adultery without turning into a Magic FM playlist.

'I'm being completely honest with you. I can't think of anything else I can do,' he said, voice pleading. Too little, too late, I thought, but I bit my tongue. 'It's been a couple of months but we've just been spending time together. I haven't been sleeping with her, I swear to you.'

'So when I asked you,' I said, more angry than I think I've ever been, 'there was still time to stop it. You could've kept out of her way, looked the other way, but you didn't. You walked right through the door.' A horrible thought struck me then, that I was the author of my own misfortune. Was I like Eve, tempting Adam to take the apple, albeit an apple who was virtually throwing herself off the tree in her eagerness to be plucked?

'I didn't, I didn't really know till you said it. I knew we were flirting, but I thought that was all it was. Don't tell me you've never once flirted in ten years. It isn't true.' He was desperate now, twisting on a rope.

'Don't you dare try and make me the liar here.'

'I haven't lied to you. She didn't tell me she had feelings for me until I told her what you'd said.'

'So, what? You thought you were just "friends"?' I shouted, making those stupid imaginary quotation marks. 'Girls like that *don't have friends. They have frenemies, they have conquests, they don't have friends. So what did you say to her when she told you about her deep and meaningful feelings?'*

'I told her I was married.'

'And you didn't think it'd be an idea to tell me then?'

'I didn't want to hurt you. Fuck, I know how that sounds—'

'And tell me, Dom, when exactly did the amnesia about us being married set in? What made you decide it wasn't really much of a problem?'

I hated the sound of my voice, its pithy hardness. I was turning into my mother. Torrents of tears were falling inside, but outside I'd become icy and defensive. I wanted to hurt him every bit as much as he'd hurt me. The last thing I was going to do was show weakness. It wasn't that love had turned to hate, more that hate had caught up and become its equal.

'Come on, Amber. It's changed between us. Long before this.'

He held my gaze, challenging me to deny it, and a wave of grief hit me. I could feel there was truth in what he was saying, but I didn't know what had made it true. Had I pushed him away or had he been looking for an excuse to run? Which came first, the chicken or the egg?

'Do you really think that?' I asked, and he gave a tiny nod.

'I'm not saying it's an excuse. There's no excuse.' He looked so pained right then that I almost crossed over to him, but I held myself back, determined to protect myself until I had all the facts. Knew exactly what he'd done to me, to us.

'You know what I can't stand? That you confided in her about me. "Poor me having to put up with my nutbag neurotic

wife. Guess what she's said now?" You handed her the axe and let her destroy our marriage with it.'

'It's not destroyed! I'm telling you to stop that happening.'

'Well, aren't you noble?'

Round and round we went, on and on. I wanted to know how many times they'd had sex (three), where (the country, her flat), what it was like (an ashamed shrug, a dismissal). Eventually, as light started to seep through the curtains, we gave in to the need to sleep. It was while he was pleading that we should stay in the same bed, that I shouldn't cast him out into the wilderness of the spare room, that his iPhone gave a fatal beep. I moved like lightning, grabbing it from his jacket before he could stop me: a single X, a single X at four in the morning. That was it.

I don't make a sound. I'm rooted to the spot, shaking uncontrollably. How do I handle this? I can hear his footsteps, and in a flat this small that affords me roughly three seconds.

'Amber,' he says, shock writ large. 'Amber,' he repeats, voice lower.

'Hi,' I say, literally lost for words.

My eyes scan him, trying to take his emotional temperature. He's wearing a navy-blue duffel coat that I can guarantee I've never seen before: if I had, I'd have burnt it. It doesn't make him look like a cool indie Hoxtonite – it makes him look like he's on his way to chess club before he races home to eat his tea in front of *The Krypton Factor*. I want to cackle mercilessly, to reassure myself he's gone to seed without me, but instead his vulnerability forms a soft knot in my stomach. There's still that mix of love and hate, hot and cold, a deep relief at seeing him, at the distance between us being breached, and then a low that far exceeds the high as I remember what he's become. My ex – two tiny insignificant letters that hold so much.

We stare at each other, and then he crosses towards me, bending down to kiss my cheek. I look at him, stricken. Is the transition really that easy for him? Am I like some long-forgotten maiden aunt at a family wedding? I've got to get a grip: he's probably longing for the decree absolute to come through and release him into some magnificent future with Rachel. If he has won round one of 'who's happy now?', I'm not going to give him the satisfaction of finding out.

'How are things?' I say, trying for nonchalance. 'How's work?'

'Oh, you know, same old,' he says, uncomfortable. 'How are you?' he adds, holding my gaze.

'Oh, fine!' I say. 'Though it turns out I'm not much good at plumbing.' I attempt a casual laugh, but it sounds more like I've choked on a fly.

'There's a surprise,' he says, and then we stand there for a bit. 'Amber . . .' he starts, but I sweep out of the room (quite a challenge in a space this small).

'Why don't you have a try?' I call from the bathroom. He follows me in, squeezes past the sink to get to the cistern, colliding with me in the process. It can only be a second that we're in close contact, but that second seems to stretch out and expand, like those two little letters in ex. I can smell his soap, Imperial Leather, a smell that can withstand the most expensive of after-shaves, mixed up with a smell that's peculiarly his. It's so familiar, that smell – it conjures up ten years of my life way

64

more powerfully than hours of reminiscing ever could – and I stumble backwards out of the bathroom before my face betrays me.

What I should do is leave, but while part of me strains to, another part of me wonders if this is the last time I'll ever see him. It would so serve Dom right if my last image of him was elbow-deep in a toilet cistern. There are loud clunking noises coming from in there.

'Come on now, you can do it,' he pleads, like he's coaxing a stubborn horse, then flushes a couple of times. 'Stupid bloody thing,' he mumbles, frustrated.

'Does it turn out you're not that good at plumbing either?' I say, standing in the doorway.

He turns round, water splashed down his T-shirt. 'All right, smart arse,' he says, and I try not to smile. 'Let's call a plumber.'

I take a deep breath and think of the icy indifference. And then somewhere on the exhale I remember Rachel, and get an image of him, post-coital, in her flat. In my imagination it's roughly akin to Austin Powers' shag pad, all leopard-skin walls and pillow mountains. I swallow down the bile rising up my throat.

'You can do that, can't you?' I say. 'It's the least you can do,' I add more quietly.

'Point taken,' he says. He looks at me, smile squashed right out of him, and I nearly go to him. 'I still call you my wife,' he says. 'I want you to know that.'

'Why would you do that?' I snap.

'We haven't got the decree absolute yet. We are still married.'

That really lights the touch paper.

'Don't *do* that!'

'Do what?'

'Get all misty-eyed and sentimental. Not now, not here,' I say, looking round the bare little box that used to be full to the brim with us. 'I can't, I actually can't hear it.'

'That's what I was trying to say, but it came out wrong,' he says. 'That it feels so fucked up and wrong that we're not married.'

'How touching. What a pity you weren't more of a fan of marriage when that ... that *slut* threw herself at you.'

Dom flushes. He looks at me, considering his words.

'All right, Amber, I made a mistake, a pretty fucking cataclysmic one. But people do come back from affairs, it has been known. For someone who's such a fan of marriage, you gave up on ours pretty damn easily.'

'Don't say that to me,' I hiss. 'How dare you try and blame me?'

I was a fan of marriage. I am a fan of marriage. I liked the simplicity of it, I liked the way it made me feel held, even when Dom was hundreds of miles away. It was like a cosy scarf I could wrap myself up in, mummify myself even. I look at him, trying to force my face so it betrays nothing. Maybe, despite my mother's affair, or even because of it, I believed too much in its endurance. I can't hold the cat's cradle up to the light, can't try and unravel it, not when I know it's too late.

'I'm not blaming you,' he says, more gently. 'I behaved like a total prick. But there were things we could've done. You could've given the counselling a proper try.'

We went once, a month after he'd moved out, and I hated every second. It was a grey-haired man we saw, and to me it felt like I'd been sent to the headmaster's office. I thought it would be about the affair, but he wanted to dig deeper, far deeper. I scrunched up tissue after tissue, and refused to go back.

'It wouldn't have helped,' I say. 'It was too broken.'

'You keep saying that, it's like some kind of mantra. Does it ever occur to you that it might be a bit more complicated?'

'Don't patronise me!' I snap.

'I'm not patronising you. You know the Gaia principle?'

'Yes, I know the Gaia principle,' I snap, even though I don't really. One of the most annoying things about Dom, unless you're doing a pub quiz, is that he knows a little bit about everything. It can make a person who mainly knows about hollandaise feel very stupid. 'What's your point?'

'So the whole world's a living, breathing organism. Everything's interconnected. A fly dying in China affects a cow grazing in Iowa. A relationship's got to be an organism, hasn't it? I'm not saying it was your fault, I'm not excusing myself, but it didn't come from nowhere.'

This is my chance, my opportunity to get the answers to all the questions that swirl round my head in the middle of the night. There's the pathetic, needy ones of the 'what did I do wrong?'/'do you think she's prettier than me?' variety, but there's also a more scary grown-up version where we really talk about what turned sour. But if I had become so sour to him then, what would make me sweet to him now? What mysterious jelly mould would I have to pour my personality into to give myself the correct contours, the winning formula, that would win his heart back? And how would I ever trust, ever know, that I wouldn't screw up again, that I wouldn't fail some mysterious test I didn't know existed at a time of his choosing?

I couldn't go through this twice. The most humiliating thing is that he never tasted sour to me, he always tasted sweet. It wasn't necessarily blinding, intoxicating passion any more, but something different, something more sustaining. I push down my hurt, seal the wound with rough, jagged stitches.

'What, so it's my fault?'

'You're being impossible. You know that's not what I'm saying! I fucked up, no question, but you can't reduce our whole marriage, our whole relationship, to one mistake.'

'One mistake? Wasn't it more like three?' I say, spiteful and poisonous. I can't stand for this to be the last thing I ever say to him.

'Amber . . .'

'You knew, you knew that an affair was . . . it was the very worst thing I could have happen to me, but you still went ahead and did it!' I suddenly feel so vulnerable, naked in this naked room. 'That's what I can't forgive, not just the stupid sordid thing you did.'

'I'm so, so sorry,' says Dom, stepping towards me and enfolding me in his arms. 'But, sweet pea, we're not your parents.' Just for a minute I give in, let him hold me, intoxicated by the affection, the familiar endearment. Too dangerous: I jerk myself out of his embrace.

'I'm going. I've got to go.' I say through my tears.

'Amber, stop,' he says imploringly, holding onto my arm. I look into his face, not even trying to staunch my tears.

'Are you still seeing her?'

'Of course not! It was over the night I told you.'

That X springs up in front of me. X = ex. Who knew I was so good at romantic algebra?

'But you still see her?'

'Only when she comes into the restaurant.'

'So you still see her.'

'Stop being so impossible. You know I can't help that.'

'Goodbye, Dom,' I say, opening the door. 'And let's stop messing around. It's time we finished the paperwork and made it absolute.'

And with that, I shut the door on my life as a wife.

Chapter 5

If you ask me, downtime's overrated. I don't know what to do with myself, so desperate am I to distract myself from thinking too hard about the last twenty-four hours. Milly's still angling for the movies, but it's too dangerous to spend two hours sitting in the dark. I'd be all right if it was *Full Metal Jacket* or *Platoon* – basically a bloodbath that's peppered with guns and action and hotties – but the best that's on offer is some Jennifer Aniston slush fest that'll push me over the edge. Instead, I go for a long run and try to keep my musings at the intellectual level of a greyhound trying very, very hard to win its race.

I'm genuinely relieved when my alarm goes off the next morning, welcoming the prospect of the familiar brutality of a restaurant. At least I know where the slings and arrows are coming from. When I arrive at Ghusto it's clear that battle has already begun. There's Mike, red-faced and furious, bawling at Tomasz like he's his slave.

'Didn't they teach you about the big and the little hand back in Warsaw?' he's shouting, jabbing an angry finger at the clock. 'Or is it just that it's an hour earlier in the motherland?'

'My bus was . . . it was . . .'

It's 7.06. There's a steady trickle of people arriving, none of whom appear to be arousing the same level of rage in Mike.

'You're lucky I don't just fire you right now. Plenty more Polacks where you came from.'

'I am sorry. It was—'

'Final warning. You're lucky I'm in a good mood. Make me the best double cappuccino I've ever had, then get on with chopping enough onions to make you weep for the fall of the fucking Berlin Wall.'

Mike gives a self-satisfied smile, delighting in the way he's laced his bollocking with a dose of modern history. God, he's hateful. Tomasz stiffly smiles his assent, then makes for the machine.

'Come back here!' shouts Mike, loud enough to attract the rest of the kitchen's attention. 'What do you say to me?'

'Er, I say sorry?' says Tomasz nervously.

'Sorry *what*?'

'Very sorry?'

'Sorry, *Chef*!'

Oscar demanding to be called Chef is one thing, but this jumped-up ginger slime ball is another matter.

'Sorry, Chef,' mutters Tomasz, and stumbles towards the machine, humiliation radiating from every pore.

What's Mike's problem? Looking at his puny form and greased back carrot-top, I can only imagine the hammering he must've got at school. Get over it, buddy. You're pushing thirty-five and it's been scientifically proven that ginger people can find love. Look at Mick Hucknall – fleets of children. Obviously I don't say that to him. Instead, I subtly edge towards the

71

machine where I can see Tomasz struggling uselessly with the milk frother. He scalds himself on the pipe, swearing viciously in Polish.

'Hey,' I say, putting a tentative hand on his arm. 'Do you want me to try?' I'm shocked to feel him shaking.

'Sorry, sorry. Hate the prick that Mike is, but can not lose job. Baby is coming at home and there will be no place for it if I don't do this.'

'Congratulations!' I say, feeling stupidly over emotional about the idea of a distant Polish baby I'll never feed a single mouthful of borscht to.

'Thanks, was mistake. But good one maybe,' he says, hastily pouring the coffee into the cup. I spoon the frothy milk on top, and we look at the chocolate sprinkles, stumped as to what qualifies as the best cappuccino Mike's ever had. I shrug and throw some on top, before Tomasz gives a wicked smirk and risks a twist of pepper from a nearby grinder. 'Just like in the motherland,' he says, 'where we are savage.' He trots over to Mike with it, standing a little more proud.

'Coffee, Chef,' he says, over-the-top obsequious. Mike barely looks at him, knocking it back before waving him away.

'Get to your station,' he hisses without a word of thanks. Tomasz makes a tiny 'wanker' gesture at me as he walks back past, and I counter with one of my own.

The trout may have sold out on Saturday night, but the sea bream didn't. There's a stack of them waiting for me in the fridge, slightly less perky than they were at the weekend. I shove them aside, knowing Oscar would hate to see them used, and get stuck into a pile of turbot, keen to keep my head well below the parapet. The kitchen's like a court, and someone as lowly as me shouldn't have come in for so much attention from the king. I don't know if said king will be here today – some Mondays he leaves Mike in charge – but I'm not going to risk asking. Mike eventually bustles over to my station, notebook clutched to his puffed up chest.

'Listen up, Fish Girl.'

I don't mind Oscar calling me Fish Girl, there might even be a tiny part of me that likes it, but this is overstepping the mark.

'I'm all ears,' I say.

'I'm thinking crab cakes as a special. Comprendez?'

Comprendez?

'Do we have any—'

'No, but as you're the fish girl, can you go out and do your fish thing.' He delivers this with some kind of irritating hand waggle that I guess is meant to translate to 'fish magic'.

'OK,' I say a tad too unenthusiastically. Crab cakes are the kind of uninspiring special that only the head chef at Fish Surprise in Wigan would jump for joy about.

'OK what?'

He's not? It's like being at the world's least funny panto.

'OK, Chef!'

'That's more like it. Now get to it.' This is accompanied by a weird little running motion. He obviously missed his true calling as a mime artist.

Where is Oscar? I was nervous about the prospect of seeing him, but now I know he's not coming in, I'm feeling oddly deflated. That might be why I take the long way round to the fishmonger's, my eyes alighting on a gorgeous red dress in a shop window that I know I could never afford. Just for a

73

second I wonder what Dom would think of me in that dress and I curse my emotional amnesia. No more dawdling: too risky.

I jog the rest of the way, cleaning the fishmonger out of crustaceans before wending my way back. I've got two massive great sacks of them, crabby claws constantly threatening to pop out through the plastic. I'm stuck wriggling through the heavy kitchen door, trying to heave both bags through without it slamming on me.

'Allow me,' says Oscar, appearing out of nowhere with a steaming cup of takeout coffee.

'Thanks,' I say nervously, aware of his hand brushing mine. He effortlessly takes a bag, holding it aloft and looking at the contents. 'Crab?' he says, looking at me suspiciously, like I've given birth to them.

'Um, Mike asked me to ...'

He pushes through the door and dumps the bag dismissively on my station.

'Mike!' he shouts across the kitchen. 'Get over here.'

Mike shoots across the kitchen, terror in his eyes. Like all bullies, he's at heart a coward.

'Did I order crab?'

'No, Chef. I sent Fish Girl out—'

'She's got a name. It's Amber.' Oscar looks at me as he says it, a smile playing round his lips.

'I sent Amber out to get them,' continues Mike, eyes glinting. 'I thought a crab special—'

'And it didn't occur to you to call me and check how special I think crab is?'

'It was your day off—'

'You still call. This restaurant's been open three months. If a fucking pea rolls under the counter, I want to know about it. You suggest specials, you don't just spend my money on retail price fish without a word. What is this fucking special anyway?'

'Crab cakes.'

Oscar silently eyeballs him, making him squirm still further.

'Um, crab cakes with a lemon and caper mayonnaise.'

I don't blame Oscar for hating Mike as much as the rest of us, but I'm faintly confused. Normally a head chef and sous chef are thick as thieves, Butch Cassidy and the Sundance Kid, following each other from job to job with slavish devotion. Then I remember how bitter Oscar's break away from Angus was. Something tells me his right-hand man must've been collateral damage.

He snorts derisively. 'Thank Christ I remembered days off are for wimps. Stick it in the freezer and I'll think up something else next week. And you,' he says, turning and fixing his gaze on me, 'are going back out for scallops.'

'Scallops?' I say, wondering where this is heading.

'Scallops, little bit hot, with a creamy avocado salsa to make sure no one's mouth gets blown off.'

He gives me a slow smile, which does something rather strange to my insides (though as I'm standing directly over a pile of two-day-old fish, the jury's out on the root cause).

'Yes, Chef!' I say, extricating myself from the awkwardness. Mike casts me a dark glance as I set back out, but I couldn't give a toss, thrilled beyond belief that Oscar would give my salsa suggestion house room. I don't care how much I have to slave over a fish slab if I'm going to get the chance to learn from a master. A temperamental master, no question, but I don't mind getting yelled at if I get the chance to stay on. If the weekend's proved anything to me, it's that I've been looking the wrong way down the telescope – it's my past that's the alien galaxy, my new life that's planet earth. All I need to do is find my centre of gravity.

Scallops prove way easier to transport, they're so light and squidgy, that I'm able to swing the bags with gay abandon. The gay abandon drains straight out of me when I spot Lydia heading towards my station the moment I get back. She doesn't even bother to come the whole way, just beckons me out to the gleaming utopia of the dining room. She blatantly looks me up and down, even though my chef's whites give her nothing to play with. She's looking as slim and elegant as ever, clad in yet another figure skimming shift dress, a gorgeous brass necklace bouncing off her perfect, triangular boobs. If I've got a body that toned when I'm pushing forty I'll feel mucho smug, but I get the feeling nothing makes Lydia jump for joy. Her mouth is permanently puckered into a disapproving moue, a look that's currently directed at me.

'Oscar tells me you're the girl in the know as far as tonight's starter goes.'

'It's a . . . it's a pan-fried scallop, tossed in chilli and coriander, with a yoghurt and mint avocado salsa on the side.' At least that's how I'm imagining the salsa, Oscar might have very different ideas.

'That's a new one on me,' she says, looking at me like I've posited pickled spiders. 'You'll have to give Johnny some idea how to write it up.'

And as if by magic, head waiter Johnny appears, jack-in-the-box-like, from behind the bar.

'Stepped off the coalface, have we? What's for lunch?'

He's a real sweetie, the kind of ruddy-faced optimist whose biggest trial in life probably consisted of a sprained ankle on the rugger pitch. His blond hair sticks up at unruly angles, framing his smiley open features. He exudes health and vitality, the kind of deep seated wellness that comes from generations of privilege. Front and back of house traditionally hate each other (they think we're roughly akin to primates; we think they're a bunch of pretty-boy out-of-work actors) but he's been nothing short of delightful ever since I arrived.

'Couldn't rightly say, beyond scallops.'

'Ooh, love a scallop. Thought Mike said something about crab?'

'The crabs crawled off. It's all about the scallops now.'

'Hmm, so I've got two hours to perfect my scallop pitch.'

'You'll be marvellous, know you will.'

'Ye of way too much faith,' he says, grinning at me as I back through the swing doors.

The next few hours pass in a blur. I prep eel after eel, part of a salad that Oscar's trying out on the lunch crowd. Tomasz and I share the odd smile across the stations. I'm positively humbled by the speed and dexterity with which he attacks his onions. At least fish represent a challenge, a chance to practise one's knife skills on a constantly changing target. Onions are a monotonous graveyard, and yet Tomasz is ninja-like in his precision. As lunchtime service slows, he cocks his head towards the door and we go and stand outside in the yard.

'Would you enjoy a cigarette?' he says, shaking one from the packet.

For a second I'm severely tempted. That's the problem with

working in this kind of high-octane environment: one can't help but crave a treat, however noxious. I know I make a nonsense of those drearily draconian weekly booze allowances, but I can't quite help myself. Even so, a fag's a bridge too far.

'I'm OK,' I tell him reluctantly, swigging from my bottle of water. I've suddenly realised how hungry I am: I hope the kitchen lunch is something vaguely edible. Maya's in charge and despite the fact we're working in a temple of culinary greatness, her penny-pinching ways mean we'll be lucky to get anything more tasty than a tureen of soggy pasta.

'How's your morning?' he asks. 'You were here and back like yo-yo.'

I tell him about Mike's humiliation at the hands of Oscar, which makes him every bit as happy as you'd expect. I ask him a little more about impending fatherhood, catching sight of a picture of the mother-to-be (Slavka, eyebrows like warring beetles) and the baby, *in utero* (hard to know, but suspect eyebrows like that are hard to shake off).

'Sorry, sorry, is all about me,' says Tomasz. 'Do you have man at home?'

My guts contract as I summon up a response.

'No,' I say, disliking the hardness in my tone. 'No, I don't.'

I wish I didn't feel such a pervasive feeling of shame at our failure to get it right. That whole first year we took such sweet delight in trying out our new monikers for size. *Would my wife like her bath with bubbles or without? Would my husband like his toast brown or white?* Now I wonder if we were just a particularly stupid pair of children, playing house.

'No worries, I am sure there is a very good man out there for you.'

Aah, the universal language of platitude has extended its reach to Poland.

'Thanks,' I say, flat. 'She's beautiful,' I add, indicating Slavka's photo. Talk about overcompensating: she looks like a hermaphrodite shot-put champion.

'Yes, very much so,' he says, tucking the photos back into his wallet with satisfaction and making to go back inside. We're at least ten minutes shy of our allocated half-hour break, but the man's almost as devoted to his onions as to his unborn child. But before we can cross the threshold, Mike comes bursting out of the door. He gives me a look of pure loathing, and I brace myself for a bilious outburst, but instead he spins towards Tomasz.

'Congratulations.'

Tomasz looks understandably wrong-footed. 'Thank you, Chef,' he says haltingly.

'You must've invented the world's first self-peeling onion.'

'We were on the way to inside ...'

'How convenient. Just as I was coming outside to drag you back to your station, you were on your way in. Where the fuck does your attitude problem come from, Polski?'

I can't listen to any more of this.

'Mike, we really were coming back in. We've only been out since two-fifteen.'

Another flash of fury crosses his features, but still he doesn't go in for the kill. That's when it hits me: he'd love to boil me in oil, but he's too worried I'm teacher's pet. Way easier to keep taking it out on his new favourite punch bag, Tomasz, an onion-slicing nobody. Me helping him out this morning was just about the worst thing I could've done.

Mike completely ignores me, jabbing an angry finger at Tomasz.

'I tried to give you a chance, I really did. I gave you a final warning, but you just threw it back in my face. End of your shift, clear your locker and get on your way.'

'But—' starts Tomasz before I charge in over him.

'That is *completely* out of order. He hasn't done anything wrong!' I should stop, I really should. Hierarchy is sacrosanct in a kitchen, and shouting at the head sous chef is about the worst thing you can do, bar mooning the boss. I lower my voice. 'Give him a break, he really needs this job.'

A nasty smile crosses Mike's mealy mouthed features and I realise I've screwed up, yet again. I've made it obvious I care, which is all the encouragement Mike needs.

'I've made my decision,' he snarls, heading back inside. 'Now get back to work before you're next.'

I go to console Tomasz, but he simply gives a stoic shrug. 'No fuss. There will be other job. Maybe I be kitchen porter next, is easier to come by.'

'But you're a chef, not a washing-up brush!'

'I am father soon. I need money, however it comes.'

I return to my station absolutely fuming. Watching Oscar sweeping around the kitchen preparing for evening service, I find myself filled with frustration. Why's he letting a nasty weasel like Mike throw his weight around? It should be so much better than this – knackering, yes; soul destroying, no – and he should know better if the rumours about his miserable life under Angus are to be believed. But my bad mood melts shockingly fast when he comes to seek me out.

'Try this,' he says, delivering a saucer of avocado gloop to my station.

I was imagining a certain taste, a rich green mulch, rendered interesting by the judicious use of a few fresh herbs and a spoon of yoghurt. What he's done is way more sophisticated. I can't identify all the flavours – they erupt through my mouth like a fireworks display – but there's no doubt it works. No wonder he's distracted. He's too busy coming up with culinary magic twice a day.

'It's perfect,' I tell him, suddenly hit by a sexual sledgehammer. Who knew that avocado was the food of love (or at least intense, inappropriate, rebound lust)? I know he's forbidden fruit, but there's something indescribably attractive about a man who can do what I do, but a million times better.

'Glad I've satisfied you,' he says, disappearing off.

God, is that sleazy, sexy or completely unconscious? If it's anything but option three, it's nothing more than him flexing his macho muscles, reminding me that the kitchen is his playground. I'm sure he'd only ever want the effortless sophistication of a Lydia type. The likes of me would only be worthy of a quickie in a store cupboard. The very thought. I've been spared so much casual kitchen chauvinism these last few years, just by having a ring on my finger. How will I ever get brave enough to don my spurs and get back into battle? And from what twisted part of my psyche did the phrase 'don my spurs' burst forth?

I force myself to get a grip, concentrating on a recipe for tonight's kitchen meal. I'm in charge, and I'm determined to trump the soggy ribbons of spaghetti doused in watery tinned tomatoes that Maya made us endure at lunch. She cooks like we're incarcerated in Holloway, rather than between the four walls of one of London's finest dining establishments. I decide to make a braised casserole with some meat that's not exactly on the turn, but is definitely looking over its shoulder. I enlist a couple of commis chefs to get braising, and call on Tomasz for some onions. He immediately offers to help, ignoring me when I point out that he doesn't owe this kitchen anything any more. Mike's taking a break way longer than our twenty minutes, and they use the freedom to blast out some music from a tiny transistor as they try to tenderise the sinewy beef into submission. Just for a moment, it's almost feeling jolly.

The meal gets eaten half an hour or so before evening service kicks in, the staff perching around the room, hastily filling their faces. Tomasz helps to ladle it out, and I look at him, wondering how he feels about his rapidly dwindling tenure here. Maybe part of him is glad to be given an easy exit without the sense of personal failure he might've felt if he'd resigned. I rather suspect that's the case, looking at how unfathomably upbeat he appears. He even goes as far as serving the loathsome Mike, loading his plate with food and calling him Chef one final time.

The evening's way more hectic than you'd expect for a Monday. It appears we've got a table of sea lions in for a birthday dinner – all I can hear is honking and clapping and requests for fish – but Johnny assures me that it's just a table of drunken blondes. Their orders come through in a great rush – sixteen starters, sixteen mains – and the kitchen immediately starts to groan at the seams. Looking at the stream of tickets coming through, Oscar rips off his hat and heads for front of house. He pulls Lydia back through the swing doors, just within earshot.

'Why didn't you give them a set menu?'

'Sorry,' she says icily. 'I think the phrase you're groping for is thank you for managing to fill my restaurant to the rafters on a gloomy Monday in the depths of winter.'

Oscar gives a guttural growl of frustration. I watch them lock eyes, and find myself voyeuristically compelled. Any husband and wife worth their salt know each other better than anyone else, bar none. They might be separated, but their intimacy still feels tangible. What gives?

'Thank you, Lydia, but could you maybe explain to me how we're going to get sixteen totally different plates out before it's her next birthday?'

'You'll manage,' she says blithely, eyes sweeping the room. Am I imagining it, or do her eyes fix on me? 'You've got a devoted team.' She sweeps out, leaving him with his fists clenched in frustration. I step towards him.

'Can I do anything extra?' I ask. 'If Michelle and her station do more prep, I can bang out some mains.'

'You were sous in your last place, yeah?' I nod. 'Get on the grill, do your fish thing. Need all the help we can get.'

Never was a truer word spoken. Front of house compounds the agony by seating an army of walk-ins, leaving us stretched to beyond breaking point. The shouting and swearing going on in this kitchen would put a chain gang to shame. As the snowstorm of tickets starts to tip into an avalanche, I hear a low moan erupt from Mike. He's stationed alongside me, even redder and sweatier than the smoking pan he's tending to should render him.

'Are you OK?' I reluctantly ask.

'Of course I'm fucking OK,' he snaps. 'Just get on with it.'

83

'Fine,' I snap, throwing another sea bream into the pan and warming some more sauce.

He's so not fine though. I can actually hear the rumbles and moans from his stomach above the noise of the kitchen. Each time I look at him he's a shade greener, but he won't look round, keeping his attention fixed on his area. Oscar appears at my shoulder, peering into the pan.

'Speed it up, Fish Girl. There's mouths to feed.'

I gently flip the fish to make sure it's evenly browned, then scoop it out of the pan. I offer up a silent prayer that I don't drop it, all too aware of how close he is. As it plops onto the plate intact, I give Oscar a stupid, goofy smile. It's relief, sure, but it's mingled with something else. I liked the proximity, the energy coming off him as he watches me cook.

'Fucking finally!' he says. 'Give her a round of applause.'

Not a compliment I grant you, but it's delivered with a lack of venom that tells me I'm still on the side of the angels. I give myself a tiny shake, force myself to concentrate. Oscar's moved his attention to Mike, who's staring autistically at a trout, one hand gripping the station for support as a bead of sweat trickles down his bulbous nose.

'Come on!' shouts Oscar. 'The sides are plated up already. What's your problem?'

'I'm ...'

'You're what, man? This isn't a fucking old people's home. It needs to go out!'

Mike turns to reply, but moving his head is obviously more than he can handle. A stream of vomit shoots from his mouth, soaking Oscar's whites and coating his shoes. He jumps sideways, a stream of expletives projectile vomiting right back at

Mike. Mike doesn't hang around. Apologising profusely, he runs straight to the staff bathroom.

'Jesus!' shouts Oscar. 'Amber, you're in charge of this station until further notice. Maya, get over here!'

Frenzied doesn't remotely convey the horror of the next two hours. I have never cooked so hard in all my life. Fish after fish passes through my pan as I desperately try to match speed with precision. I'm shouting at the commis chefs like an old-school kitchen Nazi, demanding they plate up faster and get the dishes out front. When Johnny comes out back to chase a rogue salmon fillet, I tear a strip off him, too hot and stressed to remember I'm meant to be a nice person. Maybe Mike was Cliff Richard before the stress of sousing turned him into Alice Cooper. It's hard to believe that evening service will ever end, but around ten it starts to tail off (it is a Monday, after all). Gradually the world stops spinning, affording me a moment to apologise to Tomasz for giving him so much grief when it was at its worst.

'No problem, Chef,' he says with a shrug.

'I know it's par for the course, but it's your last shift and you've had such a nightmare with Mike . . .'

A slow, involuntary smile spreads outwards across his face, making it blindingly obvious what just happened.

'Tomasz, tell me you didn't . . .'

'Is shame to waste fish just because it's, what do you say, on the turn.'

'I can't believe you did that!' I'm genuinely shocked, but he just shrugs.

'You did nice job.' He nods across the kitchen. 'The boss is thinking so.'

I turn around to find Oscar staring at me. He makes no attempt to pretend otherwise, smiling at me with a look of cool appraisal. He jerks his head, summoning me over. I walk across the kitchen, unable to hold his gaze.

'I need to speak to you. Come downstairs.'

He leads me into a tiny office that I've never been into before. Every restaurant has one of these, a chaotic tip where orders are organised and numbers are crunched. I stand there awkwardly, wondering whether I really did pass the test or if, in fact, I'm going to be summarily dismissed, guilty of myriad mistakes I'm too inexperienced to have noticed.

'I've got a proposition for you, Fish Girl.'

Something in me bridles. I might be fighting a stupid crush, but he's got no right to talk to me as if he owns me. Someone needs to remind him he's not Bluebeard. 'It's Amber by the way. You know it's Amber.'

'You're right, *Amber*. I do know it's Amber.' He pauses, smirking. 'I wasn't feeling it for Mike, even before he decided to restage *The Exorcist* in my kitchen. Whereas you, you're all right.'

'Thanks,' I say, wondering where this is going.

'You could possibly be more than all right, won't know until I've tried you.' Another loaded pause. 'Which is why, as of now, you're head sous.'

'But you can't,' I protest. 'What about Maya? And Joe – he's been a chef de partie way longer than me. You can't put me in charge over them, they'll go mental.'

'I can do whatever I like. My kitchen, my rules. The question is if you're up to the job.'

And just for a second I feel like I've been punched in the gut.

I've dreamed my whole career of making it to head sous somewhere like this and, now I have, the person who would've been most proud isn't here to witness it. Would I have told Dom if it'd happened before Sunday? Part of me thinks I would, that despite the spite and bitterness, I would've wanted him to know. Was that really going to be the last time we ever saw each other? My parting shot almost guarantees it. I dig my nails into my palm, forcing myself out of the emotional quagmire. I've got to stop caring, but caring still feels as automatic as breathing.

'Of course I'm up to it! No question. Thank you so much,' I add, reaching out to squeeze his bicep in a stupid attempt to underline how grateful I am. He steps forward, quick as a flash, and gathers me up, kissing me roughly and determinedly. Even if I wanted to stop him I'm not sure I could, and anyway lust's most definitely overthrown logic: my spurs are well and truly donned.

It feels like a lifetime since I've been kissed. Every last bit of my body engages with the feeling of Oscar pressed up against me. He smells of the kitchen, of sweat, of man and it's intoxicatingly sexy. The sheer muscular bulk of him makes me feel like I can abandon myself to it, abdicate all responsibility. I let him pin me up against the filing cabinet, one hand cupping my face. It's when he starts to get a little too keen to cup somewhere more interesting that I come to my senses. I try to pull back, but there's no room for manoeuvre so I'm forced to give his chest a gentle shove. It's like a red rag to a bull. I can feel him pulling my hair and squashing me even harder against the cold metal of the cabinet. I twist my face away.

'Oscar, stop it.'

He doesn't even reply, just drops lingering kisses on my neck.

'I mean it,' I say, desperately reluctant to stop him. 'And if you're only asking me to step up so that I'll lie down, then you mustn't. You really mustn't.'

I tail off hopelessly, distracted by the feel of mouth and stubble working downwards from my neck. If I don't press the eject button this is going to end very badly. I muster up every fibre of moral virtue and duck out of his embrace.

'Jesus!' he says. 'I heard you, OK?'

'Really?'

'Yes,' he says, looking grumpy and ruffled (and sexy. Did I mention sexy?). 'Of course I didn't promote you so I could shag you. It's a kitchen, not a brothel. I wouldn't risk my reputation for a shag. I promoted you cos you're not a vomiting liability. The fact I want to shag you is unrelated.'

'Well, you can't. I couldn't work for you if we had, and I really, really want to work for you.'

'And I really, really want to shag you but ... fair enough.' He shrugs, rootles around in a nearby drawer and pulls out a packet of fags. He lights up. 'I'll just have to pretend we're horizontal. Want one?'

The adrenalin's starting to wear off now, humiliation hurtling into the void. How can I have let him kiss me? I'm old enough and ugly enough to know exactly how sleazy the king of the kitchen invariably is, and yet I still let his hands rove over me like hungry prairie dogs. This must be why his marriage went to pot – a roving eye and a wife within striking distance is a recipe for disaster. Is the naked truth that all men would stray if they knew for sure they wouldn't get caught?

'I should go,' I say stiffly.

He takes a deep luxuriant drag on his fag, grins at me. 'Run along then,' he says. 'Dream of haddock. Tomorrow's going to feel like a whole new world.'

'Good night,' I say formally, smoothing myself down, smoothing his touch off of me. I'm feeling increasingly stupid. For all I know his marriage isn't even over, Lydia might just be playing hard to get to try and bring him back into line. I don't fancy being the ball in a game of marital ping pong.

'Come in at nine. Give me time to break the happy news,' says Oscar, leaning back in his leather chair, dragging on his cigarette. The few feet of floor space between us feel like it stretches into infinity. I'd have to do something really slutty like perch on his knee, Bunny Girl style, in order to bring him back from the land of boss. And I won't be doing that, even though the mysterious switch buried inside me has been well and truly turned back to on. Frustrating though it is, all I can do is walk on by.

Chapter 6

I step through the front door to the strains of 'Diamonds Are Forever' blaring out full blast. Milly's wailing along, but she's so off-key that she could be singing a different song entirely. A pair of red velvet slingbacks lie prone in the hallway and there's a pervasive odour of burnt toast.

'Milly?' I say, sticking my head round the living room door. She runs over, flinging her arms round my neck.

'Thank *God* you're home. Do you think you can get chlamydia from kissing?'

'Not to my knowledge, no.'

'Oh good,' she says, gulping from a brimming glass of white and making a strange gargling sound. 'Want some?'

'Oh, why not?' I say, slobbishly pouring some into a tea cup, too curious to waste valuable time foraging in the kitchen. 'What happened?'

'I'm just an idiot,' she says, heartfelt.

'You're not an idiot! Was it five-date D-day?'

'Yes, but ... you know, I'm not one of Pavlov's dogs. Though he'd probably love it if I was. There's no earthly reason to do it just because it's date five.'

'Tell Auntie Amber all about it,' I say, topping up her glass. Poor Milly looks so crestfallen. I feel rotten for her, but there's also a tiny part of me that's relieved I'm not the only romantic disaster zone around here.

'We've had a jolly time all the times we've met. You know, he's pretty good value. Not a dullard, no kids, knows loads about cows.'

'All true,' I say, 'but you were never going to spend your life with a man called Neil.'

'I know ... Anyway, I thought I should just see. I dug out some sex pants' – Milly has a complicated underwear categorisation system, whereby one section of her knicker drawer is devoted to the uncomfortable but seductive variety – 'and met him at that bar on the top of Centre Point. I got stupidly nervous. I kept sinking martinis till I felt sick as a dog.'

'Perfect! Did he give you a suppository?'

'Don't joke, it might've been preferable. He kept going on about how unpunctual the receptionist is, and how someone tried to get him to neuter a beagle for free, but how no one who could afford a beagle could possibly be on the poverty line.'

'Couldn't they just rent it out for murder investigations?'

'You're thinking of bloodhounds. Anyway, I was drunk enough to be optimistic, and I'd kind of implied last week that tonight was the night. Part of me thought maybe he's nervous too and his way of dealing with it is to ramble endlessly about beagles. I mean, it's way better for the liver than chain-drinking martinis, and he is a scientist.'

'It's so hard to know.'

As she's talking, I'm starting to feel very raw, very new. These kind of conversations used to be a spectator sport. I sympathised, not empathised, and I didn't even have to acknowledge the difference. But now I'm back in the land of mind-reading, the crazy-making place where you're left trying to divine whether someone's experiencing the same heart-melting mix of anxiety and want that you are, or whether he's nothing more than a self-obsessed chancer who wants to get his leg over. Wouldn't it be wonderful if we could call a truce, simply ask the question, but then we'd seem more insane than the most beagle-fixated psychopath on earth.

'But then he says "your place or mine?" and I start feeling like we're in a time warp. I couldn't tell if he was being ironic, and if it would be better or worse if he was.'

'So what did you say?'

'Yours. That's all I said! I am *such* a ninny. And then it turned out he had his car, and I realised he was stone-cold sober and he'd just sipped a half of lager.'

'Oh, God. He must've really wanted to perform.'

'And then it was a Skoda! I accidentally looked at it like it was the least sexy vehicle in the world since the last Reliant Robin got crushed, and then he gave me a tedious lecture about them having the same engine as a Rolls-Royce Phantom or something ...' Milly's getting increasingly wound up, waving her hands around. 'And then he said "click clunk" like the whole concept of seat belts might've passed me by. That's when I should've run for the hills.'

'It's so hard though, isn't it?'

Who am I trying to kid? I'm talking like I know the first thing about dating but I haven't been on a proper 'tonight's the night' kind of date since George Michael was straight. I don't even know what I look like when I'm dating, let alone what I look like when I love. My insides turn in on themselves at the very thought of taking that leap of faith again. When (and if) I do, it'll be a complicated backflip of believing in something new while confirming that what I once believed in ended up untrue.

'Anyway, he lives in some funny new build in the depths of the Docklands. It's really sterile and plastic, like a load of people have taken up residence in a huge chest of drawers.'

'Like the Borrowers.'

'Way less charming than that. He pours me this glass of Ernest and Julio Gallo Chardonnay, and puts a Michael Bublé album on.'

'That man is not an aphrodisiac. Someone needs to tell your date that.'

'I think he may've gathered that now.' She looks into the middle distance, lost in the horror, and I give her hand a squeeze. 'Then he sits down practically on my lap, clamps his hand on my knee and starts snogging me like he's trying to hook a bike out of a canal.'

'Yuck! But you've kissed him before. How come …?'

'He didn't have the same level of intent then. He had a dark purpose tonight.'

I feel a funny wriggle go right through me as I think of the kisses Oscar dropped down the nape of my neck. There was no slurpy hooking going on there. I know I shouldn't feel this way, but it's impossible not to.

'So was that as far as it went? You definitely don't have chlamydia.'

'I wish. After he'd drooled into my mouth for about a million years, he says, "shall we take this next door?" like he's Barry White or something.'

'I don't think Barry White would say that. It's too prosaic.'

'No, you're probably right. He'd say something like, "I know it's gonna be good, you know it's gonna be good, let's go set the sheets alight." That'd be way sexier. Oh God, it's not funny, Amber. It got worse!'

'Sorry, sorry.'

'So we ended up on the bed, and he was sort of yanking at my dress with one hand and pulling his socks off with the other. I mean, I ask you. And then he was squeezing my boobs alternately, like he was weighing up which avocado was the ripest.' She puts a protective hand to her breasts as though they're traumatised children. 'And I'm trying to slow him down a bit, but the evil intent's too powerful. He's muttering totally unwarranted filth in my ear, and I'm suddenly feeling really navy-knickered about the whole affair, but it seems too late to back out. And before I know it, he's got my dress off, and he's on top of me, and it just feels as if he's operating on me. Like I'm a particularly large dog, a retriever or something, and he's pacifying me before he does something utterly dreadful.'

'Please say you left.'

'Absolutely I left. But my excuse, Amber ...'

'What was it?'

'I don't know what I was thinking! I gave this stupid, melodramatic cough and said I thought I might have swine flu.'

'Mate! You didn't?'

'I did. I said it had been going round the office. He got

really cross and came up with all these facts and figures about how contagious it is. I guess he's been at the sharp end, right from when it was restricted to pigs. He called me a cab in ten seconds flat, and here I am, virtue intact, feeling like an utter fool.'

'Babe, you're not a fool! It's brilliant the way you keep on getting out there. You're completely fearless. Not like me, I'm such a wimp. I haven't even ...' I trail off, remembering the way my neck caught alight, little more than an hour ago. 'What?' says Milly, and I force myself back into the room, giving her the whole story from beginning (vomit) to end (sluttishness).

'Oh, my God. He sounds intensely manly,' she says. 'I told you so!'

'I wish you weren't right. I'm the fool, not you. I can't *believe* I kissed him,' I say, hitting myself on the head. 'There is literally nothing more stupid I could've done ... other than ...'

'Did you like it? It sounds like you liked it.'

'Yes, I did, but it's hardly the point. He'll probably keep trying it on now and I'll have to leave. Or worse, he'll sack me. Why would I do something so, so—'

'Fun?' interjects Milly. 'Maybe because fun's been in such short supply these last few months. Maybe because seeing Dom made you feel utterly bloody. Maybe because shenanigans' – I love Milly's vocab, it's second to none – 'reaches the parts other forms of fun can't reach. Just give yourself a break for once in your life!'

'Thanks, Mils,' I say, smiling gratefully. 'I've got to hit the hay,' I add, then notice she visibly shudders. 'Sorry, no more remotely veterinary terms shall pass my lips, I promise.'

There's truth in what Milly is saying, but it doesn't mean the lust fairy can be left to flit around unbidden, sprinkling her evil desire-dust willy nilly. I make myself a distinctly unsexy hot-water bottle, clad myself in a pair of mismatched pyjamas, and roll into bed. I realise as soon as I do, that it's the mention of Dom that sent me scuttling off. Sunday was one more degree of goodbye, but this – this is another. I know it's no more than a fumble, but Oscar's the first man I've got up close and personal with, bar Dom, since Millennium New Year's Eve (pastry chef from Romania – *big* mistake). I want to feel vindicated and triumphant, but it's more delicate and twisty than that.

Does something have a meaning and a value even if it's over, or is it only in the moment that it matters? All those shared experiences and stupid jokes that mean nothing to anyone else – do they vanish without trace, scrambled and jumbled by the passage of time and the lack of another person to vouch for what was true? And it's more than just memories. Dom's family were my family for so long, but I couldn't even bring myself to respond to the kindly messages his brother's wife left me, despite all the Christmases we'd shared. Maybe there will be a time far, far in the future where I'll be ready to go round for chummy kitchen suppers. I'll push aside the garish plastic toys loved by their unborn children, children who will never know that this strange, inconsequential grown-up would've been their aunt if fate hadn't twisted things in a crazy direction.

Let's face it, the only way I'm ever going to get to a place of such saintly magnificence is if I start moving on. So the kiss, the kiss was a good thing, even if it can't go anywhere. Maybe

I'll be like Sleeping Beauty (or at least Sleeping 'Scrubs up quite well with a decent shade of lipstick'), awoken from my pitiful self-absorption by an unusually foul-mouthed prince. Soothed by that positive take on events, I drift off to sleep, only to find myself traumatised by dreams of lobsters who refuse to die, however long I hold down the lid.

I wake up feeling just about as stressed as those poor lobsters. At least there's not much point panicking about what to wear – clean whites and hair back is about as glamorous as it gets in a kitchen. Besides, that fateful kiss has to stay a one-off. From now on, I've got to be one of the lads.

My mettle's severely tested from the moment I walk through the door. From the look on Maya's face, you'd think I'd come in wearing a swastika tattooed across my face, and Joe pushes past me without even bothering to make eye contact. At least my little team of commis chefs are more jolly. I'm sad there's no Tomasz, but Michelle tells me how pleased she and the other commis all are. Still, considering what a tyrant Mike was, they'd probably be thrilled if Joseph Stalin was taking over, fresh from his successful stint plating sides at The Ivy.

I survey the kitchen with new eyes, thinking about what I'd like to change. I know I can't start throwing my weight around just yet, but in an ideal world I'd reinstate Tomasz, then mix up all of the commis chefs so they could try out new skills. I've always had this fantasy about the kind of restaurant I would run. Dom would manage front of house and I would be out back, with a team of smiling joyful chefs who wouldn't mind the punishing hours that running the most successful restaurant in the entire universe demanded, because we would be like one big happy family. The Partridges or even the Von Trapps. I'm shaken from my reverie by Oscar, bellowing at me from the swing doors.

'Morning, Fish Girl. This is where the hard graft begins.'

I scuttle after him, gratefully accepting a cup of the poisonously strong espresso that Johnny's knocked out for us. Oscar strides to a table at the front of the restaurant, not looking back, utterly confident that I'll be trailing in his wake. I pull up a chair, forcing myself to make eye contact, but there's nothing in his demeanour that would tell you he'd been manhandling me less than twelve hours ago. I fumble around for a pen, feeling about as humiliated as it's possible to be.

'What can I handle for you?' I ask, looking up, cheeks blazing. Oscar completely ignores the fact that I've metamorphosed into an incompetent tomato.

'You can handle lunch, that's what you can handle. Richard Douglas is coming in.'

I nod sagely, but I can't quite pull it off. 'Who, who is he?'

'He's my main backer and my best mate. Plus he's Tallulah's godfather, so she'll be in too. I want to join him for at least the main course, so you're going to have your work cut out, I'm afraid.'

Great, so I'm basically responsible for the whole lunch service, plus indulging the culinary whims of a sulky teenager who most likely starves herself and a man who could pull the plug on the whole operation any day he fancies.

'No problem, I love a challenge!' I, the world's keenest Girl Guide, tell him. He saunters off to the coffee machine, giving me a moment to take him in. Why do I find him so sexy? I never find anyone sexy, and certainly not men with that in-built arrogance that comes from knowing they're handsome. Now the floodgates have opened, even looking at his retreating back is making my innards dance the tango. How lucky that he's switched straight back to cool indifference without so much as a by-your-leave.

'I want to push the boat out for Richard,' says Oscar, sliding back into his chair. 'Get a bit bloody.'

'What did you have in mind?'

'We're gonna dump the fish, I'm afraid. Come and say hello to my little friends.'

He heads out back, leaving the swing door to slam in my face. There's a crate lying on his station with a cloth laid over it. He whips it back.

'Ta da!' he says, watching my reaction to the twelve pigs' heads squashed up together like helpless orphans, snouts aloft. He grabs one from the crate, the brains sliding out and down his arm as he does so. I can see Maya surveying me from across the room, hoping I'll crumble. Not a chance.

'Lovely. What we doing with them?' I swear my voice has gone down an octave. I'm butch, baby.

'We're gonna cook every last scrap. Whole pig's head for the brave, ears and cheeks for the offal tourists. You haven't done this before, have you?'

There's no point lying. I shake my head.

'So I want you to get to know Porky intimately.' He grins as he says it, and I feel myself smiling back. Is this the world's first known incidence of offal-based flirtation? He whips a razor out from among the implements on his station. 'We're going to shave him.'

And we do. We hold their greasy pink faces and shave off the downy bristles that cover them. Peculiar though it sounds, it really is intimate. I look into their faces and find myself thinking like the worst kind of vegetarian, wondering if pigs make friends and if they get upset if their buddy gets sent to the abattoir first. If Milly got her throat slit, I'd be beside myself. Still, at least these pigs had a kindly farmer to raise them: Oscar's all about provenance (as long as the supplies aren't being delivered via my cleavage). He stays with me for the first two, showing me how to hold them so I don't nick the skin too much. I should tell him that my stubbly legs are way harder to navigate, but I'm enjoying his tutelage too much. He leaves me to it all too soon, and I pull in Michelle to help me. Everyone knows what a trooper she is, so she often gets pulled between stations. Right now I can see Jean-Paul, the alcoholic pastry chef, eyeing her hungrily, wondering if he can get her to tend to his beloved bread long enough for him to get away with a mid-morning Bordeaux break. I give a subtle shake of my head and he shuffles back to his oven.

'Don't fancy yours much,' she says as I stare intently at a particularly chubby specimen, trying to get the razor into the folds of flesh around his cheeks.

'Look at him,' I say, waggling his face at her. 'If it was midnight on New Year's Eve, I bet you wouldn't say no.'

'You saying I'm a slapper?'

'No, I ...'

She breaks into a grin. 'You'd be right. Tell you what though, there's not much going down in this kitchen.'

'I know, it's a shocker,' I agree, a little too wholeheartedly. I'm poised to shave the snout of pig six when I'm shoved hard from behind. The razor slices into my thumb, spurting blood over the counter. 'Ow!' I say, swivelling round to see Joe jostling his way across the floor.

'Sorry,' he says, a supercilious smirk plastered across his face.

'Wanker!' I say, sucking on my bloody hand.

'Jesus, you OK?' asks Michelle. 'I'll go and get the first aid box.' She lowers her voice. 'Don't worry about it. They're well fucked off, but they'll get over it.'

'Thanks,' I tell her, trying to rationalise my way through the rage. It's not like he came at me with a razor, it was only meant to be a push. Should I be going in guns blazing, asserting my new-found authority? God, it's tempting, but it'll trigger all-out war. I don't want Oscar to think the kitchen's descended into chaos the minute I've stepped up.

As I'm weighing it up, I spot Oscar looking at me questioningly. He didn't see what happened, so he probably thinks I'm just staring into space imagining what would happen if pigs really could fly. What to do? I pick up the next head with my non-bloody hand and pray that he's going to look away. Hygiene is everything and however much animal blood might be flying around, I don't think anyone's going to be wanting 'Amber's Hand on a Bed of Cabbage' any time soon (anyone bar Joe that is). Still looking, still looking. Luckily Michelle reappears and I get her to cover me while I wash my hand in the sink and stick a plaster over it.

Pigs clean shaven, I go off to talk the stations through the list of sides that Oscar's scribbled down and dumped on my station. Screw it: I'm not going to be Mike, but nor am I going to be some kind of cringing girly excuse for a sous. I'm brisk and direct, demanding about gravy and merciless about mash. Then I get back to the pigs, which are being slow cooked in the oven, warm liquid around them, ready to absorb their unique flavour. Oscar watches over them keenly, simultaneously preparing their trotters as a starter. He hates to see meat go to waste; the liver and kidneys are next up. He cuts into the carcasses like it's an autopsy, painstakingly removing the organs and stacking them up. I've got so much to do, but I can't take my eyes off him. I love his brilliance, his innate understanding of the food, the way that his focus is so absolute. I know I shouldn't, but I can't help wanting that focus to turn on me. It's not just lust I'm feeling – it would be safer if it was – it's a more complex kind of fascination. It's compulsion shot through with fear.

'Oi, Fish Girl, stop daydreaming. Get your arse out front and tell them what's on the menu.'

I think we can safely say the compulsion's one-way. How can he thrust me out there so casually when it's his wife's domain? The humiliation floods back through me, as I anxiously push my way through the swing doors. This is why I've got to extinguish all feeling as soon as I can. There's no room for it here. The gods are smiling on me: instead of Lydia's sour moue, I'm greeted by Johnny's beaming visage.

'Look who it isn't!' he says. 'How's day one as second-in-command?'

I hold out my hand ruefully. 'Other than this, it's pretty good. I'm glad I'm not a vegan.'

'To be fair, you'd probably not be hanging round here if you were.' He lowers his voice. 'How'd that happen?'

I shrug. 'You know, if I was Joe I probably wouldn't be all that thrilled at being passed over.'

'It's no bloody excuse,' says Johnny. 'You're the best man for the job, and that's all there is to it.'

'You're too kind.'

'Let's toast it after evening service is done,' he says. 'Tuesday night lock-in, perfect excuse.'

'I am going to *really* look forward to it!' I tell him, then run through the pig-based products on offer today. 'Oh, and Richard Douglas is coming in.'

'Oh, OK,' says Johnny, pulling himself up straight.

'And Tallulah.'

His face falls. 'No Lydia, and Tallulah's in? Did you ever see *Brat Camp*?'

'You'll be magnificent,' I say.

'So will you,' he says, attempting an embarrassing high-five.

The pigs are a hit, right from their trotters to their snouts. Plate after plate goes out. It feels like lunch is way busier than normal, but perhaps I'm imagining it. I step out to tell Johnny that there are only two more turbot left.

'How goes it?' I ask him, and he subtly gestures to Oscar's table.

'Night*mare*!' he mutters.

There's Tallulah, long red-streaked hair trailing in her soup. She's got an enormous padded vinyl handbag taking up the seat next to her, and is wearing the skinniest of skinny jeans. Her eyes are flicking all over the place, a perfect imitation of her mother, while Oscar stares across the table at her. I can't quite hear him, but judging by the way he's looking at her overflowing soup bowl, he's demanding that she eats up.

He's not the only one. Richard Douglas is silver-haired and

bespectacled, mid-fifties at least, but you can tell in an instant that he's refusing to grow old gracefully. The back of the chair reveals that he's wearing low-slung jeans, loose enough to display the top of his bum crack. His glasses have huge black frames like Joe 90, and a battered leather jacket is slung over his chair. His iPhone lies casually next to his plate, alongside a snakeskin wallet. You'd think he'd be exuding laid-back cool, but quite the opposite. He's struggling to spoon mash into the mouth of a screaming toddler, strapped into a high chair.

'Atticus, look, it's a choo-choo train!' he shouts over the persistent wails of his infant son. Or maybe it's his grandson, but my sneaking suspicion is that his efforts to prove how young and virile he is have reaped terrible consequences. I can't help but stare at this picture of urban horror, just long enough for Oscar to spot me and beckon me over.

'Sit yourself down,' he says. 'Richard, this is Amber. She's my new head sous.'

'Hi, Amber,' says Richard as Atticus attempts to rub mashed potato into his face. He holds onto his sticky hands. 'Great job,' he tells me.

'Thanks, though all I did was follow his instructions,' I say looking at an inscrutable Oscar. 'Did you all have the pig?' Tallulah openly rolls her eyes at me as if I've asked her if she's a cannibal. 'The soup's a good choice too,' I add hurriedly.

'Yeah,' she says nonchalantly. 'It was ... nice.'

At that moment the wailing miraculously stops. You can almost hear the whole restaurant breathing a sigh of relief.

'I need a poo,' announces Atticus helpfully into the sudden quiet. For a brief moment Richard looks as though he might start the wailing where Atticus left off. Or maybe he just needs a poo too.

I bet he saw his first tribe of children off to university in about 1992, and found himself suddenly presented with a new lease of life. His wife had probably started to look her age, their sex life was on the wane, and over time he would've begun to wonder if this really was the end of the road. After all, he still had the moves judging by the amount of attention he elicited from women twenty, even thirty years his junior. Little did he realise that it wasn't personal, that decent single men are so thin on the ground that even Quasimodo would find someone in a heartbeat if he lived in a built-up area. Was it an affair at first? Hot sex on the side, no strings attached, until the wife found out. Or did his mistress go for the sperm-bandit option, failing to announce an aversion to contraception until she was three months gone? I've no doubt he loves his son, but something tells me that potty-training an infant while fielding daily enquiries about how it feels to be a granddad was not part of Richard Douglas's game plan. I know I should stop being such a waspish divorcee, but sometimes the fertility time bomb seems so unfair. You can't blame me for experiencing a brief moment of *schadenfreude* when I witness such a prime example of an egg-based terrorist outrage.

'Well, on that note, I should probably get out back,' I say.

'Yeah, you should,' agrees Oscar, 'but tell you what, join us for dessert. Jean-Paul's bread-and-butter pudding is a masterpiece. You need to try it.'

'Oh, OK.' Is this just head chef/sous chef friendliness or is it something more? I should stop being so Jane Austen. Something more in this context would probably involve him trying to persuade me to give him a blow job while he sautés a calf's brain. Chefs are emotional cyanide and I forget it at my peril.

The lunch service is slowing down now, and we're mainly focused on the patisserie station. Apart from the lethal-looking brioche bread-and-butter pudding, there's also an amazing syllabub with lemongrass, and a prune-and-Armagnac tart with gloriously thick clotted cream.

'Try it,' says Jean-Paul, thrusting a spoon in my face.

I'm sensing he's a little bit drunk judging by the brandy breath, but I don't want to risk offending him. He's forty-five-ish and Parisian, as florid and plump as you would expect a baker to be. Up until now I've had little to do with him, stuck on my lowly station, but now I have to know every section like the back of my hand. There's naked desperation in his face, a profound need for me to appreciate what he's offering. I have a horrible feeling he's got nothing in his life except booze and baking, the fatal double helix that can take anyone down in this business. In fact, come to think of it, if I didn't have Milly ... I'm not quite at the stage of taking a nip of whisky between sautés, but I must keep remembering that I can't die old and alone, clutching a spatula to fend off the army of cats eating my face.

I swallow the spoonful, blown away by the sweetness that implodes in my mouth. 'That's incredible!' I don't normally go a bundle on desserts, particularly the pastry-based ones, but the man knows his stuff. I can see why Oscar's hired a drunk, when he's a drunk who's this talented.

'Good, *non*?' he says, a manic look in his eye.

'*Très très bon*!' I tell him in my terrible French accent. I'm heading back to my station when Oscar sticks his head through the doors, beaming.

'Get out here, Fish Girl!' he says. 'Got something to show you.'

In the restaurant, Richard is struggling with his iPhone, not helped by Atticus' attempts at a smash and grab.

'Tallulah, grab the baby, would you?' says Oscar, earning another eye roll.

'Shall I try?' I say, attempting to lift him out of his high chair. He's having none of it, thundering his feet into my abdomen and reaching for Baaaad Daaad.

'Here, take this,' says B.D, handing the phone to Oscar and wearily stretching out his crepe-paper arms. He pulls Atticus onto his lap.

'My girlfriend works on the Style section at *The Sunday Times*,' he tells me. I bet she does, all eight stone of her. 'She's just sent over Tristram Fawcett's review from next week's paper.'

'It's fucking fantastic!' adds Oscar, peering at the phone.

I feel unexpectedly choked up, like we might be teetering on the precipice of culinary history. I really think Oscar could be one of the greats, and it's only now he's striking out on his own that his true brilliance will become apparent to the world at large. A review like this is so key to him entering the premier division, a review like this and . . .

'You've got to be on red alert,' says Richard.

I know exactly what they're talking about. With attention like this, as well as the Michelin stars that his previous kitchen achieved (even if he didn't get all the credit), there's no doubt that the inspectors will be poised to visit. The tyranny of those stars – if you work in the restaurant trade it's got to be a love/hate relationship. There's nothing worse than the kind of fussy faux modern French cuisine (an 'emulsion' of crab, a 'mist' of pistachio) that's been dreamed up with no regard for the customer, but with a slavish devotion to the Gallic-tinged whims of the Michelin guide. A chef can lose all their originality and brilliance in their attempt to hit that moving target. Hell, they can lose even more than that. A French chef actually committed suicide at the prospect of losing his star. But make no mistake: if you get one, you're made. Oscar's eyes are gleaming as he pores over the text.

'Can I see?' I ask him, gently prising the phone from his meaty hand.

Oscar Retford showed great promise in his earlier incarnation as a cog in Angus Torrence's multimillion-pound machine. But it's only now that he's been (acrimoniously) released from the shackles that his true genius has been revealed. There's a deceptive simplicity to his cooking. A dish that sounds plain in description will be rendered magnificent by the subtle but utterly inspired innovations that he brings to bear on it.

On and on it goes, even going so far as to predict a star as being almost a given. I'd be weeping, but Oscar just quietly exudes his obvious satisfaction.

'Well done, Daddy,' says Tallulah, summoning up a trace of enthusiasm.

'You want to get Lydia on the blower?' asks Baaad Daaad.

'Yeah, in a bit,' says Oscar, and I see a look cross Tallulah's face that makes me feel a tiny bit sorry for her. 'I'm gonna tell the kitchen first,' he says. He shouts to the barman, 'Matt, get a few bottles of Prosecco out of the back. We're celebrating.'

As a result, evening service is a much happier affair. Everyone's a little bit oiled, and Oscar's blasting out *La Traviata* like we're on stage at the Metropolitan Opera. I'm right there on the central station, laying out Porky and his chums on a bed of cabbage. This is Oscar in a good mood, but lord knows it's no walk in the park. I'm desperate to prove I'm worthy of the promotion, but it's so much harder now he's watching my every move. I've got Michelin fear too, even though there's no earthly reason to think they'll come in tonight. I'm trying so hard to ensure that the pigs look appetising rather than like props from a particularly ropy farm-based horror movie, that I'm losing pace.

'Christ almighty, you need to speed it up!' says Oscar.

'Sorry, Chef. I'm trying, Chef.'

'Yeah, you are pretty trying,' he tells me, and I can't work out how serious he is.

I grab the next tray out of the oven, trying not to panic. 'Ow'. I am such an idiot. I've managed to burn my hand exactly where the razor cut is. I'm going to have to re-dress it, even though now is so not the moment to take a break.

'Now what?' snarls Oscar as I shout across the floor for Michelle.

'I burnt myself, it'll be OK. Just need a plaster.'

'Pull yourself together, you can't be such a fucking baby. Just put it under the tap and keep moving.'

'I ...' I can't bear to dob Joe in – it's not my inner Pollyanna, more my sense of self-preservation – but nor can I bear looking like a wimp.

Oscar waves a furious hand at me. 'If you're not up to this, you're out!' he shouts. 'Joe, get over here.'

Joe virtually teleports himself across the floor, pushing me out of the way. I glower at him, trying not to articulate the injustice.

'What can I do, Chef?' he says, giving a wolfish smile.

'What do you reckon?' asks Oscar sarcastically, moving over to grant him access.

I step out back to re-dress my stupid injured hand, swallowing down the howl of frustration that's threatening to break free. Could this be it, so soon? Am I back to chef de partie in less than twenty-four hours? I feel utterly crushed, utterly useless. I'd like to crawl into the store cupboard and never come out but I know I can't give up. I step back out as fast as I can, but Joe and Oscar have obviously found their groove.

'You're back on fish for now,' Oscar barks. 'Deal with that cod.'

It's all over before I know it. I can't believe I said I'd have a celebratory drink with Johnny for what's turned out to be the world's shortest promotion. Oscar heads towards me, sweaty and stressed, and I psych myself up for the mother of all bollockings. I try to shut up and take it, but it's beyond me.

'I know I let you down again, and I'm really sorry. I cut myself and ... It's no excuse, I know you'll say I'm a complete disgrace and I completely deserve it ...'

Oscar holds his hands up in a gesture of surrender. 'Shut the fuck up!'

This is it. I'm going to be out the door with nothing more than a plaster to show for it.

'Wasn't your finest hour, but you did OK. I reckon you'll do better tomorrow, and maybe even better the one after that. And if you can't cut it, then I'll boot you out. But I reckon I'm a better judge than that.' He shrugs. 'Get yourself a good night's sleep tonight, you're gonna need it.'

A surge of relief floods through me as his words sink in. I live to see another day, despite Joe's best efforts. Oscar grins at me, and I relax enough to start enjoying how close he is. Dom grew on me like bindweed, tendrils insidiously snaking their way around my heart. It wasn't this guttural pull I'm in thrall to with Oscar. Luckily my rational brain's got it all under control. Gotta love the rational brain. I obviously missed my true calling as a maths professor.

It's just then that Johnny pokes his head through the swing door. 'Almost a full evacuation,' he says, for some reason failing to notice that the boss is standing right next to me. 'Bugger, sorry!' he adds.

'Drinking my profits, are you?' asks Oscar wryly.

'Nothing of the sort!' says Johnny heartily. 'I'll ensure every last drop gets paid for, you have my word.'

'Fine,' says Oscar. 'Just make sure you get properly cleaned up first.'

I take him at his word. Cleaning's not my responsibility, but I'm desperate to show him how devoted I am to the cause. I'm all too aware of him in the background, poring over the order book and poking around in the fridges. Surely he's normally gone by now or am I clutching at straws? After half an hour or so, I spot him heading for the stairs without even so much as a good night. But then he turns round and crosses back to me, stopping halfway

'Night, Amber,' he says, and I wonder if that's better or

worse than Fish Girl. 'Don't stay up too late, you need your beauty sleep.'

What does that mean? Is he telling me I'm ugly or gorgeous or neither? I can't believe I flattered myself into thinking he might harass me. He's been nothing but professional, and all I feel is disappointed.

'I won't. Do you want to join . . .?' I half-ask the question, then tail off.

'Thanks, but you're all right,' he says. Oh God, why did I humiliate myself like that? 'Can't be fraternising with the staff.' Cheeky bastard. He flashes a brief smile, then heads off, leaving me none the wiser as to what's going through his stupid head.

I step back into the restaurant, trying (and failing) to shake the feeling of him off me. There's a bit of a gang sitting round the bar, almost all of whom are front of house. There's Johnny of course, and also Matt the barman, who exudes the same cocky bravado that I've witnessed in every one of his brethren. They're uniquely powerful thanks to the fact they're holding the keys to the liquor cabinet, and boy do they milk it. He's a muscular Northerner with hair that's been so savagely cropped that every bulbous lump of skull is exposed. There's something faintly ape-like about him: he gives me a primate-like once-over, but I can tell he's not remotely tempted to ask me to share his nuts. There's also a smattering of waiting staff, and Michelle, who I asked to stay for a thank-you drink.

'Has he gone?' asks Johnny.

'Yup, safely tucked up in bed,' I say, trying not to betray my disappointment.

'About bloody time, he never normally hangs round that

long,' he says, quickly introducing me to the assembled throng. Niceties dispensed with, he pours me a glass of wine and raises a toast. I chink glasses with Michelle.

'I couldn't have made it through today without you,' I tell her. 'You're a diamond.'

'No bother,' she says, but I can tell she's pleased not to be taken for granted. People say thank you way too rarely in a kitchen.

I tip back my glass far too quickly, filled with a surge of relief that I've survived day one. I top up everyone's glasses, then offer Matt some cash for another bottle.

'Leave it out!' he laughs, and I glare at him. It's so eminently predictable that he's on the fiddle. It's all too easy to fail to put a vodka tonic through the bar, then pocket the money yourself. After all, who's going to notice the bottle's one measure short, and in a joint like this you're talking about £6.50, cash in hand. What to do? Johnny organising this drink is real Glasnost, but there's no way I'm ending day one with my hand in the till.

'Matt, you can't just give out Oscar's booze—' I start, before Johnny steps in.

'Allow me,' he says, reaching for his wallet. 'Cost price at least. I promised His Nibs we'd cough up.'

Matt shrugs, nonplussed, but concedes. Johnny's bizarre turn of phrase suddenly turns on a light bulb in my brain. 'I could sneak my flatmate in, couldn't I?' I ask him.

'Why on earth not?' he says, and I quickly call Milly. She's a night owl and we're only twenty minutes away, so she eagerly accepts. As soon as she arrives I get a round of shots in, even though it's only Tuesday and I should know better.

'It's pretty swank-o-rama,' she says, taking in the well-appointed dining room.

'Yeah, it is,' I say, feeling like a Jewish mother.

'Honestly, Amber, it's gorgeous,' she says, running a hand down the chrome bar. 'You should be really proud.'

'I am,' I say, sensing a sadness in her. 'How was your day at work?'

'Oh, fine,' she says dismissively. 'Now what about Oscar, is he lurking?'

'Ssh, no, he's gone to bed,' I tell her in an undertone, pulling her towards the group. 'Johnny, this is Milly. Milly, this is Johnny,' I say, earning a well-deserved kick from her corner of the table. Subtlety's clearly been destroyed wholesale by Sambuca.

'Lovely to meet you,' says Johnny.

'And you,' says Milly, and then there's a deathly silence. Cupid, I am not. I hurriedly run round the table introducing Milly to everyone else, trying to make my strategy less obvious.

'Oi, Matt, show us how you make that rose Martini thingy,' asks Michelle, and I tag along behind them, determined to give Milly and Johnny sufficient space to realise they're a match made in heaven.

'Watch this, ladies,' says Matt, chucking a stream of vodka into his cocktail shaker from a great height. 'Watch and learn.' He laces it with a strange looking liqueur I've never seen and some rose syrup, spinning the shaker above his head like he's doing a peculiar dance. 'Now for the cherry on the cake,' he adds, pulling three Martini glasses out of a tiny little freezer unit. He pours the pinky coloured drinks in, and adds a single rose petal on top of each.

'Ambassador, you are really spoiling us,' says Milly, appearing at my elbow.

'You're meant to—' I hiss, but she cuts straight across me.

'Cease and desist. You're barking up a totally redundant tree. He's only got eyes for one person.'

'Who? He doesn't fancy Michelle—'

'You, you absolute dummy! Are you blind, deaf and dumb, or just dumb?'

I'm about to rubbish her theory when I look round to find Johnny looking at me as if he's Goldilocks and I'm a particularly appetising bowl of porridge. What's happened to me these last twenty-four hours? I was never even chased in Kiss Chase. Who knew that divorce could confer this kind of erotic mystique?

'You look like a girl in need of some serious alcoholic rehabilitation,' says Matt lasciviously, putting the third glass down in front of Milly.

'Down the hatch,' she says, eagerly gulping it down.

'Did you bring the kitty?' I ask her.

'Most certainly.'

The kitty is a genius innovation for any flatshare. Each of us puts in £25 a week, which we use for all kinds of boring day-to-day expenses (milk, loo roll) and also for more fun, joint activities (buying pink drinks, cabs home when we're too louche and late for the last tube). Occasionally there's the court of the kitty, when a purchase needs to be vetted. A DVD box set of *Mad Men*: definitely kitty-worthy if there's enough ready cash contained within. *Michael Bublé's Greatest Hits*: never, ever kitty-worthy, better to buy a leaning tower of loo roll than squander it on such musical evil.

We try to find Matt and give him cash, but he appears to have disappeared to the loos with a blonde waitress whose name I never established. Instead, I give it to Johnny, who insists it's much too much. I take a fiver back – every fiver counts – but thrust a twenty at him.

'Come and help me put it in the till,' he says, and I reluctantly follow him, hoping he won't go for the lunge. As soon as we're back there in the relative darkness, I realise that he's far too well-mannered.

'Thank you for gracing us with your presence tonight,' he says, all twinkly.

'No, thank you for suggesting it.'

There's a pause, which I break by hitting a random button on the till in a totally unnecessary attempt to open it. Lights flash and beep, a clumsy distraction from the quivering quiet.

'Gosh, I think you're best off sticking to scallops ... You're really rather good with scallops,' he adds, more softly.

'Thanks, thanks very much,' I say, stepping backwards. We are rather squashed together. 'I really ought to get going. Day two beckons ...'

'Oh yes, absolutely. But if you fancy doing this again some time, maybe *à deux* ...'

'Yeah, no, that would be nice.' He looks really pleased and hopeful, and I feel like a horrible insincere witch. I need to nip this in the bud. 'Johnny, I'm just out the other side of a ten-year ... ten-year thing, and it ended so badly and ...'

I suddenly feel more tired and drunk than a geriatric George Best. How does Dom handle conversations like these? Is he still calling me his wife, or has he put it to bed now that I've scorned him for it? It's so pathetic that despite what I said to him, part of me hopes that he does, that he isn't able to expel me from his heart. I remember how creased and crumpled he looked, his distress palpable to me. The heart is such a contradictory bloody thing, the way you can hate someone and still love them and neither cancels out the other. I reach a hand to the bar to steady myself.

'I suppose what I'm trying to say is that I'm absolutely useless right now. You need someone perky and innocent and . . .'

You need Milly, is what I'm trying to say, but of course I don't.

'OK, message received loud and clear. But don't talk about yourself like you're damaged goods. Far from it, you're top of the range. If . . . if you were butter, you'd be in London's finest food hall.'

'I don't really like food halls . . .' That is so not the point. I must be quite drunk. I grab his hand. 'Thank you, you're such a sweetie. Sorry, that's probably not all that flattering if you're a man but it's meant in the best possible way.' I lean upwards and kiss him on the cheek. 'I ought to go.'

He smiles balefully, and I go and grab Milly. We splurge the last of the kitty on a cab, even though she's only pretending it's a treat. She could afford to be taken round London on a litter if she chose to break into her trust fund. I tell her about being compared to the finest butter, and she gets a bit misty-eyed and sentimental.

'Gosh, you're pulling them in droves. I'm starting to feel like the morbidly obese cousin who never gets asked to dance. Butter indeed.'

'Have you seen *Last Tango in Paris*?'

'No! And you know perfectly well that's not what he meant.'

'A) butter's frequently rancid and b) you're not remotely like a fat cousin. No, it counts for nothing. I don't fancy Johnny and I can't have Oscar.'

I can't, I really can't have Oscar, but don't we always want what we can't have? Yet again, love turns me into a walking, talking cliché and I don't have the strength to fight it.

Chapter 7

I think it must have been the Heineken effect – Oscar's kisses reaching the places that a love-free life can't reach – but I'm officially over the worst. I'm concentrating on being chef of the year, following Oscar's gruff instructions to the letter, and making sure I avoid a stand off with the surly chef mafia. I've longed for this kind of break for so long, and I'm damned if I'm going to throw it away now. Reviews are beginning to trickle through slowly, starting with the smaller, crappier freesheets. The two that have been out this week have been absolutely respectable, but nowhere near the dizzy heights of Fawcett's appraisal. Bookings are still unpredictable – the obvious slots like Saturday night are packed to the rafters, but during midweek lunchtimes the dining room can still feel as sparse as a November garden.

On Saturday morning, I come in even earlier than required, despite the fact I'm secretly so tired I could sleep in a soup tureen. I know I'm pushing myself too hard right now, but there's a manic energy pulling me through. Joe's the first person I see, and I give him a cheery hello, determined to kill him with kindness.

'Morning, Fish Girl,' he says, a nasty smirk on his face.

Ignoring him, I sail through to the locker room, only to find the lock on my cubby is totally jammed. I wrestle with it endlessly, finally twisting it open with a knife. It springs right open, spewing out a cold cup of espresso designed to douse my whites.

'Arsehole!' I shout, catching the glass seconds before it smashes on the floor.

I breathe in, trying to swallow down the swearing and stamping that's threatening to erupt. How long is this going to go on? It's so unsettling to have a few days blissfully free of torment, and then another attack. I wish I knew who was in on it. Joe's obviously up for a full-scale vendetta, but how big is his army? Commis chef Stu comes through the door as I'm weighing it up, still coated in coffee. I watch his face to see if he's pleased but he seems genuinely shocked.

'Shit, Amber. What happened?'

I gesture uselessly at the glass in my hand, trying not to get upset.

'Stay there and I'll get a cloth,' he says, dashing through to the sinks.

I sponge myself down, thanking him profusely as he mops the floor. He even goes so far as finding me a spare top from his locker. It's way too big for me, but I could cry with gratitude.

'Trust me,' I tell him, 'you're not going to be chopping any onions over the next few days.'

Oscar barrels through the swing doors just as I'm trying to make it look a bit less like a kaftan. This look could only be sexy if you had a Mama Cass fantasy keeping you awake at night.

'There you are!' he says narkily. 'Oversleep did we? Joe told me you were still hanging around in here.'

'I ...' There's just no point. Revenge is a dish best served cold (a fact amply demonstrated by that cup of espresso).

'Come on,' he says, jerking his head towards the main floor, and we start walking towards the office. He seems especially grumpy, even allowing for him thinking that I'm late. There's a black brooding cloud around him that makes him feel utterly unreachable. Is it the lack of slavering devotion in the first few write-ups or could it be me he's disappointed in? I've done a fairly respectable first week, but I did let him down on my first evening service and I haven't been throwing my weight around like most sous chefs do. I've got to own this job, show him that I'm cut from the same cloth and make it clear to those fuckwits that I'm a force to be reckoned with.

'I wasn't late, I really wasn't,' I say once we're in the office.

'If you say so,' he replies flatly.

I push on. 'Oscar, if I really am head sous, then I've got some ideas I want to put forward.'

'Oh yeah, and what might they be?' He puts his fingers into a steeple, and leans his chin on them, staring at me through hooded eyes. He suddenly feels so infuriating to me, as judgemental and superior as my bloody mother. My mouth suddenly takes off in a whole direction I never expected.

'A) why don't you think more about vegetarians?'

'Cos they're a bunch of anaemic numpties who don't understand the first thing about food. I make sure some poor fucker knocks out a bit of rabbit food for them every day, and if they've got any sense, they'll eat the fish.'

'Don't be so backward.' I've got the bit between my teeth, which is never a good thing.

'Backward?!'

'Yes, backward. You bang on about provenance and seasonality and all that jazz. Well, vegetables are a prime example of seasonality. If you took your vegetable suppliers as seriously as your meat suppliers then you could really innovate.'

'What, so meat is murder in your book, is it? Did you go home and weep into your My Little Pony pillowcase about Porky and his mates?'

'No, I love cooking with meat and I love what you do with your meat.' Did that come out wrong? 'But have you even heard about global warming? Or fish stocks? Loads more people are going vegetarian. If you applied your powerful brain to the ways of vegetables, you'd add a whole new aspect to the menu.'

'My powerful brain?'

'Yes.'

'The ways of vegetables?'

'Yes.'

'You're fucking unbelievable. What's B? Is there a B?'

'Yes, there's a B. I want to reinstate Tomasz. He chopped onions like an automaton, he's got a baby on the way and he's nice to have around.'

I hope I'm right about this. I don't know why I'm being so sentimental about a tiny Polish foetus, particularly considering its dad's merciless use of rotten fish, but I can't bear the injustice of his firing. But it's not just that, if I'm honest. If I'm going to need an army, I'll have to recruit.

'Fine, I don't care who the fuck chops my onions. Hire who

you want, but if he's shit, then on your head be it. I'm more interested in C. Come on, Fish Girl, what's C?'

I really ought to stop talking.

'Everyone should have a voice in this kitchen.'

'Who do you think you are, Martin Luther King?'

'Hear me out—'

'Hear me out? What is it, do you have a dream?'

'I just think that it'd be great if people got to speak up more, make suggestions for the odd lunch service. If I'm going to run the kitchen when you're not here then I'd like to know what Michelle thinks ... or Stuart, or ...'

'Or Joe and Maya perhaps?'

'Yeah, or them. Obviously.'

He's looking at me hard, probably well aware what kind of treatment I'm coming in for, but I refuse to break. He leans back in his chair and pauses long enough for me to start to panic. What am I doing talking to him like this? I can almost hear Mum in my head. 'You've got no respect for authority.' Is every single day going to involve a moment where I think I'm unemployed?

'All right then, let's take this point by point. A – vegetarians are a total waste of space who shouldn't waste their time or mine coming to a joint like this. If they want to pay top dollar for the arse end of a courgette then so be it, and if you think there's some kind of vegetable main that's like the lost gold of Atlantis, then prove it. You can be in charge of the *vegetarian option*,' he makes stupid speech marks with his fingers, 'from now on. Dazzle me.'

Bollocks. I've really set myself up here. I don't know why I went on that stupid rant. I do actually think vegetarian food is

123

ripe for innovation, particularly in a high-end restaurant like this, but if I was concentrating ruthlessly on furthering my own career (which, let's face it, I am) I would try to come up with the kind of impressive meat and fish mains that would fly off the menu and make me golden.

'Good, prepare to be dazzled,' I tell him, like I'm compering some terrible talent show.

'My eyes, my eyes,' he says, but at least he's (sort of) smiling. 'Oh look, here comes your worst enemy. It's time you got acquainted.'

I look towards the swing doors, expecting hateful Joe, but instead it's Mac the Steak who appears.

'Ay ay!' he says, advancing towards Oscar. Butchery is the perfect trade for Mac, who looks much like a pig who's worked out how to stand up on its hind trotters. His nose is gargantuan and tips upwards, snout-like, while his eyes are small and beady. He's as wide as he is tall, a blood-smeared apron barely encasing his vast belly.

'How are you, my son?' he says, clapping Oscar on the back with his right trotter.

'Not bad,' says Oscar. 'This is Amber. She's replaced Mike, so you'd better remember the face.'

'Won't be a chore,' says Mac lasciviously, making me want to take a razor to his face like I did with his piggy brethren.

'What you got for us today?' asks Oscar. 'Did you bring the bellies like I asked?'

'Most certainly did,' says Mac, 'as well as a surprise. He likes a surprise,' he says to me, conspiratorial.

He goes back out to his van and Oscar fills me in. 'I've known him for years. He's the best meat supplier in the business bar none.' No wonder, knowing it from the inside out like he does. Mac comes back in with a covered crate.

'Is this the *pièce de résistance*?' asks Oscar. 'This one's got a vegetable fetish going on, she might not approve.'

'Veggies?' says Mac, like I've announced I slaughter newborn infants for kicks. 'You're not one of them vegans, are you?'

'No. I simply think they're an under-represented minority.'

Mac gives a (literal) belly laugh, as Oscar makes a 'la di da' face. I did sound like a bit of an idiot, truth be told.

'The main event!' says Mac, whipping off the cover like a magician. Oh God, I'm glad it's twenty-five years since I saw *Watership Down*. There's fifteen small brown furry rabbits lined up in there like their mum's left them to have a little doze. Only she slit their throats before she left.

'You up to the challenge, my good sir?'

'You betcha,' says Oscar, picking one up by its hind paws and holding it aloft for closer inspection.

'Lovely jubbly,' says Mac, aiming a sly grin in my direction.

'They look great,' I tell him. 'Can't wait to get stuck in.'

He waddles off, transaction complete, and I ask Oscar what he's got in mind.

'You tell me,' he says. 'If this place was yours, what would you do right now?'

I scrabble through my mental Rolodex of recipes, desperately searching for a smart reply. There's a long, deathly pause before it finally delivers.

'How about sautéing them? Do them in a bit of cream and bacon, some nice herbs, maybe a side of mash.'

He looks at me, and I wonder if he thinks I'm some kind of culinary simpleton.

125

'Yeah, very nice, very Franglais. I wanna get more down and dirty with it though.' A tremor goes through me unbidden. 'I wanna pull them apart and put the pieces back together again.'

'Humpty Dumpty rabbit?'

'Something like that.' He grabs his bashed up leather notebook from his back pocket. 'Rabbit two ways, maybe three. Use every last scrap and get maximum bang for your bunny.' The cost of ingredients versus the net return is a key concern in any restaurant. When you've factored in the overheads, a single slice of bread gets expensive. 'Let's try a risotto with it. We'll make a sausage out of it, then we'll purée the livers and sauté the kidneys. Mix that in at the end, delicious.'

'I'm sure,' I say, trying to imagine it. Silence of the Bunnies.

'I'm going to try a mousseline for tomorrow too, needs to cook overnight. Need to keep something vaguely froggy on the menu, in case those sodding judges come in.'

He doesn't look up, scribbling down ideas with fierce concentration. I get momentarily lost in watching him, loving how much he loves it, how much he innately knows. There's a confidence in him that only comes with age and experience. He looks up, catches me looking.

'Go on then, take them out back,' he says. He seems relatively cheerful now, blackness evaporated. Maybe I imagined it, but somehow I don't think I did.

'Yes, Chef,' I reply, excited about the challenge, however furry and adorable the raw ingredients look. But it's not just the rabbit I'm excited about. Oscar keeps close tabs on me all day, letting me help out on the risotto and ensuring that the mousseline prep is just so. My crush has flooded back full force, every tiny brush against me swelling out of all proportion, even though Oscar shows no sign of being similarly afflicted. It's fun, I tell myself, harmless fun. The fact I absolutely can't have him is what's letting me play. It's like watching a police chase in *Trumpton*.

Lunch is frantic, messy, hectic, just another day at the coal-face. All the time, I'm trying to solve two conundrums: a) how to come up with a vegetarian option so spiffy that it'll make Oscar herald my genius; and b) how to take down Joe before he gets there first. He's stabbed me and drenched me and it's only week one: it's kill or be killed.

I don't take so much as a crisp break, let alone a lunch break, entirely consumed with the task in hand. Eventually I settle on a lovely orange pumpkin (or four), roasted and blended with fresh herbs, chilli, breadcrumbs, and goat's cheese. The first attempt looks a bit like an industrial accident in the Tango factory, but try two looks pretty good, even more so once it's paired with a crisp green salad and some roasted baby potatoes. The net ingredients are still roughly tuppence, particularly compared with the hefty price Oscar assigns it.

'Not bad,' he says, scooping some into his bristly face. 'Only a retard would choose it over the rabbit, but there you go.'

'You see, the path of vegetables is a righteous one.'

'Whatever floats your boat, Fish Girl. Now get back on bunny duty, you can get a minion to see to this.'

I rang Tomasz as soon as I could, and he's already back at his station, keen as mustard, peeling and dicing pumpkins like they're going out of fashion. 'You do good with Oscar,' he says admiringly, and I hope he's not implying anything dastardly. That's about all he says though, hell-bent on proving my faith in him is justified. He chops, he sautés, he scrubs his station until it gleams, then does it all again.

'Is he on drugs?' asks a laughing Michelle, and I feel a sudden rush of camaraderie. They're a really good bunch. Maybe I can rise above Joe's malevolence, and my desire for Oscar, and make this whole experience the fantastic new start that I desperately need. My mind flits momentarily to Dom. I wish he didn't share this birthday week with my brother, it makes it so much harder to put him out of my mind. Enough: onwards, upwards, oven-wards.

I knew evening service would be busy, but this is like nothing I've ever experienced. When Johnny ventures out back I try and make him admit they've squashed in some walk-ins, but he swears blind they haven't.

'Come and see for yourself. It's a glorious sight, a fully booked restaurant. Just feels this way because it's never been this busy.'

'I don't mean to sound totally self-obsessed, but are they liking the pumpkin? Are the plates coming back clean?'

'As a whistle,' he says warmly. 'In fact, the girl on table twelve asked me to send her compliments to the chef. Didn't realise it was *your* cunning little concoction.'

'Did she?' I say, pathetically gratified. I love Johnny, just not in *that* way.

'She certainly did. We're getting a bit more into the pudding zone now. You should come out and let her thank you in person.'

'I'll do my best,' I say, noticing Oscar's beady eye on me and scooting back to the bunnies. I slave away for another twenty minutes or so before I realise I'm desperate for a pee. I've been on my feet for almost eight hours, and I've lost all sense of my body. I get Michelle to mind my pans, and slip off to the loo, sitting there a moment longer than necessary to regroup. I come back through, drawn from my path by a tantalising glance at the packed front of house. Surely there's time for me to take a tiny peek at the pumpkin fan?

I think I'm going to be sick. There she sits, right in the middle of the restaurant, earning every drop of vitriol that Oscar saves for vegetarians. Hateful, loathsome, husband-stealing Rachel, right there with my hateful, loathsome husband. Of course she ordered the vegetarian option. One of the few facts I gleaned from Dom before he wisely decided to never mention her name was that although she worked in corporate law, what she *really* wanted to do was human rights.

I try and tear my eyes away but it's impossible. Besides, I'm not sure my shaking legs will carry me anywhere. She's dressed in some ghastly leopard-print dress, cut low to expose her mammoth udders. She's shooting for vampy, but her big broad shoulders and middle-aged highlights ruin the effect. How could he do this to me? How could I have been stupid enough to feel bad for making him feel bad, when he's been seeing her all along? '*I still call you my wife.*' He must have been humiliating me for the sake of it, teasing me like a lion patting a mouse. I can't help but stare at him, everything I thought I knew, everything I believed, smashing to the ground like a sky-scraper felled by an earthquake. All that guilt and distress – is he really so good an actor or am I just exceptionally stupid? I wonder if I'm going mad, if I chose to see and hear what I wanted rather than the truth of what he was saying. And if I am that deluded, how far back does the delusion go? Maybe my entire marriage was an optical, emotional illusion. I stumble backwards through the doors, colliding with an ebullient Johnny. Just for a moment I really, really want to hit him.

'You spotted her then? Turns out it's a celebration. She's asked for his crème brûlée to come out with his name iced on it and candles.'

'Oh, has she?'

'Any chance you could ask Jean-Paul? Don't want to risk him biting my head off for denigrating his dessert.'

'With pleasure,' I say, a sort of madness descending. I turn to go.

'Hang on, you need his name! It's Dom,' he shouts after me. 'Thank God it's short, eh? Should just about fit.'

I go and speak to Jean-Paul, who reacts predictably badly.

'Who are these people?' he shouts. 'This is not a child's birthday party at McDonalds. *Non*. She can take him home and do her own icing with a, what's it called, Mr Keep-ling.' He pronounces it with such profound disgust that there's no room for argument. Perfect.

'Honestly, Jean-Paul, if you saw the state of her … but we need to try and do something. Between you and me, the guy she's with is quite big in the business. We don't want to seem unaccommodating.' I pretend to ponder. 'How about if I did it?' I ask after a pause. 'You don't have to touch it, pretend it never happened.'

He scowls at me, shrugs. 'Pouf,' he says, jerking his head towards a warm cornet of chocolate, and I get to work. My teeth are gritted with concentration, my mind entirely focused on the task. I stand back, wishing I had someone to share my handiwork with. TWAT it says, in big chocolate capitals. Once I've added a couple of candles, the letters acquire a lovely glimmering sheen. Who could fail to be charmed?

I'm not proud of what I do next. I wait a few minutes, figuring Johnny is about due a brief fag break, now they're on the home straight. Then I grab a newbie waiter, and give him the dessert.

'Are you sure?' he asks nervously.

'Yeah, yeah. They're old friends of mine. I promised her, he'll love it.' What is wrong with me? Turns out hell really does hath no fury like a woman scorned. I watch, riveted, as he crosses to the table. Rachel spots the dessert from a couple of paces, breaking into a rousing rendition of 'Happy Birthday' in happy anticipation. Her piercing tuneless drone reaches the next table who gaily turn their chairs to join in. Dom looks down, hating every second. She's such an idiot. Restaurant customers are his day job, the last thing he'll want is a load of them fussing over him on his night off. As she gets to 'dear Dom' the bomb lands on the table.

'Happy birth ...' she tails off, post-box mouth agape. She looks up at the hapless waiter, about to launch into a tirade.

'What the ...' starts Dom, as I sail up to the table.

'Happy birthday, darling,' I say. 'She asked for your name to be iced on. Did I spell it right? Wasn't sure how many Ts you're using these days.'

He looks me straight in the eye, white as a sheet, and suddenly it's not funny any more, if it ever was. The other table is watching, aghast. Even Rachel's been silenced for the first time in human history. I don't know quite what to expect, but I would've bet on an explosion. Instead he speaks softly.

'What are you doing, Amber?'

I narrow my eyes. 'What am *I* doing? What are *you* doing more like?'

'I know what you're thinking. You're thinking I'm a lying bastard, and I don't blame you ...'

'Oh, how very generous ...'

Dom looks at the rapt faces around us, managing to embarrass table eleven into backing off.

'Amber, please, can you just hear me out? We need to go somewhere and talk about this.' He looks back at Rachel's pasty, calculating face. 'Sorry.'

'No we don't,' I say, my voice rising. 'Quite apart from the fact that I'm in the middle of evening service, I wouldn't waste my breath blowing on you if you were on fire let alone have a conversation. Happy birthday.' By now I can see Johnny heading across the floor, alerted by my poor spotty victim to the havoc I've created. 'By the way, your dress? Looked *way* better on Lily Savage,' I hiss at Rachel as a parting shot. 'Sorry, sorry,' I say to Johnny, pushing past him to get to the relative calm of the kitchen. Oscar spots me as soon as I'm through the doors, jerking his head to beckon me over. Has news of my appalling behaviour reached him already?

'Where were you?' he barks.

I try and pull myself together, but he's not remotely aware of what a state I'm in. Besides, I'm probably no madder than anyone else here. As we speak, Jean-Paul's swilling brandy and seemingly building a replica Eiffel Tower out of meringue, while Tomasz busily conducts a full written audit of the aubergines.

'Sorry, someone was asking about the pumpkin.' I look at

him, wondering if it's my imagination or if he himself is look-ing extra mad. There's a manic quality about him, like his body can't contain what's sloshing around inside him.

'What'd you do, read them the recipe? Cook it *in front of them*!? I need you here, backing me up. Has that not pene-trated your skull?'

He's right of course, so right that I want to cry. I try and apologise, but he's well and truly on one.

'I promoted you, without a scrap of evidence you were up to the job. No fucking proof whatsoever. And going by what I've seen so far, I made a monumental mistake.'

On and on he goes. I stand there letting the tide of rage wash over me. I'm faintly aware that even for him, this is quite a temper tantrum, but it doesn't really matter to me right now.

'Think you might grace me with a response, Fish Girl? Anything going on in that head of yours?'

I look at his face, wondering what the correct reply is, but nothing seems to matter right now. It's like the colour's bled out of the picture, like inside of me is cavernous and infinite, a snowy landscape with no visible landmarks.

'No, just that I'm still really sorry. I know how much you need me, and I won't bale out on you again.'

Oscar looks faintly wrong-footed by how chastened and calm I sound. People normally quake and prostrate themselves in front of head chefs, but I just don't have it in me right now.

'What, that's it?'

'And also, could you not call me Fish Girl, just for tonight?' As I say it, I hear the catch in my voice, no longer able to block out the sadness of what's happened. How completely inap-propriate. He can call me every name under the sun if he so desires. After all, I've sold him my soul. I wait for the next round of unfriendly fire but it fails to materialise. It's like the anger's been exorcised, just like that.

'Come on,' he says. 'I need to show you something.'

Johnny's racing through the door, obviously on the warpath, but now I've got the perfect excuse to body swerve him. I swiftly follow Oscar across the kitchen, expecting him to lead me down to the office but he shoves open the door to upstairs instead. A bolt of fear goes through me but I swiftly dismiss it. He's hardly going to wrestle me to the ground, rip my petticoats aside, and ravish me like some kind of Regency villain.

As I reach the top of the stairs, a fat black and white cat barrels into my legs, mewing vociferously. Oscar scoops it up.

'Chill your boots,' he says, 'not everyone's got food.'

'I didn't know you had a cat!'

He's lovingly stroking its head, crossing to the galley kitchen and pulling a tin of food out of the fridge. 'Meet Moriarty. Lydia wanted joint custody but I was having none of it.'

I take a look around the room. It's compact and neutral, but manages to avoid being bachelor bland. How could it be when there's a huge painting of a nude above the fireplace? Despite the subject matter, it manages to be tasteful, an impressionistic line drawing of a woman lying backwards. There's a big, silver-framed picture of a younger Tallulah in school uniform, perched on an inlaid coffee table, and a pair of comfy sofas arranged in an L around it. I risk perching on an arm, wondering if Oscar really did bring me up here to meet his cat. I think about asking him but I'm too unsettled by the shifting sands of his moods. I probably should have said no when he set off up the stairs, but there was no way I was going to. An image of Dom sitting opposite Rachel flashes across my mind and my insides wrap themselves up like a poisonous snake.

'Is Moriarty sated?' I ask, crossing towards him.

'Yup.'

'What did you want to show me?' I'm flirting, I can't deny it. Anything to hold back the avalanche of anger that's poised to engulf me the minute I give way. 'And what's the wine situation?'

He opens the fridge, pours a glass of white for me without asking what colour I want. I'm not a big white drinker, but as soon as I take a swig, I'm blown away. It's like nectar, honeyed but still dry enough not to be sickly. Definitely not on special at Costcutter.

'Wow, it's amazing,' I say, but Oscar's not listening.

'Have a read of this,' he says, thrusting a glossy supplement at me. 'I got one of the porters to get an early edition from King's Cross. More fool me.'

Close But No Cigar reads the headline. It's Tristram's review, but not as we know it. *Oscar Retford's a chef with years of experience under his belt, but as a restaurateur, he's a new kid on the block. Unfortunately for him it shows. Ghusto shows definite promise, but it lacks the killer combination of flair and polish that made Violet such a bonafide hit with critics and diners alike.*

And so it continues, slyly suggesting that Oscar's talents were far better served when he was part of the Angus Torrence empire. When I get to the section on the cooking, I really start to feel the ouch. I look up at him, wanting to sympathise, but he nods for me to continue reading. *The night's designated*

135

special, a pan-fried trout in herb butter, wasn't quite special enough to merit the moniker. Pared down perfection is one thing, but this tasted more like peasant food. The wife fared better with her plate of lamb's kidneys, but this dish would also have benefited from a more radical approach.

'Since when do peasants eat trout? Has he been hanging out in a gulag in Knightsbridge?' Oscar looks grim, and I worry I sound flippant. 'I'm gutted for you,' I add, laying the ghastly thing down, 'for all of us.'

Oscar looks at it murderously, then screws it up and hurls it at the wall. 'I should've fucking known,' he says. 'There was no way Angus was gonna let me off the hook.'

'Why, is he . . .'

'He knows everyone. His organisation's like the mafia. He's got spin doctors so ruthless they'd make Alastair Campbell piss his pants. They've got inroads with the *Sunday Times*. There was no way they were gonna let that review get out there.'

Is he being paranoid? Looking at the evidence, I fear not. For one brief, egotistical moment I wonder if trout-gate is responsible, but the review's faint praise is broader than that. I search for the right words of comfort, but I'm all too aware what a body blow it is, how real the impact might be on Ghusto's future. As I'm groping for the right response, I'm suddenly struck by how weird it is that he's made me his shoulder to cry on, even though he was bawling me out fifteen minutes ago.

'Oscar, your cooking's amazing, one bad review can't change that. Word of mouth, other reviews, stars . . .'

He gives a half-smile, obviously thinking I'm a simpleton. I don't entirely blame him – I know I'm downplaying the impact, offering him a false kind of comfort – but I can't quite help myself. I'm like a cheerleading squad that won't get off the pitch, refusing to accept it's a wipe out.

'What did Lydia say?' I ask, giving up on the up-spin.

'Haven't told her.'

'You haven't *told* her?!'

'She never wanted me to leave, thought it was a stupid idea when we'd just got the second star.'

'So how come she came with you?'

'We're a team, just not in that way any more. Besides, Angus would've made her life hell if she'd stayed.'

I sit backwards on the arm of the sofa, trying to work it out. Who wants who back? Surely someone must. 'So you and Lydia . . .'

'Why are you so fascinated by me and Lydia?' he asks sharply.

'I don't get it, that's all. If I had to work with my ex, I would stab him with a steak knife before the end of day one. Or I'd force his face through the meat mincer . . .' I'm getting way too into this.

'We met when we were too young, worked 24/7, got older and wiser, realised it wasn't the thing any more. It was more than twenty years ago, for Christ's sake. She was doing her A levels, working some kind of Madonna look that didn't play all that well in Putney.'

I subtly try and do the maths, suspecting Lydia's one of those women who stubbornly insists she's thirty-nine until someone prises her passport out of her dead hands.

'I was cooking with her brother,' Oscar continues. 'I took her out on a date, think it was U2 at Wembley Arena. The rest is history.'

'Exactly!'

'Exactly what?' he says, pulling a chair towards me.

'Well, you've got all that history. How can you bear to have a lesser version of what you had? If it isn't the relationship it was, isn't it agony?'

'Agony?' He laughs. 'Things change, people change. We still get on, better than we did when we were trying to pretend we were still love's young dream. I'd be lost without her, to be honest. We just don't want to shag each other any more.' Little bit too much information there. 'You're a bit of an idealist, aren't you, Fish Girl? Sorry, *Amber*.'

He smiles condescendingly, wondering at my sheer naivety. Still, I'd rather be naive than cynical any day of the week. Surely you should hope for the best, and shoot for the best, rather than kidding yourself that the consolation prize is good enough? I hope, with every fibre of my being, that Dom knows he's got the consolation prize.

'I wouldn't have shouted if I'd realised what a sensitive flower you were,' he adds, smirking.

'I'm not some shrinking violet,' I say, a tad too acidic. 'I can handle myself.'

'I know you can,' he says more softly. 'But I shouldn't have lost my rag. I just wanted you there when I read that shit. Dunno . . . I guess I'm getting used to having you around.'

He holds my gaze a second too long and before I know it, I've sprung across the room and kissed him. What am I doing? I should pull back now, but I'm not yet ready to resume normal service. The world feels topsy-turvy and strange: nothing and no one can be trusted.

'Slow down,' he says as I slip a hand inside his shirt. 'Are you sure about this?'

'Yes,' I insist, pushing myself against him.

'Have it your way,' he says, pushing me back so I'm sprawling on the sofa.

There's something distinctly dominating about Oscar, a sense that he can't be denied. Once I've given him the green light, there's no stopping the train. He kisses me roughly, deeply, slipping a hand under my top without much preamble. But it's not like he's a testosterone-ridden teenage boy with no ability to pace himself. He strips my clothes off seamlessly, kissing the exposed flesh so seductively as he does, that I couldn't resist even if I wanted to. By the time I'm naked, he's naked, at which point he scoops me up in his arms and carries me to his bed. It's then that I ask for a time out, momentarily stunned to find myself in bed with any man, let alone this man. I look up at him, taking in his stocky muscular body, so different from Dom's whippet-thin frame. The physical realisation of where I'm going sets the topsy-turvy world spinning again, and I wonder if my bravado is going to hold up.

Oscar must sense it. He strokes my face, suddenly tender. 'How you doing?' he asks, and in doing so makes me OK.

I didn't realise quite how sexually frustrated I was until I had sex. The poor man. Once I've recovered my memory, I won't leave him alone. We lie in the inky semi-darkness and I try not to think about how little of the night is left for sleep. He runs a finger across my temple.

'What's going on in that powerful brain of yours? Still thinking about pumpkins?'

What's going on is me trying to hold back the panic about what the likely consequences of this madness might be.

'No, moved on from pumpkins.'

'Thinking about my pumpkins?'

'I reckon it's time I left your pumpkins alone.'

'Yeah, maybe for tonight. But not permanently.'

'But, Oscar, what about ...'

'It'll be fine. Don't get your knickers in a twist.'

'Haven't actually seen my knickers for about two hours.'

'They're lovely. Black scrappy things.'

And with that he drifts off to sleep, leaving me to lie there wondering what the hell just happened. It takes me ages to get comfortable, too used to sleeping alone to accommodate another body, let alone such an unfamiliar one. Eventually I squash myself up close to his sleeping bulk, the side of my face alongside his chest. Ultimately it's comforting, this big, powerful man breathing over me. Tonight of all nights, I don't think I could handle flying solo ...

Chapter 8

It takes me a good ten seconds to remember where I am when I wake up. My snout is buried deep in Oscar's flanks, my arm flung across his chest. Please, God, let me not have dribbled. I'm trying to work out how to extract myself when he stirs, leaning down to kiss my hair with unexpected tenderness.

'Morning, Fish ... morning, Amber.'

'Morning,' I mutter, face turned down, embarrassed about my nakedness, my morning breath, the grease that's surely coating my hair.

He places his thumb under my chin, pulling my face upwards. 'Shall we try that again? Good morning, Amber. Would you like a cup of coffee?'

'Good morning, Oscar,' I say, giggling despite myself. 'That would be delightful.'

'Well, make me one while you're at it.' Unbelievable! 'Joking,' he says, taking in my thunderous expression. 'I'll be back in five.' He rolls out of bed, totally comfortable in his nakedness. He grabs a grey waffle robe from the back of the door, busying himself in the kitchen. I can hear him grinding beans, shooting frothy milk out of the machine. He might not be an idealist about relationships but he sure is about coffee. Better not tell him that more often than not, I start the day with instant. He comes back in with two cups and saucers, and places one next to me.

'I'm warning you, it's rocket fuel. Today's gonna be tough, I need everything you've got.'

'I hate to break it to you, but I think you might've had everything I've got,' I say, drawing the sheet a little more tightly around my breasts. He grins at me.

'And as you might say, it was delightful.' He runs a finger round the side of my face. 'More than delightful, pretty fucking spectacular. But now I need your other talents.'

'Don't forget I'm only down for a single. I've got evening service off.'

Oscar looks royally put out. 'Today is not the day to let me down,' he growls. 'Not after that dirty bomb of a write-up . . .'

'I booked it ages ago. I've done so many doubles this week, I'm on my knees.' Wrong, wrong and thrice wrong. Never complain about the hours, particularly when you're naked. 'It's just because it's my brother's birthday dinner. There's no way I can skip it.'

'How old is he?'

'Um, thirty-four.'

'And how old are you?'

'How old do you think I am?'

'I'm not falling for that one,' he says, wry.

'I'm thirty-one.'

'Ten years,' he says, taking a hasty swig of his coffee. 'So you were fourteen when I became a dad. That's it, put your clothes on.'

I look at him, face full of trepidation. This is obviously a disaster, but I can't quite cope with any more humiliation.

'Joking!' he says again, setting down his coffee and rolling towards me. 'Joking,' he says more softly, kissing me, hands roaming my body. He's like a drug. As soon as he's on me, I'm completely lost in it all. Was I always like this or is he especially good at it? To answer that question I'd have to think about Dom, and there's no way I'm going there when I've got such a good means of distraction.

Half an hour later I'm under Oscar's power shower, trying to get my head round the realities of spending the next eight hours trilling 'Yes, Chef' to a man who's spent the last eight hours exploring every nook and cranny of my body. There's no point projecting forward – I've just got to get through today as professionally as I can and then take a view. I wish to God I didn't have to go to Ralph's dinner on three hours' sleep. I can imagine the pity overload that's going to be coming my way. *Poor Amber, divorced in infancy yet looking every bit as raddled as Ronnie Wood*. I am going to need a factory's worth of foundation to look remotely presentable.

I swaddle myself in a thick towel, suddenly poleaxed by the practicalities. How the hell am I meant to get downstairs without anyone noticing where I've emerged from? And it's not like I've got any clean clothes. I'm going to be reduced to turning my knickers inside out like some binge-drinking old slapper. Oscar's in the kitchen, whites on.

'I've got bad news for you,' I tell him.

'You've got syphilis?'

143

'No, don't say that! You're going to have to tie your sheets together and lower me out of the window.'

'Don't be stupid, you're not escaping from Alcatraz. I'll go downstairs, check the coast's clear, then you pretend you came through the front.'

'It's not that simple! What if Lydia's on the floor? Or Johnny, or ...' I can tell it's bothering him way less than it is me and for one mad, jealous moment I wonder if he's trying to rub Lydia's face in it. Perhaps I'm a pawn in some twisted game between them, a revenge shag designed to remind her who's winning.

'I could be wrong, but you don't strike me as much of an abseiler so I can't see you've got many options.' He shrugs. 'It's your own fault for taking advantage of me. If you hadn't been so up for it, we'd have been down there an hour ago.'

God, he's infuriating, but luckily he's right about the coast being clear, and I get out back without too much trouble. We studiously ignore each other for the first half hour or so, with me rushing round the stations dispensing the kind of over-enthusiastic chivvying you'd expect from a Brown Owl with a coke habit. When I get to Maya's station, she looks at me as if she can see into my very soul and it's not pretty.

'Everything OK here?' I say, then notice that she's shoving a copy of the scathing review back under the station while a couple of her commis chefs slink away.

'All good,' she says coldly, and I back off, feeling for Oscar.

I sneak a look in his direction, but he hasn't noticed. I hope they're not taking that review at face value, mocking him for how much of a performance he made about draft one. How much do the kitchen like him? He's not the most approachable man, gruff and growly unless there's cause for celebration. I know him better than that now (way better) but if you're just frying his onions, you'd have no idea how funny or charming he can be. He needs their loyalty right now, even more than he ever has.

I am extra subservient all shift, determined that Oscar doesn't think I've forgotten my place in the hierarchy now he's had sight of my knickers. He's super focused today, insular and uncommunicative, and I can't help but feel a band of paranoia tightening itself around my heart. It was more than a revenge shag, much more, but I can hardly put the timing down to coincidence. Now that I'm chopping in the cold light of day, my logic (or lack of) feels wildly flawed. How to get over a crippling rejection – jump into bed with a man who's ninety-nine per cent guaranteed to reject me, and will then remain inescapable unless I commit career suicide. Pure romantic genius.

It's taking all my strength to keep a stiff upper lip, particularly when Oscar snarls at me that his rock salt's gone missing (what does he think, I've snuck off to bathe in it?). I'm not remotely prepared for the arrival of Lydia, who sails majestically into the kitchen, oblivious to everyone bar Oscar. Suddenly it all feels hyper-real, a love pentagon lit up in neon lights. She's left the field clear, separated from Oscar enough for me to infiltrate and colonise. But I never would have done that if Dom and I hadn't drifted, allowing Rachel to slip in under cover of darkness and set up camp. All five of us, intimately connected, however much we're pretending those ties have been severed. Whatever Oscar says, I can't believe Lydia wouldn't be devastated to know what happened last night, that it took place under her nose.

The fact I know that, that I can see I might be *her* Rachel, makes the surge of jealousy I feel utterly hypocritical. When I see Oscar stop dead in his tracks, focused entirely on what she's got to say, it hits me like a truck. His respect for her is second nature, world's apart from his casual rudeness to me. I couldn't have cared less this time yesterday, it was the most natural thing in the world, but now it feels like a slap in the face. I've got to slam on the brakes before it gets more messy than it already is. But something's happened, something fierce and illogical has sprung up inside me. Caging it may require more strength of will than I can lay claim to.

They disappear into the office, no doubt to discuss the review, and I study their retreating backs to see how intimate they look. They're stuck in there for a good fifteen minutes, and I become insanely convinced that he's seducing her. The mental hamster wheel is short-circuited by the arrival of a sober-faced Johnny.

'Good morning, Amber,' he says coldly, sounding posh and authoritative enough to be Prince Charles' chief equerry. I jump in feet first, no time for niceties.

'Johnny, I am so, so sorry for my appalling behaviour last night.' And that's only the half of it. 'There's no excuse for me compromising your operation like that, but ...' I grind to a halt slightly, slapped in the chops by the memory of Dom and Rachel's dinner à deux. I'm not sure I can bear to eviscerate myself in the way I need to explain my sin, but I don't seem to have much choice. Johnny's as silent as the grave, waiting for me to dig myself one.

'It was my ex-husband. We split because of that, that … woman.' Normally this would be the space to insert an expletive, but the fight's rather gone out of me today. 'He swore to me it was over, so when I saw them out together for his birthday … I, I just lost it. You know how it is when love turns to hate?' I look at him pleadingly, and his expression starts to soften.

'It was Leo's first day on the job. He wasn't remotely qualified to cope with what ensued.' He pauses, anger dissipating. 'Thank God Lydia wasn't there.'

'So you haven't told her?'

'I'm not a snitch.'

'Thank you so much. I really don't want to lose this job. Not any time, but not now.'

He smiles. 'It does sound gruesome, I give you that. I had no idea you were a divorcee.'

'It's hardly something to shout about,' I say quietly.

'You know what I think?'

'What do you think?'

'What I told you. That you're the best butter there is. Butter of kings, divorcee or not.' A smile cracks his face in two like a sunbeam hitting water, and I get to wondering how much he feels for me. He barely knows me so it's all going to be a fantasy wrapped around an illusion, but I get the sense it's more than a crush.

Today of all days I should be longing for a quiet shift, but the fact that it's less manic brings me no joy. There's a bunch of late cancellations and a couple of no-shows, which has to come down to the faint praise heaped on us by Tristram.

147

Oscar crashes around the kitchen like a bear with a sore head, barking orders. Nothing anyone does is right, there's no music, no laughter, just cowed chefs trying to look busier than they are. I stay longer than a single shift demands, a pathetic part of me longing for reassurance. Eventually I have to leave. Oscar's rootling around his station, jaw set. He looks up, eyes as black and cold as midnight in Siberia.

'Um, Oscar, I've got to get going soon. It's my brother's birthday and—'

'I know.'

I glance around, wondering if anyone heard. Would it make sense for him to know where I'm going?

'I'm sorry,' I say, though I really shouldn't be apologising for taking one measly shift off. 'It's just I haven't seen him for ages and . . .'

'And he's thirty-four today. Yeah, got it.'

He's so brutal when he's like this, so unyielding. I wish I could hurl myself into the water, force a ripple from him, but he's giving me nothing. I feel that familiar scorch of humiliation. I've got only myself to blame – the rules have changed back, and I'll have to abide by them.

'Is there anything I can do for you before I go?' I can feel a crimson tide flooding my face. 'Like menus? Are you happy with the specials for tonight?'

He looks at me stony-faced, then breaks into a smirk. Who can blame him, what with my purple face and the way I'm twisting a tea towel around like a string of worry beads.

'OK, Fish Girl, let's talk specials. Step into my office please.'

When we step through the door it's more like we've stepped through the looking glass into a parallel universe. He's kissing me like I'm life support while attempting to strip the clothes from my body.

'Slow down,' I say, unclamping his hand from my cleavage. I couldn't bear to feel he was impervious to me, but this is no less complicated.

'I can't lay eyes on you without wanting to shag you,' he mutters, and I'm struck by three parts lust, one part fear. I need to look after myself.

'That could make working in a kitchen quite a challenge. I'm pretty sure there's a nudity clause in my contract.'

'Yeah, I wrote one in especially,' he says, slipping a hand downwards.

I sidestep him, wanting to hold onto a tiny bit of power. He might be setting the rules, but I can still umpire. 'Did you really want to talk to me about the specials?'

He scowls at me, but in a way that doesn't feel too mean. 'Yeah, come on then. Take a look over what I'm thinking through for next week.' He fires up his laptop. 'I'm not having that arse-wipe Angus destroy me. If those judges come in, we'll be ready for them.'

'It's just one review ...'

'Don't want to talk about it,' he says determinedly. 'Read if you please.'

And I find myself utterly absorbed in the dishes he's created, amazed as ever by the pairings he's come up with. I venture a few suggestions, some of which he snorts at, some of which he grudgingly considers. It's only once we've got to Thursday that I realise that I've wasted an hour. Well, not wasted, but ...

'Shit! I'm literally dead, I've got to go. I'm meant to be in Ealing at seven-thirty.'

'You'll be fine, just jump in a cab. Bags of time.'

He so doesn't get it. I've got to make an emergency pit stop to discard my skanky smalls before I even set off for deepest suburbia. And the chance of me being able to afford a cab to take me that far is roughly equal to the chance of me casually hiring a rocket to whizz me to Mars. I could scoot, but I really can't face this particular soirée stone-cold sober.

'Yeah,' I say, kissing him one final time. 'I'll see you tomorrow.'

I burst through the door, determined to de-pant and re-pant in a matter of seconds. Forget all my grooming aspirations – a lick of mascara, a spray of dry shampoo and I'll be out the door. Instead I nearly go head over heels, ankle snared by a gigantic Selfridges bag. It's the first of many, stretching like a gaudy procession down the length of the hallway. This bodes ill.

'Milly?'

I texted her this morning to reassure her that I wasn't dead in a ditch, and got a bald *OK x* back. I thought the lack of curiosity was worrying, but I didn't have the headspace to engage.

'Hi,' she says quietly. She's huddled on the sofa, wearing a grey cardi with a large price tag. I won't tell you what the price tag says because you'll be horrified, but she's basically spent half my weekly salary on a piece of school uniform (cashmere, I grant you).

'Are you OK?' I say, even though I know full well she isn't. That's the essential contradiction of Milly. She's all highs until suddenly she's low. And when she's low she's subterranean.

'Yeah, no, I'm fine.'

If I was a really good sister I'd take her at her word, spruce myself up and dash out the door, but then I'd be a really bad friend. I cross to perch on the arm of the sofa and reach for her hand. She doesn't make eye contact.

'No, you're not. Tell me.'

'You're in a hurry.' At that exact moment my phone beeps angrily, just to illustrate the point. 'And anyway, there's nothing really specific, just . . .'

'Just?'

'A general sense that human existence is a pointless and futile exercise.'

'I see, a full-blown existential crisis.' I squeeze her hand, trying to get her to smile. 'Yes, that definitely qualifies as nothing.'

She manages a tiny upward turn of the mouth, hugging the cardi more tightly around her slight frame, and I wonder what to do. I've known her since we thought corduroy OshKosh dungarees were a fashion statement and she's always had a tendency to slip down the snake of gloom.

'I know it's stupid, Amber, and I don't want to pin it on being single. I mean, I might meet someone who doesn't tranquilise horses for kicks any day now, but it all seems a bit much of a muchness.'

'What does?'

'The treadmill of it all. Working, dating random individuals, buying rectangular plastic dinners from Marks and Spencer.' This time she smiles properly. 'Apart from when you save me from myself on your days off.'

I feel a stab of guilt at how often she is left with the

rectangular plastic option. I stand up, taking her hand to pull her to her feet.

'Amelia Arbuthnot, I'm officially saving you from yourself. That cardigan needs an outing. Come with me, I'm not leaving you here on your own. We can tackle the essential pointlessness of human existence on the way. And I can tell you exactly why I didn't make it home last night.'

'I'm not sure if I ... And anyway, it's a sit-down dinner.'

I give her a tug. 'No buts. They can borrow a stool and we'll share my portion. It'll be a blessing to be honest, Beth can't cook to save her life.' I can see she's wavering, but isn't quite there yet. 'Come on, Mils, I'm not belittling how you feel, but I know stewing won't help. Trust me, I'm a doctor.'

I've won her round, and we blast out Beyoncé as we slather ourselves in make-up. It's not just altruism that motivates me: gloomy or not, I'm really grateful to have a companion. It's a bit of a step down from a husband, though come to think of it I'd rather have Milly by my side than that cheating scumbag. Don't think about it, don't think about it ... Luckily a sexy text from Oscar comes pinging its way through the electronic airways before I get too obsessive.

Once we're safely ensconced in a cab (bless Milly for offering), I try and dig a little deeper.

'Has something happened?'

'No, not really.'

I feel a bit out of my depth, truth be told, I always have. Ephemeral gloom isn't really my thing: when I'm miserable it's specific, a clear target rather than a hazy mist of sadness. And even then it's misery, not depression. Depression sounds like a boggy, marshy place, a swamp that holds you down against

152

your will. Misery might be cold and sharp but at least you can swim through it, keep moving until you collapse, exhausted on the other side.

'Actually that's not completely true . . .'

I'm relieved. If there's a cause then there's got to be a solution. 'What was it? You can tell me.'

'It'll sound so awful. You'll . . . you'll just think I'm a spoiled cow.'

'I would never think that!'

She pauses, looks at me. 'I just got this great wodge of money through that I wasn't expecting.' She looks at my expectant face. 'You see, it doesn't make any sense! It's pathetic.'

'*That's* what's made you unhappy?'

'Sort of. I just sat there staring at my bank balance feeling a tiny bit sick. It feels faintly obscene. I'm going to give a ton of it to Oxfam, even though I know my dad would be furious with me.'

'I still don't get why it makes you sad.' I wish it worked in reverse. I wish my overdraft made me so mad with joy that I danced down Oxford Street in only my pants.

'It makes me feel like I've been neutered.' We break into giggles, and I breathe a sigh of relief. 'Bad choice of phrase. It's just . . . it makes whatever I do a bit pointless. I could never earn that kind of money, never in a million years. Maybe that's why I've never tried. And now look at me, I'm a thirty-one-year-old sort of do-gooder, with a rackety personal life and a great line in cashmere cardigans.'

'Don't be so hard on yourself,' I say as it finally clicks into place. I'm sure some people would say Milly is the last person who's entitled to moments of extreme misery: no financial

153

responsibilities, elfin face, no cellulite, four limbs in perfect working order. I'm ashamed to say I've occasionally been one of those naysayers. But now I can see it's exactly that that takes her down these dark corridors – the sense that she should be happy, and that she has no earthly justification not to be. It's a crippling case of psychological stage fright. 'Who you are isn't what you do anyway. I don't mean to sound like I've time travelled from Woodstock, but you being you, being so lovely, is enough.'

'How can you, of all people, say that? When your career's everything?'

'It's not everything,' I say quickly. Is that really how I come over? Like the Tin Man, with a Moulinex mixer where my heart should be?

'No, not everything. Sorry ... but it does make you happy.'

'Yeah, and I do think a real job would give you something you need. But all I'm saying is you're not worthless without one.'

'Thanks darling,' she says, squeezing my hand. 'And I know you won't take it, but I want you to know if you did want me to pay off your overdraft, I'd do it in a nanosecond.'

'You're already charging me buttons in rent. Save your fire-power for the tiny African children, honestly,' I say, still rattled.

There's not much of the journey left, but I manage to squeeze in the potted highlights of the last twenty-four hours, leaving Milly open-mouthed. 'Promise me you'll be careful,' she says, as the cab wheels into Ralph's road. 'Treat yourself like you're bone china.'

She's right of course, and I need to hear it. As we clatter up the path I get another text from Oscar – a little sweeter, a little less filthy – but I hold back from replying. While he's got every right to call the shots at work, there's no reason I should give him that privilege wholesale.

The door's opened by Ralph, looking distinctly merry. His shaggy blond mop of hair is sticking up at a tipsy angle, and his checked shirt is half undone. That won't be Beth's doing, it'll be that adorable bundle of toddler he's effortlessly holding. Ralph's always been stupidly tall and broad; he could carry sextuplets without breaking a sweat.

'Feltopp anko dip?'

'Hello, Frank,' I say, leaning in to kiss my two-year-old nephew. God, he's gorgeous, all fat cheeks and blond hair. He reaches sticky fingers out towards me.

'Kuptic,' he adds, beaming with pleasure at his contribution to the conversation.

'Still speaking only Frankish?' I ask.

'Not a word of English has passed the boy's lips. I lie, we think he might've said "nana" last Wednesday, but I couldn't swear to it.'

'And anyway it's an abbreviation. Doesn't really count.'

'I'd take an abbreviation any day,' says Ralph, handing me his offspring so he can embrace Milly. 'Hello, stranger,' he says. 'Haven't seen you for ages.'

'You should come and visit,' she says.

'Fat chance of an audience with my sister,' he says, tapping his watch. 'Slaving over a hot pan were you? Don't even start trying to blame this one on your job.'

Slaving under a hot boss more like. I experience a little jolt of pleasure at the thought of that last text, but there's no way I'm telling Ralph about my indiscretions.

'Hang on, I read something about your Führer, I meant to tell you.'

'What? That horrible *Sunday Times* review? It was total crap.'

'No, not that. It was something Beth saw, I'll ask her.'

I follow him down the hall, raining kisses on Frank's round, pink face while he giggles delightedly. This boy is definitely Ralph's progeny. The thing about my brother is that he was always the star of the show, the adored first-born son who me and Ben followed round like an anointed king. He decreed what games we played, who got the top bunk, whether or not fishing was cool (it was, then it wasn't). It was the same at school. Fiercely bright and fiercely sporty, Ralph was always a natural leader. When he got into Cambridge, it was no great surprise, but I suspect that he was deeply unnerved by the unfamiliar sensation of being a small fish in a big pond. Cue the acolytes.

'Hello, everyone!' I trill brightly, casting a reluctant look around the assembled throng. Every year it's the same old bunch: 'Big Greg', so-called because he's, well, big; Posh Anthony and Gay Bryan, plus their other halves. I cast a hopeful eye around for Beth's older sister Laura, a foreign correspondent with a wicked sense of humour. Every year I'd say to Dom that I couldn't understand how someone hadn't snapped her up yet, a comment that only now, ringless and vulnerable, strikes me as intensely patronising.

Beth's got her head stuck deep in the oven. 'Don't do it!' I quip, but she's too stressed to laugh. She kisses me hello, a dusting of flour in her hair giving her the look of a deranged geriatric.

'Should I put milk in carrots?' she hisses, urgent.

'For Frank? I'm sorry but I wouldn't have the foggiest . . .'

'No, not for Frank! For the carrots. I'm mashing them.'

'*Milk* in carrots? Mashed carrots?' I try my hardest not to look repulsed. 'No, I really wouldn't.' I can't bear to witness Beth's desperation. Scrub that, I can't bear to risk mass food poisoning. 'Have you got an apron?' I ask, and she gratefully thrusts one in my direction.

As I'm rescuing the poor, innocent carrots from looming liquidisation, I can see Ralph introducing a beaming Milly to Posh Anthony, who seems to have come alone this year. And why wouldn't she be? He's tall and dark, with a painfully chiselled jaw and a smile so white it could blind you. He's a fellow medic, with a cut-glass accent and a lovely flat on the river to boot. Tragically, he's also the most charmless individual you could ever hope to meet. It's too late to warn her, she'll just have to suffer the disappointment.

Ralph leaves them to it, bringing a singing Frank over to the cooker. I think the tune is vaguely akin to 'Baa Baa Black Sheep', but you'd never know from the words; 'Huu Har Burpoy' seems to be the main refrain. Maybe we should all give up and convert to Frankish. Maybe it's the new Esperanto.

Beth looks mightily relieved at the distraction. 'I'll pop him into bed in a sec if you really don't mind holding the fort.'

I think about asking if I can do it, but quite apart from the risk of food poisoning, I see him so rarely he might mistake me for the child catcher. I settle for tucking his blond hair behind his ears and kissing him good night, feeling a little sad as I do so. As I pull away, Ralph pokes me hard in the ribs.

157

'So, anything to report? Any sex-yuw-al intercourse on the cards?'

'Ralph!' snaps Beth. 'Don't be so crass. Don't pay any attention to him, Amber.'

'It's fine,' I say, whacking Ralph back. '*Shut up!*' I know he's taking the piss out of Dad and the time he embarrassedly sat us down with a book called *How Babies are Made*, and for ever burned the phrase 'sex-yuw-al intercourse' into our brains.

'How are things though?' adds Beth, unpeeling Frank's chubby paw from her nose. 'Stop it, darling,' she protests as he pokes a probing finger up her nostril. I know she's trying to be kind, but I can't help feeling that motherhood means you're only ever half there. Even if your children aren't sticking a finger up your nose or into a plug socket, if you're doing it properly, you have to give over a large proportion of your heart and your brain for all eternity.

'Yeah, basically fine,' I say non-committally.

'That's great,' she says distractedly. 'I better get him upstairs.'

'You didn't tell me Marsha was getting married,' says Ralph after she's gone.

'How did you know?' I ask, guiltily aware that I've done absolutely nothing about her engagement drinks.

'She sent a "save the date" email. Didn't you read it?'

I've worked so hard these last couple of weeks, I've barely had time to brush my teeth, let alone check my emails. I vow to get on with coming up with a venue, pushing away a tremor of sadness about Dom. Being a maître d' extraordinaire, he'd have known exactly where she should hold it, and been able to negotiate some fabulous deal for her. I keep blocking out what I saw, and then having to remember all over again. As if to remind me that life's moved on, my phone gives an angry beep right on cue. It's Oscar, natch. *Where are you?* he's written, no kiss. There's something a little bit gratifying about the hint of obsession that his agitation implies. *At dinner, in the burbs, like I said* I text back, with an *x*.

'Who's that?' demands Ralph.

'Mind your own beeswax,' I tell him smugly.

'You are! You are having sex-yuw-al intercourse!'

I give him a death stare.

'I'm not having a go, you can tell me,' says Ralph.

'Maybe I am, maybe I'm not.'

'I won't tell Mum and Dad.'

Oh, God, I can't begin to imagine what they'd think if they knew how I've chosen to celebrate my promotion.

'Don't look like that,' adds Ralph. 'She's not the enemy.'

'I didn't say she was.'

'You didn't have to.'

We stare at each other in sulky silence.

'It's way harder than it looks,' continues Ralph. 'I mean, I love Frank to bits, but sometimes he's *such* a little fucker. I thought reasoning with a drunk with a head wound was a ball ache – it's got nothing on wrestling a Snickers bar off a toddler.'

'Don't be so mean!' I laugh, despite myself.

'All I'm saying is that perfect parents are a myth, you only get them in Enid Blyton books. Everyone screws it up.'

'Not literally, not like Mum did.'

'Jesus, Amber, you're like a dog with a bone sometimes,' snaps Ralph. 'You never let things go.'

'Fucking hell, Ralph, that's so unfair!' I'm almost crying, aware I'm overreacting, but unable to regain control. It's the echo of Dom that's done it, the way that my inability to forgive him became as big a crime as his affair. How could he let me feel that way when he was seeing Rachel all along? 'I'm the one who found out, not you! I'm the one who had to tell Dad . . .'

'I'm sorry. OK? I'm sorry!' says Ralph, putting his arm round me. 'Forget it, forget I said anything.'

It's like the two events knock against each other like wind chimes, each making the other reverberate harder inside my brain. I was twelve when Mum had her affair, and was just beginning to get interested in boys and take pride in the fact I almost merited a bra. My needs were simple, all I wanted was to be the first girl in our gang to get their period (why?!) and to marry Blake from *Home and Away*. Dad was running a pub restaurant in the village while Mum was working in Manchester, punctuated by frequent trips abroad. She was meant to be in Germany this particular half term, which meant I could get away with far more (Dad was always a soft touch). That was how I came to be in Leeds, came to spot her having a way too cosy lunch with a man I'd never seen before, who most definitely wasn't my dad. She was in the window of Café Rouge, bold as brass, fingers intertwined with his, laughing at something he'd said. I was with a gaggle of my mates, but something stopped me telling them, made me take the information away and bury it. I was ashamed I think, ashamed that my family wasn't what I thought it was, that my whole sense of myself was built on a lie.

I watched her obsessively – how she spoke to Dad, how she touched him. Suddenly the comforting mundanity of their relationship felt like a living, breathing lie. There was no intertwining of fingers, no caresses – to me it felt like Dad was being sold a terrible falsehood. Mum soon picked up on my silent resentment (my permanently narrowed eyes and flaring nostrils might've been a clue) and tackled me about it on the way to my piano lesson. I was always a bit scared of Mum, intimidated by her quiet authority, but I raged at her now, spoke to her in a way I could never have dreamed of. And she, she stepped out of being my calm, controlling mummy and became a weeping mess who begged me not to tell my dad, to give her time to end it. I was so confused those next few days, waiting for the bomb to drop. It was greed that gave me away. I stopped eating, wouldn't touch Dad's most special and delicious Victoria sponge. His kind, concerned face was too much. I told him everything, watched the shock spread right through him, then watched him try and pull himself back so as not to distress me.

At first there was a relief that it was out in the open. Mum and Dad sat all three of us down, promised that it was over, that they still loved each other very much. But of course we couldn't step through the looking glass and go back to being the family we once were. We were kids, selfish kids, who hadn't had to worry about much beyond ourselves and our petty battles up until then. Suddenly it felt like everything at home was under the microscope, that we couldn't take anything for granted any more. We all seemed to find more and more excuses to be away – I went from being a total piano dunce to a wholehearted belief that I could be Beethoven if only I took enough lessons, and Ralph played enough football to be a shoo-in for the World Cup. It was Dad who crumbled. He had what I now realise was a mini-breakdown, giving up his job and spending all his time around the house. While we all whirled around, finding more and more ways to fill our already packed schedules, he seemed to get stranded there, inert and uncommunicative. It was like the house was the past, and he believed that if he waited it out, we'd all return to our proper roles. It scared me, it scared me that he still said the right things, but that the lights had been extinguished.

Gradually he came out of himself, doing the odd shift at the pub and dabbling in local politics. Things went back to a kind of normal, a fragile peace, until one by one we peeled away to start our own lives. It's not something we ever talk about now. I don't know if it's because everyone else is truly over it and I'm nothing but a stupid and stubborn mule, or if it's because they've all taken a trip down the most alluring of rivers: denial.

Beth comes bustling up with the final guest and as it's emphatically not Jerry Springer, I refrain from any more grue-some family gut-spilling. Instead, it's Laura. I hug her much too hard, desperate to discharge my upset.

'Amber, lovely to see you,' she says, a trifle bemused.

I unpeel myself, taking a proper look at her. What I love about Laura is that she's not one of those women who destroy their life in the pursuit of eternal youth, blithely ignoring the fact that it's as likely as a unicorn taking up residence in the back garden. I like that she's got lines around her eyes and the odd hint of grey at her temples. I'm not saying I'll be brave enough myself, but it feels like a strike for womankind. She is attractive, but her appeal comes as much from how sharp and quick she is, a keen mind that's been honed by journalistic postings in some of the scariest places on the planet.

'Lovely to see you too! Tell me your news,' I say as Beth subtly hustles us towards the table and away from the burning smell that's emanating from the oven. Oh dear, I shouldn't have got distracted.

'My news ...' says Laura. 'I'm happy to report that finally I've got some news! And he's about to arrive.'

She quickly fills me in as we take our places. She's told me about the odd high-octane fling, but she's never had anyone significant enough to cut it as a serious plus one, not in the five years I've known her. It's only now that she's finally met someone, or rather reassessed someone – James, a work colleague she's known for more than a decade. Recently separated, she's been his shoulder to cry on, and gradually it became more. Six months on, he's moving in and it's all systems go.

'That's fantastic,' I say, struck, yet again, by how quickly life can flip over. I push away my stupid mental snakes and ladders board, trying instead for the Pollyanna assessment. Fate moves in mysterious ways – you can go from miserably single to blissfully coupled in the blink of an eye. All those years I spent lamenting the fact that someone as fabulous as Laura hadn't met anyone, and now justice has been done. Unfortunately the way it's come about makes me think about Rachel and how she cannibalised my marriage and built herself a cosy nest out of the skin. I don't think Pollyanna ever had to find an up-spin for flesh-eating monsters.

I manage to keep Laura on my left, but my right's less of a success, swiftly colonised by Gay Bryan (how gay do you have to be to spell Brian with a Y?). Don't get me wrong, I haven't metamorphosed into a hate-filled homophobe. It's just that as Bryan's so clearly gay, I don't understand why he insists on being married to a woman. Milly, meanwhile, is in hog heaven, seated to the left of Anthony's chiselled jaw. She gives me a tiny, imperceptible thumbs up, blissfully unaware of the coma-inducing conversation coming her way.

'Hi,' says Robin, Bryan's intense American wife, as she sits down next to him. Short and dark, with a bob so helmet-like that you'd swear she was fighting in the Norman conquest, she never ceases to intimidate me. She sticks out her hand like it's a weapon, enfolding my own in a vice-like grip. 'Long time no see.'

'It's a year of course,' I say, forcing a smile, reminded yet again of how much can change in twelve months. Robin's bright beady eyes flick momentarily towards Milly, my gonad-free plus one, and I can see she's thinking the same thing. Beth will have told her I'm sure, and now she's wondering whether to raise it. I can't bear it. 'You probably know me and Dom have divorced,' I tell her, my voice sounding foghorn-loud in my clumsy attempt to be breezy.

Robin struggles for the appropriate response, sticky red lips pursed uncomfortably. 'That sucks,' she says. 'I'm so sorry'.

'Yes, yes, it does suck,' I reply primly. I'm frantically casting around for another topic of conversation, but my brain's frozen over.

'What happened?'

She's not honestly asking me to gaily rattle off a breakdown of the breakdown between courses, is she?

My face obviously conveys this, as she draws back, taking refuge behind her husband. 'Dumb question, I'm sorry.'

'No, no, don't worry!' I say, digging an even bigger hole for us both. Since when did I become such a social liability?

Luckily the arrival of James creates a distraction. My sheer joy at meeting him is even more OTT than my greeting of Laura. She must be starting to think I'm fixated on her. He's utterly English, tall and sandy-haired with impeccable manners. He immediately launches in with some politely interested questions about my work. Beth's subtly watching him out of the corner of her eye, her relief palpable. I bet their family's fretted endlessly about Laura's terminal singledom. Having met their mother, I suspect her myriad professional achievements will have paled into insignificance. I hope I'm not going to become the spinster aunt *du jour* now there's a vacancy. I know it doesn't count, but I sneak a look at my phone, and am thrilled to find another text from the man of the moment. It's not a solution but just for today, it's paracetamol.

Sadly, I didn't arrive early enough to rehabilitate the starter, a peculiar prawn mousse that's topped with a crest of parsley. Beth passes it round, and we all poke an exploratory fork in, trying to make appropriate noises. I push it round my plate, turning reluctantly to Bryan so that James and Laura don't think I've turned into a Single White Female. I swear he's fashioning a swan out of his paper napkin.

'How are things?' I ask him. 'It's *your* birthday quite soon, isn't it?'

'Yeah,' says Robin, leaning across. 'I'm throwing him a party.'

'Fancy dress?' I ask simultaneously with Bryan's eager, 'Fancy dress!'

Poor Bryan, there is nothing in life he likes more than an excuse to don drag, but there are so few day-to-day excuses for a straight man. University at least provided a regular stream of musicals and farces for him to appear in, but now he really has to work hard to contrive a reason. Still, the man's nothing if not inventive. Their daughter's third birthday party was an ideal opportunity to try out a Mary Poppins costume for size, and last Halloween, when he took her trick or treating, he dressed as Carrie, complete with a blonde wig, voluminous white nightie and hyper-real blood splatters.

'What are you going as?' I ask wearily.

'It's a world leaders party,' he says. He's a civil servant so I guess there's some logic to it.

'Bill Clinton?' I ask, knowing perfectly well he'd never squander an opportunity this good. 'David Cameron?'

'Angela Merkel,' he says, leaving me open-mouthed. Even for Bryan that's quite a brave choice once you factor in his thick coating of stubble and stocky, muscular body. It's much easier when there's an obvious costume to do the work for him: I'm not sure pearly highlights and a skirt suit are going to cut the mustard.

'You should swing by,' says an unperturbed Robin.

'That sounds great,' I say, half tempted, suddenly feeling way less sorry for myself. Surely it's better to be a divorcee than a beard? I subtly turn back towards James and Laura, hoping there'll be a gap in the conversation I can slip into, only to find there doesn't seem to be much of a conversation. They're both pushing the prawns around their plates in silence. Maybe it's an intense lustful silence but it doesn't feel quite like that. Besides, James is wearing a tank top.

'So give me the lowdown on Oscar Retford!' asks Laura eagerly.

'The lowdown ...' I say. I wish for a selfish second that Laura was still single, and we could get all drunk and conspiratorial, but it's not to be. 'He's brilliant.'

'Come on, you can do better than that,' says Laura, journalistic instincts too sharp to stand for being fobbed off.

I tell them how he makes ingredients that seem gross taste mouth-watering (our eyes flick imperceptibly towards the prawn gloop on our plates), how spectacular the restaurant is, how the critics are starting to take notice.

'But what's *he* like?' demands Laura. 'Do you actually like him?'

I blush, despite myself. 'He's an arse some of the time. He's a real shouter, completely uncompromising. But yes, I do like him. Watching him cook is like nothing else, he's a proper genius. And he's got charisma like you wouldn't believe.'

Laura smiles at me, and I know she knows. Like I said, she's clever. Oh yes, and there's the fact that I'm red in the face and grinning like a loon.

'It's such a cliché though, isn't it?' says James. 'These celebrity chefs and their temper tantrums. Surely they'd achieve just as much if they behaved civilly?'

I fight down my irritation. Give him one Saturday night shift in a busy kitchen and he'd be begging to go back to the Gaza Strip.

'It's a pretty tough environment,' I say evenly.

167

'I'm sure,' replies James, obediently finishing his starter before Beth arrives to clear the plates. I construct twin peaks out of mine, hoping it'll look like I've consumed more than three tiny mouthfuls. I take the break between courses as a chance to check in with Milly, who's looking a little less chipper than last time I saw her.

'Hi Anthony!' I say brightly, pulling up a chair. 'How are things?'

'Can't complain,' he says flatly, handsome face impassive.

Silence reigns for a long minute, before Milly leaps into the breach. 'Anthony's been telling me about all the fascinating things he does with bones!'

'What kind of things?' I ask.

'Usual stuff. Cobble them back together. On occasion, I even break them again to make the join better. That seemed to impress your pal no end.'

If I end up sharing a cab home with him, I'll be tempted to push him out and then try reassembling his bones as badly as possible.

'I don't know how you do it,' says Milly. 'I'm so squeamish, I've been known to cry at a paper cut.'

Anthony finally musters a smile, thrilled to find someone who's time travelled from the decade that feminism forgot. She doesn't mean it, I know, but her ability to mould her personality into whatever shape some random man wants is deeply unnerving.

'I'd come and crack a few femurs with you,' I say bullishly. 'I butchered a whole brace of bunnies yesterday and I'm pretty nifty with a pig carcass.' God, I sound like some kind of 1950s lesbian in plus fours who strides round her country estate

168

shooting things and ripping them asunder with her bare hands.

'Would you really?' says Anthony sneeringly. 'I'll bear it in mind.'

My butchery skills are more popular with Beth, who's pulling a large dry-looking chicken from the oven. 'Do you want me to carve it?' I ask, and she hands me a knife, scooping some soggy-looking roasties into a bowl.

The knife's on the blunt side, but I love a culinary challenge, whizzing it round the wings, skimming off the multiple burnt patches en route. Everyone valiantly tries to chomp their way through it, but by now the birthday boy is losing interest.

'Shots, shots, shots!' he chants, soon joined by an eager Bryan. Maybe he thinks this is the year he'll get Ralph drunk enough to convert him. I swear he's been in love with him since Freshers week.

I use the cover of vodka to send another text to Oscar under the table. I'm finding myself becoming more and more forward as the evening progresses, almost matching him for naughtiness (though not quite). *Come back here* he texts. *Can't* I text back. *I'm your boss and it's an order* comes the reply. Back and forth it goes, until Ralph spots me.

'I'm going to put that thing down the toilet if you don't put it away. If I don't give someone a blood transfusion, it's life or death. If the kitchen runs out of tomatoes, it's no big deal.'

'Leave her alone,' says Beth. 'You've got no idea who she's texting.'

'Busted!' I say. 'It's work. I'll stop.'

Luckily Ralph's distracted by his cake coming out. 'Make a wish, darling!' says Beth.

Ralph shuts his eyes, as if he still believes in Father

Christmas. 'I wish for *SingStar*!' he shouts, then rushes off to get it set up. Trust Ralph to find a form of karaoke that's competitive.

He kicks off by belting out 'Livin' On a Prayer', arguing fiercely with the electronic Simon Cowell who decrees (rightly) he's totally out of tune, and can't see him thrashing about and trying to crowd surf off the side of the sofa. No prizes for guessing who's up next: Bryan, singing Britney. Once I've watched him sing two choruses of 'Hit Me Baby One More Time' almost exclusively to Ralph, I decide to take a sanity (and vodka) break. I wander into the back garden, grabbing my bag en route. Three more texts from Oscar. Don't drink and dial, don't drink and dial, I chant to myself, then ring him.

'The wanderer returns,' he drawls.

'I wish. I'm still in the 'burbs.'

'How is it?'

'Carnage,' I say, holding the phone out of the door for a second so he can hear Ralph murdering 'New York, New York'.

'So do what you're told, and come back here.'

'Oh, Oscar, I can't. I'm worried my flatmate's going to cop off with my brother's mate and—'

'The follies of youth.'

'I can't just leave her! He's awful and—'

'You're not her mum. Bet you they'll be glad you're out of the way. Just get in a cab.'

I take a deep breath. 'I know it sounds lame but I can't afford a cab.'

'I'll pay for it when you get here.'

170

'No,' I say firmly. And I mean it. I'm not going to start feeling like a kept woman. That's way too fur coat, no knickers for my liking.

'Then you leave me no option. I'm coming to get you.'

'No, don't! I forbid it.'

'Forbid it, do you? Unfortunately for you, forbidden is one of my biggest turn-ons.'

Resistance is futile. Before I know, it I've given him the address, hoping that Ralph won't kill me for bailing. I'm about to go back in when I'm waylaid by Laura.

'Join me for a sneaky one?' she says, pulling out a packet of fags.

'Thanks, but I really don't smoke. I'll keep you company though.'

'Fair enough, but if James comes out you've got to swear they're yours.'

I look at her askance, and she smiles apologetically, but doesn't elaborate. I bite my tongue, swallow the urge to tell her that once you've turned the soil, prepared the ground with small white lies, you'll inevitably end up fending off the big black ones.

'So where are you off to next?' I ask her, shivering. 'Tell me it's hot, even if it's littered with hand grenades.'

'I'm actually going to stay a bit more office-based over the next few months,' she says quietly. 'Calm things down a bit.'

'Oh. That's good,' I say, surprised. She's always been so full of her work, the injustices she's exposed. 'Did you feel like you needed a break? I guess with a new relationship you're going to want to be in one place for a bit.'

'Yeah, of course,' she says, taking a sharp drag on her fag. There's something subdued about the way she says it, a total lack of animation and I'm suddenly not quite sure this relationship's the romantic salvation that it's being billed as. If James really was the man of her dreams, wouldn't she'd have realised it years ago, found it too painful to hang out as chums? Could it be that the game they're playing isn't kiss chase but fertility chicken: how long can you risk not settling before the big bad wolf comes along and gobbles up your eggs? Ralph comes out to drag me in for a duet, only to get distracted by the lure of Laura's fag smoke.

'I can't believe a medical professional such as yourself is willing to risk furry lungs and imminent, sudden premature death,' I say, paraphrasing the dire warning on the side of the packet.

'Happy birthday to you too,' he says, fishing one out of the packet. We all stand there shivering and giggling, the two of them sucking on their fags like naughty teenagers. Ralph throws an arm around my shoulders.

'I didn't think you'd make it tonight.'

'It's your birthday, of course I made it!'

He raises an eyebrow, gives me a cynical smile. 'And you're still here, which is a total miracle too.'

'It's not a miracle! But I am actually going to go soon.'

'Oh,' he says, disappointed. 'Shall I get Beth to call you and Milly a cab?' There's an awkward silence. 'Oh!' he says, grinning. 'Are her and Anthony on a promise?'

'No!' I say. 'No, it's just that ...' Bollocks, I don't want to put Milly on the spot. 'Someone's coming to collect me.'

'Oh my God, you are having sex-yuw-al intercourse!' he

172

says, triumphant. He considers me for a second, more serious. 'Is it Dom? Are you trying again? I want to fucking kill him, but if he really fucking made it up to you ...'

Ralph and Dom were always mates, right from the get-go. I think he feels almost as betrayed as I do.

'No, no, it's not Dom!' I say, increasingly stressed. I wish I'd never got into this.

'Who? Who? I might have to tickle you until you tell me.'

'For God's sake, how old are you?'

I've put my phone on loud so I don't leave Oscar stranded. It beeps self-importantly, ready with a text. Ralph tries to read it, but I shield myself, wondering if he's outside. I don't know who it's from at first – the number's not saved in my phone any more, wiped in a fit of rage. But as I start to read it there can be no doubt.

I know there's no point calling you, you'll never pick up, but please spare me seven seconds before you press delete. I am so, so sorry for last night. I can't stand that I've hurt you all over again, it makes me wretched. It's happened since toilet-gate, I swear to you, not before. Please, please let's meet and talk. I heard what you said, I know it's over, but this can't be how we remember each other. We were better than that. xx

I stare at the screen, the words spinning in front of my eyes. That little intimacy 'toilet-gate' – that stupid prefix we'd put on our rows to take the heat out of them. It infuriates me that he uses it, infuriates me how much it evokes, delivering as much of a sucker punch as that lungful of him I inhaled in the tiny bathroom. I can't compute the information, can't face trying to unpick it, and having Ralph looming over me is really not helping.

'Give it,' he says, but before we can get into a full-scale scrap it rings. Oscar.

'Hello?' I say, voice shaking. 'Are you outside?'

'Outside?' says Ralph keenly.

'Think so,' says Oscar. 'Do you want me to come in?'

'No!' I say hurriedly, amazed he'd even suggest it.

'Get him inside for a glass of vino,' shouts my eavesdropping, interfering brother.

'Wait there, I'm coming out,' I say, pushing Ralph's head away from the phone. I've got my coat on, and my bag's to hand too. Perhaps I could just slip away? Too rude – I go for a general goodbye, then hug Milly close.

'Are you OK?' she whispers.

'Not really, tell you tomorrow.'

I head for the door, only to find Ralph tailing me. 'Ralph, fuck off!'

'Come on, Amber. Let the dog see the rabbit.'

'If you were a dog, I'd've put you down years ago. Go away!'

'He wanted to come inside. Why are you such a spoilsport? Is he ginger? Don't tell me you're shagging a ginge, we don't need any ginger genes.'

'He's not ginger!' I try to close the door on him but he jams his foot in it. 'It's early days, I don't need an audience.'

But Ralph won't let it go, tracking me down the path, running after me when I make a break for it. I jump into Oscar's vintage Merc, slamming the door behind me.

'Where's the fire?' he says, leaning over to kiss me, but I shake him off.

'Just drive!'

'No!' he snaps, 'I'm not a bloody chauffeur.'

Ralph's reached the car now, and I slam the lock down so he can't get in.

'I know you're not a chauffeur but please will you drive?' I ask pleadingly, hoping it's too dark for Ralph to get a decent look.

'No, you're being ridiculous. I suppose this maniac is your brother.'

'Yes,' I say in a small voice.

Oscar winds his window down. The car's so old it requires the cranking of a handle, leaving long enough for both me and Ralph to realise how pathetic we're being.

'Hello, Amber's brother, I'm Oscar. Pleasure to meet you.'

Ralph's rendered speechless by someone more confident than him. Or maybe it's the overwhelming evidence I'm shagging my boss. Either way, he's got even less to say for himself then Frank.

'OK then,' he replies finally. 'Do you … do you want to come in for a drink?'

'No', I hiss.

'That'd be lovely,' says Oscar in unison.

'It wouldn't be lovely!' I say, almost wailing. 'Trust me.' How did I get myself into this?

'Come on,' says Oscar. 'One drink won't hurt.' He deftly parks the car, walks round and opens my door. 'Cheer up, princess,' he says, amused by my sulky face. I suppose I shouldn't sulk, I should be pleased that he's treating me as more than a one-night stand, but I'm dreading taking him inside. It's taken Laura five years to decree someone serious enough to stand up to this kind of scrutiny: how can twenty-four hours possibly qualify him?

We step back through the door to the sound of Big Greg destroying 'Bohemian Rhapsody', fists pumping the air and sweat spraying off him like a sprinkler system. What an urban sophisticate I must seem.

'What are you drinking?' asks Ralph. Despite the fact he invited him over the threshold he's looking about as friendly as an Alsatian. I'd expect Beth to be all over the situation, smoothing out the ruffled edges and making sure she'd got the inside track, but for some reason she's hanging back.

Oscar's eyes rove over the wine bottles on the table and clearly finds them wanting. 'Vodka and tonic if that's all right,' he says, still looking faintly amused.

How can he be so cool? Maybe it's the absolute reverse of what I first thought. Maybe I'm such a minor notch on his mammoth bed post that this is nothing more than a funny little vignette that he can swap with his poker buddies as they swill beer and gamble away their houses. Jeez, I'm out of practice. Bless Milly, despite all the dire warnings of earlier, she comes dashing over as soon as Ralph's gone to get Oscar's drink, full of the joys of Spring.

'I'm Milly, Amber's flatmate. You must be Oscar.' She manages to sound a little unsure, brilliantly covering up the Inspector Clouseau-style dossier of photos she managed to summon up when I was going to interview.

'Lovely to meet you,' says Oscar, warmth and chivalry radiating from him. He's a totally different animal from his workplace Barbie persona. When I think about the terse interrogation he gave me, the conversational curve balls ... he compliments Milly on her dress, asks where the flat is.

'I love your restaurant,' she says. 'I mean, actually love it, not generically love it.'

'Thanks,' he says, face lighting up with pleasure. 'That's very flattering.'

'It must've cost a fortune to do that space up.'

'Don't, I'm fucked if it fails. I'm staking my life on it, my family's future on it.'

My family? That means Tallulah, right? Laura appears at my elbow, allowing me to tune out. It's probably a good thing, as there's a green-eyed monster snapping at my heels, baiting me to wonder if he fancies Milly more than me, if his ready charm is a laser he turns on any pretty girl he meets outside his kitchen.

'Knew it,' mutters Laura. 'Excellent work, my friend.'

Despite myself, I feel a little jolt of pride. It's undeniably gratifying having a bona fide hottie in tow. He's wearing a buttery leather jacket, unzipped to reveal an expensive-looking, grey marl T-shirt, muscles taut beneath. I love how comfortable he is in his own skin, those powerful hands wrapped around his glass. It's a conscious effort to look away.

'Sing with me!' pleads Laura.

'No way!' I tell her. 'James can sing with you.'

'He says he's tone deaf.' He's deep in conversation with Beth, earnestly interested. What can they possibly be talking about? I think it's just his listening face. I bet he'd arrange his features in exactly that configuration to discuss the highlights of last night's *Jersey Shore*.

'Go on,' says Oscar, 'treat me.'

'No!'

'Tell you what, I'll sing with you,' he says to Laura, picking up the box.

Who am I to mock James? I'm normally something of a karaoke diva by the time I've sunk this much booze, but I'm far too self-conscious to strut my stuff in front of Oscar. My love handles are enough exposure for now, I'll save my throat nodules for a later date.

'You asked for it,' he says, giving me a sexy shrug. 'What do you fancy?' he asks Laura, tossing her the box.

'Fly Me To the Moon' is what they pick, with Oscar pitch perfect and playful. For most of the appalling caterwauling, people have only lent half an ear, chattering away in small groups, but this particular duet merits everyone's attention. I can see people looking at me, and back at him, trying to get the measure of the relationship. Do they recognise him? I'm not sure, but even if they don't, he's got a certain star quality. He plays it beautifully, performing with Laura but directing enough of his lines to me so that by the time he returns to my side I feel like I'm in some kind of Rat Pack retro fantasy.

'You were amazing!' says Milly.

'I was in a band about a hundred years ago,' says Oscar quietly, and uncharacteristically modest. 'I'm rusty though.'

Ralph's watching him closely from across the room. 'Well done, mate,' he says, still guarded. I smile at him, touched by his protectiveness despite myself.

'Thanks,' says Oscar, not remotely rattled. 'But you're the birthday boy. Why aren't you up there?'

Ralph doesn't need telling twice, but I don't need to watch him twice. We four retreat to the garden where Oscar holds court, regaling us with outrageous stories about the great and the good. The thing is, I couldn't repeat a single one. My brain's marshmallow soft, my body moulded by the feel of him pressed against me. As the evening dwindles and we pre-pare to leave, Dom's text floats further and further away from my consciousness, an abandoned helium balloon swallowed up by the sky.

Chapter 9

That blurry, squashy feeling carries me through the next few days. It's a comfort blanket, a blindfold, insulation against all the things I don't want to think about. Catering can do this to you at the best of times. Working the hours we do, there's not much time for reflection, but I know that it's more than that. Living in the moment is all I can manage, and for the first time in a long time the moment is fun.

In other news, it turns out I'm Britain's Worst Bridesmaid (admit it, it's a reality show waiting to happen). I've done some half-hearted Googling of venues, but I'm nowhere near finding somewhere that's simultaneously special and affordable on Marsha's measly budget. Maybe I'd be rubbish anyway, but I must confess that immersing myself in all things wedding is about the last thing I feel like doing. I haven't replied to Dom's text, but nor can I bring myself to wipe it. My finger has hovered uselessly over the delete key a few times, but something's paralysing me. I'm infuriated with myself. It's so pathetic that I'm clinging onto a melting flake of nothingness, but I detect a trace of the Dom I thought I knew contained within it, and holding onto it makes me feel like I'm not going mad.

The time we spent together was like a string of beads, moment upon moment that added up to a life, and I never thought to hold an individual piece up to the light and ask what it said about him. I didn't act as judge and jury; I was swept away by the tide of my feelings, and then unceremoniously dumped back on the beach. I never asked myself if Dom was a good person, a worthy recipient of that love, I simply loved him. Now I've turned into a souped-up historian, combing through the past, trying to work out if the man I married was nothing more than a fiction I created. I don't think I'll ever love, or at least fall in love, with the same degree of village-idiot innocence, but maybe that's no bad thing. So happy though I am for Marsha, the thought of manning the buffet car on the marriage express is slightly killing me.

I'm ashamed to say I'm having another moment of paralysis in the locker room on Wednesday morning. Oscar slips in, surprising me, and I thrust the phone in my pocket. Is he boss or ... not boyfriend, definitely not boyfriend. Lover? How gruesome a phrase is that, but going by the Eskimo kisses he's dropping down my neck it's the most appropriate one I can find.

'What are you doing here?' I say, reluctantly peeling myself away from him. 'Someone'll see us.'

'Let 'em. I've taken you off the rota for tonight, we've got a date.'

I look at his grinning face, the unrepressed childlike glee, and sense my heart's lights turn not from red to green, but definitely to amber. I've been trying so hard not to invest, to keep

181

reminding myself that head chef invariably equals commitment-phobe workaholics, but it's hard not to feel pulled. I've been cursing it with watchfulness, constantly holding up the dark against the light, but I suspect that – unlike with Dom – what you see is what you get with Oscar. The rains might be torrential, lightning-ridden, but when the sun comes out there's nothing but blue sky.

'What kind of date?' I say, squeezing myself tight against him and kissing his handsome face. Feeling starts to flood through me as I feel the warmth of him, the numbness beginning to thaw.

'Threesome with Mimi.' I pull back. '*La Bohème*, you dumbo! It's at the Opera House.' He drops his voice. 'Front row seats.'

I spy the door swinging open behind us, cold dread flooding through me. 'I'm sorry, I know the starters were slow out,' I gabble. 'I promise you, hand on heart, we'll raise our game tonight.'

Oscar swings round, spotting Joe. He turns back, smirking. 'Fucking hopeless! I expect a lot more from you than that sorry performance. You'd better start thinking about how you're going to make it up to me.' He gives me a wink, striding off, pleased with himself.

'Not as easy as it looks, is it?' says Joe. 'I give you a week,' he adds, his small, mean mouth twisted like he's sucking on a raisin.

'Luckily, what you think counts for absolutely nothing round here,' I snap. 'Why don't you go and dice some celery or something? It's about your level.'

'Fuck you, you jumped up little bitch,' he spits, his venom

taking me aback. 'Coming in here and throwing your weight around. We'll see who's got the power round here. This time next week you're going to be scraping plates in buttfuck nowhere.'

'I'm not going to dignify that with a response. I don't want anyone with an anger problem like yours in my kitchen. Consider yourself warned.'

He gives a horrible, mirthless laugh. Part of me sees why: if you banned anyone with anger-management issues from catering, there'd be a global famine.

'Seen the rota yet, Fish Girl? Oscar personally rang me to get me in for the late tonight. He's off and he doesn't trust you to do it. Your kitchen?! I'd resign now if I were you, spare yourself the humiliation.'

I resist the temptation to throw the truth in his face. It's also tempting to use that leverage to sack him, but I can't bring myself to do that either. I don't want to get all Lady Macbeth about it, particularly when the first Lady Macbeth is still very much in the building. Besides, Joe's spiteful focus means he keeps his station pushing out plates like they're on fire. It's not easy to find chefs who deliver every time, I don't want Oscar to think I'm losing him good staff because I can't handle the authority.

'I agreed a night off with him, family emergency'. I'm so bad at lying, no wonder he looks unconvinced. 'We're right under the spotlight now, we can't waste energy on in-fighting.' I hold his gaze, trying to appeal to his better nature, but there's no earthly sign of one. 'Oh, just get on with it,' I snap, banging my way through to the kitchen.

I'm fearsome today, aware that Joe will be briefing against

me, making a meal out of my mystery absence. Every now and then I forget to rally and cajole, hit by a splash of pleasure at the romantic night that Oscar's planned for us. What to wear? I'm mentally rootling through my wardrobe, shamed by the high-street knock-offs that are nestling in wait. An unwelcome appearance from Lydia, closely followed by Baaad Daad, only heightens my anxiety. She's wearing a scarlet wrap dress, perfectly cut and offset by a pair of skyscraper heels. Even if I *had* the money, I've never had the natural style that women like her effortlessly possess. The mischievous joy starts seeping out of me as I watch her strutting towards Oscar's office like she's walking the catwalks of Milan. I hadn't really thought about what tonight means, the fact that we're saying goodbye to the bubble we've created, immune to the messy realities of a life beyond Ghusto. What Oscar looked for in a wife was a woman with perfect poise, a woman who could handle herself at the Cartier Polo or the Queen's garden party. How can I, with my split nails and split ends, be anything but a fling? Even if it hasn't occurred to him yet, when he sees me outside the comfort zone of the kitchen, I'm afraid his desire will wither on the vine. I'm not sure if I can induce further withering. It's not good for a girl's *joie de vivre*.

My phone registers yet another missed call from Ralph, the fourth this week. I know, I'm a bad sister as well as a bad daughter and a bad friend, but I can't face the inevitable lecture about the fact I'm shagging my boss. I hoped my thank you text would keep him off my back, but knowing how dogged he is, it's better I call him than have him punish me by snitching to Mum and Dad. He answers after a couple of rings, Frank babbling fluent Frankish in the background.

'At long fucking last,' he says, exasperated.

'Don't swear in front of Frank,' I say. 'What is Frankish for fuck anyway?'

'Mumphgrrup, I think. Anyway, shut up, I need to talk to you.'

'Let me guess, don't shag your boss, blah blah. It's too soon for you to have another relationship blah blah, let alone with him, continue ad infinitum. I know, and I know it's because you care, but I don't always need a big brother.'

'Amber . . .'

'And please don't tell Mum and Dad. I can't bear Mum thinking I'm a slut as well as a divorcee.'

'Amber, stop talking! I need to tell you something.'

Just for a minute my tummy rollercoasters downwards. What if Dad's got cancer and I've been too busy screening my calls to notice?

'What is it?' I say, tremulous.

'That article Beth read . . .'

'Yeah, the review. You can't clap the man in irons for one mediocre write-up.'

'It wasn't that,' he says soberly. 'It was a piece in *The Times* diary. I've got it here.' He reads it out, my heart sinking as the words hit home. '"Oscar Retford's come home to roost in pumped up offal eatery, Ghusto, after making a sharp exit from his star-laden tenure at Angus Torrence's Violet. But did he go or was he pushed? Retford's implied he had to battle Torrence for his freedom, but some say his fondness for his female staff made him too much of a handful to keep on the payroll."'

I feel completely sick, the excitement I felt this morning a distant memory. Do I never learn? How stupid must I be to marry a philanderer, then fall straight into the arms of a man with Lothario written right through him like a stick of rock.

'OK,' I say, trying to sound cool, calm and collected. I can't bear being the accident-prone baby sister for the whole of my life: scraped knees are one thing, a mangled heart is quite another. 'Thanks for telling me. I'll talk to him.'

'Don't try and style it out. You need to dump him. I knew there was something shifty about him . . . Cocky fucker.'

'All right!' I snap. 'There's a whole load of back story you don't know about.'

Maybe this is nothing more than the latest round of unfriendly fire from a bitter and vindictive megalomaniac.

'Sounds more like there's a whole load of back story *you* don't know about.'

'You need to let me deal with it.'

'Yeah, but I'm saying you need to end it now, Amber. Right now.'

'I don't go round telling you how to run your relationship!'

'What, shock horror, I'm married with a kid.'

'Well, bully for you,' I say, my voice cracking.

'I didn't mean it like that. We all wanted that for you, it's a total bastard. I just don't want you to miss out on a second chance.'

'Thanks for telling me. I've got to go. Really, Ralph, thanks.'

'Amber . . .' he continues, but I'm halfway to hanging up.

I'm on autopilot for the remainder of the afternoon. My first instinct was to storm into Oscar's office and demand the truth, but Lydia's presence is kind of a drawback. Now I've had a bit more time to think, my anger's mutated into something sharper and sadder. It's not as if he's broken any promises, he's simply confirmed the incontrovertible truth about chefs the world over. I'm disappointed, really disappointed, aware that however much I've been trying to pretend to be a pistol-packing sexual renegade, I've summarily failed at keeping my heart out of the equation.

By the time my shift's over, there's still no sign of Oscar emerging from the bat cave. Rather than stand him up, or call him up to call him off, I'll go along as planned. I'll summon up the best outfit my mildly pikey wardrobe can offer, sweep in majestically and tell him it's our last assignation, looking as magnificent and dramatic as Joan Crawford collecting an Oscar.

Despite my fighting talk, I trudge back home feeling distinctly stupid. Now I'm having to accept that Oscar's most likely a dead loss, I'm finding myself even more plagued than normal by thoughts of Dom's sparkly new life. What if he's already moved into the shag pad, except now it's all neutral fabrics and Norah Jones, nesty and domestic? Maybe they spend their Sundays trailing round Waitrose, arguing about whether or not to spend the extra on happy chicken breasts, already well into stage two of the relationship, speeding down the slippery slope towards the inevitable moment when there are horrible little replicas of Rachel screeching round the playground stealing other people's Tonka toys. I force myself to stop fantasising and start concentrating on the evening in hand. One trauma at a time, form an orderly queue.

The biggest trauma actually turns out to be the parlous state of my wardrobe. I'm staring into the recesses balefully when Milly arrives home.

'OK, wardrobe 999. Is it possible to wear 2005 Topshop to the Royal Opera House?'

'You're going to the opera?! Oh, how gorgeous. Oscar, I take it?'

'The very same,' I say, flat.

'What's up?'

And I tell her about Ralph's phone call, a tear rolling down my cheek despite myself. 'I just feel like such a muppet. As though it's all happening again, only this time I've only got myself to blame.'

'Sweetie, why are you so hard on yourself?' It's sort of a good question. Tough on me, tough on the causes of me. 'You'd have to be made of iron not to find Oscar sexy, I told you that before you even met him. You've had a lovely time with him, and yes, he might be a shag nasty and if he is, you're out of there. But he might not be, it might just be evil Angus wreaking his revenge. So just go along and see how it plays out.'

'I might have to go in my whites at this rate,' I say, holding up my first choice critically.

'Shall we have a rootle in my wardrobe?' says Milly delicately, not for one second making me feel rubbish about its self-evident superiority.

'Could we?' I say gratefully.

Milly's a much braver dresser than me. It's all either elegantly utilitarian (like the school cardies) or wildly *outré*, and I'm far too scared to consider the first few frocks she pulls out. There's one that looks to me like a tea towel, all checked and rough, that she swears develops a whole new aspect once it's on, and a silver number that I know would make me look like

Danny La Rue. What I do alight on is an understated grey shift with a gold zip slashing the front of it, a zip I know that Oscar will ache to rip downwards. I get that shudder again as I put it on, blindsided by the memory of the chemistry. What a waste.

'Oh, Amber, that's divine on you!'

'Are you sure it's OK for me to borrow it? I promise not to drop spaghetti sauce on it.'

She waves a dismissive hand. 'Honestly, I can't remember the last time I wore it. In fact, I got it on eBay, not sure it's ever had an outing.' God, the idea that I'd have something this gorgeous and have so many options that I'd never even have worn it. 'No, it's perfect on you.'

Milly grabs some clips from her dressing table, pinning my hair up into an artfully messy bun. I look at myself properly, caught unawares by the image staring back at me. The gap between me on the inside and me on the outside has never been so yawningly large. It scares me a bit, truth be told. I'm not sure I'm ready to graduate.

'Very coquettish,' she says. 'He'll be weeping into his champagne if you dump him.'

I don't want to dump him, I really don't, but it's hard for me to believe he's not guilty as charged. If a stringy, geeky specimen like Dom can't keep it in his pants, what chance is there that a man who oozes sex appeal is going to be as pure as the driven snow? It's time I found out. It's six o'clock and I'm meant to meet Oscar in the bar half an hour hence. I ignore the turnovers my tummy's doing and steel myself for whatever's coming my way.

*

189

I probably could've learned A level calculus from scratch and still not been late. I cut a lonely figure at the bar, sipping a glass of tap water (it's £11 for a glass of house white) and hoping no one thinks I'm a high-class hooker. Oscar's phone appears to be off, and I can't possibly ring the restaurant ('Hi Lydia, I was just wondering why your husband's stood me up?') The bar staff are casting me pitying looks, the last drinker standing. It's only once the whole place is deserted, the bell ringing for curtain up, that Oscar deigns to make an appearance.

'Where were you?!'

'Got held up,' he says, leaning in to kiss me. I pull away, glaring at him, but he doesn't apologise. 'Come on, else we'll miss the start,' he says, subtly cupping my breast as I slide off the stool. I was relying on this window of time to eke the truth out of him – to make a dramatic exit if I didn't like what I heard – but now it's been wasted. I give him another scowl, but he just laughs at me.

'Cheer up, you're in for a treat.'

'I know.'

'Have you ever been here before?' he says, grabbing my hand. He's never held my hand before, but then we've never been properly out before. I think about pulling it away, but it feels too nice.

'No, no, I haven't,' I say, taking in the opulent surroundings. What I don't tell him is that the only opera I've ever attended was the Macclesfield Players doing *The Mikado*. I'm not quite sure that counts. We're in the auditorium now, where the lights have already been dimmed. The usher gives us a disapproving look, pointing out our seats. They *would* be right in the middle of the row. We pick our way past, with me feverishly apologising to the line of pissed-off poshos we're inconveniencing.

Once we're sat down I expect him to drop my hand, but he doesn't. Instead he interlaces his fingers with mine, giving it a squeeze as the plush red curtain sweeps up from the stage. And then the music begins. Don't tell them, but it turns out the Macclesfield Players have got a lot to learn. The music dips and soars, the singing is utterly beguiling. The girl playing poor, destitute Mimi gives the role total conviction, absorbing me totally in her doomed love for paramour Rodolfo, despite the fact that I don't understand a word of Italian. I'm totally rapt, disbelieving that I've denied myself such an amazing experience for the first thirty-one years of my life. But then I glance at the ticket Oscar thrust in my hand and understand why: £190!

When the interval comes, I lean in close. 'Thank you,' I say, and he gives me the loveliest smile.

'Not too shabby, is it?' he says, and pulls me up from my seat.

The bar's a well-heeled scrum, and I assume drinks will elude us, but Oscar somehow manages to command the bar girl's attention right from the back of the crowd. He won't let me pay, and I can tell as soon as the wine hits the back of my throat that it's not the house plonk. It seems utterly wrong to temper the loveliness of it all, but I can't allow myself to sink back into this until I know the truth. It needs to be real.

'Thank you,' I say. 'I know I've already said it, but this is amazing. It's … it's much better than any of the opera I've seen before.' Please don't ask which, please don't ask which.

'You're very welcome.'

We stand there looking at each other before I hurl myself into the breach.

'Oscar, I've got to talk about that stupid thing in *The Times* diary.' His face immediately tells me he's read it. My heart sinks like a stone. If he didn't instantly seek me out and reassure me, then surely it must be true. 'I can't stop thinking about it. I know ... I'm not your girlfriend or anything ...' I am making such a hash of this. I can see every drop of bonhomie draining off him. 'But if you are, I dunno, one of them, I've got the right to know.'

'One of who?' he demands, voice dangerously flat.

'A ... a shag nasty.' Curse Milly and her stupid expressions.

'What the fuck's a shag nasty? Oh, don't answer that. I can't believe you've got the nerve to ask me that when I've brought you here.'

'I don't want to believe it, but it's there in black and white. I don't know you yet, I ...' I want to tell him how out of my depth I feel, way more like an awkward teenager than his own teenager, but it sounds too pathetic.

'I've told you about Angus, what he's like. It's just another potshot he's taking at me. I can't believe you're even bringing it up.'

'Of course I'm bringing it up! If you'd told me it was bollocks rather than letting me stew, then I wouldn't have to.'

'I didn't want to talk about it! I didn't think you'd be brainless enough to believe it.'

'Brainless?!' I say, just as the bell rings. 'Don't you dare call me brainless.'

'Well, don't you go round accusing me of being some kind of sleazebag when I'm treating you like a bloody princess.'

'I didn't accuse you, I asked you—'

An usher comes sliding over at this most inopportune moment. 'Sir, madam, if I can just ask you to take your seats. The performance will be continuing in less than two minutes.'

'Yeah, thanks, got it,' snaps Oscar, gripping my elbow and steering me towards the entrance. So much for a dramatic storm off, he'd probably rugby tackle me to the ground if I dived for the exit.

'Don't be so rude, he's not a kitchen porter,' I hiss.

'Don't think I asked for your opinion,' he snaps back.

It's almost impossible to concentrate on the second half. I try to get back to the absorption I had before, but I'm way too mad. Is he protesting too much, trying to cover a guilty conscience with bluff and bluster? And even if his conscience is clear, the fact that he's congenitally incapable of empathy isn't a great sign. I pull myself as far away as I can, but as he's stubbornly refusing to look at me it has absolutely no effect.

Gradually, gradually the music starts to creep up on me again. It's almost against my will, its beauty too seductive to resist. Rodolfo pushes Mimi away, leaving her heartbroken. It's only when she seeks him out and eavesdrops on his conversation with his best friend that she discovers that it's not that he doesn't love her. He believes that his poverty will leave her too vulnerable to the ravages of consumption (I know, ridiculous, but trust me it works in Italian). Eventually, I can't help but sneak a peek at Oscar, wanting to share with someone how lovely it is. My eyes flick towards him, expecting to find him as rigid and aloof as he was when we sat down, but the Oscar who sits beside me now is quite a different proposition. He's utterly rapt, staring at the sickly Mimi with complete absorption, tears coursing down his calloused cheeks. He feels my eyes on him, and gives a sheepish smile, wrapping my hand up in his powerful grip. The warmth of his rough skin against mine spreads right through my body, melting my anger like a pat of butter.

I've always found men weeping a bit nancy-ish, but his tears aren't turning me off. Quite the contrary, they're making my heart rise and soften like the most accomplished of Jean-Paul's sugary concoctions. He moves his hand up around my shoulder, pulling me towards him, and despite the discomfort, I stay as squashed up against him as I can until the curtain call.

'Thank you,' I whisper as we clap, and he kisses me on the lips.

What was it that moved him to tears? Is it his own marriage break-up, the tragedy of the fact that love isn't always enough? Can't think about it now. I squeeze his hand, waking him up to the fact we're the last people in our row.

'Come on then,' he says, hauling me up like I've been dawdling.

Outside, we stand on the pavement and I feel suddenly awkward again.

'Could I prevail on you to accompany me home?' says Oscar, mock posh. 'Rest assured I have the utmost respect for your maidenhood.'

'Shut up,' I say, giggling. 'Shall I hail that cab?'

'No,' says Oscar, pulling my extended arm down, and wrapping me up for a snog. 'Let's take the long way round.'

We cross Covent Garden, me struggling to keep up with his determined stride, then we navigate the Strand and arrive at the river. 'Look at it,' he says. 'Just look at it.'

And I take in the peaks and troughs and glittery lights of the buildings that make up the skyline, suddenly conscious of London's beauty. It's so rare I have time to drink it in, to drink anything in. Oscar holds my hand a little more tightly, and starts off north.

'Talk to me, Fish Girl,' he says.

'Not if you call me Fish Girl.'

'Dearest, sweetest Amber, I beg you to share with me your hopes, dreams and aspirations.'

I'm not an idiot, I recognise irony when it slaps me hard round the chops, but I feel a sudden panic. What are my hopes, dreams and aspirations? It was always opening my own restaurant, with *Amber's* written above the door in my more narcissistic fantasies, but I never dreamt of doing it solo. Even if it did still exert the same pull, I'll feel a fool telling a chef as accomplished as him that I believe I can scale the same dizzy heights. So what do I want? Do I want him? The truth is I probably can't have him, and I'm not in the market for any more crushing disappointment.

'Dunno,' I say, sounding like Kevin the Teenager.

'Hey, didn't mean to tease,' he says, giving my hand another squeeze. 'I wanted to talk to you. Properly,' he adds, voice dropping like it's a dirty word. 'What you said about not being my girlfriend . . .'

'I don't know what this is,' I say, truth bursting out of me like a geyser. 'Do you know what this is? I haven't been someone's girlfriend since the dark ages. I suppose I thought it was a fling, but I'm not sure how good I am at getting flung.' I look at him, searching his face for clues. 'So now I don't know.'

He smiles down at me. 'Have to disagree with you on that. I think you're very good at getting flung, just not really sure what a fling actually means.'

'Oh, you know, short-term, lots of flinging, no strings attached. Fun but meaningless.'

He pulls his hand away, turns to look at me. 'Is that what you want?' he says, deadly serious. Jeez, the handbrake turns don't make for a relaxing ... fling.

'Um, no, not really.'

'Why not?'

Is this a trick question? Mysterious and dangerous, mysterious and dangerous.

'I don't know if I'm slutty enough. I suppose if I want to ... fling, then I also want to talk. And hang out and ...'

'So you want to be my girlfriend?'

How did I get tricked into this conversation? It turns out I am about as mysterious and dangerous as a golden retriever.

'What do you want?' I ask back.

'I asked first.'

Fuck it, I think, I'll stick with the truth, before making the unnerving discovery that I couldn't rightly swear to what it is. I love being with him (mostly), I love flinging with him, but the idea of being his girlfriend floods me with fear. There's the impossibility of it, the fact that his life is so different from mine: a not even ex-wife, a teenager, a slew of column inches. How could I ever carve out a space for myself in the midst of all that? But that's just the tabloid headline version, the spin that makes me feel thoughtful and measured. The truth is that stepping forward involves a whole new level of acceptance, a silent and secret goodbye.

Oscar crowbars his way back into my consciousness, slipping his arm more tightly around me and twists me to him so we're eyeball to eyeball. 'Tell me the truth, I can take it,' he says, pulling a strand of hair out of my face and smiling with a gentleness I've never seen in him. He's searching my face, tracking his effect on me. There's something so utterly melting about his vulnerability, about the fact that he shouts like Bluebeard one minute, then weeps for Mimi the next. My internal musings feel like a swarm of hateful wasps that I need to dodge at all costs.

'Yes. I want to be your . . .' Girlfriend sounds so pathetic, but I'm sure as hell not saying lover. 'Lady friend.' Why did I say that?

Oscar hoots with laughter. 'Lady friend it is,' he says, kissing me hard. 'Now is that gonna stop you getting all tortured and screechy cos you think I'm putting it about?'

'Screechy?!'

'You know what I mean,' he says, teasing.

'Then tell me the truth. Give me the headlines since you and Lydia called it quits.'

Even saying her name sends a shudder of dread all the way down to my wildly uncomfortable heels. How would we ever survive her finding out? Whatever he says, I know she'd be murderous. And who can blame her? They had a family together, she'll want to protect what's left of it, ensure I don't try and usurp her position as the mother of his child.

'I definitely want ages, not so bothered about names.'

'You're in luck cos I can't remember any.'

I swat him on the arm. 'Seriously, Oscar, what's your story? I feel like I need to know.'

I realise as I say it how much store I set by a person's romantic CV. A thirty-eight-year-old man with no dependants might seem like a perky prospect, but not if it's because he's madly in love with his mother. Or his best friend Tony. Couple of bruising rounds of loved and lost is way more reassuring than a psychopathically sterile romantic roll call. Or maybe that's just me trying to make myself feel better about my own failed union.

'OK, Fish Girl, from the top.'

More dread, as I wonder what I've let myself in for. If he's shagged a succession of 'exotic dancers' or voluptuous customers, I think I'll curl up and die.

'Hang on,' I say, partly playing for time. 'When did you and Lydia actually split up first of all?'

'First of all? Should I be expecting a full interrogation here?'

'Nooo. Just some gentle probing. More Jessica Fletcher, less Cracker.'

'Gentle probing is it? OK . . .' And the dread starts up again. Maybe I care more than it's safe to care. 'I moved out eighteen months ago, but there hadn't been any funny business for quite some time before that.'

It bubbles up inside me to ask why, but I stop myself. I feel a sudden wave of sympathy for Lydia. Did he just go off her? No wonder she's fighting off ageing with every weapon she can lay her hands on. It's so much harder for women, so much harder to know that fifty is the next big birthday when you haven't got the option of re-classifying yourself as a silver fox. I know it's a very unspiritual way to look at it, but I can't help believing it's true. As soon as I can afford it, I'm going to submerge my face nightly in Crème de la Mer.

'Then there was a little bit of a dalliance with Veronica.'
Veronica? She sounds about 105.

'Who's she?'

'She owns a vineyard in Umbria, that fabulous Barolo we were knocking back that first night comes from her gaff. Should take you out there some time.' I involuntarily snatch my hand away. 'Or maybe not,' he laughs. 'We're mates now, we were just scratching an itch.'

'How delightful.'

'What do you want? Me telling you I fell madly in love?'

Does he love? Does he ever have the space and time to let it grow? I suppose the fact he parted with Lydia implies a marriage of convenience wasn't enough for him. Even though I know that loving him would be deeply unwise, I feel like I need to know the ground's not too dry and infertile to rule out the very possibility.

'So she was transitional girl.'

'Come again?'

'You know, the person after the person who gets you back on the horse but you could never really be with.' He looks at me a second too long, and I feel myself blush. You're not that, I want to say, but it sounds too presumptuous.

'Something like that. Lovely lady, but it was more of a physical thing than anything else.'

A bolt of insecurity shoots through me as I imagine the kind of filthy continental moves she must've had up her sleeve.

'Oh,' I say, running out of steam.

'What?' says Oscar.

Jessica Fletcher never falls at the first hurdle like I'm doing.

'Nothing.'

Silence reigns for a long moment, before Oscar turns me round towards him again. 'Do you want to know the terrible truth?'

Not really, I think, but I give an uncertain nod.

'I met Lydia when I was twenty. I'd had a couple of girl-friends, but nothing serious. She was my first love, sap that I am, and I never ever strayed. That's why that article makes me so livid. I came out the other side knowing fuck all about dating, fuck all about women: I'd only ever been with one. Since Veronica there's been nothing, and she doesn't really count.' He continues more quietly. 'And now there's you.'

'Now there's me,' I repeat, looking up at him. I wonder if he's going to ask me more about my history but no questions are forthcoming.

'Come here,' he says suddenly, yanking me towards a bench. He pulls me down, holds me close. 'Listen, Columbo, you've asked enough. I'm talking now.'

'What do you want to say?' I whisper, the hairs on the back of my neck standing up as he gently strokes it with two fingers.

'What do I want to say? I want to say that I don't want to fuck around, in either sense. I didn't think it through when I jumped you first off, but since then ... since then it's changed. I'm really falling for you. Fuck knows why, you drive me mad, but it's a fact.'

And my heart does a flip-flop long before the wasps can catch up with it. I grip his free hand tightly, snuggle in closer.

'Me too,' I say, knowing it's true, but also fearing the impossibility of it all.

'Ringing endorsement there, Fish Girl. Glad I put myself on the line for you.'

'I mean it, but—'

'No buts,' he says. 'We should go public soon.'

'Jesus no!' I say. 'I'll be dead meat in that kitchen, no one will have any respect for me.'

'They'll have me to answer to if they give you any shit. They'll be out the door before they've blinked.'

'No, Oscar, I mean it,' I say, cold fear gripping me. I'd have to leave, surely I'd have to leave, and I don't want to leave.

'We'll talk about it later. I'm not sneaking around like this is some kind of affair much longer. Not my style.'

'What about Lydia?'

'She'll live. She's been a naughty girl since we called it a day.'

'How does that make you feel?'

He shrugs. ''Sall right. Not sure she wasn't getting serviced by the barman at Violet, if I'm honest. It's part of what made me say we should make it official.'

'Weren't you furious with her?'

'Briefly, but it'd been over for years. We'd just both been too lazy to admit it.'

My insides plunge unexpectedly downwards. Is this the grown-up response? Maybe that's how Dom felt, that he'd been driven into Rachel's arms by the desiccation of our relationship. It's scary to contemplate my own blindness, to fear what it might be hiding from me now.

'What's going on in there?' says Oscar, lightly tapping my head.

'Nothing useful,' I say, tiptoeing upwards guiltily to kiss him on the lips.

'There's some other stuff I need to talk to you about,' he continues. 'Business stuff.'

'What like?'

'Let's walk and talk,' he says, standing up, 'chop chop.' We set off at quite a lick, suddenly purposeful. 'Thing is,' he says, not looking round, 'the bottom line's not working right now.'

'But we're packed!'

'I know, I know. It's picking up now, but it's hard to know how sustainable it is. And my way of doing things ... I'm not going to compromise.'

'What do you mean?'

'Pricey ingredients, the best suppliers. But it's not like five years ago, you can't charge the kind of margins you could then. Richard came in earlier for a bit of a summit meeting.'

That's why he and Lydia were in the office so long. It's such a selfish response, but I can't help feeling miffed that she's still so much at the core of Oscar's business.

'And said what?'

'That the backers are worried, that we need to be turning a bigger profit margin by now. Dunno, I left Violet so I wouldn't be Angus's bitch, and now I've got a load of suits breathing down my neck.'

'But what about the reviews?'

'It's swings and roundabouts – they're mixed reviews, no stars yet. And Angus won't rest until he's buried me.'

'Are you sure you're not being paranoid about that?'

'No, babe, I'm really not. I wish I was. He'll do whatever he can to screw me over. Trust me, this press stuff won't be the end of it.'

'Richard will keep the backers on side though,' I say, grasping at straws, painfully aware of the weight he's carrying. 'He'll make sure you're protected.'

'Hope so, but ...'

'But what?'

'I kind of lost my rag with him today.'

'Oh, Oscar.'

'I know, I know. Couldn't help it. Gonna have to eat humble pie tomorrow.'

'Now *that* sounds cheap.'

He finally looks round, grinning at me ruefully. 'You're a real sweetheart, you know that, don't you?'

I smile back at him. 'I will help you, I really will. I know I'm a baby compared to you, but I'll try and work out how we can cut down costs on ingredients. There must be other things we can do.'

'Think we might have to lose a couple of commis.'

'OK,' I say, thinking of poor Tomasz and hoping he's not in line for another impromptu exit. 'It'll be fine ... what you're doing, it's amazing. They should be so lucky as to back you. It might not turn a profit for a year or so, but then it could be a total cash cow for them.'

'Thanks for the vote of support,' says Oscar, leaning in to kiss me.

'I mean it, Oscar, I really want this to work. Let's start now,' I add, getting caught up in it all. 'Let's get a cab back, and work on the menus for the week. You may mock the ways of vegetables, but they do exactly what you're talking about.'

'You're not wrong,' says Oscar, effortlessly hailing a passing cab.

I squeeze up to him in the back seat. 'I know it'll be all right,' I whisper, but I can tell from the way he's distractedly looking out of the window that he's not convinced. Surely it can't be over when it's only just begun?

Chapter 10

Oscar brews espresso when we get back, a bit like we're pulling an all nighter before an exam. It's amazing to watch him work, the way he throws out ideas and then riffs on them, innovation on top of innovation. He's trying to work out how some of those cheaper cuts of meat can be given the kind of culinary twists that make them feel like luxury. I make the odd suggestion, but most of my time is taken up scribbling like a maniac. Eventually, once shards of light are starting to illuminate the zinc bar, I beg to go up to bed and Oscar reluctantly agrees. It's like his battery never runs down.

'Hang on,' I say, as he puts his key in the lock. 'What's that?' There's a door opposite his front door that I've never paid much attention to.

'Nothing. There's a load of junk in there, I thought it might work as a private dining room at some point.'

'Why not now?'

'Kind of the problem, isn't it? We can accommodate pretty much all of the bookings in the restaurant.'

'How about if it was more of a function room? It's just

sitting there, there's a real dearth of nice upmarket spaces to hire,' I say, Marsha's face appearing before my eyes, a familiar look of quiet disappointment writ large.

'Function room? It's not the sodding Dog and Duck in Loughton,' he says, prickly.

But over the next couple of days I manage to convince him it's worth a try. He also eats said humble pie with Richard, but gruffly reports back that one of the key investors is still toying with pulling out, scared that offal wizardry isn't recession proof.

I find myself stalking Lydia, watching her at every available opportunity to try and get the measure of her feelings for Oscar. He's insisting we have to come out, and I'm not sure how long I can hold him off without risking his wrath. My feelings have been bubbling to the boil ever since that opera night, but I'm still petrified of throwing myself over the cliff. It's certainly starting to feel more normal – he's even coming round to the flat for dinner tonight – but I'm still finding it hard to believe we've got a shot at the long-haul. Part of it's sheer cowardice, a fear of putting my heart back out on the slab, partly it's fear about whether we'd have a real chance at a future. He's already had his family, lost his twenties to nappies and night shifts, surely he'll want a shot at a second youth? And having watched his family destruct before his very eyes, how keen would he be to commit again? However much he plays it cool, I'm sure living apart from Tallulah must hurt, a fact evidenced by the embarrassingly lavish dinner he's throwing at the weekend for the end of her mock GCSEs. I know I should live for the moment, but it's hard to jump when you don't know what's going to break your fall.

I've had a day off today, welcome respite from the playground politics of the kitchen. Joe's not letting up. So far this week I've had my phone mysteriously turn up in the dishwasher, and my bike helmet pitch up in the wine cellar (as I'd stayed over I had quite a hard time explaining how I hadn't noticed). I cast an anxious glance at the pot bubbling away on the stove. I don't think I've ever had such performance anxiety as I've got tonight. Not even my catering exams worked up this much of a sweat. I decided to go for something simple, a spaghetti puttanesca, otherwise known as a whore's sauce because it's so easy that a prostitute from Naples could knock one up between punters (I don't think I'll share that with Oscar). I can't bear him to think I'm a culinary simpleton, so I've also committed myself to a peanut butter cheesecake for pudding, for which Milly has doggedly ground down a ton of digestives.

In a moment of sheer insanity I also suggested to Marsha that she should come round to talk party plans. She's booked it for three weeks hence, and I haven't got another evening off for a week, but it wasn't the brightest of ideas. She's started a knitting class (Marsha's big on self-improvement), so I've afforded her the six to eight p.m. slot, giving me a full hour before Oscar's even due (he's sure to be waylaid by some kind of culinary emergency like a world tripe drought). Much as I'm relieved that I'm out of the romantic graveyard, I'm not remotely ready to introduce them. The very idea makes me feel like a pair of scales that can't quite find a way to balance.

The doorbell rings, predictably punctual, on the dot of six-thirty. Marsha's ruddy-faced from the cold, a peculiar purple knitted hat perched atop her head, like the first craft from an alien landing.

'You like?' she says, pulling it to a jaunty angle. 'It's the first fruits of my labours.'

'Yeah, it's ... it's very fetching,' I say, ushering her in out of the cold.

'Why thank you. It's been cancelled tonight though. The old dear who teaches it is a knitting goddess, but prone to chesty coughs.'

'Oh no!' I say, a little too heartfelt.

'I know, but at least we get a chance to really chew the fat.' What a disgusting expression. Should I try and put off Oscar? It's tempting, but I can't justify it. It's insulting to one or both. I take a deep breath, pulling some white wine.

'So I've got some news,' I say, then proceed to give her the bare bones of what's been going on. I can feel I'm draining the colour from it, squeezing out the fun like I'm in the confessional.

'Oh, good for you,' says Marsha, fiddling with the brim of her woollen spacecraft. I wait for her to continue, but she doesn't.

'What?'

She pauses, awkward. 'Sounds like there are quite a lot of challenges ahead. The huffy daughter, the mother still being on the scene ...'

Even though it's exactly what I've been thinking, I can't help but be irritated. Why can't she rejoice in the fact I'm back on the horse?

'Love doesn't necessarily come in the perfect package,' I say drily.

Oscar might not have the world's best track record but at least he doesn't look like Mr Potato Head.

'So you love him?' she asks, eyes keen and bright.

Oh, good God, maybe I do, at least a bit. I certainly think about him a lot, even if much of that thought is of the neurotic variety. I can't say it aloud yet, not even to myself.

'I don't know ... I could do.'

'What, you could do in a hypothetical future, or you could do now if you were prepared to admit it?' Damn Marsha and her presidency of the Bristol University debating society.

'Either, both ...' I say, flustered, overjoyed to hear Milly coming down the corridor.

'Hello,' says Marsha, forcedly jolly. Milly goes to kiss her on both cheeks, but Marsha doesn't hold with such continental frippery and inadvertently pulls back before the second one lands.

'Congratulations!' says Milly, and we're soon lost in an absorbing discussion about wedding arrangements. Marsha's gone and bought the dress, totally unsupervised, from Cowthorpes, a tiny department store near our parents that is like stepping onto the set of *Are You Being Served?*. It's the shopping experience that time forgot.

'The sale was extraordinary,' she says, triumphant. 'It was a bona fide bargain.'

'How much?'

'Ninety-nine, ninety-nine. And it fits perfectly. Well, almost perfectly. The dry cleaner can work his magic and it'll be right as rain.'

'I guess at that price, you can keep looking,' I say. 'I mean you could get some fabulous vintage number for not much more.'

'Vintage is nothing more than a fancy way of saying second-hand,' says Marsha tartly. 'No, it's perfect, very simple. I mean you looked lovely, but it starts to look faintly ridiculous when you're thirty-plus and trussed up like some kind of virginal prize turkey.'

A little jolt hits me as I remember stepping into my full-on princess bride number. It was a bit ridiculous, but I wanted to suspend disbelief for the day, banish irony and lose myself in the most traditional version of love I could think of.

'Let's talk about the drinks,' I say hurriedly. 'The room's still got to be set up, but I think it'll be perfect.'

'Now I know what you've been up to, it all makes sense! Have you met the man of the hour?' she asks Milly.

'Oh, he's divine! I'm completely smitten.' Marsha looks askance. 'Not literally,' adds Milly, flustered. 'He's Amber's boyfriend.'

My head jerks towards her, the phrase still alien to me. I'm relying on the fact that soon it will start to feel normal, but it feels strange coming from someone else's mouth. I take a sneaky peak at my watch. I haven't told Marsha Oscar's due, perhaps if I dish up the whore's sauce now, I've still got a fighting chance of running tonight like restaurant sittings.

'Hungry?' I ask brightly.

'Always for your cooking,' says Marsha, with a warm smile. 'What are you making?'

I hurriedly warm the sauce through, tossing the plates table-wards like a frisbee champion. 'Delicious,' declares Marsha, tucking in heartily, and I feel like the most perfidious of friends. Of course I'll introduce them, but timing is everything.

'So we should work out a rough plan for the party. You

210

must come in and see the room, but what are you thinking? How many people for starters?'

'Eighty to a hundred? Most of them are Peter's friends.'

That's the thing about Marsha: she's always been quality over quantity when it comes to friends. It's something I really like about her.

'And booze. Champagne? Or something like Prosecco that won't break the bank. Oh, God, the wines Oscar's got. If you do feel like splashing out—'

'Oh, goodness no. I'm sure the house wine will be absolutely fine.'

I hope I'm not heading for another roasting from Oscar. I need the party to turn some kind of profit. If it's nothing more than an unwelcome distraction for his already overworked staff, I'll never hear the end of it, but Marsha seems to want something roughly akin to an Amish engagement party, so pared down and basic are her requirements. Remind me not to book a naked butler for the hen weekend.

The up-side is that the planning takes barely half an hour. I'm slurping my pasta up like a badly behaved toddler, watching the big hand and the little hand creep towards eight p.m. Marsha's a big fan of an early night, and I'm sure she won't last much more than another hour. So confident am I that I've got away with it, that I half kid myself that the insistent ring of the doorbell is the clock striking the hour. Milly raises her eyebrows at me, and I reluctantly peel myself off my seat. Oh, please let it be the Jehovah's Witnesses. If it is, I'll buy *The Watchtower*'s entire print run.

It's not, of course. There's Oscar, handsome as ever, clad in his buttery leather jacket. I still get that rush just from laying eyes on him, knowing he's mine. Unfortunately he's accessorised said jacket with a scowl that would curdle milk. I reach up to kiss him but it's like putting my head into a lion's cage.

'What's wrong?' I say, trying to detain him on the doorstep for a conflab, but he pushes straight past.

'I need a drink,' he says tersely, bursting his way into the kitchen, leaving me to scuttle after him.

'Hi, Oscar!' says Milly, crossing to kiss him. 'How are things?'

'Fucking awful!' he snarls, body-swerving her in favour of the open wine bottle and not even bothering to acknowledge an open-mouthed Marsha. Why, oh why, couldn't he be the charismatic charmer of Ralph's birthday? I pour him a glass, and slip a cautious arm around him. He's quivering, radioactive with rage, so nuclear I'm tempted to pull back, but I don't dare.

Oscar takes an angry swig. 'Fucking bean counters.' He stares at me accusingly. 'I've been calling you all afternoon, you realise?'

'No, I didn't realise,' I say, trying not to sound snappy. There's no point in fanning the flames. 'This is Marsha by the way. You know, who's having her drinks at the restaurant.'

'If we're still in business,' says Oscar, giving her a brief grimace of acknowledgement. He slams his hand down on the counter. 'Why did they bother to back me if they don't trust me enough to let me do what I'm paid to do?'

'What happened?' I ask, looking guiltily at Marsha's congealing pasta. This hardly constitutes a fun girl's night in. Yet again, I've let her down.

'Swings and fucking roundabouts,' he says, swinging his

212

arms to demonstrate. If I didn't know him, I'd think he was drunk. He is in a sense, intoxicated with rage. 'If you'd answered your phone you'd know about it. First, we got the nod that we're on the shortlist for the *Evening Standard* restaurant award.'

'That's amazing!' I say. It really is. That kind of profile boost is exactly what Ghusto needs. Marsha continues to fix Oscar with a beady stare.

'Thank you!' says Oscar. 'Not that John Follett seems to think so. He's still pulling out his investment. If we can't find another backer in the next fourteen days, we'll be out of business within three months. How am I supposed to do my best work when I'm scrabbling around for pennies? Arsehole!'

It's so not the time to remind him that this kind of precariousness is the price you pay for going it alone.

'But now you're on the shortlist surely there'll be backers queuing round the block?'

Oscar shakes his head at me like I'm a simpleton. 'Does the phrase global recession mean anything whatsoever to you, Fish Girl?' He's so infuriating.

'Yes, obviously—' I say, before Milly interrupts.

'I'll do it!' she shouts, eyes bright, cheeks flushed like she's got a full house.

'Milly—'

'No, I mean it. Oscar, embarrassing though it is to admit, I've got money sloshing around that needs a good home. It's not going to earn any interest, and I don't want to accidentally buy guns for dictators.'

'Green energy is a copper-bottom winner,' says Marsha, but no one except me acknowledges her contribution.

'Let me,' says Milly emphatically. 'I don't mean to be syco-phantic, but it's abundantly clear you're a genius. And also,' she looks at me, boundless affection writ large, 'I've never seen Amber like this about a job. She's always worked her socks off, but she adores working for you. If I can help sustain that, I feel I absolutely should.'

'Hang on,' I say, earning a scowl from Oscar. 'That's so lovely of you, but you need to fully understand the risks. It's a huge decision.'

'Oh, I'm a risk, am I?'

'Not you in particular! Any start-up is a risk.' He pulls away from me petulantly, takes another slug from his glass.

'Yes, of course we need to go over the figures properly, get my financial adviser to cast an eye. But it'd be a tragedy if Ghusto went down the tubes. And there's no question I need something sensible to do.'

To do with her money or to do, full stop? I'm sounding like Marsha now, but the distinction worries me. Oscar's face has lit up from within. He crosses to the table, envelops her in a hug.

'You're a godsend,' he says. 'An absolute godsend. Give the girl a round of applause!'

I obey him, as always, conscious of Marsha's limp attempt to join in. I'm trying to force down my misgivings, to concentrate on the positive, all the time fearing that work and friendship are like oil and water. I couldn't bear for Ghusto to go under, but I can't help hoping for a last-minute backer to come galloping round the corner on his white charger.

'I really ought to make a move,' says Marsha, taking a final mouthful.

'Oh no, stay!' I say. I mean it. I can't bear for her to walk away with such a bad impression of Oscar. She doesn't know him like I do, she won't appreciate that his moods are nothing more than a turbo-charged revolving door. Besides, I'm actually finding her presence quite a comfort.

'Yeah, stay,' adds Oscar. 'I need to get the inside track on this one,' he says, pulling me in close and wrapping his arms round my front. 'Was she always in detention? I bet she was a naughty girl.'

'Rarely actually,' says Marsha, refusing to take the bait. She pulls on her green serge coat, buttons it right to the neck.

'And you need to tell me all about the party,' he adds. 'It's our first, wanna get it right.'

'It's very kind of you,' she says, polite, 'but I do need to get back to my fiancé.' Again, that beaming smile of contentment. Not smugness; contentment. 'I wouldn't want him thinking I've eloped.'

'Are you sure?' I say, holding onto her gloved hand.

'I'm sure,' she says, and I walk her down the passage. 'I'll call you tomorrow,' she says, with a tight smile.

'Do!' I say. 'I'm sorry about that, he's very passionate.'

'Evidently.'

'And we need to make a date for you to see the space.'

'Absolutely. Good night, Amber. Delicious as ever.'

I close the door behind her, wondering why I feel so bad about releasing her into the charcoal darkness. I stay at the door a moment, my forehead pressed against the glass, until the pop of a champagne cork propels me back to the kitchen. Oscar and Milly are laughing like drains, him regaling her with a story about six months spent in a Roman kitchen.

'I didn't know you were a sous in Rome,' I say, stacking our plates.

'Yeah, I told you that,' he says.

'No, no, you didn't. Do you want some of this? I'm sorry we ate without you.'

'Thanks, sweetheart, but I'm fine. I had some of the kitchen meal.' I look for an apologetic smile, but there's no trace of one. 'And the head chef is this guy from Naples, mafia crawling all over the joint . . .'

I'm glad I didn't spend my day off slaving over a beef Wellington. I contemplate the cheesecake, sat proudly centre stage in the fridge, but the very idea of it makes me feel faintly nauseous.

'So he sets me up in this dive of a flat in Trastevere,' continues Oscar, pouring me a glass of wine that's close to overflowing. He hands it to me, tries to pull me down alongside him, but I'm focused on trying to impose some semblance of order on the kitchen. It suddenly seems very important.

We head to bed an hour later, though I get the feeling Oscar could spin stories indefinitely. I lead him to my bedroom, only now conscious of how exposing it feels to be inviting him into my private space. I have obviously artfully arranged everything, down to the last speck of dust, but I still find myself trying to see it through his eyes. There's that barbecue snap on the dressing table of Dad with his comedy fork, but there's not much else save a couple of boudoir-tastic velvet cushions and an overpowering scented candle. I blow it out, my eyes alighting on the photo. Dad must've been younger than Oscar when that was taken, even though he felt the very definition of a grown-up. What a strange thought.

'So this is you then?' he says.

It isn't really. It actually feels a bit sterile and rented now that the pools of discarded undies have been confined to the wash basket where they belong. It's not like Oscar's *pied à terre*, where every square inch feels imbued with his foxy musk. My flat was like that, a chaotic merging of Dom and me, his noirish French classics battling for space with my popcorn romantic comedies.

'Sort of,' I say, wondering if I should explain some of that, but worrying that it leads too directly back to Dom. Before I can work out a sanitised version, Oscar's on me, pushing my dress down from my shoulders, as fixated on my neck as Dracula might be.

'Slow down,' I whisper. 'Talk to me.'

'Talking's overrated.'

Don't get me wrong, I love being this desired, but it feels vital I get through to him. Make contact.

'You will think this Milly thing through properly, won't you? Not just jump into it?'

'Jesus, what are you worrying about?' he says, pulling back. 'What is it, do you think I'm some kind of con artist?'

'Of course not!'

'Or is it me? Are you not sure about me? Wanna make sure you can make a clean break?' His jaw's set now, eyes flinty.

'No, not at all. I just think it's a big deal ...' Saying how anxious I feel about the work/friendship cocktail will sound too selfish, like his livelihood takes second place to me having someone to play hopscotch with in the playground.

'Obviously it's a big deal; that's why she needs to properly

217

check it out. But if she's happy, I'm happy. And you should be happy,' he adds, emphatic.

'OK,' I say, backing away from it. 'You're right.' I kiss his sandy cheek, stroke his face.

'That feels nice,' he says, hands slipping downwards.

I catch his wrists. 'Can we just lie here for a bit?' I say, feeling a sudden nostalgia for those teenage relationships where the most complicated part was sneaking a boy past my mother so we could lie on my bed for a bit of light snoggage. I felt like such a temptress, particularly once I'd read *Forever* and gleaned a few tips. Judy Blume's got a lot to answer for.

'OK, sweetheart, if that's what you want.' He rolls towards me, faces me.

I'm liking just looking at him, examining his face in repose, but I sense an impatience. The panther of paranoia pads around me. Was Lydia more scintillating company than me? Maybe he finds me woefully unsophisticated, girlish when he's used to a woman.

'Tell me stuff,' I say, tracing the lines on his palm. 'Tell me about your first girlfriend.'

'That was basically Lydia.'

I try not to care how seminal she is, how all-encompassing.

'What about at school? You must have had a high-school sweetheart?' I ask the question in a silly cod American accent, a clumsy attempt to conceal how much I mean it. I want to know more about him, make the moments of calm among the chaos deliver something sustaining, something we can build a structure on top of.

'Miriam Chalmers. Long brown hair, legs up to here.' He sees my face, laughs. 'Not a patch on you of course.'

'I get it, but how did she make you feel?'

'Dunno. Horny?' he says, mildly exasperated. 'I hate to break it to you, but that's pretty much the only feeling teenage boys experience. Thank Christ I've got a girl. Why do you care so much about Miriam Chalmers anyway? I haven't thought about her for twenty-two years.'

'Did she meet your mum?'

'She did, fatal mistake. She looked her up and down like she was roadkill.'

'Were you a mummy's boy then?'

'Nah, it's just Irish Catholics. Love is the devil and all that.'

'I didn't know your family were ...' I start, but then he's kissing me, making my mouth fairly much redundant (at least for Columbo-esque purposes). Trust me, I'm not complaining, but I'm a tiny bit distracted by how little I know about him and indeed how little he knows about me. I know how he makes me feel, but I don't know entirely why yet. I need to undertake a thorough archaeological dig among all the crevices and cracks of his past.

No time for that. By now he's peeling my knickers off in one seamless movement, pushing me backwards. I lose myself to it, let myself be in the moment. He envelops me, every part of me possessed by him.

'I love you,' he mutters, emphatic. 'I love you.'

'I love you too,' I breathe, fingers twisted deep into his dirty blond hair, relief overwhelming everything else.

Chapter 11

'What's the end goal here? I'm dying to know. Do you actually want to make a Michelin judge throw up over my restaurant?'

Like he said, he loves me. He's staring at my deflated blue cheese soufflé like it's a steaming cowpat.

'No, obviously ... No, Chef. It was my first attempt, it hasn't worked. I'll start again.'

'No, you will *not* start again. When will you finally realise that vegetarians are bottom of my list of priorities? Concentrate on cooking proper food that's got some kind of shot at winning awards. And you ...'

He's turned his gimlet eye on Tomasz now. As you may have gathered, Tuesday afternoon at Ghusto is even further removed from the Garden of Eden than it normally is. The *Standard* award judging involves an ex-chef coming to watch an entire evening shift, examining every aspect of the operation in forensic detail. Oscar's obsessed with drilling everyone so they don't miss a trick on the night, but seems incapable of realising that his ferocity is guaranteeing the exact reverse. Tomasz has lost himself in chopping chives, wielding his knife like it's a Cossack sword. He doesn't notice Oscar until he's looming menacingly over the board, peering down in disgust.

'What's this? You're pulverizing the fucker!' shouts Oscar. 'There's no flavour left once it's a pulp. It's not compost.' He sweeps the entire contents of the board onto the floor, leaving Tomasz open-mouthed. '*Start* again.'

'Yes, Chef,' he says, stooping to clean it up. 'Sorry, Chef,' but by now Oscar's long gone, eyes out on stalks looking for his next victim.

'If those judges come in and find anything we've cooked is less than perfect, I will find out who's responsible and break their neck. You have been warned.' He jabs a finger in my direction. 'And that goes for you too.'

And breathe. Maybe it's more than naked ambition that's stoking his fire. Tallulah's dinner is scheduled for tonight, sixteen Sloaney teens slap bang in the middle of evening service. I know if my dad had been in charge of something so important to me he'd have wanted it to be absolutely perfect. My wedding was a case in point; Mum was much too busy to get buried neck-deep in wedding arrangements, but Dad threw himself into making sure we had the best of everything. Perhaps Oscar's desperate to make up for the lack of time they get together. In the six weeks I've been seeing him I've only known her stay over once, with the rest of their 'quality time' limited to the odd meal in the restaurant. I'm sure tonight means more to him than he's letting on.

He's stormed out back, giving me a chance to take a sneaky peek at my watch. Yet again, I've scheduled Marsha for the worst possible moment. It's gone five, she's sure to be here. I slip my way through to front of house, a bastion of calm in comparison to the war zone I'm leaving. There's Marsha, tap water at her elbow, poring over the wine list with Johnny.

'Here she is!' says Johnny, smiley as ever.

I take a breath. Marsha looks so incongruous sitting there, and it's not just down to those ill-advised cords. It's a collision of worlds, but it's nothing in comparison to the Milly situation. The paperwork's being rushed through, already close to signed and sealed, despite it being less than a fortnight since the idea was even mooted. Quite a contrast to my divorce papers, which are languishing in my bedroom like indolent teenagers. As fate would have it, they arrived the day after Oscar and I declared ourselves. It should have been perfect timing, a poetic antidote to a bitter pill, but I can't yet bring myself to sign them. I can't just scrawl my name and shove them in a postbox – I need a moment to honour what it is that I'm doing. Unfortunately, the string of shifts I'm signed up for means deep and meaningful reflection time has been cancelled for the foreseeable future. Or at least until next Wednesday.

'Hi, sweetie,' I say, leaning to kiss her. 'Have you picked something?'

'House red, house white,' says Marsha firmly. 'We're done and dusted. Shall we go and check out the space? I'm sure you're frantic.'

'You're not wrong,' I say, looking at my cheese splattered whites. 'I wish I had longer—'

'No matter,' says Marsha, standing up. 'Let's get underway.'

I approach the door with some trepidation. The cleaners are meant to have given it a really thorough spruce up, but I haven't had time to double check what's been done. I breathe a sigh of relief as soon as I see it. All the junk's been cleared up, the windows cleaned and polished so that you can really appreciate the fabulous river view that it affords. It feels light and airy, the high ceiling giving it a sense of space.

'It's perfect!' says Marsha, face glowing. 'Thank you.'

'We can improve on the lighting, maybe string fairy lights around? Or candles?' I feel myself choking up, I'm not quite sure why.

'You're much more visual than me.'

Absolutely true, I think, observing the way the corduroy ruches around her bottom.

'I'll leave all that in your capable hands if you think you'll have time.'

Is there a barb in there or is it just practicality?

'Absolutely,' I say, aware how little time I've got right now. 'I'm really sorry, but I'm going to have to get back—'

'I know you do. But, Amber, before you do . . .'

'Yes?'

'I want you to listen carefully to what I'm about to say, please just hear me out. Have you considered the possibility that you're in an abusive relationship?'

'What?! Marsha, you're being ridiculous. This is exactly why I didn't want to . . .' I take a deep breath, try and calm down. 'This is what chefs are like. They're passionate, they're temperamental. It doesn't make them bad people.' A rogue's gallery flashes before my eyes as I make that statement. Not Oscar though.

Marsha looks at me dubiously. 'I don't think that excuses the way he talks to you.'

'He was upset!'

'He's so, so dismissive. So patronising.'

'He's joking half the time.'

'Forgive me, but there didn't seem to be much laughing going on.'

'If anyone's being patronising, it's you! I didn't ask for your opinion, and even if I had, you can't judge him on one meeting. You don't know him. He's ...' I chase after my feelings for Oscar like they're frisky sheep. 'The reason he can sound so obnoxious sometimes is because he cares so much. He sees everything in bright colours, nothing's grey. I'm not grey, not to him. And I love feeling loved again.'

'You're not grey to anyone!'

There's a moment's pause. If I had more time, I'd talk to her about Dom, tell her about how much the papers are demanding that my feelings crystallise and make sense. But there's no time.

'You're not yourself with him!' adds Marsha, cheeks flushed. 'You're like, you're like ... Mrs Tiggy-Winkle the way you fuss around him.'

There's a stand off where we both stare at each other, before I laugh.

'Mrs Tiggy-Winkle. Oh, Marsha.'

She smiles apologetically. 'I don't mean to interfere, I really don't. I just worry you're not ready.'

'Don't you think I need to be the judge of that?'

'Of course you do,' she says unconvincingly. I know what she's like, she's prepared her closing argument and she'll be damned if she doesn't get to deliver it. 'It's just when I look at how you are with him, and I think about how you were with Dom ... You were such a team!'

I dig my nails into my palms. 'I thought that too, right up to the point where he fucked someone else.'

224

She at least has the grace to look sheepish. 'Oh goodness, Amber, look at me with my size nines. I'm not belittling what you've been through, quite the opposite. All I want is for you to be happy.'

'Snap,' I say, trying to stop my voice shaking. 'I can't talk about this now. I've got the day from hell—'

'I'm so sorry. It's just I see you so rarely, and I, I've been really worried.'

'Thank you for worrying about me, but don't. I'll be fine. I mean, I am fine.'

And I walk her out, trying to regain my composure, get myself psyched up for battle. She hugs me goodbye, still sheepish, and I give her a proper hug back. She is infuriating, but she's infuriating for all the right reasons.

That said, I'm more shaken by our conversation than I can afford to be. I know I've got to get back to the field, but I need a moment. I stand outside in the freezing cold, gulping in cold air, willing myself not to cry. Maybe I'll go and seek Oscar out in his office. I feel like I need to reassure myself of the flipside, of that warmth and affection that Marsha isn't remotely aware of. I can see his outline through the frosted glass, and I slip through the door, thinking I'll throw myself into his arms. Big mistake. Lydia's perched elegantly on the desk, strips of Sellotape fixed to her long, manicured fingers. There's a huge Selfridges box between them, which she's wrapping in extravagant gold paper.

'Darling, you need to write the card,' she's saying. 'They're due in half an hour!'

I want to turn on my heels, but it would be too rude.

'Sorry, I'll come back later,' I say, trying to pull the door back too.

'No need,' says Lydia with that exasperating air of *noblesse oblige*. She's wearing a long silken sheath, split up the front. You'll be shocked to hear it's significantly sexier than my whites. 'Do you need Oscar?'

She pushes the card towards him as she says it, not even turning to look at him. The unconscious intimacy of a long-term partnership can survive almost anything. I think I heard the same thing about cockroaches and nuclear holocausts.

'Go on,' she says, chiding him, and he picks up a pen. He looks at me, smiles, but not his normal smile. He's as scared as me of her finding out, even if he can't admit it to himself.

'Um, yes,' I say, brain contorting with the effort of coming up with an excuse. 'There are no ... no courgettes left. None at all.' How is it possible for me to be this stupid? They both look at me blankly. 'So we won't be able to use them in the soufflé. Or as sides.' Stop talking.

'Thank you, Amber,' says Oscar stiffly. 'I'll be out in a few minutes.'

'Oh good.' Like I said, stop talking. I back away. Is it my imagination or do Lydia's cat-like eyes narrow as I do so?

No time to worry. The kitchen is frenetic, working at full tilt to cater for our new pre-theatre menu. Oscar reappears after twenty minutes or so and I have to force myself not to get utterly distracted. It's not that I think that he and Lydia are secretly together, but nor do I think that they are truly apart. No wonder he's so *laissez-faire* about his marriage break-down, he's not had to say a proper goodbye. Could I survive, could we survive, being the catalyst for that?

226

Tallulah's party is booked for seven-thirty, with later diners staggered to allow for the rush of orders, but by seven-fifty there's just one forlorn toff marooned on the table with only a top-of-the-range iPhone for company.

'Should we start plating up some cold starters?' asks Michelle sensibly, and I force myself over to the pass to ask Oscar.

'No,' he snaps, pulling his phone out of his pocket like a cowboy grabbing his gun. It rings out, Tallulah's message trilling out.

'I'm busy right now, you know what to do. Ciao.'

It'd be enough to make anyone want to shout, but Oscar keeps his anger on a low simmer. 'I've been waiting half an hour for you to grace us with your presence. You've got five more minutes before I give the table away.'

He looks through the double doors menacingly, and right on cue Tallulah comes tripping in with a troop of stick-thin henchwomen trailing in her wake. She looks fabulous, no question, a bandage-style black dress skimming her thighs. Chunky heels prevent it looking too girly, and hair and make-up are perfectly done. I can't imagine having had the poise to carry off a look like that at her age. Hell, I'm not sure I'd have it now, but part of me's still nostalgic for the youthful thrill of splurging a month's savings on some misjudged high-street monstrosity. No teenager should be exercising their virgin credit limit at Prada.

'This is Pops,' she says, crossing to kiss him. 'And this is Jemima, Persephone, Antonia ...' She trails off, laughing. 'This is everyone.'

Everyone laughs, even Oscar. 'Looking very lovely, ladies,' he says, all bonhomie. 'Let's get you seated.'

'Thanks, Mr Retford,' says one particularly gorgeous swan of a girl. 'So sorry we were late, terribly rude.'

'Don't worry at all,' he says, holding eye contact, 'and please, it's Oscar.'

I notice Tallulah watching him charm her friends, waiting for him to properly acknowledge her. Finally he kisses her hello, and her face relaxes. He leads them over to the table, the babelicious one glued to his side, unaware of my eyes burning into his back. It's very hard to feel alluring when you're dressed in a flour sack. Johnny comes bustling over, all smiles. At least he doesn't hold it against me.

'Lucky old us, eh?' he says wryly. 'Think we're in for a long night.'

A crowd of cockatoo-haired boys are swarming in now, not in the slightest bit intimidated by the glamour of their surroundings or the lateness of their arrival.

'Johnny, for the love of God, make them order fast. We're going to be totally stuffed if we don't get their tickets in the next ten mins.'

Lydia's circling the table, herding people into their seats.

'We'll be a pincer movement,' says Johnny, pointing over. 'We'll lick them into shape.'

He's as good as his word, coming back through with the orders in seven minutes flat.

'You're brilliant!' I say, pleased as punch, but then he starts with the adjustments.

'Girl at the end with the nose stud wants the dressing on the side, girl to her left—'

'So no dressing?'

'No, dressing on the side. Girl next to her wants the

goat's cheese and blanched chicory salad without the goat's cheese—'

'But that's the whole point of the dish! Johnny, we don't have time . . .'

'I know, I know,' he says, laying a conciliatory hand on my arm, 'but Lydia was there for the order and she didn't step in. We can hardly say no.'

As Oscar's also got no complaints, all I can do is instruct the chefs to follow the ridiculous list of instructions and hope they don't get derailed by the next tranche of tickets. It's not long before Johnny's running through with a whole handful of them, the doors parting to afford me a view of Matt Nutkins popping open a bottle of something fizzy for the assembled throng.

'Please tell me that's not Cristal,' I hiss.

'Put it this way, it's not Lambrusco,' grins Johnny, backing out hastily.

I shout out the orders, finally finding my focus. The starters come back half-eaten, and are scraped into the bin like rubbish. Meanwhile, we're struggling with mains that are every bit as dicked around with as their predecessors. Stu's yelling with frustration as he tries to sauté fish in olive oil, not butter, while the mashed potatoes that accompany it languish uselessly, condemned as a crime against Atkins. By now, Oscar's absented himself entirely. He's either skulking in his office or flirting with jail bait, and either option is making me seethe. The kitchen's deadly quiet, everyone intent on turning round the vast volume of tickets that are hitting the decks. All I can hear are the braying shrieks of Tallulah's hyena pack. Johnny comes back through with yet another sheaf of orders, and I pull him to one side.

'Is Oscar out there? I'm not being funny, but if I can hear how much that boy's birthday Porsche cost from here, the other diners are going to be doing their nut.'

'Haven't seen him for a good half hour. Lydia had a quiet word with her royal highness, but it doesn't appear to have done the trick.'

'I'm going to hunt him down. She might ignore her mum, but would you risk winding up Oscar?'

Johnny pulls a face. ''Fraid that's not the only pressing concern. I've got a creeping suspicion there's a judge on the loose.'

'What?! Why?'

'Peculiar little woman with a bun on table six. I only remember her because she's so uncannily similar to my great-aunt Phyllis, God rest her soul. Second visit in four days, I'd swear to it.'

'Has she ordered? Who's she with?'

'Greying chap, nondescript. Last set of tickets I think, the ones Jason brought through. Turbot and beef, with crab and asparagus as the starters.'

I literally sprint to the pass, shouting to the stations to tell me where the orders have got to. The asparagus starter comes with a poached duck's egg, and as soon as it comes through I can see it's imperfect. The yolk looks too hard, not the soft inviting mulch that should bathe the stalks in yellow goo. I grab Bobby, the commis chef whose station it emerged from.

'Hopeless!' I shout. 'Useless. You heard Oscar. We're on red alert right now, and you're not even delivering on the basics.'

He prods the unyielding yolk. 'Sorry, Chef. There are just so many orders—'

230

'Yeah, it's a tough night, deal with it. Get back to your station and get that turned round in three minutes flat. Michelle, you're on the pass until I get back.'

I push my way out of the kitchen and head for the office. Oscar's hunched over a ledger book, an inevitable fag dangling from his fingers.

'I know you're busy, but I really need you.'

'Hold your horses, I haven't seen you all day, not properly. Leave them to it for five minutes, come and talk to me.'

'No time. Tallulah's mates are virtually rioting, and now Johnny thinks we might have the inspectors in.'

His jaw clenches. 'What the fuck are you doing here then? Who's on the pass?'

'Michelle, I only left her so I could come and get you—'

'You should've *stayed* there, I would've been back through in a couple of minutes.' He's on his feet now, stubbing out his fag.

'How was I supposed to know that? The kitchen's on its knees with their off-menu bullshit. Why invite a group of girls who clearly haven't eaten a square meal since primary school for a three-course dinner?' Too rude. Maybe I mind more about him and Lydia than I thought.

'Are you saying my daughter's anorexic?'

'No, I—'

'Good, because you don't know the first thing about her,' he says, jabbing a finger in my direction. I've clearly touched a nerve.

'That wasn't what I was saying ...'

I may as well talk to a sea bass. Oscar's already out the door, and most of the way to the kitchen. He takes over on the pass, making my comments about the egg sound like the minutes from a Women's Institute meeting in Surbiton. As the plates barrel past us, the noise from the party seems to reach a crescendo. I watch Oscar, wondering how long it'll take him to react. Eventually he breaks, striding through the doors and heading straight for his shrieking offspring. I'm nearly brained by the door springing back open, as Oscar drags her to the side of the pass.

'Daddy, please don't be cross. Everyone's having such a lovely time, that's all it is.'

'You can't ruin it for the other punters, it's not TGI fucking Fridays!'

'I know!'

'I'm busting my balls to make this work. You do know that, don't you? You won't be getting any more posh frocks if we go under.'

'Sorry, Daddy,' she mutters.

'It's a real possibility you know.' I find myself feeling a tiny bit sorry for her. They're loud, no question, but does he need to load her with worry about his precarious finances?

'Off you go,' says Oscar, more kindly.

'Will you come out and have a drink?'

'I'll try,' he says, non-committal.

'OK,' she says with a petulant moue. I think she might even roll her panda eyes, but Oscar's already turned away.

Service continues apace, each dish inspected to within an inch of its life. Great Aunt Phyllis and her companion send their starter plates back clean, but however much Johnny tries to eavesdrop, it's impossible to identify them. The party noise continues at the level of a dull roar, but Oscar ignores it, focused on Phyllis's mains. He sends back the first attempt at the beef and personally supervises the turbot, shoving both plates towards me once they're done.

'I reckon they're perfect,' he says, satisfied.

'Yeah, they are,' I say.

'So why are you looking so mardy?'

'I'm not! I just think that they'll want to eat their meal in peace, and whatever your daughter promised you, they're still bellowing at each other.'

Oscar looks momentarily murderous, but he can't deny the truth of what I'm saying. 'Fine, you go and ask her to keep it down.'

'Me?!'

'Yes, you. Or find Lydia and tell her to do it. I'm not leaving the pass.'

I stare at him, dumbfounded. What's really going on here? Is it a natural reaction to the judge jeopardy, or does the prospect of having to do some real parenting scare him witless? I can't face coming over all *Supernanny* on Lydia, but Johnny's too deep in conversation with bun lady for me to pass the buck. I weigh up the odds. Surely fronting up to a sixteen-year-old has got to be better than taking on Cruella De Vil (particularly when you've been dallying with Mr De Vil). I cross to the table, only to find Tallulah's vacated her seat.

'Hi,' I say loudly, but no one pays the slightest attention. 'Erm, excuse me, I'm looking for Tallulah.'

A heartbreakingly handsome boy turns long-lashed eyes on me. 'Think she's in the bog,' he says, ruining the effect at a stroke.

I take the sweeping staircase downstairs, admiring the

233

twinkly lights that are recessed into each and every step. The overheads on this place are too scary to contemplate. I get inside the bathroom, to find that only one cubicle is locked. Should I wait or knock on the door? She's entitled to pee in peace, but then I've got to get back quickly enough to avoid a roasting. I hear an audible sniff coming from behind the door. Oh, Jesus, is she crying? I don't think I'm up to counselling duties. Perhaps I should just back away. The sniff is swiftly followed by a giggle, a thud, and the unmistakable sound of Matt Nutkins. 'You don't often get muscles this defined in a man of my age,' he says.

Cold dread seeps through me as I imagine Oscar's reaction to this charming vignette. 'Matt, it's Amber. Get back out here. If Oscar finds out—'

'Shit, shit,' he says.

There's some frantic scuffling sounds before the door's hurriedly opened. I couldn't swear they'd been taking drugs, but I'd need all my fingers and toes to count up the restaurants where the barman's moonlighted as Doctor Feelgood. Even so, could he really be stupid enough to be getting high with the boss's daughter?

Matt scoots straight out, giving me a smile that's more of a grimace. I give him a murderous look, resolving to get to grips with him later. Tallulah's righting her dress, shaking out her hair. She's doing a good impression of someone who's unconcerned, but when she defiantly pulls out a lipstick I detect shaking hands.

'Your dad sent me to find you,' I say. 'What do you think you're doing?'

She turns, limpid blue eyes circled with rapidly smudging

kohl. 'I appreciate your concern, I really do, but spare me. I can handle myself, whatever Dad thinks. And if you do start, I dunno, tipping him off, I'll tell him you're mixed up. You're just another chef, you'll probably be gone in a few weeks, he's not going to want to believe you. And I bet you need this job, you look like you do.'

'What's *that* supposed to mean?' pops out of my mouth before I've got time to come up with something mature and measured.

'Nothing,' she says, stowing her lipstick. 'Don't upset him, yeah? He really doesn't need it. And I promise you he'll hate you for it.' She swings open the heavy door.

'Leave it with me,' I shout after her, refusing to let the snide little cow have the last word. She doesn't even bother to respond, leaving me to hang onto the sink taking deep breaths. What am I going to do? There's no time to decide, I've been gone a good fifteen minutes. I race up the stairs, grabbing Johnny en route to the kitchen.

'Where's the fire?'

'Everywhere. Keep Matt under lock and key, and please get Lydia to make them shut up.'

'I'll do my damnedest. Phyllis is called Dorothy by the way. She's delightful. If she is a judge, she's got to be the nicest they've got.'

'Perfect double bluff,' I say, throwing myself back through the doors.

Oscar's grinning widely and telling knock-knock jokes to Jean-Paul. Of course he's not. He's glowering at a haunch of venison presented by poor old Michelle.

'It'll do,' he growls, turning his attention to Stu's next fish.

235

'There you are!' he says, spotting me. 'Nearly sent a rescue party.'

I kind of wish he had.

'Got a result though,' I venture, relieved to notice that the braying's abated.

'Yeah, dunno why it took you an hour to get there though,' narks Oscar.

Slowly, slowly the mayhem starts to abate. Oscar does the rounds up front, presenting the illusion of a man who does so every night rather than just when he's up for best in show, while I keep things on track out back, quelling Jean-Paul's rage at how little of his meringue exam paper got eaten. Job done, I peek through the doors to find Oscar's taken up residence next to Tallulah, filling up glasses and plying people with dessert. He actually looks happy.

'Grab a glass,' he says to a passing Lydia. 'Johnny's got it covered.'

I watch her slide into a chair, surreptitiously kicking off her heels. I wonder if positioning herself opposite eyelash boy was intentional. I step back from the door, a little saddened by it. Tallulah's probably right, Oscar won't want to know what she's up to. This is the best version of his family he's got – an ex who wants to stay stitched into the fabric of his life, a daughter who shows him what he wants to see. With the kind of pressure he's under, he hasn't got the emotional capacity to deal with a more complicated kind of truth. Can I really bear to carpet bomb his fragile peace? I take another look at them all sitting there, playing their roles to perfection. Is wicked stepmother really the part I'm born for?

I step away, scouring the kitchen to work out where I'm

most needed. 'How you doing, Tomasz? What'd you think we need to put in the order book?'

'Aubergines, courgettes, peppers, red and green, and I hope also for yellow, red onions, white onions—'

'Amber?' says Michelle, mercifully interrupting. 'There's someone out back asking for you.'

'Who?'

But as I say it, I know. I shouldn't know, but I do.

'You're in charge until I get back,' I tell Michelle, forcing my shaking legs to carry me out through the door.

Chapter 12

There he is, hands clasped tightly together like he's praying for benediction. He's looking at the ground, and I wonder if he's rehearsing what he's going to say. A dirty messy mix of feelings swirl up in me as I take in his obvious discomfort. Part of me's thrilled he's experiencing a modicum of the pain he wrested on me, but the dumbass part of me wants to take it away, like it's still my job to protect him from any hurts that come his way. In sickness and in health: keep remembering he was the one that brought the sickness. I stand there watching him, refusing to be the one to speak.

'Thanks for coming out,' he says quietly, holding my gaze but making no attempt to step closer.

'I needed some air.'

There's a pause as we stare at each other, sizing each other up. Maybe I should just go home and sign those damned forms rather than waste any more emotional energy on him. But I don't.

'Thanks for not punching me in the face,' he adds, cocking his head to try and win a smile.

'My left hook's not what it was'. I'm not letting him joke his way out of it. 'What are you actually doing here, Dom? It's bad enough you brought that vile woman into my place of work, without you coming back and ambushing me. Fuck off and start your shiny new life, just spare me the details.'

'I've been texting you for two weeks, I even tried calling you. Nothing.' That'd be because my phone landed up in the dishwasher, but I don't tell him that. 'I couldn't sign those bastard papers without, without ... we've got to have a conversation.'

'Can't see there's much to talk about. You met someone else, we split up, you're with her. Beginning, middle, end.' I can feel a sob rising up, but I force it down. 'And I met someone else too,' I add, willing my voice not to wobble.

'Did you?'

'Yes, yes, I did,' I say, high-pitched. 'So we've both moved on.'

I've had many a vindictive dress rehearsal of this moment, but it's not playing as well as I'd hoped. I'd imagined I'd feel victorious and triumphant, ideally accompanied by Dom beating his breast and gnashing his teeth like some kind of lion/gorilla crossbreed, but what I actually feel is guilty, like I've vandalised something.

He pauses, looks at me. He can be very unreadable sometimes, Dom. He packs things up inside, squirrels them away in some hidden nook, then goes away and examines them in private. I always felt there was an aspect of himself he held back, a part of him I was left hankering for. I think in a funny way it made me love him more, kept me hanging on.

'Who is he?' he asks eventually.

I pause, looking back towards the restaurant. Part of me is so used to telling him everything that I almost do. 'It's not your business any more,' I say, wishing my insides felt as hard as my outside.

'Not Oscar Retford? Oh, come on!'

'Of course not'. I'm a terrible liar, and he knows me better than anyone. *Knew* me better than anyone. Was it my subtle turn Oscar-wards that gave me away?

'It is, isn't it? Jesus, Amber, is it serious?'

'Yes.'

'But he's a shagger, he's notorious for it.' He at least has the good grace to look sheepish. I was starting to think he'd developed premature Alzheimer's.

'You're not seriously saying that to me, are you?' I snap, protective and defensive in a way I couldn't have predicted. I trust Oscar implicitly now, love the way he wears his heart on his sleeve. 'It's not true, and even if he was, you do realise the blatant hypocrisy when you're going home to the woman you left me for?'

'Wrong on both counts. I didn't leave you for her, and I'm not going home to her.'

'*Metaphorically* then.' I hate Dom's verbal trickery, the jousting he forces me into.

'Amber, I'm not going home to her. It's over.'

I wasn't expecting that, I wasn't expecting that at all. I feel a whoosh of breath leave me like a balloon that's been waiting to pop. I nearly dance a jig of joy, but let's face it, unless you're in *Riverdance* it's not a good look. The spurt of satisfaction only lasts a second as I remember that we're still standing on a street corner, nearly divorced. A soft little 'Oh' is all I can manage.

'I know how it must've made you feel seeing us together but ... I'd bollocksed up my whole life for letting myself have feelings for her, and I wanted ... I don't know, I suppose I wanted to know if it had actually meant something.'

'And did it?' I ask, voice wobbling.

He pauses, chewing his lip. 'Not enough,' he says eventually.

A jab of pain hits me in the solar plexus. 'So it meant *something*?' I ask, jagged.

'There's no right answer to that, is there? I haven't got my head round what happened between us, what I did to you, and I don't want to fuck someone else up trying to work it out.'

He still had feelings for her, just 'not enough', whatever that means.

'But surely I wasn't good enough either? Are you still hoping Maggie Gyllenhaal's going to ask for your phone number? I hate to break it to you, but I'm not sure it's going to happen for you guys.' Maggie was Dom's special dispensation celebrity in the halcyon days when infidelity was still a joke.

'Tell you what, can we have a moratorium on sarcasm for, ooh, I dunno,' he makes a big show of looking at his watch, 'five minutes? And I know you won't go anywhere with me, but can we at least sit on that bench?'

It's freezing, but I still sit right at the other end, pulling my coat round myself and wishing my whites were thermal. I'm almost envying Dom his duffel coat, but despite imminent hypothermia, I still have some standards. Besides, the cold I feel isn't just the cold, it's also cold dread. Self-righteous anger has kept me warm but frankly I'm bored with it, bored of sniping and wisecracking. I look at him sitting there, woollen

241

cuffs pulled down over his long bony fingers – there's something so vulnerable about the sight of them. Those hands have
been all over my body, gripped the steering wheel of our series
of crappy cars, wrapped themselves around a million cups of
tea (black, one sugar).

'Look, Amber, I'm the arsehole, we both know that. It's
just ...' he peters out, looks into space. 'I felt like I lost you.
Like work swallowed you up whole.'

'What, poor diddums didn't have some 1950s throwback at
home, ironing his shirts and cooking his din dins, so he had to
play away?' Again I think of Oscar, the encouragement he
offers when he's not shouting. He doesn't make me feel bad
about being ambitious.

'That's not what I mean. I work hard, these jobs are hard.
It wasn't just about the hours, Amber. Sometimes I think you
hide behind it, that it's too easy for you.'

'It's not easy!'

'Yes, it is. You're a fucking brilliant chef, you always have
been.' He reaches his hand across the bench, thinks better of
it. 'Please don't take this the wrong way.' God, I hate it when
people say that. I sit there, shivering, waiting for the firing
squad. 'What am I trying to say?' He chews his bottom lip the
way he does when he really wants to get something right.

'Just say it!' My tummy's in knots now.

'You're always going to be top of the class, a legend in your
own lunchtime. Part of the reason you're so fucking brilliant is
because you won't admit it to yourself, you just keep driving
yourself to be better, to be the best. And I love that about you,
how determined you are. But the rest of life's not like that, is
it? It's messier. And you hate the mess.'

I don't bite straight back at him. I sit for a second, feeling an echo of truth reverberate inside me unbidden. He smiles apologetically.

'Where'd you get that coat, the PDSA?' I say, desperate to change the subject, even momentarily. 'Sooo trampy.'

'That's the loveliest thing you've ever said to me.'

'Don't mention it.'

There's a pause, broken only by the sound of my teeth chattering.

'There's nothing wrong with trying hard,' I say. 'I tried hard with you as well.'

'I know, I know you did,' he says, voice gentle.

The tears come now, unstoppable suddenly. He knows I tried, how much I cared, and still it wasn't enough. What made me so wrong in his eyes, so unworthy of loving? He puts his arms around me and I don't have the fight to stop him.

'Why wasn't that enough for you? Why wasn't I enough for you?'

'I know you cared about me, course I knew that. But it was like you couldn't hear me, as though you didn't want to look me in the face any more. My job ... it's not exactly going to change the world, is it? Whether or not some footballer gets a table in the window? I think I've been having a shitty, paltry early mid-life crisis.'

I think about our last holiday, a snatched week in Sicily. He was quieter than normal, no question, but I thought it was just because he was as exhausted as I was. I should've probed further. I must've known there was more to it than that. Maybe I was scared, scared that if he did start talking I wouldn't have the answers.

'Do you honestly think I would've left you if you changed jobs? What kind of monster do you take me for? I'd have loved you if you'd cleaned toilets, Dom.'

He pauses again, sighs. 'I'm sure that's sort of true, and you're the opposite of a monster.' There's another interminable pause, presumably while he tries to work out what the opposite of a monster is. 'I didn't talk to you enough,' he continues. 'We always had that dream, that restaurant. You always wanted this.' He gestures towards Ghusto, looming over us in the darkness. 'And I didn't want to take it away from you. It felt like I'd be taking your dream away from you, like I'd be betraying you, and for what? It's not like I've got a Plan B.'

'How is that not you saying you had an affair because you didn't like your job any more?'

'Amber, listen!' says Dom, pulling away, fists balled up. 'Don't be so reductive. It became symbolic I suppose, that I couldn't tell you. I started realising how much I've always protected you, wanted to stop you getting hurt.'

'Yeah, you did a great job with that by the way.'

He shrugs, rueful. Touché.

'You don't even like watching the news, Amber. You can't bear anything too painful, too horrible.' It's true. Despite the fact that my working life is like a war zone, I can't bear hearing about real war zones. 'You keep asking what you did wrong, but that was how I felt. Like I'd end up really disappointing you, or life would disappoint you and you wouldn't be able to cope. So I stopped being honest, I stopped telling you the truth. And that's where the rot set in.'

I think back to that holiday again, a dinner we had. It was a mamma-and-pappa type trattoria, perfect pasta for tuppence, and an elderly couple casting a benevolent eye over the idyll that they'd created. I loved it, absolutely loved it, but I could feel a detachment in him, a sense he was humouring me. I was frustrated by it, filled with resentment at his predictable squirrelling, but maybe I'd left him no choice. Was I some kind of quiet tyrant, dictating what could and couldn't be said? A tear rolls down my cheek.

'You were lonely,' I say. 'Being with me made you lonely.'

'Yeah, I was. No excuse though.' Dom properly puts his arm around me again, comes close. 'All I wanted was not to disappoint you, and the stupid, the stupid fucking thing is, I ended up really, really disappointing you. That's what I hate myself for the most. When you asked me how I could've done the worst thing you could imagine, on some fucked-up subconscious level I think that's almost why I did it. Does that make any kind of sense?'

I don't answer. I just look at him, trying to process the torrent of answers to the questions I've silently asked myself.

'Like that experiment where people are told not to think about a white bear, and all they can think about is a white bear. I knew it was the worst thing, the very worst thing ...' He pauses, eyes far away. 'Amber, however much you hate me right now, I promise you I hate me more. That's why I'm not going to be inflicting myself on anyone else for a good long while.'

And then I really start sobbing. Painful choking sobs that come from somewhere even deeper than this.

'You should talk to your mother,' he says quietly.

'I know I should,' I say, my damp face stuck to the blue wool of his jacket. I pull away guiltily. 'Did we just get married too young?'

He pauses again. I can feel his breath moving in and out, thoughts moving in tandem. 'Maybe being married gave us too much to lose,' he says.

'What, you got stage fright?'

'I was mad when I met you, manic. My dad was only just gone and it felt as though you loved me back to life, like you were the future. When you used to ask me about it, it wasn't just about me sparing you, I think I was blotting it out. I had some insane idea that I'd do the same thing for you, that I'd protect you like I was some kind of fucking knight in shining armour, like I could preserve that idealism I fell in love with. But it's impossible.'

'I'm not a child, Dom.'

'Of course you're not a child. That's what I'm saying, that it was me as much as you. Some part of us got stuck in those roles we were playing when we met, but we'd got too long in the tooth for them.' He grins a lopsided grin. 'Like if Joan Collins was playing Juliet.'

'With Lionel Blair as Romeo.'

'Exactly.'

We hold each other's gaze, so much swirling around in the ether. A wave of frustration hits me.

'Why the fuck didn't you say all this to me before it happened? Talked to me, instead of going off and shagging someone else? Jesus, Dom, I'm so glad you're not with her, I couldn't *stand* it if you were with her, but at least we'd be over for something real. It's such a waste. It's such a bloody waste.' My heart sinks in on itself like my terrible soufflé. It was easier being angry, easier than tracing out the contours of the truth.

'Because I didn't know it then! I didn't know what I was

doing, I was just doing it. It's only now I've had time to think ... too much time to think.'

I look to the restaurant, aware of how long I've been gone. How would Oscar feel if he knew where I'd been? That I'm out here with Dom while he's in the nest of his fractured family?

'I should go,' I say, feeling suddenly guilty, knowing that I won't be sharing any of this with him. Does he tell me everything that comes to pass between him and Lydia? I wonder. I think he probably does, I'm just not sure he always knows what really has come to pass.

'OK.' Dom looks up, pained. 'I hope this isn't it, Amber.' I look at him, praying my eyes don't convey how much that statement muddles me, even now. 'I hope we'll be able to be in each other's lives in the end.'

I feel winded, despite myself. I think it's just wounded pride, the creeping suspicion I've always loved him more than he's loved me. He's already teeing us up for the grown-up post-divorce badinage ('Hi, Dom, so sorry to call you, but I wasn't sure whether to take my army of blonde, Boden-clad children plus perfect hubby to Puglia or Tuscany this year, and felt sure you and Fenella would have the inside track'). I honestly can't imagine anything worse, can't imagine a time when it wouldn't cut into my soft flesh like a knife.

'Yeah, me too,' I say, sounding as sulky as Tallulah.

'I'm not sure how much longer I'm going to be sticking around ...'

'What do you mean?'

'I'm thinking about going travelling with my half of the fifty pence we're making on the flat. We never had the chance to do

247

anything like that . . .' I feel a little pinprick of responsibility, as I remember the volley of high-pressure jobs I took that kept us firmly embedded in the capital. 'I thought it might clear my head a bit.'

'Oh, right.' Stupid as it sounds, considering we've exchanged about four texts in six months, I'm feeling a wave of panic at the thought of him being in some faraway land that I don't even know about. 'Be sure to send me a postcard,' I say, infuriated that the sarcasm's sneaked back in on me.

'Amber,' he says, voice catching. 'I'll always be your friend. I would always come if you were in trouble.'

I'm so deeply relieved to know it, but it still feels like a mixed blessing. Whichever way I try to hold it, it can't help but cut. 'Even when you're a sex tourist with a badger beard?'

'Even then.'

I smile at him, step forward to hug him, kiss him on the cheek like the grown-ups we are, but before I know it we're kissing properly. I couldn't swear who started it, but I lose myself entirely. The feeling of his mouth is so utterly familiar, that smell of him caught in every part of me. He pulls away, bringing me back to myself with a bump. What the hell have I done?

'Sorry,' he says, 'I didn't mean—'

'It's OK,' I say, flustered. 'I shouldn't be here.'

How could I do that to Oscar? I can't believe I've gone and committed the very crime I've spent months being self-right-eously angry about. OK, a kiss is only worth a hundredth of a shag (I think we've already established how good I am at romantic mathematics), but I worry that this kiss was even more of a betrayal. Not in the gross physical sense of writhing

248

bodies and discarded undies, more in its pure and simple intimacy.

I make my way back into the restaurant, forcing myself not to look back, hoping that my heart will stop beating like a bird that's been trapped in a tiny box.

Chapter 13

I want to leave right there and then, let my team do the clearing up, but my keys are back in my locker. Michelle hurries over as soon as I'm through the door.

'You all right? Oscar's been asking for you but I told him I didn't know where you'd got to.' Oscar. 'You're not OK, are you?' she says, giving me a much needed hug. 'Babe, you're shaking.'

'I'm fine, honestly,' I say, trying to get a handle on myself.

'Is he still through there?' I say. She nods. 'OK,' I say, taking a breath. The stupid thing is that, had I not lived the last hour, I might've slipped off without saying good night, spared myself the exposure to his all too present family. But now, now I've kissed my not even ex-husband within yards of him, I feel like to do so would be a betrayal. After all my sanctimony about Dom, I'm poised on the shore, ready to cast the first stone of untruth into my new relationship.

I peek through the double doors, hoping I can just catch his eye. There's Lydia, right at home on his left-hand side, while Tallulah and a trio of stragglers continue to guzzle the

European wine lake down the other end of the table. He spots me, and I try to get away with a twee little goodbye wave.

'Amber!' he booms, grinning. It's wildly inappropriate, but I can't help loving his open-heartedness. I look down at the ground, ashamed. 'Grab a pew and have a taste of this.' He signals a bottle of red that has that musty, dusty, super-expensive look about it. 'Matt'll tell you how good it is.'

He should be keeping me and Lydia as far apart as is humanly possible. If, I mean when, she finds out, this is exactly the kind of incident that will compound her rage (trust me, I'm an expert).

'It's a blinder, boss,' says Matt slimily, filling up a glass. A glass that's located right next to Lydia's seat. Oh joy. Just for a second, Dom's damning assessment comes back to haunt me. Could they be upmarket swingers, laughing behind their fans about their latest scalp? I try to smile at Lydia but my top lip gets stuck, leaving me looking more like a churlish horse baring its teeth. I shuffle into the chair, muttering about only staying a minute, scraping it across the floor in the process. Tallulah scowls briefly, before resuming her analysis of a girl called Martha who apparently has 'the *worst* cellulite in the whole lower sixth.'

'No, in London!' adds a mean-looking blonde, and they all dissolve into fits of giggles.

Poor old Martha, sight of the saddlebags would soon cheer her up. My mum would never have stood for that kind of casual bitchiness, but Lydia doesn't break a sweat, imperiously beckoning Matt over to top up her glass.

'So how are you finding your tenure here?' she asks. My mind goes into overdrive. Even if she doesn't know Oscar and

I are together, surely she must know about Milly's cash injection, or has he put it down to some kind of Secret Millionaire random act of kindness?

'I love it.' Lydia looks at me, doesn't volunteer anything else. 'I absolutely love it. You must ... you must be very proud.'

As I say it, a little piece of me crumbles at the incontrovertible truth of the statement. It is hers, as much in spirit as it is in practice. Just watching them together, I can tell how much he needs to know she's holding the fort out front so that he can work his magic. I think of Dom, how much I wanted to fuse personal and professional into an all-encompassing life, a blanket we could wrap ourselves up in. Perhaps he was right not to want it, but it doesn't mean I'm not still sad that my dream's landed on the scrap heap.

I pause for a second, let myself actually taste the sadness. It feels vivid, makes me realise how much the constant rush cuts me off, renders me a human doing not a human being. I can't help feeling for Dom in this moment. However much of a fuckwitted fuckwit he's been, he would've known how sad it would be for me to say goodbye to the fantasy paradise of Amber's, would've hated to deliver that blow. I couldn't have borne having to take something equally precious from him – though maybe in his darker moments it felt to him like I did.

'I am,' Lydia demurs with a gracious smile. 'And how's the step up?'

'I was a sous before—'

She cuts across me. 'I meant joining the big league.'

Patronising cow. 'I think I'm doing OK. Oscar, are you pleased with me?' I shouldn't have risen to the bait.

'Very pleased,' he says, eyes locking with mine for a second. Silence reigns for what feels like an age.

'Did you enjoy your night, Tallulah?' I ask, just to give you a measure of my desperation.

She peels her head round, looking as baffled as she might if I'd asked her to come up with a solution to world peace. 'Er, yeah.'

'Bit more gratitude wouldn't go amiss,' says Oscar.

'It was fabulous, Daddy,' says Tallulah obediently, and he gives her a swift smile.

These two have got a well-worn routine going on, a version of a relationship that does a job: Tallulah gets abundant pocket money; Oscar gets a smiley offspring who doesn't call him on his workaholic elusiveness. I swallow sharply, suddenly wanting to ring my dad right this minute, even though he's always tucked up in bed shortly after *Newsnight*. I take a hefty slug from my glass.

'Not too shabby, is it?' says Oscar. It really isn't. I can't get too used to wine like this though, considering how often my paltry pay package reduces me to Czechoslovakian Rioja from the corner shop. I blew the best part of half a week's wages on making sure Oscar wouldn't gag on what I offered him at dinner.

'Not shabby at all,' I say, keeping eye contact as brief as I can. Surely she'll guess: I'd guess. Why is he doing this?

'You look like you need a top-up,' says Oscar to Lydia, signalling to hateful Nutkins. 'Oi, Matty-boy, what's with the wine drought?'

Matt hurries over, watched very subtly by Tallulah.

'Can *I* have a top-up?' she asks coquettishly.

'Darling, you've had enough,' says Lydia.

'Half a glass more won't kill her,' says Oscar. 'Don't forget it's a celebration.' They silently square up, eyes locked. I hate this.

'Give her the tiniest of drops,' says Lydia snippily. 'And when I say tiny, I mean tiny'.

Tallulah subtly smoulders at Matt as he pours, leaving me feeling faintly nauseous. The number of hidden agendas going on at this table would put the Cold War to shame. For a mad moment, I think about confessing the kiss to Oscar, but I think better of it. It would hurt him, and for what? Just so I can clear my conscience? It's not just that, of course, there's also a hearty dollop of self-preservation. Considering how angry he can get about chives, I wouldn't fancy my chances with this particular revelation.

'I should go,' I say, standing up abruptly. 'Early start.'

Oscar tries to catch my eye, but I can't risk looking at him. 'Night,' he says, sullen. What does he expect me to do, stick around to challenge him and Lydia to a game of naked Twister?

'Bye!' say the blonde chorus, but Tallulah doesn't so much as raise a smile.

'Say good night, Tallulah' says Oscar sharply.

'Night,' says Tallulah, in a tone which translates to 'die' in school-girl.

I reluctantly climb aboard my scooter, wishing it were a Tardis. All I want to do is reach the sanctuary of home. I keep thinking about Dom's face as he tried to unpick his journey, searching for a palatable way to explain his infatuation with someone else. I know, I know, there's no right answer, but a bit of me would rather he'd had some gross whipped-cream rid-dled shagfest than felt tentacles of love start to creep around his heart. I wish I didn't care, disloyal harlot that I am, but I can't exorcise it. Maybe this is what grown-up, second-time-round relationships are like – walking an uneasy path through the graveyard of past loves, trying not to stop to gaze at the headstones.

Milly's asleep when I get home, but I wander down the hall with my electric toothbrush whirling on full blast until she surrenders. What can I say, I am pure evil. She wanders out, eye mask pushed up like a velvet bandanna.

'Morning, darling.'

'Sort of. Two in the morning.'

'Amber, I was dead to the world!' Then she spots my stupid, crumpled face. 'What is it?'

'Can I sleep in your bed?' I ask, utterly pathetic.

'Of course you can,' she says, putting her arms around me.

Milly's room is positively gothic, filled with family heirlooms as mottled and ancient as her grandmother's four-poster bed. Huge and wooden, you have to climb aloft like it's a ship. I haul myself up, comforted by how safe and enclosed it feels.

'I'm going to put my eye mask back on, but it doesn't mean I'm not listening. Oh, and your mum rang.'

'My mum rang?' I say, feeling a pang at the memory of Dom's comments. I resolve to call back first thing rather than make her play telephone tag like I normally do.

'Yes, now tell me what's gone on before I fall into a coma. I was having a highly distracting dream about George Peppard before you cruelly ejected me from my reverie.'

'*Breakfast at Tiffany's* era George, not *The A-Team* George?'

'Obv. What's going on?!'

'Dom.'

And I try to recount our conversation word for word, but once I get to the part about the white bear I realise that you really had to be there.

'Oh, Amber, thank God it's over. Imagine if he'd been coming to tell you that he was moving in with her or ... or worse.'

She's right, of course. If he'd pitched up to salve his conscience before wedding number two I'd be distraught.

'I know but, Milly, he loved her. It wasn't some tawdry fuck, he actually loved her.'

'You don't know that.'

'I do know that.' And I do. It's hard to explain to someone who hasn't ever lived, breathed and pooped alongside the same person for a decade how you can just know these things.

'And you love Oscar.'

'Yes.'

'Lovely Oscar,' continues Milly, before I have time to try and express how confusing it is, how perhaps you can love two people at once, even if one version of love tastes more like grief shot through with a trace of fury. 'I'm coming in tomorrow by the way,' she continues.

'Are you?!'

'Yes, Oscar's talking me through his business plan for the next eighteen months.' She pauses. 'That's not too bizarre, is it? It's just that now I really am getting him out of this pickle, I need to understand what it is he's doing.'

Of course it's bizarre. It's beyond bizarre.

'No, no, that's fine. It's great you're doing it.'

'Amber?' continues Milly, sounding close to sleep. 'Why'd you think Dom really turned up tonight?'

I think of that kiss, feel myself flush in the dark. I still can't believe I did that. Milly's my best friend and yet I can't get the words out. Not now I'd be betraying her business partner.

'To salve his conscience? To get some kind of closure?' I remember those papers stacked up under my bed. I'm glad I'm not sleeping above them tonight.

'Closure? He's not Oprah.'

'You're right, he's most definitely not a middle-aged black woman.'

And with that knotty issue satisfactorily resolved, Milly drifts off back to sleep. Unlike me.

I slip out of the bed while Milly's still dead to the world, snuffling snores escaping from underneath the velvet mask. I stop for a second and look at her, meanly thinking how much easier it is to invest rather than doing the hard graft. I can't go down this track … Dom's words are still swirling round my head on the way to work. Work: maybe it really is a four-letter word. I never meant for it to cost me everything. If Oscar and I really do have a shot then I've got to make sure we don't make the same mistake, and that surely means telling him about Tallulah. I needn't tell him about the kiss, about Dom even turning up, it'd only hurt him, but he needs to know what he's too frenetic to see. My stomach clenches at the very thought. There's no way I want to sail too close to his complicated family life, but how can I profess to love him and let him make the same mistakes I did? Priorities, people.

He's pacing the kitchen like a papa lion when I arrive, emitting the odd growl. 'Finally!' he says, even though I'm dead on time. Annoying though it is, his face tells a different story. He looks almost pensive, unsure of me. That's the problem with secrets and lies; they poison the well before you know it. Even if he doesn't know what's making him edgy, couldn't articulate the feeling, some animal part of him has picked up that something's amiss.

'Can I talk to you?' I say, then hear my tone – way too intimate when Michelle and Tomasz are both in earshot. 'About, about our vegetable suppliers?'

Tomasz smiles with quiet satisfaction as I wait for a predictable explosion about anaemic numpties, but it's not forthcoming.

'OK then, shall we go through to the office?'

I follow him, aware of Michelle's eyes burning into my back. She's no fool, I suspect I'm going to have to 'fess up soon and keep all my fingers and toes crossed that she's still batting for my team.

I'm rehearsing my opening line in my head, trying to work out how to say what I need to say without sounding interfering or judgemental, but I'm snapped right out of it by the slam of his door.

'Why did you walk out on me last night?' he demands.

'I didn't walk out on you! What did you want me to do? Come and sit on your knee and feed you cocktail cherries?'

'Don't be such a smart arse. You were out of there without so much as a look backwards.'

There's truth in what he says, but I can't go there. I'm ashamed to say I take the coward's way out and go on the attack.

'How do you think it feels for me seeing you with Lydia? She's everywhere; on your desk, telling you off at dinner. I feel like some random serf tugging my forelock in the background. Please, sir, can I have some of your delicious wine before I go back to my hovel?'

'That's it,' he says, slamming his hand down on his desk. For a second I wonder if he's dumping me. 'I'm telling her later. I'm not having this.'

'Are you sure—'

'You can't have it both ways, Fish Girl.'

It's a fair point but nevertheless, the very prospect of it is making me feel physically sick. 'It's just I know how angry she'll be.' Though it's another one of those pesky unsquareable circles: the longer we keep it from her, the angrier she'll be.

Oscar waves a dismissive hand. 'Why would she be? We're over, I'm moving on. She's got every right to do the same.'

'But it's not that simple—'

'Isn't it?' he snaps. 'How's so?'

I find him genuinely scary when he gets that look in his eyes. Still, I can't bear to censor myself. That can't be right.

'It just isn't. You might be OK with the idea in principle, but it might still feel weird when it happens. Just because ... because you've got all that history, not because you want her back.'

'*What* are you talking about?' says Oscar, and I realise I shouldn't have gone there, not today.

Would it be easier if I could be honest about the graveyard, or would it in fact be harder? If he said he was sometimes confused by his split, despite his feelings for me, I don't know if I could handle it. Particularly not after Rachel. Perhaps his emphatic, straightforward version of love is exactly what I need: a man I can read, not even like a book, but more like a copy of *Closer*.

'I promise you I couldn't care less,' he continues. 'Not unless she exhumes one of the Krays and moves him in. Then I'd care, but only because I care about my daughter. No, I'm going to talk to her. She'll be fine.' He looks at me, gives me a smile that makes me feel like silly putty. 'We'll be fine. Come here.'

And I do. I kiss him, bury my hands in his hair, feel the warmth of that powerful body. I can hear his heart beating, the frailty of that, the fact that life is short. I put my hand on it, kiss him more fervently.

'Everything's resting on this month,' he says, talking into my hair. 'I know I said it before, but this is when I really need everything you've got. We'll get through it, we're a killer team.'

I break away from him. 'We will, but talking of Tallulah—'

'What is it now? You're the queen of angst today, aren't you?'

'Oscar.' I pause, wondering whether to back off but I can't. 'Last night ... when I went to find her. She was with Matt, down here in a cubicle, which is bad enough, but I'm not sure they weren't taking something ...'

I watch the colour drain from his face, his jaw clench. I remember the first time I stayed over with my sixth-form boyfriend, my dad trying to be cool about it. No father ever wants their daughter to grow up, let alone like this.

'You're fucking joking! Are you sure?'

'I'm sure they were in the cubicle, I can't be sure about the rest. It was just the noises … she asked me not to tell you,' threatened more like, but I'm not going to make this any worse, 'but I had to.'

He doesn't speak for a few seconds, emotions building up like a grenade that's set to explode. I put my arms around him but it barely registers.

'I know it's a shock but …' I tail off, unwilling to say any more. What I mean is that perhaps it needs to come to a head: there's a tangible unhappiness about Tallulah buried beneath that sub-Paris Hilton shtick, and maybe this is nothing more than a cry for help, a chance for them to reconnect. But I don't know whether that's a step too far, too stepmother-tastic. Besides, surely it's obvious?

'Right!' he says, slamming his fist. 'You,' he points at me, 'you're going to call Matt and fire him.'

Oh no.

'Don't you want to do that?' I ask hopefully.

'I haven't got time, I need to deal with this. I'll call him later, don't you worry. Lydia's not in today, I've got to track her down. That little madam will be at school, so it'll have to wait until home time.'

Don't be too hard on her is what I want to say, don't treat her like an army recruit gone AWOL, but I'm struggling to find how to pitch it when it's patently none of my business. I remember her sneering dismissal of me in the loos, not entirely unlike her mum's *noblesse oblige*, but I still can't help thinking she needs compassion more than punishment. I'm about to blunder on in there, when there's a smart rap on the door. I step back from Oscar, retreat to the right side of the desk.

'What?' shouts Oscar.

'Sorry, guv,' says Mac the Steak, sticking his tragically porcine features round the door. 'I really need to speak to you.'

'Not a good time.'

'Five minutes,' says Mac pleadingly.

Oscar waves a hand, allowing it. I move to leave. 'No, stay,' growls Oscar, and I look apologetically at Mac, who looks … he looks positively suicidal. What's with today?

'Oscar, mate, you've been nothing but good to me,' he starts, reddening. 'I want you to know this isn't my choice. Far, far from it.'

'Spit it out,' says Oscar.

'I can't supply you any more,' says Mac, visibly shrinking back from him.

'*What?!* I've got fucking judges crawling up my arse, the most important competition of my career in less than a month. You can't do this to me.'

'Angus Torrence's people have been on the blower. They've offered us, like, thirty times over what we make here, three-year contract to supply all his restaurants, but it's an exclusive. It's a family business, mate. My brother says we can't turn it down.'

'That, that *clot*.' He doesn't actually say clot, but for the sake of modesty, let's pretend he does. 'He's trying to ruin me. Well, fuck him, this is war. And you, you can fuck off,' he says, jabbing his finger at Mac.

'Hang on,' I say, going to lay a hand on Oscar's quivering arm before I remember I'm meant to be a lowly serf. 'Mac, I get you're in an impossible situation—'

262

'How's it impossible?' interjects Oscar. 'When I've done so much for you.'

'My business is on its knees,' says Mac, emotional.

'Mac, could you give us a month at least?' I ask. 'Just let us get through the competition? You know Oscar's all about provenance, we can't just replace you overnight.'

'I wish I could, but the deal's off the table if we don't close down to other customers by the end of the week. You don't have to pay me the last month, it's the least I can do.'

'Get the *fuuuck* out!' shouts Oscar, throwing a book at him.

'Oscar!' I say, trying to stop him from grabbing a huge glass paperweight that's to his left.

'I'm sorry!' says Mac, beating a hasty retreat.

The paperweight shatters all over the floor behind him, shards of glass cascading like a fountain.

I can safely say that this particular Wednesday is the most stressful day at work I've ever had. I try to call Matt, but his phone's off, so all I can do is leave him a message. Johnny is Lydia when Lydia's not here, and front of house is really their jurisdiction, not mine. When I tell Johnny what I've done, he's horrified.

'What possessed you?' he asks.

'I had to,' I say lamely. If you don't know about me and Oscar, it doesn't make much sense. All I am is a teacher's pet and a snitch. Nice combo. 'He needed to know.'

'You're a chef, not a social worker! How the hell am I meant to cope without a barman?'

'Oscar won't have him through the door.'

'Well obviously, but he's not the one having to deal with

the drinks orders. Jesus, Amber, what have we ever done to you?'

For a brief second I think about telling him. Odds are it's going to come out, and at least he wouldn't think I'm some kind of Bible-bashing moraliser who doesn't understand the first thing about the harsh realities of restaurant life. But I can't face it, not now, and not when he's held such a candle for me (a candle I've well and truly snuffed out).

'Well, if you had any bright ideas about me doing it, you can think again. Matt might be a naughty boy but he's also my friend. Anyway, I'll be too busy calling round to try and get some cover.'

I don't blame him for being furious. Did I do right? Maybe I should've waited until the next three weeks were out of the way, and not thrown another curve ball into the mix, not to mention causing Matt to lose his job at a time when they are so few and far between. I just couldn't bear holding back that knowledge from Oscar, hypocritical though it sounds when my lips have so recently gone walkabout.

He's stormed out in search of Lydia, leaving me waiting, stomach and buttocks clenched in tandem, for the incommunicado Matt to turn up for his shift. I've fired people before, but not like this. As I'm making my four millionth call to a butcher, I remember the promise I made to myself this morning. Mum. There was a time when she would've been the first person I'd have called when I felt like this. Admittedly, not since Stacey Kingsman left me off the invite list for her ninth birthday party (bitch!), but nevertheless . . . She answers on the second ring.

'Amber!'

'Hi, Mum. Sorry I haven't rung for a few weeks.'

'Yes, well ... you're busy.'

There's an awkward pause. There often is. Then I hear her manicured fingernails hit her keyboard, an email having landed.

'Mum, don't,' I say, suddenly emotional. 'Don't look at it, talk to me.'

I hear an intake of breath.

'What would you like to talk about?' she says, flustered.

'Tell me how you are, how you actually are.'

She hesitates.

'What were you doing on Sunday at four o'clock?' I prompt.

'Sunday at four o'clock? I was planting out my parsley. It's silly I know, but I like to do it on St David's Day. The azaleas are starting to bud now, and the pond's overrun by frogs ...'

On and on she goes, and I'm not bored at all. I imagine them there, planting and bickering, Dad reading out the odd outrageous piece of public policy from the *Observer*, old lefty that he is. I really, really want to go home.

'And what about you?' she asks eventually, and I decide not to hear her gearing up to judge me. Maybe she isn't gearing up to judge me.

'Well, I've been seeing someone, but that's a longer conversation. And today, today I've got to sack someone.'

Who better to call than an HR manager? Now she's really on a roll. When I hang up the phone, a good fifteen minutes later, she's given me three good pieces of advice, including how to deadhead roses. I vow to come home, trying to calculate how long it is until I get a free weekend. I can't imagine Oscar letting me out of his sight before the competition, that's for sure.

Matt turns up at 11.45 and it's even worse than I imagined. I take him into the office, which is still peppered with shards of glass despite my best efforts to sweep them up. It's like the rage is still palpable, the air thick with it, but it's nothing compared to the tsunami that hits me when Matt grasps what I'm saying. Looking at the shock on his face, I can't help but feel guilty. Of course he can't understand why I'd do this, I just look like a cackling witch who'll stop at nothing to further my own cause. The accolades come thick and fast: I'm a clot, a furry clot, a talentless whore, a kiss arse. I shrink further and further back into the chair, but the more I do, the further he leans in, spittle erupting from his mouth.

'Don't try and run away from me!' he shouts. 'You haven't got big daddy to hide behind now. I want you to tell me why you really did it.'

'Because she's a just kid! Because you shouldn't be exploiting a kid.'

'She can handle herself, I promise you,' he says, with a twisted kind of smile. 'The question is, can you?'

I'm glad he's small and wiry, not big and burly.

'What's that supposed to mean?'

'I will ruin you,' he says, jabbing a finger at me. 'I'll ruin you here, I'll ruin you wherever you go next. It's a small world, you know it is, and people have a long memory.'

He's obviously watched *The Godfather* far too many times, but I still can't help being intimidated. 'Matt, I'm really sorry,'

I say, standing up in the hope I can calm him down and hustle him out. 'But I didn't have a choice.' Stupid thing to say, of course I did, I just thought it was the right one.

He flushes with rage, draws himself up to his full height (five-foot six roughly). Oh, God, is he actually going to attack me?

'Matt—'

'Knock, knock,' says a familiar voice. 'Is Oscar at home?'

If only. There's Milly, dressed in some kind of strange skirt suit, hair scraped back, brandishing a laptop as big as the Enigma machine. It's the world's most incongruous sight but, under the circs, a very, very welcome one.

'Come in!' I say, 'Matt was just leaving.' I look at him, trying to bring my breathing back to normal. 'I'll make sure you get paid up to the end of the month. I know you don't believe me, but I am sorry. And I really hope you find something else. We'll give you a good reference.'

'Don't fucking patronise me,' he hisses. 'I meant what I said, you'll be next.'

'OK, thanks, Matt!' I trill, conscious of Milly's saucer-wide eyes flicking between us. He slams out, and I collapse backwards onto the side of the desk.

'Golly, just another day at the office?'

'Something like that.'

'And breathe! Do you need a tot of brandy?'

'Nice thought, but no,' I say, looking at my watch. I need to get back upstairs. I give Milly the thirty-second précis of the morning's events, assuming she'll want to reschedule, but she settles herself into a chair.

'What's this?' she asks as her towering, shiny, black stilettos

267

crunch glass deep into the floorboards. She must've watched *Working Girl* on loop before she left the house.

'Um, a ... a water glass smashed.' More lying to those I love. Oh, the lies. 'Maybe it'd be better if we arranged another day? He might need ages with Lydia.'

'He'd have texted surely, if he wasn't coming?'

'Well, maybe ...'

'I'll give it twenty minutes,' she says stubbornly. 'I really think we should get started if we can.' There's an awkward pause. Started with what exactly? 'You never know, he might be glad of the distraction.'

'Oh, OK. Well, I'll have to leave you here.' I think about that for a second, aware that Oscar would never want an investor left alone in his lair, filing cabinet unguarded. Milly wouldn't dream of snooping, but he won't know that. 'On second thoughts, why don't you come upstairs and we'll get you a drink.' That's the last thing I should offer. 'Or, or a cup of tea.'

Milly totters up the stairs behind me, arriving on the floor at the exact moment that Oscar erupts through the front entrance.

'Fish Girl, five minutes,' he says, jerking his thumb towards the stairs, before clocking Milly. 'Hello there,' he says, a nerve pulsing at his temple, only visible to me. 'If it isn't my favourite lunch date. You'll be glad to hear we've got the best table in the house.' He steps aside, ever the gentleman, and Milly beams with delight.

I watch them together, remembering that article, wondering if I should feel threatened, but I feel relatively sure that Oscar's charm comes more from confidence than lechery. He knows

268

he's handsome, doesn't even have to think about it, the proof is on the back of every ladle or passing shop front. It allows him to glide through, knowing that his good looks will effortlessly oil the wheels. I give my left saddlebag a sneaky pat, hoping it might've gone into remission, but no such luck. He must sometimes compare me to Lydia, whatever he says, notice how much less slickly packaged I am. They were gilded, the two of them, still are when they're caught in the same frame.

I try and tear my eyes away, but can't fail to notice the glow that Milly's got now her new chapter's begun. I immediately feel less of a grumpy old curmudgeon seeing that flash of real pleasure, the purpose in her wobbly stride. She really, really wants to be achieving something. Maybe this is fine, maybe Oscar can charm her into thinking her input's invaluable, listen to not a word, and then make her a tidy return. That way everyone wins.

You wouldn't think so if you were judging by today. Johnny's put a newbie waiter behind the bar, leaving the main floor short, and a raft of drink orders muddled up and misplaced. I take the odd peek through the double doors, watching Milly's eyes swivel around the room, however much Oscar tries to keep her front and centre. That soft thrum of anxiety creeps back into my bones. Ditsy she may be, but it doesn't make her unobservant.

She comes through to the kitchen before she leaves, incongruous in that tweedy pink suit. 'Bye, darling,' she says, flinging her arms around me. 'Lunch was super delicious.'

'Oh good,' I say, 'good.' I wipe my greasy paws on my whites, eyes roving the room for the next disaster.

'So I'll be off-ski' says Milly. 'See you at home?'

I notice a few people, notably Joe, staring over, and I suddenly realise how dangerous this is. Or maybe it isn't, not if Lydia's about to blow the whistle anyway. It's so hard to know whether she'll opt for icy silence or a public service announcement, designed to convey how little she cares while royally screwing over my command of the kitchen.

'Ssh, and yes,' I say in an undertone.

Milly safely dispatched, I go in search of Oscar but he's left without saying goodbye. I feel like a cat on a hot tin roof for the rest of the afternoon. Joe wastes no time telling the rest of the kitchen what I've done, with predictable results. No one says anything, but I feel about as welcome as Angelina Jolie might if she pitched up at Jennifer Aniston's birthday party on a whim (surprise!).

I silently curse my lack of self-preservation, but I still can't see how I could claim to love Oscar and leave him in the dark. I wish he'd come back. I'm desperate to know what's going on, what's been said. That article Milly found suddenly comes back to haunt me as I'm hauling a side of beef out of the cold store. Could the cards fall the other way? It might be that their need to come back together for Tallulah could bring them back together for real. Maybe it would serve me right, I think.

Eventually Oscar reappears. He comes straight to the kitchen, grim-faced, and barks orders at any poor unfortunates who look like they might be slacking. He jerks his head in my direction and I follow him to the office.

He slumps down in his chair, face turned away. I've never seen him like this – it unnerves me. I've got super adept at soothing his rage, but this is a quickstep I'm yet to learn.

'Baby, what happened?' I say, slipping my arms around him from behind and laying my head on his shoulder. 'What did she say?'

'She said you were lying. Then she said you weren't lying, though she does swear she wasn't the one taking drugs. Then she said we didn't understand her. Then she bawled her eyes out and said she hated us. Well me, anyway.'

'Darling, she doesn't mean it. She's upset, she wants attention.'

'Well, she's grounded for the next month so she should have plenty of time to think about it.'

Oscar lights up a fag, body rigid and unyielding.

'For a month?' I imagine her rattling around Lydia's no doubt picture perfect apartment, waiting for her to finish evening service. 'Won't that be a bit lonely for her?'

'She should've thought about that before she came over all Lindsay Lohan in training. We need to come down hard on her now before she goes off the rails.'

I think about my sixteen-year-old self, the endless battles Mum and me had over the length of my skirts and the exact definition of an alcopop. There was nothing more likely to make me sin than knowing it would wind her up.

'Did you *properly* talk to her?'

'Of course we talked to her!'

'Yeah, but about why she did it?'

'She did it because we haven't been tough enough with her. Those schools,' he shakes his head, 'I would've been scared of a joint at her age, let alone anything else.'

'It's been a tough year for her though. You two splitting up, moving apart.'

'No excuse,' says Oscar definitively. 'Tough love is what she needs and tough love is what she's going to get.'

'You could try and spend some time with her at least. Maybe if she's grounded she could be at yours more, you could cook her dinner and stuff.' I am actually Mother Teresa. What could possibly be worse for me than that? ('Budge up, Tallulah, *EastEnders* is on in a sec.') I'd be leaving the flat in a box.

'Once the competition's out of the way.' He grinds his fag into the ashtray, knuckles white. 'Need to start seriously planning.'

'Yeah, we do, but ... You must be feeling terrible. It's such a shock, I'm so sorry that I had to tell you.'

'We're dealing with it,' he says, pulling out his battered notebook from his breast pocket. 'Lydia's on it. If Tallulah's good I might take her on a trip in a couple of months, New York or something. Reward her for doing as she's told.'

When I was a twelve or so, I used to beg Dad to take me to Pizza Hut, even though chain restaurants make him want to curl up and die. I loved the salad bar, piling on tomatoes until they skittered over the floor like marbles and earned us death stares from the staff. It's not about glamour, I want to say, it's about knowing your dad actually wants to be with you, will put himself through things he doesn't like just because you do. I look down at Oscar from above, see the sadness that's pooled in the blackness of his eyes, but also feel the way his body stiffens under my touch.

'Talk to me,' I say, doggedly massaging his knotted-up shoulders.

'I am talking to you. I'm talking to you about the competition.'

I draw back, defeated. I would literally be the world's worst therapist; my couch would have tumbleweed blowing down it. I know he's cut up about it, but I can't get to him. I think about that night at the opera, the tears he shed for Mimi. Why is it so much easier for him to openly feel for an imaginary urchin? Or is it me? For all his professions of love, perhaps he feels I haven't yet earned the right to see all the way through. Maybe I was too hasty, too patronising thinking he was my own personal copy of *Closer*. Each way I look there's another reminder of what he and Lydia share, another doorway that's been designated out of bounds.

'Got the date through today,' he says, lighting another fag and pulling on it sharply. 'Thirteenth of March.'

We knew it would be in March, but they've kept the precise date back for as long as possible so they can really catch us on the hoof and see how we react to the pressure.

'Friday the thirteenth?' I say. 'Oh God, Friday the thirteenth.' Shit. Shit, shit, shit. Why did it have to fall on the day of Marsha's engagement drinks? I tried to talk her out of picking such an inauspicious date, but she dug her heels in. In fact, I think it made her all the more determined. 'Superstitious nonsense,' she'd said, returning to the guest list with brio.

'Unlucky for some,' says Oscar. 'Won't be for us though.'

'No, no, it's not that. It's Marsha's drinks that night.'

'Unlucky for some, like I said. You'll have to cancel her. We've lost Mac, we've got enough to contend with.'

'But I can't,' I wail. 'She'll be so disappointed. It's not much more than a week away, we won't find anywhere nearly as nice for a Friday night, and Peter's family have booked flights so she can't even change the date.'

'Amber—'

'I don't want to let her down. Not again.'

Oscar finally looks at me properly, eyes studying my face. 'Do you remember your interview?'

Like, every last millisecond. I nod mutely.

'What you said to me? About wanting to learn from me? Well, one thing I've learned, the one reason I got that second star, is that you can't be half-hearted about making sure you're the best. And that means making big sacrifices.' He smiles at me, that smile that still makes my insides curl in on themselves like a snail heading home. 'It's hard, I know, but you are a fucking incredible chef. I probably should have laid it out sooner, but I didn't want you getting too cocky. You've got the most raw talent I've ever seen and you can't afford to be wasting it.'

I try and hold myself down, poleaxed by the echo of Dom's words from last night. Maybe it is true, and if it is, how can it mean such different things to each of them? I look at Oscar, search every crevice and contour of his face to check he means it. I would've done anything, anything, to hear those words from him when I started here. It's like winning *The X Factor* and *Strictly Come Dancing* all in one night. I can't let him lose faith in me, I need to prove myself worthy.

'We need this award,' he continues. 'It could change everything for us, take the pressure off so I don't have to take arse-over-tit suggestions on board from people who don't know the first thing about catering.'

I feel rueful about letting Milly blunder her way into this. I should've been fiercer with them both, protected her better.

'Was it that bad?'

'She's a lovely girl, total diamond, but asking me if I need more waiters? Does she really think I can't work that out?'

I refrain from reminding him that lunch service was roughly akin to a prison riot.

'You need to put Marsha off,' says Oscar, waiting for me to respond.

'OK,' I concede reluctantly.

It's a direct order, what choice do I have? It's the most important night of Ghusto's short life, and I've got to do all I can to make sure we triumph. That's what my head says, but my body says different. 'I was only following orders' has already been proven to be an indefensible defence. I'm robbing Marsha of the party of her dreams, letting her down on the one thing she's asked me for. I'm not even going to be able to attend whatever woeful, warm Chardonnay-ridden excuse for a celebration that she pulls together. At least if it had been here, I could show my face. I'm going to have to throw myself on my sword, offer bridesmaid duties to someone who actually deserves it.

'I'll do it now,' I tell Oscar. She needs as much notice as I can give her, and I need some time out.

'Good girl,' he says. 'I'll go and share the good news with the troops.'

I don't go out to the yard, it feels too ghost-ridden, like some trace element of Dom and me will still be freezing their butts off on that uncomfortable bench. Instead I go out the front, watch a few curious passers-by peer at the menu and stare through the plate glass at the opulent interior. When a Hoxton geek (hair like a great crested grebe; glasses a pair of

275

twin aquariums) makes a disgusted face at the ample offal that's on offer, I almost go over and take him on. Ignorant fool. Little does he know that the kidneys would tickle his taste buds and tease his mouth like nothing he's ever eaten before, that the blood in the ice cream would give it a tang that you couldn't imagine. That's why, I think, determinedly staring at my phone, that's why Oscar's brilliance needs a wider audience. There's so much stacked against him, he doesn't need me loading the deck.

There's no answer on Marsha's mobile, and I nearly wuss out, but I know I've got to strike while the iron's not hot exactly, but at least lukewarm. I wish I didn't have to do this. I dial her work number, and she swiftly picks up.

'Marsha Thorogood,' she says, all clipped and business-like.

'Marsha, it's Amber.'

'Hello, Amber,' she says, warmth flooding into her tone. She's probably still feeling self-conscious about our row, wondering if she overstepped the mark. I hope she knows me better than to think this is revenge.

'Hi,' I say. I can't bear to strike the blow.

'I'm so glad you called!' she says. 'I've got tickets for a private view of Inuit wall tapestries at a new gallery in Camberwell and I was hoping you might be able to make it. There's a new veggie place we could go to after.' Her voice softens. 'My treat.'

Inuit wall tapestries and mung bean casserole: the perfect Marsha-shaped olive branch. I can't think of anything worse, but still my heart slides closer to my boots. Thorogood is the perfect surname for Marsha, it never occurred to me before. I should probably be re-named Amber Blackheart and forced to live in a self-constructed shelter made entirely of chickpea tins in the midst of a rubbish dump.

'That sounds lovely,' I say. 'But, Marsha, there's something I've got to talk to you about.'

'Not the party, please don't tell me it's been derailed.'

The fact she guessed first time tells me everything. A hot backwash of shame spreads through me as I realise how little she relies on me, and yet still she asked me to be a bridesmaid. I take a gulp of air, try to find the courage to carry on.

'It has rather, Marsha. We're up for an *Evening Standard* award, and they've just sprung on us that that's the night they're going to inspect. They'll be crawling all over us, front and back of house. We're going to be under so much pressure, and Oscar doesn't think we can handle both. He, he . . . needs this so much, Marsha.'

'And you didn't have the slightest inkling this could happen?' she asks, voice sharp. She's right, of course. I should've factored it in.

'It's no excuse, but the odds were so slim.' A skein of silence spreads out between us, infinite. Then I hear a strange choking sound.

'Marsha? Marsha, are you crying?' There's a sharp intake of breath.

'No, no, of course not. We'll just have to make do and mend. My flat's not quite big enough, but there's sure to be some kind of recreational,' she gulps, 'recreational hall that I can hire. Any commercial venue will know they've got us over, over a barrel and—'

I can't bear it. I can't bear her woeful stoicism, the resignation of the fact that I've let her down yet again. She's not even

277

asking me to help find a solution, even though I would literally call butchers and bars in tandem until my fingers were no more than bloodied stumps. Oh, stop with the melodrama, if you care this much then prove it.

'Marsha, Marsha,' I jump in. 'It is too late, you're right. I'm going to find a solution, we just need it to be two separate operations. Get in extra staff. I'll ... I'll get Dom to help if I have to.' I feel a warm spark inside at the realisation that he will help if I ask. I'm not sure that I can bear to, to face up to another reminder that he's worked out all the answers and limped on, but I'm still happy that I could.

'No, no,' says Marsha tartly. 'You've got your reasons. A little bit more foresight would've been helpful but I appreciate you can't shut the door after the horse has bolted.'

'No! I'm lassoing the horse.' Where did that come from? 'It's in the paddock, munching its nosebag. I'll, I'll talk to Oscar.' A finger of dread trails down the back of my neck making the hairs stand up. 'I'll take full responsibility.'

'Without wishing to sound like a doubting Thomas, or even Thomasina, are you really in a position to make that promise?'

It's a fair question, more than fair. Can I say yes? It feels suddenly imperative that I do, that I shake my fist at the universe and tell it I've changed. What is more important than loving those we love, not just by uttering meaningless platitudes we've learned by rote, but by what we do for them? And if Oscar loves me, surely he'll let me do this for Marsha if I can find a way to avoid compromising the operation? And if he doesn't get it, well ... well at least I'll know.

'I promise. By the power of Greyskull.'

Marsha didn't have older brothers so she doesn't really appreciate the solemnity of that promise, but with ten minutes more chat I persuade her both that I mean it and that Inuit wall tapestries are my number-one passion – two for the price of one. Now all I've got to do is sell the deal to Oscar.

I don't get the chance to speak to him until midnight, after the horrors of evening service. I was made to feel so untouchable that at one point I nearly bellowed 'I am not an animal', Elephant Man-like. I haven't even got my support team to cheer me up. Michelle's totally got me and Oscar sussed, which means I'm avoiding any meaningful interaction beyond the skillet-passing variety, not yet able to face her disbelief. Tomasz is not so much narcissistic as onion-cistic, which makes him a poor candidate for a heart-to-heart and Johnny ... well, Johnny appears to hate me. It's a thin line between love and hate, that's for sure.

I've sneaked up to the flat, trusting the kitchen porters to ensure the restaurant's left spick and span. Oscar's unbuttoning his whites, revealing that taut, muscled chest. I want to run my fingers down his midline, feel the shock of electricity as he responds to my touch. Is the tremor I'm feeling desire or fear?

'So I called Marsha ...' I start tentatively.

'Well done. And what about butchers? How'd you do with that?'

'I need to talk you through options on that tomorrow. Nothing's ideal, but I've got some ideas.'

'Tell me now,' he says, pulling his all too familiar notebook from his back pocket.

'Not now,' I say. 'It's bedtime.'

'It's like that, is it?' he says, unbuttoning his whites in a seamless movement.

'Oscar, wait,' I say, 'I called Marsha but—'

'But what?' he says, eyes flinty. Who can blame him? I'd probably feel exactly the same. I'm relying on the fact that he's my beloved as well as my boss, hoping that love trumps work, but do I have the right to expect that of him?

'I just … I couldn't bear to do it to her. It's too late. She'll end up stranded in some dive in Stratford when I know I can find a way to make it work. I've already warned her it'll push the cost up a bit, and she's prepared for it,' I gabble on, trying to hold back Oscar's mounting rage, 'so I can hire in a couple of extra people, and make the food as simple as possible. I'll pay a couple of people overtime, pull an all-nighter beforehand. You won't have to think about it, I promise.'

'Stop right there,' says Oscar, fists clenched. 'You are *not* doing any of those things. You had no right, no right at all, to disobey a direct order. This is the most important night of my life, and you think you've got the right to play fast and loose with it—'

'The most important night of your life? What about the night Tallulah was born? Or, or the night your dad died?'

He shakes his head at me. 'I can't believe you, you're shameless. Absolutely shameless.'

'No, I'm not! I know,' I step towards him, but think better of it, 'I know how important this is, and I will make sure that no one takes their eye off the ball. I will give you everything I've got, just as I promised, but I love Marsha. She's stuck by me, even when I've been a selfish, workaholic bitch.' Here a sob escapes from me, unbidden, but I swallow it down. Now

280

is not a time to show weakness. 'And maybe I should never have promised her this party, but now I have, I can't let her down.'

I look at his uncomprehending face. No, his expression is more than uncomprehending – it's betrayal that's registering, his handsome face rendered ugly by its toxic assault. I feel a sharp stab of guilt at the thought of that stolen kiss. Maybe this is about more than loyalty to Marsha, maybe it's me trying to prove to myself, to Dom, even though he'll never know, that I do know the real order of events.

'How touching,' says Oscar, with a smile that could curdle milk. 'I'm so glad that you love Marsha so much. But *what about me*?' He slams his fist down on the kitchen counter, causing Moriarty to run from the room with a yowl. 'It's not the fucking Girl Guides. You haven't taken some premenstrual pledge of allegiance. You're meant to love me, meant to work for me – do neither of those things count for *anything* in your warped little brain?'

'It's not a competition!' Oh, God, poor choice of words. 'Sorry, obviously it is a competition but ... I do love you, I do, and I don't blame you for being furious.' I try to soften him, smile at him, but his face is an unyielding mask. 'If you love me, then please let me have this, trust me not to let you down. Trust that if I love you I won't let you down.' Again a sob threatens, but I defeat it. Oscar grabs his fags from the counter, scrunches the empty packet up in his powerful grip like he's King Kong plucking a blonde from the streets of Manhattan. I can hear Moriarty coming back up the stairs, even though I could've sworn he ran bedroom-ward. Oscar turns back towards me.

'Jesus, Lydia ...'

There's no time to take recover from that little verbal bombshell, no time at all, because before another word has time to cross my lips, Tallulah's framed in the doorway, eye make-up torrenting down her cheeks.

'Daddy ...'

Chapter 14

'Tallulah,' says Oscar, scrabbling to button his whites back up. 'Sweetheart, what are you doing here?'

I'm frozen to the spot.

'I came to tell you that I don't hate you,' she says quavering. 'But it turns out I do.'

I want to tell her to sit down, to calm down, make her a cup of tea, but obviously my only job is to stay mute until I can make a break for freedom.

'Course you don't hate me,' says Oscar, smiling at her. 'You can't hate your dad.'

'I do!' she screeches. 'I actually do. Is this why you and Mum split? Is it all true, what all those horrible people say about you? That you go round *fucking* waitresses?'

'Don't you dare talk to me like that!' Oscar spits back. 'This is a relationship, I was waiting for the right time to tell you and your mother. And if you hadn't ambushed me, I would've found it.'

I see her face crumple in on itself. How horrible to feel that your dad's house is a fortress, a place you have to ambush even to tell him you love him. I involuntarily reach an arm out towards him, wanting to calm him down, earning a look of pure hatred from Tallulah. Did she hear him call me by her mum's name?

'I should go,' I say, stupidly scrabbling around for my shoes.

'Yeah, you should,' says Tallulah belligerently. 'Go and fuck over someone else's family.'

'Don't go,' says Oscar, gripping my arm, a look of desperation in his eyes. Is he scared he's out of his depth? 'And you,' he says, jabbing a finger at Tallulah, 'stop talking like a gutter snipe.'

'No really, I should,' I say, casting him an apologetic look. Staying would be a disaster of monumental proportions. Tallulah needs unadulterated Dad and I need to avoid becoming some kind of wax effigy stuck with more pins than in *Eraserhead*. 'This is between the two of you. I'm sorry,' I add, directly addressing her. 'I really am.'

The look of black rage I get as I hotfoot it down the stairs and out the door reminds me of one person, and one person only: Oscar. What a colossal mess. I should've encouraged him when he said we had to come out, though part of me wonders if he was as keen as he was claiming. He must've known how Tallulah was likely to feel, the hurt he'd be inflicting – scalding your beloved is one thing, but wilfully hurting your child must be almost unbearable. I should've talked to him more about the potential emotional fall-out, not spent so much time worrying about my status in the kitchen. OK, enough with the self-flagellation. Seeing a black cab sailing past, I impetuously stick out an arm: tonight is not the night to contend with tequila-buzzed students on the night bus.

*

I've got the next morning off, but my eyes ping open at six like they're on stalks. Last night is playing on a loop. I couldn't bear it if Oscar feels doubly betrayed, my insistence about Marsha's party followed by my leaving. I text him. *Sorry I left you, but I thought you two needed space. Call me when you can xx.*

I go and make myself a gallon of coffee, trying to focus on Googling butchers. I nibble on dry toast, trying not to retch at the stream of pictures of dead, bloody cows suspended by their hooves: it's probably exactly what Tallulah's got in mind for me. At seven a.m. there's an even more shocking sight: Milly, fully clothed, wandering in with a copy of *Business for Dummies* tucked under her arm.

'Morning, darling,' she says, flicking on News 24 on the portable television in the corner, the television that's almost exclusively used for watching the *EastEnders* omnibus in our pyjamas. Within three minutes we've learned about a devastating Asian flood and a fatal stabbing: I'm not great at staying informed at the best of times, but certainly not before eight a.m.

'Could we turn it down a bit?' I venture.

'Mmm?' says Milly, watching it with rapt attention. 'They're going to get to the FTSE soon.'

I concentrate determinedly on smearing marmalade on my toast, remembering that she also vowed she was going to pay proper attention to her other investments. I'm sure her accountants are enjoying her new-found financial zeal as much as I am. Stop being such a bitch, I tell myself. It's good she's found a new sense of purpose.

'Yesterday was fascinating,' she says, once we're safe in the knowledge that copper prices have rallied after yesterday's temporary blip.

'Oh good,' I say, before grinding to a conversational halt. I diligently take down a number for a farm with some deliriously happy Gloucestershire Old Spots.

'What are you doing?' asks Milly.

'I'm trying to find a new butcher, it's an absolute nightmare. Our supplier's walked out, and trying to find someone with meat that's as good and not exorbitant . . .'

'So many balls to juggle,' she says. 'I did have a few thoughts,' she adds, and I try to make my face look more encouraging. 'For what they're worth.'

'Yes, Oscar said.'

'*Did* he?' she says, pleased as punch. 'I wasn't sure if they'd fallen on deaf ears, but I do so want to help.'

'I know you do,' I say, smiling for real.

'Like, are you missing a trick not catering for the more squeamish?'

'What do you mean?'

'Well, don't take this the wrong way,' I hate it when people say that, it always precedes something bad, 'but there were quite a few empty tables.'

'It's mid-week lunch. We're relatively new, it's the nature of the beast.'

'Mmm,' says Milly, looking annoyingly doubtful. 'It's just, I don't know, if you had something like a bolognese for people who don't like the more *outré* stuff. The pickled brains and so forth . . .'

'Oscar doesn't pickle brains, he's not Frankenstein. And besides, it would make the menu completely incoherent.'

'I'm exaggerating,' says Milly with an airy shake of the hand. 'But you get my point.'

No, I don't. Deep breaths.

'I think he might have other things on his mind today. Tallulah walked in on us last night.'

'Noooo!' says Milly, aghast. Normal service has been resumed.

'Oh God, not walked in walked in,' I say, 'but she knows.'

I give her the highlights of both rows, realising as I do that the only Retford who didn't yell at me last night was Lydia. Something tells me today might make it a hat trick.

'Oh, Amber, what a nightmare,' she says.

'It had to happen. I mean it is a nightmare, but the person it's a real nightmare for is Tallulah. She's deeply hard to like.' A whorl of dread opens up inside me as I imagine a future where it's compulsory. What if my lack of orange robes stymies me yet again, and it turns out I haven't got enough good in me? 'But I still feel desperately sorry for her. It must feel like the end of her childhood.'

'Aren't you giving yourself too hard a time? She's sixteen, surely it's over anyway?'

'I know what you mean, but her fantasy version of it is over. Her mum and dad together – even though she knew they'd split up, it'll feel way more real now she's seen him half-naked with another woman.' I shudder; no one needs to think of their parents as sexual beings, let alone sexual beings with anyone other than each other. I know that better than most.

'See what you mean. And I'm afraid I still think it's a nightmare for you, trying to negotiate all of that.' Milly looks at me, my face plastered with trepidation. 'But if anyone can manage, you can! You're a trooper, Amber, look how you've handled the divorce. And you and Oscar love each other. Love conquers all, and all that!'

Milly raises her coffee cup to mine to toast this joyous fact, her face wreathed in smiles, and I say it back to myself inside, trying to bolster myself up for whatever's in store.

I try not to be consumed with paranoia as my phone remains resolutely silent. Instead, I use the adrenalin to fuel my hopeless research. It's so hard to get a sense from a website, and no chef worth his salt is going to want to share his prized supplier. As I'm calling some kind of pig correctional facility in deepest Norfolk, Milly comes bursting into my room.

'Geronimo!' she shouts.

'What?'

'Jack Foster-Cuthbert. His father was at school with my father. He dutifully toiled his way through a few years in the City, before throwing it all in and devoting himself to live-stock. It's not been easy, but that rather works in our favour as I'm sure he'll be open to negotiation.' She taps her nose in a rather strange way, like she's a particularly posh bookie. 'I've just called him. We can just whizz down there in the Clio.'

'Wow. Thanks, Mils!'

I'm a bit nervous, to be honest. What if it's a duff lead and I have to try and extricate myself without causing Milly mortal offence? But once we've looked at his website, I start to feel more positive. We're still combing through it when Oscar finally manages to pick up the phone. I snatch it up so fast it positively jumps to my ear.

'What happened?' I ask. I hear his Zippo click open, his poor abused lungs drag in the smoke. It feels like an eternity.

'We got there,' he says. 'I'm sorry you got talked to like that.'

Oh, the irony!

'It's OK, she was upset. It's completely understandable.'

'See? Like I always say, you're a sweetheart.'

I breathe out as he breathes in, so relieved that he seems to have declared a truce.

'But, Oscar, what about Lydia?'

'Will you stop worrying about her? I drove Tally home once she'd calmed down, told Lydia, it was all very civilised. You've got nothing to worry about.'

Apart from him having actually called me Lydia, but I decide not to mention it. And Marsha's party. Talking of which . . .

'I've been thinking,' he says, 'if you promise me I won't hear a word about it, and you keep it six-thirty to eight-thirty, I'll let you have your way. But you can't be off the floor any time I need you. I mean it, Fish Girl, I own you that night. You pull in a couple of Johnny's team we don't need and they run it. *Not* you.'

'Really?! Really? Thank you so much, I . . . I love you.'

'Good,' he says gruffly. 'Now what's going on with the meat?'

There's so much more I want to find out – what Lydia actually said, how he resolved it with Tallulah – but as per, there's no time. And maybe only half of me wants to know: I've still got the feeling that feminine intuition will give me access to nuances he's blissfully unaware of.

'The meat!' I tell him all about Jack Foster-Cuthbert and his happy-looking sows.

'What time you going?'

'Kind of now. I wanted to be in by two.'

'Come and pick me up. I'm not having any pigs crossing my threshold who I haven't seen *in situ*.'

'But I was going to take Milly—'

'They're mates, it's too complicated. I need to negotiate myself. This is about business, not friendship.' I feel horrible about chucking Milly off Team Meat, but I know she hasn't acquitted herself well enough for me to argue the toss, as with so many things it comes down to the fact that Oscar's the boss. 'And hurry up, we haven't got long,' he adds, putting the phone down.

I recount what he's said to her, full of apology. She looks utterly crestfallen, but remains stoic.

'I'm not sure I believe in his strategy,' she says. 'Friendship has oiled the wheels of many a business deal, but I can see his word is law.'

'I'm really sorry.'

'Do give Jack my best. He's a thoroughly good egg.'

'I will,' I say, hugging her and putting on my coat in one seamless movement. At least I've scored a goal for Marsha.

I've got no inclination to enter the restaurant – way too many landmines – but as Oscar's not picking up his phone, I've got no choice. I gingerly pick my way through front of house, heading for the office. He's outlined through the glass, and I push through.

'Hi, darling!' I say, planning on covering his face with kisses in gratitude for the party reprieve.

Only it's not him. It's Lydia, talking close into her phone. She whips round.

'I'll call you back,' she hisses, killing the call.

I'm beetroot red, shifting from foot to foot. 'Um, hi, Lydia,' I say. 'Are you, are you OK?'

Curses. I meant about Tallulah but of course it'll sound like I'm commiserating about Oscar. I expect a withering put-down, but she seems wrong-footed. Has distress punctured that icy reserve? I feel a stab of guilt at the thought that I might truly be her Rachel. I don't want to be anyone's Rachel (damn the fact I'm even thinking about her).

'I'm fine. I'm sorry you've been dragged into our family dramas these last couple of days.'

'Don't ... don't apologise,' I say, attempting a smile. 'Um, I'll ...' I start, backing towards the door. Honestly, she renders me positively Neanderthal, all I seem to be able to produce are a series of incomprehensible grunts. I might as well start picking fleas from underneath my armpits and wrestling mammoths.

'I assume you're looking for Oscar,' she says, too clever for vitriol. 'He's upstairs.' There's a tiny pause. 'You know the way.'

'Thanks,' I say, tomato red.

He is upstairs, shaving his sexily grizzled face. He's wearing jeans set off with a moss-green V-neck of the softest cashmere. 'Hello, gorgeous,' he says, though it's patently clear who's the more gorgeous of the two of us. I shouldn't have let him rush me, should've spent long enough on my outfit to ensure that I didn't alight on this bobbly purple polo neck, vintage in the worst sense of the word. I give him a hesitant kiss, paranoid he'll feel like he's being date raped by a mutant blueberry. Lydia could never look like a sexually deviant forest fruit; even today, she could give Grace Kelly a run for her money.

291

'Thank you,' I say, risking another rapey kiss. 'Thank you, thank you. The car's on a single yellow, so we ought to go.'

'Let's take mine.'

'I can't leave it here.' He looks at me like he's waiting for me to come up with a solution. 'Besides, I want to drive. I haven't driven a car in ages.'

'This should be interesting,' he says, grabbing his jacket and taking the stairs two at a time.

'I'm a very good driver, I'll have you know,' I tell his retreating back. 'I passed first time thanks to my dad's excellent tutelage. Neither of my brothers did.' Like anyone cares.

We don't talk about anything much in the car, probably because I've landed myself with the worst case of performance anxiety ever recorded. Milly's Clio is way too old to have retained any Gallic charm it might once have had, and I crunch the gears and bunny-hop the clutch like a pensioner who's gleefully come upon her licence at the bottom of a coronation biscuit tin. It's such a relief to park up and breathe in a few lungfuls of country air, it feels like forever since I escaped the smoke. I get a pang as I think of my conversation with Mum. The minute, the very minute, this competition's done and dusted I'm going to insist on four days off. I sneak a look at Oscar, who's surveying the terrain like we're planning a smash and grab. Will he want to come with me? He should, and I should want him to, and yet the idea makes me feel a little breathless. Maybe it's just a reaction to the lack of carbon monoxide.

'Look at those cows!' I say. It's blue and crisp, with fields spread out as far as the eye can see. 'Shall we go and give them our regards on the way to the office?'

We stand by the fence, and Oscar slips an arm round my waist. The other one's unavailable as he's using it to comb through his BlackBerry.

'So come on, Oscar, what actually happened? I need details, not headlines.'

'Why?'

'Because that's what relationships are!' I say. 'They're about the details, about sharing the details. And these details are critical ones. If we're going to have any kind of shot I need to know what ... what your wife feels. Whether Tallulah is coping. Real stuff.'

His wife, she's his wife. Am I being hopelessly naive not to read more into the lack of divorce proceedings? Those papers, still marooned in the chaos of my bedroom. I must send them off.

'I gave Tallulah a cup of coffee, sat her down on the sofa.' He looks at me, sarcastic. 'I think it was around four steps she took to get there but we can restage it when we get back if you like. I told her that I was glad she didn't hate me, and that you were a great girl. That she should be happy about it.'

'That's a pretty big ask, Oscar! She's still getting her head round the div ... separation. Are you and Lydia ever going to actually get divorced?' I can't contain the thought any longer.

'Yeah, 'spose so. No rush.'

'It's just ... it makes me feel a little bit like we're having an affair even though we're not.'

Lydia. He called me Lydia.

'Couldn't that be a little bit sexy?' he asks, cocking his handsome head.

'I'm afraid I don't find affairs all that sexy,' I say, sounding

293

woefully sanctimonious. I did mention in passing that an affair ended my marriage, but I was petrified of going into detail – scared that I'd crumble, start avalanching snot. I'm not sure he'll even remember, I think I was gaily tossing my bra skyward to prove just how unconcerned I was. 'I just, I don't know, I struggle with it.'

'You're not divorced yet.'

'I am nearly,' I mutter, imagining those pesky papers leaping up and doing a demented dance. 'Sign me, sign me', they sing, possibly to the tune of 'Call Me' by Blondie.

'Nearly's not divorced,' says Oscar smugly. 'Come back to me when you are. Anyway,' he says, smirking down at me, 'what's the panic? Is this some kind of Fish Girl version of a proposal?'

'No!' I snap back, a little too fast.

'Glad we've got that straight,' he replies, looking down at his BlackBerry.

He was taking the piss, wasn't he? I haven't hurt his feelings? I just didn't want him to think my bunny-boiling tendencies extended beyond the confines of the kitchen. What does he think about second time around? Now isn't the time to ask, but when is? Maybe I need to try and drag him away for a few days before I prioritise going home. No, home is too important to endure any more postponements.

'So then what happened?'

'What?' he asks, distracted.

'With Tallulah!'

'She calmed down, agreed she'd knuckle down at school. I told her we'd have a weekend at the Mercer in New York if she racked up some decent AS levels.' I want to go to the

Mercer! I don't know what it is, but it sounds Carrie Bradshaw fabulous. 'We sorted it. She's my princess, she knows that. She's just a bit over-emotional – can't think where she gets that from.' He grins, waits for me to melt from the sheer wattage of his smile. I steel myself against its power.

'And what did Lydia say?' I ask, trying my hardest not to sound whiny, but he's turned back to his emails.

'Yeah, all good. She said I should've looked further than my own kitchen, but she's OK with it.'

I could scream with frustration. 'What did she actually say? Word for word?'

'I'm telling you, that was basically it. Chop chop, Fish Girl, we'd better go and find Farmer Giles. We've got to get back,' he says, striding farmward. I scuttle after him, as ever, shoes splatting their way through the mud like a pair of flippers. His battered leather loafers look perfect of course, a dusting of mud does nothing but add another layer of lived-in chic.

Jack's a man who farms for the pure love of it, you can tell the second you meet him. He's spattered with mud from head to foot; it erupts from his fingernails, mottles his face, sprays across his jeans like a Jackson Pollock canvas. He's not much older than Milly and me, but there's something ageless about him, like it's the farm that time forgot. He has a profound earnestness as he strains forward from behind his wire-rimmed round spectacles, as though he can barely contain his enthusiasm. His office is chaos, feed piling up in the corner, and coffee cups and calculators strewn around with gay abandon. He's scattered a few steaks on his desk, and then festooned it with a couple of strings of sausages, like it's Christmas Day round at Sweeney Todd's house. I don't know if I should defer to

Oscar, but as it was me who got the introduction, I jump in there. Besides, Oscar shows no sign of adding to his gruff 'pleased to meet you'. He's too busy peering around the room, checking it all out.

'Milly sends her love.'

'Amelia's such a treasure,' he says, and I start imagining her in full milkmaid garb finding romantic fulfilment in some kind of Victorian rural idyll.

'What an amazing place,' I add, before I get too carried away. 'Have you had it for long?'

'Long story,' he says, and I sense Oscar shifting in his chair with sheer impatience. 'It was my dad's, but he's pretty much stopped farming, given in to the big boys.'

'The big boys?'

'The factory farms, rows of pigs on death row, cows so pumped full of hormones that the bulls grow tits.' He's virtually foaming at the mouth, eyes ablaze. 'I couldn't stand coming down here and seeing it going to seed, so when I lost my job in London I decided to take a punt. Live off the land, see if I could make a difference. It's only been a year, we're no way out of the woods, but we're giving it our best shot.'

So OK, he's a little bit like Che Guevara, the way he's erupting with revolutionary zeal, but surely that's what we want – someone who cares so passionately about his pigs that their meat will ooze happiness and joy all over the plate. Oscar's passion for food was the first thing I loved about him, and here it is again, re-presented in a rather muddy package. I sneak a glance at him hoping he's feeling it too, but he's not giving much away. He's watching, intent, but his face doesn't yield. I feel a stab of annoyance at the fact that he's my boss, at the way in which every aspect of our relationship is criss-crossed with complications: even now it still matters so much to me that he thinks he's made a good hire.

'You obviously are,' I say fervently, overcompensating for Oscar's extended silence. 'Those Old Spots are a sight to behold.'

'Let me take you to the back field,' says Jack, eyes lit up. 'We've got a breed that was set for extinction, *literal* extinction, before we delivered them from evil.' He sniggers, a little like Muttley, going halfway to reassuring me that he's not some kind of Bible-bashing pork-crazed zealot who's going to tie us up in a sty and force-feed us sausages until we admit that his porcine god is a righteous god.

'We're a bit short on time,' says Oscar, putting a strong hand down flat on the chaotic desk, 'so let's cut to the chase. The livestock looks great, the cuts look great.'

Jack beams with joy, and I grin back at him like a loon, every bit as pleased that the man from Del Monte, he say yes. 'The prices you're talking aren't so great.'

Where's that come from? I showed him the figures en route and he didn't say a word. It's a little bit more than Mac, but that's to be expected when it's such a small operation. I wish he'd warned me, let me lead in differently rather than snatching the rug from under him.

'Yes, but if you think about the size of the farm, the conditions that each and every animal lives in …' Jack's red, blustering, but Oscar remains impassive.

'Yeah, sure, got it, but I'm running a business. I need quality *and* value.'

'That's what I'm trying to tell you,' says an increasingly upset Jack. 'It's both, but you have to allow for the size of the operation. The prices I've given you are absolutely the best I can do.'

'I really think—' I start, but Oscar waves me away. Actually waves one of those meaty paws in my face like I'm a fruit fly.

'Well, in that case I'm sorry we wasted your time,' he says in a tone of voice which doesn't sound remotely sorry. He stands up. 'Come on, Amber, we'd better take our leave.'

'Are you sure?' I say, looking at Jack's stricken face.

'Yes, I'm sure,' says Oscar, halfway to the door.

'Bye, Jack,' I say, heartfelt. 'It really is an amazing farm.'

He looks utterly crushed. 'Bye,' he mutters, barely looking up from his coffee cup. As soon as we get out of the door I turn on Oscar.

'You behaved like a total arsehole!' I snap. 'He's a start-up, same as us. He's doing what he loves, trying his best to put quality before everything else, same as us. You could at least have heard him out.'

'Stop yapping,' says Oscar, who's actually got the temerity to grin at me. 'Trust me, you've got a lot to learn.'

And there, right on cue, is Jack, pelting across the muddy courtyard. 'Wait,' he says, 'hold up.'

Oscar and Jack go round and round the houses until they've thrashed out a deal, with Jack accepting Oscar's measly price on the basis that it'll be renegotiated in six months if he's kept on, with a potential increase in volume. I literally don't get a word in edgeways, despite having brokered the deal. It might as well be 1955, with me relegated to girlishly transcribing their manly genius while occasionally breaking off to mix them a mid-morning Martini.

'Pleasure doing business with you,' says Oscar, reaching out a hand to a weary-looking Jack. 'I'll get a contract drawn up.' Jack reaches out his hand. 'Oh, one thing,' Oscar adds. 'I need a guarantee you won't supply anyone else within five miles of us.'

'I can't do that!'

'Oscar, he's building a business,' I say, unable to stop myself.

'Three miles then, I need exclusivity.'

I get it now. He's willy waving, just like Angus.

'Are you honestly expecting me to get out an *A–Z* and a ruler?'

'If you like,' says Oscar, dangerously cocky.

'Right, that's it!' snaps Jack. 'I won't be bullied. Send my regards to Milly, but there's no deal to be made.' He stands up, refuses to even look at Oscar. 'I enjoyed meeting you,' he says to me, shaking my hand.

'Oscar, say something.'

'I offered him three miles, he turned it down. It's his look out,' says Oscar, holding up my coat for me to slip my arms into, even though this is no time for chivalry. 'Bye, Jack. Good luck with the pigs.'

I round on him once we're outside. 'What the hell have you done? He's perfect for us, you don't need that bloody exclusivity clause.'

'It's fine, he'll come round.'

'No, he won't!'

Oscar pauses, uncharacteristically quiet. He looks back towards the office, but this time there's no sign of Jack.

'Phone Milly,' he says, subdued.

'And say what? Sorry Oscar totally offended your boyhood friend, do you mind clearing up his mess?'

'Yeah, roughly.'

I roll my eyes, make the call. I'm expecting Milly to be horrified, but she sounds oddly energised.

'Well, he did jolly well to get the price down,' she says.

'They were already rock bottom.'

'One should never accept the first offer, it's the first rule of business.' She's literally turning into Lord Sugar. 'And as for the exclusivity, I can absolutely see his point ...'

'I know, he was really upset.'

'No, I mean Oscar. Definitely worth a try, but it's not worth losing the deal for. Leave it with me, Amber, I'll do my utmost.' She hangs up smartly, full of entrepreneurial zeal. I look at the phone, slightly open-mouthed.

'Sorted?' says Oscar hopefully.

'We'll see.'

'Oh stop sulking!' He's probably right, but it's all started to feel like a matter of principle. 'It's business,' says Oscar, giving me that smile. 'Simple as that.'

'OK, fair enough, the figure is business. But he'd already virtually agreed cost price. It's his livelihood. Look at this,' I say, windmilling my arms in the direction of the cows like a demented Heidi. 'He's trying to create a thing of wonder. If the world's one big, living breathing organism we should do everything we can to support that, know it'll come back to us.'

'What *are* you talking about?'

'Um, Gaia principle.'

'I see. Thing is, I am helping him. I'm teaching him about the realities of business. It's a big bad world out there where wolves will eat all your sheep given half the chance. He needs to learn to protect his corner.'

We're at the car now, its wheels deeply embedded in the churning mud. He looks at me, holds out a hand, but I clench the keys tight to my bosom.

'Sometimes,' I say, 'sometimes it's like you harden your heart. Like it's an advent calendar, and you've slammed all the tiny little doors shut even though it's Christmas Day.' Jesus, what's wrong with me today?

'Thing is, Fish Girl, you have to keep the doors shut, or else that big bad wolf,' Oscar drops his voice, 'he comes along and steals all the chocolates.' He takes my face in his hands, kisses my mouth like it's the most delectable chocolate he's ever been offered. 'But they're not shut all the time. They're never shut to you.' There's a catch in his voice when he says it, a clear bell of truth that rings out, makes me sure he's not the big bad wolf.

'Good,' I say, stroking his face, turning the key, backing away from tackling him further about the lick of Angus I detected.

I'd like to say that we speed down the motorway, my driving as sexy and zippy as James Bond in pursuit of a moustache-twirling villain, but the truth is that we do no more than putter. I can sense Oscar's frustration, but there's only so much poke you can get out of a car this small and this ancient.

'Just pull over,' he says. 'I'll floor it.'

'It's Milly's car! Anyway, I'm going at the speed limit.'

'Exactly my point.'

My phone starts up, and hoping it's Milly, I clumsily sling it onto my lap and hit loud speaker.

'Amber, you're not driving are you?'

Oh no.

'Dom?'

'Yup. Has Steve the Slime not got hold of you?'

'Dom, can I call you back—'

'The flat's fallen through. I mean, we can hardly blame fully grown adults for not wanting to live in Oompa Loompa Towers, but I still can't fucking believe it. A week from exchange . . .'

I try not to laugh at the thought of a troupe of Oompa Loompas ranging around my horrible avocado bathroom. This is, after all, no laughing matter, particularly considering the size of my overdraft: I should definitely care more. Maybe my caring about the flat is overshadowed by my caring about the horror of Dom's voice blaring out in Oscar's earshot.

'Bollocks,' I turn to Oscar, give him an apologetic smile, 'huge hairy gonads. Dom, I really have to call you back.'

'Is it Milly's car?'

'Sure is.'

'I can't believe that shit heap's still mobile. You can only be going thirty tops. Can't we at least discuss whether we sack The Slime?'

'Obv, he's got to go. But, Dom, I'll call—'

'You need to modify your financial expectations to bring them in line with the current economic climate,' says Dom, butting in with a pitch perfect impression of hateful Steve. 'With chocolate production in a recessionary hammock, Oompa Loompas are in the grips of a literal credit crunch.'

How is it that I'm yet to end this call?

'Dom, I'll call you later.' I look round at Oscar again, but he's staring fixedly at his BlackBerry. 'I'm not alone.'

There's a pause. 'Oh, OK then.' And then, suddenly more formal, 'Call me whenever's convenient.'

'Will do!' I say, gruesomely perky, but I'm met with a dial tone. There's pretty much a dial tone from Oscar too.

'That, that was my ex.'

'You don't say.'

Silence reigns, bar the unrelenting chug chug of the Clio's tinny engine.

'Please don't be grumpy. You see Lydia every single day, you've got a child together, it's in my face 24/7.'

'I'm not grumpy,' says Oscar in the grumpiest voice ever recorded.

'You are grumpy, Oscar, and I don't blame you, it must be weird hearing me talk to him.'

'Oh, must it? Why's that then?'

I pause, wrong-footed. 'Well, because it's weird hearing your person talking to their ex-spouse, it just is.'

'It shouldn't be.' Not this again. 'What's weird is listening to my girlfriend flirting with another man when I'm inches away,' he says, voice steely. 'Now that's weird. Or disrespectful. You choose.'

'I wasn't flirting with him.' I try and spool back through the conversation but I can't recall a single moment of bona fide flirting.

'No, Amber, you didn't tell him you'd biked round your knickers, but trust me, every single thing you said to him was coquettish.'

'Coquettish?! Excuse me, precisely what decade do you think we're living in?' I look round, furious. 'You do realise I can vote, don't you? I've even been known to show my ankles in polite society.'

'Keep your eyes on the road.'

'I would, if you'd stop being such an arse.' I pause, realise how tense I am, how wrong this is. I continue more softly. 'What you heard was intimacy, and I can't help that, just like you can't help it. Do you not think Lydia perching on your desk holding out her hand like she's some kind of sex siren Sellotape-tree is intimate? We've each of us got a proper past, and it's always going to be a little bit weird.' I breathe out, relieved to have said it out loud. If we both admit to the presence of the graveyard – confess we get a little bit scared walking through the valley of death, to paraphrase either God or Coolio, depending on your leanings – perhaps we'll have a chance of making it out alive.

'Flirting,' says Oscar, voice leaden.

'Well, I'm sorry you feel that way,' I say, which is surely the most passive-aggressive comeback in the history of comebacks.

But is he onto something? I didn't flirt, I know I didn't, but it doesn't mean that my heart didn't jump out of the river like a frisky fish when I first heard Dom's voice. It didn't last of course, but just for one Pavlovian puff, it betrayed me, betrayed Oscar. Stupid, stupid Amber. It's just familiarity, which for some reason has decided it's over that whole breeding contempt jag. It's the dying gasps of our marriage exerting their final pull. I'll sign those papers the minute I get home, and find an estate agent so ruthless he'll make Steve the Slime look like my trusty compadre the Dalai Lama. I stamp my foot down hard on the accelerator, wishing it was my rogue emotions, and take us bunny-hopping back to London at a truly spectacular seventy-two m.p.h.

Chapter 15

'I worry that fairy lights might push us over the edge,' says Marsha, head cocked towards the large gilt mirror I've had hung over the function room's fireplace. 'They're verging on vulgar.'

'Marsha, you're not Lady Bracknell!' I say, predictably exasperated. 'They're romantic. They're, they're tiny, shiny beacons of hope.'

As you can see, I remain slightly unhinged, every single emotion ten degrees more vivid than it should be. Take this morning, when I woke Oscar up at five a.m. to serve him breakfast in bed, complete with a white tablecloth and a single flower in a vase. No porridge, I tried a boiled egg on him, but he still growled like Daddy Bear at being roused a whole hour early. I couldn't really justify it, realising as he reached for a fag and stubbed it out in the egg cup, that I was loving him too hard, walloping him with a sledgehammer, instead of subtly wrapping him up in a gossamer scarf.

'I'm hoping we don't need hope,' says Marsha, defensive.

'Oh, we all need hope,' I say, and I mean it. Marriage is the longest of long-hauls, a marathon not a sprint. It's a garden in which even the hardy perennials need to be tended and watered. Marsha and Peter are better starred than most – they love each other dearly, neither of them is a thrill seeker, and even if they were, they'd have to find a corrupter with a corduroy fetish – but even so, they still need to keep turning the soil. I look at myself in the mirror, swallow down a wave of self-flagellation at my late stage realisation of these self-evident truths.

'Hope it is then,' says Marsha, flicking the switch. The lights bathe the mirror's frame in their warm and shiny glow, lighting up the reflection of her delighted face. 'They are rather jolly,' she concedes. She turns to me. 'Thank you, really and truly thank you. I know you put your head on the proverbial chopping block, and it's much appreciated.'

'I'm really glad I could do it for you,' I say, giving her a squeeze. It's true, I am. It feels like the first action of the rest of my life, and action's the best defence I know against self-flagellation.

'Now canapés,' says Marsha, keen to hightail away from the pesky sentiment that's crept in. 'Can you guarantee me, absolutely stake your life on it, that tuna sashimi won't lay anyone low with a dicky tummy?'

Argh! How would she feel if I asked her if one of her root-canal surgeries was likely to kill her patient stone dead? But before I've had a chance to make my point, I'm distracted by the cut-glass tones of Lydia.

'Forgive me if I'm mistaken, but I thought I'd made my position crystal clear. Anything less than £200,000 would be an insult.' She strides into the room, ramrod straight and full of purpose. 'Oh, hello,' she says, almost recoiling at the sight of us. 'I'll call you back,' she hisses, hanging up.

Oh God, oh God, oh God. When will this bone-crushing awkwardness go into abeyance?

'Hi, Lydia. This is my friend Marsha.' Lydia mine-sweeps her, taking in her ill-fitting mushroom trouser suit, worn with a clumpy pair of black shoes, which hover on the end of her legs like a pair of hooves. Lydia's wearing grey satin stilettos so high she might as well be wearing a £400 pair of stilts. She's as elegant as ever, but I'd still rather be Marsha. 'She's one of my oldest and dearest friends,' I add unnecessarily, 'and she's having her engagement drinks here tomorrow night.'

'Oh, yes, *those* drinks' says Lydia slyly. 'What impeccable timing.'

'I'd like to think we've got it all under control,' I say, even though I'm not sure we have. Tomasz has recruited a Red Army of Poles for me, but it's still a big ask. To keep things simple, everything's cold hence the suspicious sashimi.

'Well, keep up the good work,' says Lydia, in a tone that suggests I'm running a jumble sale for MENCAP. 'Lovely to meet you, Moira.'

'Yes, you too. And it's—' says Marsha, but Lydia's already out the door. Marsha turns to me, outraged by Lydia's rudeness, but I'm too distracted by Lydia's uncharacteristic lack of cool. It's unlike her to be quite so openly hostile, she's normally cleverer than that, but she was obviously rattled by being interrupted. What was the £200,000 she was talking about? I know, whatever Oscar says, there's inevitably going to be a strike back. Maybe she's pushed the button on the divorce, is gearing up to take him to the cleaners. That said,

£200,000 probably doesn't represent a full dry clean, but with money slipping fluidly between his business and his personal account, it might be enough to rip the rug out from under him. Should I warn him? I've been trying with all my might to keep out of that side of his life. I haven't even commented on the fact that he's only had one solitary Starbucks meet-up with Tallulah since their heart to heart, respected his decision to give the kitchen everything he's got until tomorrow's competition is done and dusted. For all I know it's a perfectly legitimate business conversation about matters I know nothing about, but there was a miasma of guilt that surrounded her, a disturbance that tells me there's more to it than that.

I take Marsha out the front, relying on the fact that Oscar's holed up in his office. He may have given the party his reluctant blessing, but I don't want to rub his nose in it. Once she's safely dispatched, I go in search of him.

'If it isn't my early bird. Caught any worms?'

'Don't call me a bird, it's not the 1970s,' I say, kissing him. 'And you're not Paul Raymond.'

'Spare me,' he says, 'never liked a woman in dungarees.' That's abundantly clear, I think, Lydia still troubling me. 'Have you tried the lamb's kidneys? Jack's come up trumps. We did well there. The menu should go out like clockwork.'

Milly was as good as her word, getting Jack to honour Oscar's cut-to-the-bone price and sign an additional clause, of her own making, that he wouldn't enter into discussions with Angus's evil empire. Oscar couldn't help but be impressed, and is way less grumpy about the regular brainstorms she's insisting on having. I'm still feeling like a bit of a forelock tugging serf, but that's my own childish problem.

Despite Oscar's jolly tone, I can tell by the whiteness of his knuckles as he clutches his stubby pencil that he's holding down a whole heap of stress. He's been all about the competition for the last week. It's not just Tallulah that's been neglected; we've talked nothing but tripe, literally. My trusty sword of truth seems distinctly blunted as I have to admit it's been a relief. I expected him to nurse a grudge about my spitting distance conversation with Dom, to continue to needle me about the perceived flirtation, but he hasn't said a word since that day. Perhaps he replayed it and realised that it was nothing more than matey frustration about our mutual housing woes. Mates, mates, jolly old mates. I finally forced myself to sign the papers that will render us mates once and for all, shed a tear as I shoved them through the letterbox outside Costcutter in Bethnal Green. It seemed an inauspicious ending to all those hopes and dreams, so I comforted myself with a discounted Kit Kat just to compound the gloomy mundanity of it all.

'Oscar?'

'Mmm.'

'Lydia was having a very peculiar conversation earlier.'

'It's not the Cold War, Fish Girl. Stop hanging round in doorways imagining evil mutterings and expecting her to poison you. News flash, paranoia doesn't turn me on.'

'I'm not being paranoid! And anyway, who says I want to turn you on?'

'Charming,' he says, smirking in what I must admit is rather a sexy way. 'Look, me and Lydia are grown-ups. There's no drama, nothing to see.'

'Just listen to me.' I describe the conversation as accurately as I can, but he barely seems to listen, just keeps on scribbling away. He looks up once, but it's only so he can find his fags.

'Dunno, maybe she's buying a flat. We've got separate bank accounts.'

'But that doesn't make sense, why would she be negotiating the price up?'

'Don't know. Don't care. I can ask her, but she'll think you're a sticky beak and I'd have thought that's the last thing you'd want. Now tell me if you think we should put that bunny terrine back on the starters.'

'The bunny terrine,' I say, remembering the sheer thrilling romance of us ripping their tiny furry bodies asunder when all we'd done was stolen a kiss. It was all so much simpler in those days.

'Consider that question properly,' says Oscar sternly. 'I'm staking my life on this fucking competition. If we win it, we're straight into the big league. We'll be in with way more chance of a star, we'll be permanently booked out, we can hike our prices. And most of all—'

'Most of all?'

Oscar stands up, unable to contain himself. 'It'll be a massive *fuck you* to fucking Angus.' He's shaking, face contorted with the emotion of it. 'I will even the score,' he adds, voice molten and deadly, 'however long it takes me, I swear to you, I will even the score.' It's not what he says so much as his face that scares me. I hope I never fall out with him.

I try broaching the subject of Lydia one more time, but he's one hundred per cent focused on the competition. Maybe his lack of concern is entirely justified – after all, she's his spouse not mine. My stomach lurches at the very thought; separated or not, there's something about the fact that she's his wife that still casts an evil spell. He needs to pass go, net his celebratory cut-price Kit Kat. I can feel in my bones it's going to be different once I really am in my life post-wife. However much I've declared myself a divorcee, the fact that it's not been a total truth has allowed the air to seep out of the balloon gradually. But now, now it's going to pop. I head to the kitchen, hoping someone might pay more attention to my earth-shattering words of wisdom there. My phone beeps en route, almost like Dom's been eavesdropping on my internal dialogue (jeez, perhaps I am paranoid).

Steve the Slime is no more. As it's a ball ache, I've taken an executive decision and hired Wet William from Hardacres. Trust me, he's worse than he sounds. Talk to you soon x

God, does he actually think I have balls? He's so jolly, so energised about putting it all to bed before he sets off round the world and meets Ursula Andress strutting magnificently out of the Indian Ocean. I'm glad we're no longer throwing knives at each other, but the matey-ness, the sheer unadulterated matey-ness, kind of kills me. Am I really that forgettable? I blush at the thought of that catastrophic kiss – I'm increasingly convinced I'm remembering it wrong and I lunged dementedly, with him kissing me back for the briefest time possible to spare me any more abject humiliation. Every communication serves to remind me how spectacularly over me he is. I know he still loves me, I can sense it, but I suspect it's like a cousin you're always really glad to see at Christmas. Or a gout-ridden but devoted Labrador that you can't bear to put down, even though it keeps peeing on the priceless Persian rug.

I love him already. Thanks for sorting it out. And I finally sorted out the papers. They should be with your solicitor any day x

Thanks x is all that comes back. Oh, the sheer, heady romance of modern life. I wonder how Shakespeare's sonnets would've worked out for him if he'd had to compose them via the medium of text, with a sprinkling of emoticons for added poignancy. Enough. I gulp down my Molotov cocktail of feelings and prepare to bust a few balls on the floor.

Everyone's working at full capacity, the kitchen spookily quiet. We've been road testing various new dishes for the last week, but we're all on tenterhooks waiting for Oscar's final selection. The open hostility's lessened since Oscar and I got outed, but oddly it's a lonelier place to be. Before there were friends and there were enemies, but now everyone (bar Tomasz) is kind of a frenemy. I hoped Michelle would stay constant, but I think she's embarrassed about how rude she's been about him, even though I can totally understand why working with a man who erupts more randomly than Mount Etna doesn't induce the warm, fuzzy stuff.

Even if the hostility's gone underground, it hasn't disappeared. Joe's eyes still narrow as I approach the fish station, despite him being choir-boy polite. I rally the troops, do my very best to tee them up for evening service, and just as I've finished, Oscar comes striding in. There's a palpable energy change as he does, a standing to attention that automatically happens. Could I ever command a kitchen like he does? Is it a man thing, or is it an Oscar thing? Maybe his capriciousness works in his favour, ensures that everyone's working so hard to keep up that they never have time to question his authority.

'Right, listen up,' he shouts, clapping his hands. 'Tomorrow night is gonna make or break us, no question. I don't say it enough, but we've got talent in this kitchen. This competition needs everything you've got, *I* need everything you've got. I'm gonna be here every step of the way, I promise I won't be leaving you in the shit. But the flipside is I'll be watching every last one of you like a hawk, and if you aren't pulling your weight, I'll be down on you like a ton of bricks. Come on, people, let's get ready to go out there and show those judges we're the best fucking kitchen in London!'

A cheer goes up, a cheer that mutates into a standing ovation. Oscar drinks it in, a manic glint in his eye. He's exuding that determination to prove to Angus who's the boss, the prodigal son returned triumphant. I can't bear to contemplate what the consequences will be if he loses. He won't, I tell myself, he's brilliant and he's got the kitchen behind him. Surely the judges will see it like I see it? He takes a mock bow, loving the momentary adulation.

'Thank you, people. Now get on your marks, because this is my final selection.'

And he reels off the menu with all the confidence and brio of a circus ringmaster. Bunnies will be massacred, hearts and kidneys will be taken off the transplant list, trotters will be trotted out. It's not a menu for the faint-hearted, some might say it sounds more like a prop list for a horror film, but I love its audaciousness. It's only once he's reached the end I realise the 'anaemic numpties' have been left to fend for themselves (or eat their own body weight in salad).

'I can see the cogs turning there, Fish Girl,' says Oscar, and everyone's head swivels between us like it's the Wimbledon final. 'I tried to think of a vegetarian option but I ended up in a fucking coma. They're your department, make your selection and get it banged out.'

'Yes, Chef,' I say, face fixed. Oscar gives me one of those looks, one of those smiles, but I don't break. Not here, not now.

His tone wouldn't give it away, but the chance to choose a dish for the competition, brussels sprouts reliant or not, is a hell of an honour. I pull Michelle in to help, rootling through the menus from recent weeks to work out what's gone down best. There's a tense excitement after Oscar's speech, a sense of anticipation that seems to finally overwhelm the kitchen's hostility to me.

'That night, you know,' Michelle's voice lowers, 'when your ex came in.' I still haven't told Oscar about that. I sneak a look at him, but he's demonstrating how to mutilate a pigeon, and couldn't be less interested. 'The pumpkin dish you did, it sold out.'

'It did,' I say, remembering the cold, dead horror I felt when I found Rachel was its number-one fan. 'You're right, we could try that again.'

But of course I can't settle on option one. Instead, I get obsessed with the idea that the perfect dish is just beyond my grasp, some kind of bastard love child of Elizabeth David and Nigel Slater. I try various things out, so absorbed that I don't notice Oscar's left again. The level of orders tells me lunch is pretty frantic, but I don't venture out front to see for myself. It's the last place I want to go.

Around five I go to try out my top three suggestions on Oscar, but as I approach, I can see Lydia through the glass. At least she's not doing her sexy desk mascot act. Instead, she's sitting opposite him, face a picture of seriousness. His head's bent over his notebook, the whole tableau spookily reminiscent of my attempts to get through to him this morning. I creep backwards, grateful for my battered old Converse: as any good spy knows, stilettos are not designed for stealth.

I'm halfway down the corridor when I hear a roar. It really is a roar, so guttural and intense that it doesn't feel entirely human. There's a crash of the desk upending, as the door is flung open. Lydia bursts out, flushed.

'Come back here,' shouts Oscar. 'Don't you dare walk away from me.'

'You can handle this one,' she hisses, sweeping past me towards the restaurant floor. 'He's all yours.'

Oscar comes barrelling after her, snatching at her, but she's hurrying out as fast as her stilettos will take her. Thank God the restaurant's empty, the tirade that's coming out of his mouth would be enough to land him in court. I chase after him, but I know I can't get too close. Before he can stop her, she's stepped into a cab, slamming the door in his face. He's standing out there on the pavement, rooted to the spot. I go to him, steeling myself for the stream of bile that's going to hit.

'Oscar? Oscar, what is it?'

He turns slowly, his face stricken. I go to hold him, feel him shaking. The rage seems to have drained out of him. He clings to me, silent.

'Darling, tell me. What is it?'

We're like a tiny urban island. Cars honk and screech around us, while tunnel-vision commuters elbow us out of their way in their desperation to get to the tube. Still we stand there, me waiting to take my cue from him. Eventually I loosen my grip, look up at him, shocked to discover the tears that are streaming down his cheeks.

'Come on, let's go inside. No,' I add, thinking of the effect it might have. 'Let's go over the road.'

There's a city boozer just around the corner, which is permanently overflowing with grey-looking men in identikit suits. I install Oscar at a corner table, hoping no one recognises him. If someone comes over and asks him for a table, I think he might deck them. Or perhaps not. Maybe I don't know him at all. I take a guess at a shot of brandy, buying myself a glass of the least offensive-looking white wine. I sit back down next to him, put my hand on his.

'Please tell me,' I say. 'I can't help if you don't tell me.'

'She's leaving,' he says, and I try and get my stupid little brain to compute. Surely she's already left? They've been split up for a year. 'She's going to work for Angus.' He grips his glass, long since emptied, so tight that I fear he'll crush it.

'Oh, Oscar . . .'

'He's been after her for months apparently. He wants her to run the front of house operation for the whole group.'

'So what, she's been planning this for ages?'

'Oh no, she'd turned him down, but since she found out about us . . . we're rubbing her nose in it apparently.' He clinks my glass, a mirthless grin. 'Congratulations, Fish Girl, turns out you were right.'

Of course I was, though I wish I wasn't. It was never going to be the Topsy and Tim version of divorce, the human heart is far too messy an organ for that. Look at him, the sadness in his face, the grief that's finally hit him like a battering ram.

317

You can only put it off, you can't escape it, and the only way past it is through it.

'I'm so sorry. I know how much it hurts.' I'm walking a fine line here, aware how much I've downplayed my own emotions about Dom for the whole course of our relationship. I can see him trying to man up, and I wish I could tell him not to, to just feel it. Not a chance.

'The competition's good as lost,' he says. 'It's front of house as much as the cooking, so we're fucked.'

'Johnny's brilliant, Oscar, he can—'

'Don't even mention that little shit. He's going with her.'

'He's not?! I can't believe he'd just walk out with no notice.' I look at him. 'You didn't?' I say, remembering the violence of her exit. Of course he will have summarily ejected her, his pride too wounded for logic.

'I'm not having her sorry, treacherous arse on the premises after this. The only communication she'll be getting is via my lawyers.'

'But you can't ... darling, you need to think about Tallulah. I know it's hard, but when the dust has settled you need to try and keep it civilised. Even now you do, with her in such a bad place.'

'Sweetheart, I know you mean well, but if I want parenting advice I'll ask a parent.'

Do not snap, do not snap. It's just so bloody infuriating that he's fenced off a whole part of himself that he's deemed me too naive to comprehend. I think about reminding him that I was a teenage girl, that that alone gives me some insight, but there's no point.

'At least your party will go with a swing.'

318

'OK, stop it,' I say, slamming down my drink. 'You are not going to throw away this competition.' Is he trying to punish her or is he acting out his hurt because he can't allow himself to say it? There's no time for Doctor Amber Freud to put him on the couch: I need to focus on the practicalities.

'Me and Johnny have always been mates, let me try and talk him round. He's the definition of decent, I can't believe he won't help us. I don't think he's on today, but I'll call him.'

Oscar looks at me, mutinous and miserable.

'Oscar, what I love about you is your self-belief, your passion for it. That speech you gave earlier was amazing, and I know you meant it. You're brilliant, and Angus knows it, that's why he's doing everything in his power to destroy you. It'll kill him if you win this.'

Oscar pauses, his face still etched with sadness. Imagine if I'd had to, I dunno, win the women's final at Wimbledon in the week after Dom moved out – this is roughly the equivalent.

'Go on then,' he says, looking at me properly for the first time. 'What are you waiting for?'

I hug his big, unyielding body. 'I'm not,' I say. 'You deal with the kitchen, and I'll fix the rest.'

I shut myself in the office, but I decide to use my mobile. If it's the work number he'll figure it's Oscar, and who in their right mind would pick up that call? He answers on the second ring.

'Hello?' He probably doesn't have my number in his phone. I take a breath in, tee myself up.

'Johnny, it's Amber. I've heard your news.'

'Right,' he says, ice-cold. I wish I had a Tardis, and could swoop back to those days when all he could do around me was twinkle.

'It sounds like a great opportunity. I'm not ringing to have a go, but please, please, don't walk out before tomorrow. You're brilliant, you've done such amazing work here. This could be the culmination of all of it, Johnny. Please don't throw it for us.'

Silence reigns for what feels like an age. I've gone too far, he'll think I'm emotionally blackmailing him.

'Amber, I'm curious, since when did you metamorphose into Lady Macbeth?'

'Sorry?'

'You heard me. "We" this and "we" that. Are you surprised Lydia feels like she does? It was bad enough when you were going round sacking people.'

'Johnny, I had to tell him, she's only sixteen. You'd do the same, I know you would.'

'Oh please, spare me the ten commandments according to Amber. You lied to me. You told me you weren't ready, when all the time you were screwing the boss.'

'I wasn't when you asked me out. I wasn't ready—'

'It's not really the point for you, is it?'

'What's that supposed to mean?'

'Landing Oscar's hardly doing your career any harm.'

'Don't you dare talk to me like I'm some kind of hooker, I love him. I didn't fancy you, it's not a crime.'

'You're right, it's not. But don't expect any favours from me. It was Lydia who hired me at Violet, it was Lydia I came over for. If she's out the door, then so am I.'

It's absolutely pointless talking any more. I say a polite

320

goodbye, wondering if his anger is also a useful defence. What is it with men and hurt: why can't they just express it? If you ask me, hell hath no fury like a man scorned, not a woman. A woman will go off and bore her girlfriends to death, eat her own body weight in Bountys, and watch her favourite episodes of *Sex and the City* back to back until she believes she's channelling the Post It dumped spirit of Carrie Bradshaw. But then she'll get over it, get some perspective. Talking of which – could I?

I remember Dom's face when we were sitting on the bench, the promise he made that he'd always be there for me. Maybe now, before Ursula Andress has jiggled her perfect boobs in his direction, is the time to cash his promise in. He's the one person I know who could sort us out, could come in and run a completely unfamiliar restaurant like a military operation. I stand there looking at my phone like it's got magical sooth-saying powers. I can't ring him without asking Oscar.

He's back in the kitchen, bawling and barking so belligerently that those words of praise seem like a hallucination. I drag him to the corner of the kitchen, outline my plan. I'm steeling myself for a tirade, but his eyes are glassy, his gaze elsewhere.

'Do it. I can't lose this competition, it can't happen. I don't give a fuck what it takes right now.'

'OK then,' I say, slightly taken aback. I'd expected a heated debate, at the very least. I believe it's the right thing to do, but I'm perversely insulted that there's not so much as a flicker of jealousy. Ridiculous.

I try Dom's phone, but unsurprisingly it's switched off. I think for a minute. If he does agree, he'll have to switch things round to get himself rota-ed off, and if he needs to do that, the sooner I can tell him the better. I grab my coat and hightail it out the door, trying my best not to over-analyse any of it too much. Amber Freud has left the building.

It's only once I'm walking up Piccadilly that the stomach churning kicks in. I've done everything I can to avoid Marquess since we split up and the uncanny lack of invitations to tea at the Ritz has meant I've managed quite well. I can see the lights blazing from here, the top-hatted doorman smoothly hailing taxis for over-fed customers. It's gorgeous this place, and so resonant for me. Oh God, oh God, oh God. What if Rachel's here? I almost turn back at the very thought, but I force myself onwards, talk to myself as sternly as I did Oscar. For the next twenty-four hours I need to stay focused on the competition, displaying roughly as much emotion as a cyborg. Only then can I start to search for the balance I'm craving: go home and remind myself I'm a daughter as well as a chef, think about what posting those papers meant, not just rely on the dubious healing powers of a Kit Kat. Not quite yet, though.

I reach the doors, aware how scruffy I look. Luckily the doorman recognises me.

'Hello, Shaun,' I say, wondering how much he knows.

'Amber!' he says, his face lighting up. 'Lovely to see you again. Come right through.' I love Shaun, actually love him.

Marquess is truly glorious, high ceilinged and beautifully lit. It's like an old-fashioned European bistro writ large and is always filled to the gills with the great and the good. The buzz is deafening, big round tables stretching out as far as the eye can see. I grind to a halt at the reception desk. There's a new door bitch in charge, who casts a disparaging glance at my bike-friendly puffa jacket.

'Hello, madam. Do you have a reservation?'

I freeze, the nerves I've been forcing down coming back full force. Narcissistic and ridiculous though it sounds, I'm convinced every last one of them knows my husband left me for a trannie (or something).

'I ... um,' but just as my stuttering reaches a crescendo, Shaun appears at my side.

'This is Amber, Dom's wife. Can you track him down for her?'

I could almost cry with gratitude. Soon I'm ensconced in the cosy bar, with an unaffordable, expensive glass of ice-cold Chablis nestling at my breast, waiting. Waiting for Dom. I'm on tenterhooks, eyes constantly swivelling to the door. What if he can't be arsed? Maybe he's prepping someone to come and let me down gently. After all, now the paperwork's in the bag he doesn't have to play nice. Paranoia be gone. Once I've necked all but a trickle, a pretty waitress approaches. She's kooky pretty rather than drop-dead gorgeous. Big, intrusive glasses frame her clear green eyes and her dark hair is fighting a losing battle with a battalion of pins that are holding up a cascade of corkscrew curls. She's basically a mash up of Maggie Gyllenhaal and Annie Hall: no wonder Dom hired her.

'Amber?' she says, unable to disguise the fact she's checking me out. She's curious, not mean, so I try not to mind.

'Yup.'

'Dom sends his apologies,' my heart sinks, 'he'll be with you as soon as he can.' Her cute, innocent little face lights up. 'He's dealing with some über-demanding Russians, you know

323

what it's like.' She loves him, I just know it, and I can't even hate her – it'd be like hating Thumper.

'Thanks,' I say, grief engulfing me. Why did I do this? Was it pure altruism, or was part of me looking for an excuse to catch a final glimpse before he's off limits for ever? Either way, it's backfired spectacularly. I'm not tough enough to watch his life carry on without me in it, even though my own life's ticking along quite nicely, thank you. And here he is, rushed and harassed. He thanks Maggie Hall, who blushes with pleasure, then kisses me on the cheek.

'To what do I owe the pleasure?'

'Dom, I'm so sorry to turn up on the doorstep,' I babble. 'I just, I didn't know who to call.'

'Tell your creepy Uncle Quentin everything,' he says, laying a flaccid hand on my knee. It's a stupid old joke about the weird uncle in *The Famous Five* who had to be either a closet case or a paedophile, and it immediately puts me at my ease. A shared history can kill you or cure you, that's for sure. I do tell him everything, right back to Mac the Steak's walk-out and then leave him to ponder what part he can play. He looks out onto Piccadilly, playing with the stem of my glass.

'So basically you want me to save your new boyfriend's arse?'

'In a nutshell,' I say.

'Poetic justice, I suppose.'

'Dom, you said I could call on you if I was stuck, and I'm sure you meant if I was stranded in a burning building, or if, I don't know, I was drowning in Loch Ness,' he looks at me askance, 'but in a way I am. We've worked so hard for this competition, it would be criminal if it was over before it began. And there's Marsha's party too, that's the nightmare. If only I'd pulled it in the first place but I didn't—'

'It's great you didn't,' interjects Dom softly. 'I always liked her.'

'You did, didn't you? It's the last thing I'll ever ask of you,' I say, feeling that sadness again. I hold off any emotional blackmail, but I suspect my cocker spaniel eyes are doing far better than my mouth could. There's a long pause.

'Thing is,' says Dom, 'I've handed my notice in now so I'm a bit demob happy anyway.'

'Have you?' I say, trying not to think about Ursula or Maggie or any of the other myriad women who'll cross his path.

'Sure have, I'm out of here in a month. And I'm training up this total keeno, who'll bite my hand off for an extra shift.' He pauses. 'And I owe you a lot more than this. A lot more.'

'So you'll do it?'

'You're on,' he says, shaking my hand. Shaking my hand! I shouldn't be complaining: the road to success has been infinitely simpler than I was expecting, but it feels a bit anti-climactic. Of course, part of me longs for them to wrestle like bears for me, beating their manly chests at the moon, but I'm not that kind of girl. I'm turning to go, but Dom calls after me.

'Amber, the papers . . .'

'I've sent them off, I told you that!' I know I'm being snappy, but I can't help myself. He wants the marriage over and done with, I get it.

'I know—'

But before he finishes his sentence Maggie comes darting up, shyly tugging on his sleeve.

'Dom, sorry to interrupt. Freddie Flintoff's called for a table and we need you to do a rejig.'

He gives a tiny, imperceptible shake of his head, and I finally appreciate his profound weariness with it all. I can't believe I'm heaping on a whole turbo-charged second helping; he must feel really guilty to have agreed. Or really determined to make sure I play nice.

'I'm there,' he says, giving her the loveliest of smiles. She responds with a toothy equivalent, each one like a piano key caught mid-scale. Why is it that every single one of her imperfections only serves to amplify her cuteness? 'Sorry, Amber,' he says, giving me a perfunctory kiss on the cheek. 'I'll see you at five, all being well. I'll call you if there's a problem.'

'Thanks,' I say, but he's virtually out the door. I slosh back the last sip like the terrible slut that I am, then make my own exit.

I wander down Piccadilly, not in the mood to rush. It's all so confusing. I retrieve my phone from the recesses of my puffa, conscious of exactly who it is I need to speak to. Dad picks up on the second ring, *The Archers* theme tune ringing out in the background.

'Perfect timing!' he says. 'I'm not just surfing the web these days, I've diversified. I'm using it to listen to all kinds of things at all kinds of times.'

'Very good,' I say, luxuriating in the familiarity of his voice. God, I miss him. 'Dad, I'm coming home.'

'Believe it when I see it.'

'No, I am. As soon as this sodding competition's over. I'm

switching the rota round and coming home. I'm forty-eight hours away.'

'Really?' he says, disbelievingly.

'Really, cross my heart and hope to die.'

'And will that Retford fella be in tow?'

'Ralph told you?'

'Well, when you told Mum … been trying not to call and bother you, but we've been worried, pet.'

Pet. He never calls me pet, not since I couldn't see over the top of the barbecue. He really must've been worried.

'Don't worry, Dad. He loves me. He's, he's nice to me.' Well, most of the time, but now is not the time for clauses. 'I might bring him.' I try to imagine Oscar round our kitchen table, his expensive jacket flung over the back of a pine chair. It feels incongruous somehow.

'That's all I need to know.' He pauses, 'Well, not all I need to know. There's a great deal more, but we'll save that for when you get here. Do you want me to book your ticket? That's another thing I can do now.'

I hear the eagerness in his voice, the need to snare me into certainty. It's tough being a parent. You're a rock star when your kids are tiny, everything to them, but before you know it, the power balance has swung violently the other way. Suddenly you're not the one setting the agenda, longing for five minutes' peace. Instead, you're left trying to lure them into spending time with you, laying a trail of breadcrumbs to bring them to your gingerbread house.

'No, Dad. Honestly, I promise I'm coming. Now I need your help.'

And I hit him with my culinary challenge, wishing I could

tell him the rest, but knowing that the whole debacle will only send him into a tailspin. Keep it simple, keep it one hundred per cent courgette-related.

'Now you hang on,' he says, loudly pulling recipe books off the shelf, like he's some kind of mad scientist. 'We can crack this.'

I settle myself down on a bench next to Eros, and lose myself in the challenge. We're riffing off each other like we're Lennon and McCartney, throwing out ingredients instead of chords. Some of the time I zone out a bit, listen to the cadence of his voice instead of what he says. It's the closest I've felt to him in so long. Eventually we nail it: a dish that feels complex enough to impress, but pared down enough to work with the ethos of Ghusto. It's an interpretation of a Nigel Slater, a butternut squash and breadcrumb affair with chilli and orange to add a slightly Moroccan angle to proceedings.

'Delicious,' says Dad, satisfied. 'You'll knock their socks off with that.'

'Do you really think it's got the wow factor?' I ask, suddenly doubtful.

'Will when you've cooked it.'

'You're biased,' I say, laughing.

'You're right, I am,' agrees Dad. 'Doesn't mean I'm not right.'

'Thanks, Dad,' I add. 'We've been on the phone for an hour!'

'I've always got an hour for you,' says Dad. He pauses. 'Whatever happens with this Retford fella, what's gone on with Dom, you're more than their other half, don't ever forget that. We're born alone, we die alone. You're your own person, and a lovely one at that.'

'That's a bit gloomy, isn't it?'

'It's the truth. We'd all do well to remember it, not expect someone else to hold our heart in their hands.'

I feel myself choking up. 'I haven't been lovely, Dad, I really haven't. I've been a horrible, neglectful prodigal baggage. But I'm going to change.'

'Course we'd love to see more of you, but you don't have to change.' He pauses, I suspect thinking about me and Mum. 'Course it'd be nice if some things changed.'

'They will, they will,' I say, emphatic.

'OK, poppet,' he says, holding back from delving deeper. 'Well, you cook like a maestro, and then get yourself on the first train north. We'll be waiting with bated breath.'

'Thanks, Dad,' I say, my freezing fingers curled tightly round the phone. 'I'll see you then.'

I'd always planned to sleep at home the night before the competition – I'm determined not to move out by stealth, go all muff before mates on Milly – and to my surprise Oscar doesn't object. Maybe he needs space too, time to lick his wounds and think about times I was most definitely not a part of. It's all flying around inside me like a kaleidoscope: his stricken face when Lydia left before he retreated into anger; the time he called me by her name. If there is feeling left there, will her walkout shake up the bottle, make it impossible for him to deny it any more? It seems naive now, that conviction I had that I could read him like a book. The thing about graveyards is that it's impossible to know what's lurking in the shadows.

I'm up at stupid o'clock, of course, but Milly's already in

the bathroom listening to the *Today Programme* while she lathers up.

'How's the Dow Jones?' I ask, as she pads out wetly.

'Don't tease!' she says. 'I'll put some coffee on.'

She does better than that, making me a round of toast and even marmalading it for me like I'm Paddington Bear.

'You need to keep your strength up,' she says. 'Big day. Ooh, I meant to tell you, Marsha emailed to invite me.'

'Really?!' I say. 'I mean, really?' I repeat, squashing the shock out of my voice.

'I know, I was surprised too. What did she say?' says Milly, awkwardly paging her way through her box-fresh BlackBerry. '"As you're part of the Ghusto family now, and very much part of Amber's friend family, it felt remiss to leave you off the list."' Milly cocks her head, reading it again. 'Bless and so forth, but why does she always sound like she's writing a memo?'

'That's just how she rolls.'

'How she rolls?! She's the person least like Puff Daddy that I can think of.'

'Get with the programme, he's just Diddy these days. Anyway, it's great you're coming.' And it is great, as long as she doesn't start giving me notes on how the restaurant's running mid-competition. 'And you're not the only surprise guest.' Milly can't believe my news, can't believe that Oscar is magnanimous enough to be allowing Dom into his domain.

'Should I be worried?' I say, my paranoia returning full-force. 'Do you think he's not that into me?'

'I don't think it's that,' says Milly. 'It's just that he knows that the show must go on, that's why he's so brilliant.' She's

330

got a faraway look in her eye as she contemplates his sheer brilliance, her rampant crush on him abundantly clear. Weirdly I don't really mind: she's about as likely to act on it as she is on her Cary Grant obsession (and he's dead as a doornail).

'You love that drive he's got, don't you?' she adds.

'Y-yes,' I say, more aware than I ever was what a complicated blessing it can be.

'Still, two of them under the same roof ...'

'Don't,' I say, gulping back the dregs of my coffee. 'What the hell have I done?'

'You're a saint, Amber Price. A wimple would actually look very fetching.'

'That's nuns, isn't it? I'm *not* a nun.' I take a final bite of my toast, go to leave, then turn back. 'Mils,' I steel myself, 'will you call me if something all official and divorcey plops onto the doormat?'

'Sure,' she says, crossing to me. 'But do you really and truly want to know that today?'

'I just can't bear it if Dom knows we're divorced and I don't. Can you imagine? "Someone sent the kidneys back, and have a nice life."'

'I see your point,' she agrees.

'Thanks,' I say, fervent, thanking her for way more than being on post patrol.

There's a superstition that a bad dress rehearsal precedes a great first night, and for the purposes of today, I'm choosing to believe it. Ghusto is utter chaos, the kitchen tense and silent, with Oscar more explosive and exacting than I've ever seen him. Meanwhile front of house is full-blown carnage. Johnny's woefully inexperienced number two is in charge of lunch service, and 'couldn't organise a piss-up in a brewery' doesn't begin to cover it. I run between the two halves, calling on the knowledge I've gleaned from living with a maître d', soothing the ruffled feathers of customer after customer. I'm pushing down my anxiety about spending a night with Dom all day, but by the time he arrives, sheer practical relief takes precedence. I tell him the true horror of Stephen's inept stewardship, a secret I've managed to keep from Oscar, and step back to let him take control of his temporary team.

'Stop a sec,' he says, grabbing my arm. 'Are you OK? Come on, deep breaths, you can do this.'

'Can I?' I say. 'There's Marsha's party upstairs, a kitchen who all think I'm Lady Macbeth and a butternut squash special that's got my name on it and probably wants to hurl itself back through the window of the Cranks.'

Dom gently takes my wrists, turns my palms upwards. 'Look, no blood,' he says, soft. 'You'll be fine. I'll lick this lot into shape and then sort out upstairs. I'm sure I can keep half an eye.'

'Good, cos I'm trusting Tomasz's Polish army with no hard evidence.' I pull my wrists from his grasp, self-conscious. He turns away, claps his hands to rouse the troops.

'Listen up, people. You've had a rough twenty-four hours, and you've got no good reason to trust some chancer who's just walked in off the street.' He gets a laugh, which can only bode well. 'But I need you to go with me. Amber tells me you're brilliant, and one thing I know about her is that she always tells the truth.' He looks at me, rueful, and I give him

332

a half smile. I shouldn't have done this, it's making me sad, and sad is a luxury I can't afford. 'This competition is just as much about you as it is the kitchen. Let's go out there and show them how it's done.'

His speech seems to have the desired effect, despite him sparing them the dire warnings and threats of assault that lace Oscar's pep talks. The waiters pick up their heels, laying the tables and running through the specials with renewed vigour. Oscar strides into this hive of industry, the swing doors almost knocked off their hinges by his velocity. He looks around, surveying the scene with a look that feels almost violent. I cross to him.

'Let me introduce you,' I say, awkward. The problem with having no time is that I've had no time to prepare the ground, to suss out how he's feeling. I'd hate this, but he's not me.

'You must be Dom,' he says, sticking out his hand like it's a weapon.

'I am,' says Dom, shaking it firmly. 'Your reputation precedes you.'

Oscar looks at him suspiciously. 'Thanks,' he says. 'And thanks for stepping in. We were desperate.'

Touché. They stare at each other, then seem to think better of it. I catch a smirk on Oscar's face as he turns away, and I could almost swear to why. He knows he's sexy, it's part of how he negotiates the world, while Dom's ... Dom's Dom. He's a random jumble of things that add up to an unexpected combination. But if Oscar wants to dismiss him, that's much the best result.

Just as Oscar exits, Marsha appears stage left. She looks between Dom and me, flabbergasted. It's rare that Marsha's rendered speechless, but the moment has officially arrived.

'It's complicated,' says Dom, which triggers a little lurch inside me. Is it complicated for him? And is the part of me that hopes it is pure ego or something equally complicated? 'Amber can explain. Shall I take your coat?'

'Long time, no see,' says Marsha coldly. 'Well, obviously.' She peers at him suspiciously, pulling her coat closer around her. She's giving him nothing. I go over and hug her, try and break the ice.

'We're so incredibly grown up that the very week of our divorce, Dom's stepped into the breach. You would've been back in Tiger Tiger if he hadn't been racked with guilt.' I give him a half smile, aware I'm being tricksy. I must stop it, keep it ruthlessly professional – the thing is, it's almost impossible to wall myself off like that. Marsha slowly peels off her coat, wary. Or maybe it's just reluctance to reveal the mustard-coloured prom dress she's wearing, complete with hip-widening tiered ruffles and Peter Pan collar. Honestly, it's like she's ram raided Ann Widdecombe's wardrobe.

'You look lovely,' says Dom, which definitely counts as a little white lie rather than a big black beetle. 'Amber is Oscar's slave tonight,' I look at him sharply but he doesn't look round, 'but I'll take you upstairs and get you set up.'

'I'll pop up for five minutes,' I say, knowing I'm directly contradicting what I promised Oscar. Surely five minutes won't hurt? We troop up there, greeted by Tomasz's merry band. Well, fairly merry band. There's only two of them, but they reassure us that the other two will be rushing on from their day jobs within the hour.

'Fantastic,' says Dom, all confidence, and Marsha's nervous

expression unknots itself. It unknots a stage further with the arrival of Peter, who goes to shake my hand at the exact moment I go to kiss him. Dom's briefing the staff, adjusting the lights, spreading calm and order.

'I ought to go,' I whisper. 'Do you think they'll be all right?'

'They're perfect for each other.'

'Not them! The waiters.'

'If there's four, they'll be fine.'

'But what if—'

'Let's cross that bridge when we come to it,' says Dom. 'You go, you've got culinary greatness to create.'

'Greatness might be pushing it.'

'Have it your way. You've got culinary mediocrity to create.'

I laugh, despite myself, grateful for a moment of not feeling like it's life and death. I'm just about to leave when Marsha's older sister appears, hot and bothered. Who can blame her: she's got a fractious baby wriggling in her arms who's recently accessorised her black velvet dress with a swag of vomit.

'I'm so sorry,' she says, trying simultaneously to hug Marsha, the baby and a huge carry cot. 'The au pair's ill, and I couldn't bear to not be here at least for the toast. Is it OK to have a baby here?' she asks me as the baby's wails reach a crescendo.

'I'm sure it's fine,' I say, trying not to sound thrown. I promised Oscar no disruption, and I'm not sure this qualifies. I look at its red face, its mouth a black O of need, its tiny hands flung out in protest. Dom comes back up, bearing a tray of drinks.

'What's she called?' he asks, smiling at her. How did he

335

know she's a girl? I wonder if the baby feels his acceptance, his welcome, because her cries immediately become less frantic.

'Allegra,' says Hannah, smiling gratefully. 'God, I would actually kill for one of those.'

'Shall I grab the cot?' says Dom, swapping it for a glass of wine. 'If we put it in the corner here you never know, she might grace you with a nap.'

Hannah sinks back on the sofa, effortlessly put at her ease, and as she relaxes so does Allegra.

'She's gorgeous,' says Dom, and I can see in his eyes that it's no word of a lie, black or white. 'Hello, Allegra.'

'Do you want to hold her?' asks Hannah. 'Correction: please, for the love of God, will you hold her?'

'No problem,' says Dom, taking her tiny body in his arms. 'How old is she?'

'Three months.'

I have to turn away, the irony not lost. Maybe I should've stuck with hating him, kept my bogey-man version of him as the enduring image. No, I would've loathed that, loathed what else I'd have had to tell myself – that he was a shit, that all those years of happiness were a fairytale – what it would have done to me. Black and white is comforting, but it turns out grey's very in this season, at least for me.

I arrive back to find the kitchen working at full tilt. Oscar casts me a sharp look, but he stops short of bawling me out. There's fifteen minutes until the judges arrive, and I make my way round the stations, checking there's no last-minute problems with any of the dishes. This is not a night when we can afford another Trout-gate. That said, I rather hope we do run low on the lambs' tongues that Oscar's put on the starter menu. I love the uncompromising extremity of it, but I worry the judges will view us unkindly if the vast majority of diners are too squeamish to partake.

'You're assisting me,' says Oscar tersely. He's never the one at the stove, but tonight's different. 'Michelle can run with your vegetarian option.'

'Did you like it?'

He wrinkles his nose. 'Sounds like baby food, but then it all does to me.'

I wish he liked it, wish I could squeeze a tiny bit of praise out of him. 'Babies don't eat chillies' is my quietly pathetic comeback, but he's too busy pulling rabbit carcasses out of the fridge to hear me.

When the judges do arrive, they're not at all what I was expecting. There's a Roman restaurateur who's lived in England for the past five years, and a nondescript middle-aged woman who will confide no more information beyond the fact that she's had 'a lifetime in the food industry'. I rather suspect that might've been spent on the Haribo production line, as she displays no passion for food whatsoever. She creeps around the kitchen suspiciously, staring silently at the various stations like a wraith. Giorgio is all together more engaging.

'Lovely premises,' he says, beaming. 'You give me the tour?'

'Of course,' says Oscar. 'We've got a private function on upstairs though. Perhaps you could see how that's going?' he asks me, casting me a black look. Oh God, it better be going well. We might not be being judged on it, but it'll be hard to keep Giorgio out, and it won't reflect well on us if it's an under-staffed bun fight.

'Very good,' says Giorgio. 'Oh, and one little surprise for you. We've ensured the restaurant is fully booked, but a number of those tables are with our surprise diners. They'll be giving their scores afterwards so we can see how you cope with keeping up quality when you're at capacity.'

'Great!' says Oscar with a plastic smile. 'Where did you find them?'

'They're just average punters – that's the point.'

Average punters who hopefully don't feel queasy at the sight of a brain, wobbling gently like a blancmange. Being judged by professionals is one thing, but this? How much easier will it be for a restaurant like the top class Italian we're up against? Oscar's thinking just the same, I can feel him tensing up, but he doesn't go postal.

'We love a challenge, don't we, Amber?'

'That we do,' I say, like I've suddenly metamorphosed into a leprechaun. I make my excuses and dash upstairs, encountering Milly at the door.

'Have you just arrived?' I ask her, taking in the crush.

'No, I was having a breather. Honestly, darling, it's an assault course even trying to get a drink.'

'Oh God, Oh God,' I say, as Dom appears beside us, finally looking anxious.

'No waiters, I'm afraid,' he says. 'I've been doing some ringing round, but it's too short notice.'

'There's no way we can spare anyone from downstairs ...'

'I'll do it,' says Milly, quick as a flash.

'Don't be silly,' I say, simultaneous with Dom's 'Fantastic.'

'She can't,' I tell him. 'It's crazy. You're here as a guest!'

'I worked behind the bar in the student union,' says Milly.

338

'I'm more than capable. I want to help.' She does, I can see it in her face, and I suddenly feel overwhelmingly guilty about how snippy I've been about her transformation into Donald Trump. All she wants is to feel useful.

'Amber, come on, desperate times,' says Dom, 'there's still loads of guests to arrive. It's not rocket science, is it, Mils?' He holds my gaze, and I feel myself give in. It's funny how one part of me trusts him more than anyone, while another part of me still watches him through narrowed eyes.

We get Milly kitted up with a uniform and a tray of drinks, send her into the fray, and the sense of frenzy gradually subsides. Marsha gives a big grin of relief, and taps her glass.

'Unconventional though it may be, I'd like to say a few words on behalf of me and Peter.' Peter smiles proudly, firelight bouncing off his NHS-style specs. 'It's been something of an uphill struggle finding the one, you might say it's almost like pulling teeth!' There's a polite titter from the assembled throng. 'But I know that both of us feel it was very much worth the wait.' They smile at each other, lost to all of us for a few seconds. 'And we're immensely pleased you'll all be there to share it with us. I just wanted to give a special mention to my most special and bestest friend.' I look over to Lisa, whose bump is now protruding roundly. 'Amber.' Me? How can I be her best friend when I've been so rubbish? 'Amber sometimes feels like a firework, who burns brightly but briefly, sometimes as rarely as annually,' she looks at me, a Marsha-like note of reproach tempering her outpouring of emotion, 'but she's far, far more than that.' Dom's watching her intently – not soppily, intently. 'She risked career annihilation to make tonight happen in a spectacular act of unselfish friendship and for that, and for so much more, I will always be grateful to have her in my life. So let's charge our glasses and raise a toast to all of you, our treasured friends.'

Oh gosh, I'm weeping. I'm not at all sure this counts as ninja-like focus. Milly hands me a napkin and I do an emergency repair job on my eye make-up in the seconds before Giorgio and Oscar come sweeping in. Milly quickly hands Giorgio a glass of the distinctly average Prosecco, but thankfully he's distracted by his extremely Italian interest in her cleavage.

'A tiny sip,' he says flirtatiously, 'I'm working. Good use of the space,' he continues. 'It adds another dimension to the business.'

'I like to think so,' agrees Oscar, ignoring my smug smile. It does look nice now. There's a roaring fire in the grate, casting a lovely glow, and although it's very busy, it doesn't drown out the palpable joy. People are crowded around Peter and Marsha, and there's an ever-expanding pile of presents in the corner, even though they're only at the engagement stage. Dom's gone back downstairs, which is probably a good thing, as I'm finding it almost impossible not to think about our engagement drinks, held in a skanky pub in Islington in the depths of winter. We were very much the pioneers, and I would've felt embarrassed to hold a soirée as sophisticated as this. We all drank cheap white wine, played pool and tried our best to control the random choices on the jukebox. I was naive and happy in equal measure, but I was definitely happy.

Soon I'm back down the mine, braising rabbits and sautéing livers like my life depends on it. Oscar's utterly absorbed in the cooking, barely looking up except to demand ingredients, but my eyes are constantly roving the room. Susan is still stalking around the stations, silent and deadly, with her notepad at the ready. Diners are streaming in, but Dom seems to be ensuring front of house deals efficiently with the deluge. Maybe, just maybe, we'll be all right. But as I exhale, relief gives way to something more complicated. There's something scary about stopping, about the trip home I know I must make and the space it'll give me. I haven't had time to think for so long, each emotion allotted a tiny amount of time before I jerk back to keeping the show on the road.

Once we've successfully got the first barrage of mains out, Oscar graces me with a smile. The judges are sat at a two-person table where they can savour a tasting-sized plate of each dish, and have so far declared both the rabbit and the monkfish a great success, with the miniature plate of pig trotters we sent out as an amuse-bouche having come back clean too.

'Think we're nailing it, Fish Girl,' he says, swigging from a bottle of water he's got to his left. I don't want to tempt fate, but I think he might be right. And much as he's been tunnel vision-tastic, I've loved watching him actually cook, rather than just command operations. His consciousness of when a cut of meat is perfectly cooked, his understanding of his ingredients – he's a real magician. I look at him for a second, conscious how much in awe of him I still am. 'You should be on the pass,' he adds.

'Joe's fine there!'

'Go on, I need every plate looking perfect. You're my eyes and ears.'

I cross over, trying not to feel like I've been relegated to

341

understudy, and give Joe the good news. It's hard work up there: plates are coming through thick and fast with waiters pinging back and forth like rubber bands. It gets more and more frenetic and harder and harder for me to keep my cool, particularly now Susan's back in the kitchen. She's made a few acidic remarks about the speed of service, but I know that we can't allow standards to slip. Oscar certainly won't have it, and has already thrown out a couple of his own plates, even though they looked absolutely perfect to me. Can we really hold it together now we're at maximum capacity?

'No!' I'm telling Stu, frustrated. He's brought out three below par plates in the last hour. 'That mash looks like school dinners, you need to keep it to the left, not let it bleed all over the plate. For fuck's sake, Stu, you're better than this.' I look up to find Dom at my elbow. God, he must think I'm such a shrew.

'Amber—'

'Yes?' I say, trying to keep the stress out of my voice.

'There's a call—'

'Dom, can you deal with it?' I say.

'Well, no, not really. It's the police.'

I look at his sober face, try to keep down my panic. 'What's happened? Is it my dad?'

'Your dad? No, it's for Oscar. His daughter's been arrested.'

Oscar patently ignores my attempts to draw him away. I have to virtually shout to get his attention, hoping against hope that Susan's too busy frightening the sauce section to hear me.

'Oscar, listen to me, Tallulah's been arrested.'

He looks me full in the face, white. 'What?!'

'It's OK, it's OK, she's all right. She crashed a car into a lamppost—'

'She can't fucking drive,' he says, a wild look in his eye. Everyone's looking round, and I try to subtly signal to them to keep working. The last thing we need is to look like a kitchen in crisis.

'She's OK, but she's been arrested for driving without a licence.'

Oscar can barely contain his fury. He looks at Susan, crashes his fist down on the station and releases a tirade under his breath. 'She's fucking well grounded, she knows that. Not only does she disobey me, but she disobeys me in the most disrespectful way possible.'

Why are we having this conversation here? I want to tell him that that's absolutely the point, that she's sticking two fingers up at him in the most spectacular way she knows how. I lead him out, pull him to just through the swing doors where Susan can't see us, and try my best to convey some of that.

'All she wants is attention,' I tell him. 'She wants to know you care, and she's going about it in the most teenage way possible.'

'Of course she knows I care. For fuck's sake, I spent a fortune on that dinner.'

'She needs time with you,' I say, 'particularly now. She must be in bits about what's just happened between you and Lydia.'

'And where is fucking Lydia?' spits Oscar. 'I'm doing all of this for them,' he pauses, 'for Tallulah,' he pauses, 'and this, this is how they repay me.'

No time. No time to tell him what I'm starting to suspect,

that delayed gratification is a pact with the devil. It's the worst kind of pension, working yourself into the ground with the idea of a rosy retirement, then finding you're fatally estranged from everything and everyone who might've made it meaningful. Who wants to be a lonely old bird in a gilded cage?

'They can't get any answer on her phone, and anyway ...' I take his hand, then look round almost unconsciously, scanning the room for Dom. He's on the far side of the restaurant dealing with a fussy-looking couple of business men. 'It would be the best thing in the world if you turned up together.' Oscar's eyes are almost popping out of his head with sheer incredulity. 'No, listen, Oscar. She's part of each of you, it'll be horrible for her to feel like you hate each other. How unbelievably confusing to have to try and choose a side.'

'I haven't asked her to do that.'

'No, but,' I pause, trying to not get dragged back into my own story, 'she'll still feel like she has to. She can't hate her mum, even if you do, and God knows, you don't want her to hate you.'

Oscar gives me a hard look and I wonder if the clock's ticking on his internal detonator. I really should stop, but I don't seem to have an off switch these days.

'We need to get back to the kitchen.'

'Oscar—'

'It'll do her no harm to cool her heels in that cell for a couple of hours. I promised her tough love and tough love is what she's going to get.'

'It won't feel like love.'

'How many times,' he starts, frustrated. He changes tack. 'I know you're trying to be caring, but you haven't got kids.' It feels stark when he says it, harsh. Dom's laughing with the be-suited ones now, backing away once he's sure they're happy.

'No, I haven't. But I have loved people and . . . you've got to put this first. There's nothing that matters more than the people you love, and certainly not this competition. We can handle it for a couple of hours.'

Oscar looks doubtful and I give it one final shot.

'Oscar, you will never have this night again, never have the chance to show her that you love her unconditionally, no matter what she does.' Dom's close now, making sure the judge's table is cleared and ready for their next course. It's hard to be sure, but something tells me he's eavesdropping. I'm hit by a wave of self-consciousness. 'Obviously it's your choice,' I add, sounding less like a Hallmark card and more like one of Marsha's verbal memos.

'Fuck's sake,' says Oscar, grimacing. 'OK, I'll go. You're in charge. Do *not* fuck this up.'

'So no Big Macs for the judges?'

'Don't joke,' he says, stripping off his whites. He's sweaty, grimly determined – still sexy no matter what. 'I'll be back as soon as I can.'

And he's gone. I stand there a second too long, long enough for Dom and me to catch each other's eye.

'Everything OK?' he says. 'That looked pretty intense.'

What did he hear? Knowing Dom, knowing how quietly cunning he is, I bet he heard everything. He loves information, it's part of what makes him so good at his job. I smile at him, so glad he's there, despite everything. There's something about being known as well as he knows me that's incredibly comforting, the fact that he knows all my flaws, many and varied, and is still here for me. And of course, he might be a cheating scumbag, but it doesn't turn everything off. Maybe one day I really will be magnanimous and mature enough to be friends.

'Not really,' I say, smiling despite myself. 'Onwards and upwards.' I turn towards the kitchen, then turn back, touch his arm. 'Thank you.'

'Don't mention it.'

'OK, I won't.'

And with that, I step back into the inferno.

'Listen up, people,' I shout, eternally grateful that the judges are seated at their table rather than listening to my rallying cry. I experience a blip of panic at the knowledge that they've reached their mini-portions of my vegetarian special, but I push it aside. 'As you may or may not know, Oscar's had a family emergency.' A murmur starts up, but I carry on. He also told Giorgio, who seemed fairly sympathetic, but it's hard to know for absolute certain that he's not just committed competition hara-kiri. 'I know my promotion's been deeply unpopular with some of you, but I'm begging you to work with me here. Let's not fuck this up. Ghusto's not just Oscar, it's all of us, and so is this award. Let's go out there and get it!'

I look straight at Joe for the end of my speech, wanting to see if he's dripping poison into the surround, but it doesn't look that way. Perhaps I really am over the worst. I don't earn an Oscar-style standing ovation, but there's no slacking off, everyone works their absolute hardest, turning round plate after plate of impeccably cooked lambs' tongues and pig spleen. Despite the Sweeney Todd gruesomeness of it all, most plates come back clean. Maybe the mystery diners are more hardcore than I anticipated?

Dom comes barrelling through with a pair of those said clean plates when I'm supervising the sauce section.

'Look!' he says, holding them up.

'Oh what are they?' I say, scratching my head. 'It'll come to me. They're plates!'

'No, stupid, they're not any old plates. They're your butternut squash plates. I heard the judges discussing how delicious it was.'

'No!' I say, flushing with pleasure.

'Yes!' says Dom. 'I'd better get back out there, but I thought you'd appreciate some good news.'

I watch his retreating back, taking a few seconds to bask in the glow. He swings out the doors and I watch them swing back, poleaxed by the strangeness of the situation. This is like a bizarro version of what I always dreamed of: Dom effortlessly brilliant out front, me out back waiting graciously for the rapturous accolades. It's like *Jim'll Fix It* (*Oscar'll Fix It*? Somehow it doesn't have the same ring), like I'm getting my dream for one night only. Dreams can change, I suppose. I can devote myself to cooking alongside Oscar, occasionally breaking off to unpeel Tallulah's fingers from around the neck of my first-born son. Hell, maybe Dom can be godfather. Happiness comes in unexpected packages. I look hard into a rabbit's cavernous tummy and remember what I'm here to do. Oscar texts obsessively, still unable to free the Kensington strangler from the cells. I reassure him it's going well, and I think on the whole it is. Jean-Paul pulls off a magnificent

347

selection of desserts, and gradually, gradually, the pace starts to slack off.

I risk a brief trip upstairs, finding Milly stretched out on the big purple velvet sofa, her feet stuck up high on the arm. There are only a few stragglers left now, but the atmosphere feels mellow and relaxed.

'God, I love wine,' says Milly with feeling.

'It's Beelzebub's best invention.'

'That was *the* most exhausting three hours of my life,' she adds. 'I don't know how you do it.'

'I'm not actually a waitress.'

'No, the whole thing.' She pauses. 'My helpful tips are officially at an end,' she says. 'Don't think I haven't noticed you rolling your eyes when you think I'm not looking.'

I jump in, deeply embarrassed by my churlishness.

'You totally saved our bacon – sorry, bad joke – with the meat. We'd have been up shit creek without you talking Jack round.'

'Thanks.'

'What you've done is incredibly generous. And I'm sorry if I've been ungracious.'

'Maybe Oscar would give me a couple of shifts.'

'Would you really want to do that?'

'Well, sort of. I'd like to actually understand it from the frontline.'

'OK, I can ask him,' I say, giving her a hug. She's so without ego sometimes, so much more Lama-worthy than I'll ever be. I look round at Marsha, flushed and contented, presents spread out around her like she's a mother hen with a clutch of eggs. I love my friends. 'I better get back downstairs,' I say reluctantly.

I want to be here in the warm with those who love me, but as normal there's not enough time.

It's nearly all over. The team clear up while the last few desserts go out, the judges circulating around the remaining tables. Most of the score cards have been filled in, but of course we're not allowed to see them. The results are out tomorrow afternoon, so there won't be long to wait.

'How'd you think we did?' I whisper to Dom.

'They all seemed pretty merry,' says Dom. 'I'm not sure how popular the blood ice cream was, but the sheeps' kidneys went down a storm.' There's a teasing undertone to his voice, though his face is deadly serious.

'Do you not like it then?'

'What?'

'Oscar's cooking.'

'He's talented, no question,' says Dom thoughtfully. 'I don't know . . .'

'Spit it out.'

'Is he not a bit style over substance? All mouth and no trousers?'

'Not at all,' I say hotly.

'No, I'm sure you're right,' says Dom. 'I should go. You don't need me any more.'

There's a pause.

'Stay for a drink?' I ask, hoping I don't sound too pathetic.

'No really, I should go.'

'OK.' We stand there like lemons: the hills are aliiive with the sound of silence.

'Have a nice trip?' I venture.

349

'I'll speak to you before I leave.'

'Well, we need to talk about Wet William, check on his progress.'

'Yes, of course.'

There's another gut-wrenching pause, before Oscar appears through the main doors, a sheepish-looking Tallulah in tow. And is that . . . ? Yes, Lydia's here too.

'I'm out of here,' says Dom, giving me a quick kiss on the cheek. Lucky old him.

I'm rooted to the spot, wondering where to put myself. Oscar is glad-handing Susan and Giorgio, full of apologies, while Tallulah and Lydia cross the floor and head straight for the flat. I attempt a smile but as neither of them look at me, it must seem like I'm either smiling into thin air or at my imaginary friend. I hope the judges don't have me down as some kind of half-wit (*Ghusto's charitable policy of employing care in the community chefs can only be applauded.*)

It's over, it really is. As soon as the judges are dispatched, Oscar heads upstairs with barely a word, and me . . . I slink off home.

Mercifully I've got the morning off. I arrive at the last possible moment, not long before the results are due. I haven't heard a peep from Oscar since last night. I wonder about staying away, keeping myself busy in the kitchen, but it feels heartless. I tentatively knock on his office door, slip inside. He looks up, face grey and strained.

'Darling, what happened? Tell me properly.'

'It's OK. They're not going to press charges. It was Persephone's mum's Mini, so I've told her I'll pay for any damage.'

'And Tallulah?'

'It's been a real wake-up call.'

'That's brilliant! If you guys have more time together, really talk to each other—'

'For her, not for me! Her actions have consequences, I think she *finally* gets that now.'

Oh God, he is sleepwalking into a terrible relationship with his daughter, and there's nothing I can do about it. I can't hold back the whisper of foreboding any longer – it's suddenly horribly, blindingly clear that this is not the man I want to father my children. It hits hard, but there's also a relief in finally admitting what I've been trying so hard to suppress. Truth in beauty and beauty in truth. I try to stop my face from betraying my inner revelation.

'And are you and Lydia on better terms?'

'We were civil,' he spits, 'but she's still a devious bitch.'

'Oh, OK.' I guess she is, but she's also the mother of his child – the really, really angry mother of his child. And he's angry too, you don't spit like that if you feel nothing. If I'd had a bit more imagination, I might've tried pretty hard to fuck Dom over in the immediate aftermath, I just wasn't prepared to pull some *Daily Mail* scorned-wife type trick, like cutting the crotches out of all his trousers. Besides, most of them are so bashed up, he probably wouldn't have noticed.

'Anyway, come on, Amber, tell me exactly what the judges said to you. Any impressions you got, anything.'

I try my best to describe it all, but it's hard. 'I think we did a really good job,' I say, once I've exhausted my knowledge. 'And D ... front of house seemed to think the mystery diners were really impressed.'

'You can say his name.'

'Dom.' There was no need to actually say it. All he meant was that he's not unmentionable. Now I've proclaimed it at the top of my voice, like a town crier. Dom-m-m. It reverberates magnificently, like I'm wandering the streets of Lincoln in a fetching piped coat, ringing my enormous bell. Oscar ignores me, rifling through a pile of papers on his desk.

'I've been pulling up reviews for all the other restaurants, trying to work out our odds.'

'There's no way of knowing,' I say, 'besides, the results will be in any minute.'

He looks grumpy. 'Don't you care?'

'Of course I care! It's just a waste of energy speculating.'

As if to illustrate the point, the rest of the staff come streaming in, crowding around Oscar's desk in tense anticipation of the press release. When his laptop finally pings to signal its arrival, you could hear a pin drop. Oscar's face is set.

'Can't read it,' he says, his fearlessness in abeyance. 'Fish Girl, do the honours.'

I go from the top, trying not to skim my way to the bottom.

'The judges were faced with an almost impossible choice, as the five shortlisted restaurants were of such a uniformly high standard. This is why they have taken the unusual decision to award a "highly commended" place as well as declaring an overall winner.'

'Go on, go on,' says Oscar, fists clenched.

'So while Mario Cardino's Three Bridges ultimately takes the crown, Oscar Retford's Ghusto is recognised as a close enough second to merit this lesser award.'

A cheer goes up from all the staff, just as Oscar erupts with a furious 'Fuuuuck.'

'Oscar, it's still amazing!' I say. 'They've invented a whole category for you. For us. Well done, everyone. Of course it would've been great to win, but . . .'

There are muted smiles all around, no one able to celebrate when Oscar looks so murderous. I cock my head to encourage them to leave, mouthing 'well done' one more time as they file out.

'I don't do second best,' says Oscar mutinously. 'After everything I've been through, I needed this.' He looks at me accusingly. 'I should never have left. That's why we lost.'

'You don't know that!'

'Yes, I do.' He jabs a finger at me. 'If you hadn't piled on the emotional blackmail—'

'I was trying to help you!'

'Well, you didn't. Two more hours and we'd have won.'

'You did win!'

'What the fuck is that supposed to mean?'

'You won at the other bit, and that's more important. You showed your only child how much you loved her, that she matters more than work, and that's a much bigger prize.' Oscar continues to glower at me. 'Can't you see that?'

I really don't think he can. He hasn't got the internal space to experience love as a living, breathing thing of beauty. It's like the difference between tending a rose garden – fertilising it and watering it even when there's nothing to show – versus buying a huge, flashy bunch of the things wrapped up in cellophane and dead from the stems down.

'This isn't going to work,' I say quietly.

'Sorry?'

'No, I'm sorry. I just know this isn't going to work.'

'You're dumping me? I've just lost the most important competition of my life and now you're dumping me? Am I not the big man any more, is that it?'

Am I a cold-hearted bitch? I don't think I am – I just know for sure what I've suspected for a while and I can't live a lie, not even for a day. It wouldn't be fair.

'It's not that, of course it's not that. Oscar, I don't think either of us is ready to really, properly love yet. I think we wish we were, but that's a different story.'

'I do love you.' He shoves his chair back angrily. 'At least I did.'

And I do sort of believe him. But I think what we've been experiencing is the top note of love multiplied by the infatuation of lust.

'But we're both holding so much back. There's so much that's too raw for us to really show each other.'

'I'm not holding anything back. What you see is what you get. I thought you knew that.'

'But you shut me out all the time!'

'No I don't! I have to work like a dog to do this,' he throws his arms out into the space, into his domain, 'I told you exactly who I was, I've never lied to you. I haven't changed, Amber.'

I don't know how to express what true intimacy means, what words I need to communicate it to him. I know that we don't have it, but then I don't know if he's ever had it. Perhaps it really is the price you have to pay for having the kind of fiery ambition that powers a career that burns as fierce and bright as his does.

'Do you ever worry about what it all costs you?'

For a second I sense that sadness again, but then his jaw clenches like a vice.

'Oh spare me the cod psychology, Fish Girl! Just spare me! Stop making pathetic excuses. If you're still in love with your husband, then just say it.'

Oh God, is it really as simple as that? How unutterably sad.

'I'm still in love with my husband,' I whisper, a lone tear rolling down my cheek. But it isn't why I'm walking away. Even if I felt utterly and completely resolved about Dom, if I was going for mani-pedis with Rachel and helping her pick out the perfect shade of slut red, I know this still wouldn't be right. It might've been right for the person who walked through the doors of this restaurant, who hero-worshipped Oscar and respected that a job like this takes everything you've got, but that girl's not me any more. I'd want to slap that girl round the face and shout 'get a grip'.

'Then get the *fuck* out of my restaurant,' shouts Oscar, red in the face. 'And don't you ever, ever come back.'

I don't need telling twice. I race out of the door and through the restaurant, stopping long enough to take a last look at it. It is beautiful, an incredible stage for Oscar's creations. I wish I could have been part of it for longer. Then I'm in the kitchen. I can't just disappear: I grab Michelle and Tomasz, tell them some of what's happened.

'Shit!' says Michelle. 'I really don't want you to go. He's such a fucking—'

'He's not, Michelle, he's really not,' I say. I wish I wasn't leaving him the way I am, but I'm not sure there's any other way to leave Oscar. 'He's brilliant. If you show him you're loyal, he'll look after you.'

'I cannot believe this comes to pass,' says Tomasz, looking genuinely heartbroken. 'If you go somewhere else, I will always chop your onions.'

'You both made this for me,' I say, pulling them into a group hug like we're at a rave. 'I couldn't have done it without you.' Tears again. I pull back, head for the locker room for the final time.

As I come back through, ready to make my silent exit, a cheer goes up. 'For she's a jolly good fellow ...' they sing, every single one of them, even Joe. Of course it's easy for him to sing now he'll get my job, but still ... I blow them kisses, and say my last goodbye.

Sometimes I'm unutterably happy that Milly doesn't have a proper job.

'I should never have tried so soon,' I say, digging my nails into my palm.

'You didn't know! Besides, maybe he shouldn't have tried so soon.'

The reality of what I've done suddenly hits me. I can't believe how abruptly it's ended. The thought of never seeing him again is incredibly weird. I do care about him, more than perhaps he realises, but I can't blunder into the long-haul knowing I won't be able to go the distance, knowing a part of my heart's broken off somewhere else. I think of his reaction to Lydia's walk-out: however much he forced it down, I know he was devastated. And when I think about it, I feel sure he's withdrawn from me since then. He's said the right things, but he's pulled away from me on some level. I look at my blank phone, dead and textless.

'He might just be waiting for you to text him?' says Milly.

'I will. Well, I won't text him, I'll email him a proper message. There was loads more I would've said if he'd let me. But I'll wait for the dust to settle. I'll wait until I've found a job at least. I bloody well hope we sell Oompa Loompa Towers soon.'

'Well, you know you don't have to pay me any rent until, ooh, until they come with wheelchairs and transfer us straight to our adjoining bath chairs in the nursing home.'

I laugh, but it's a laugh shot through with terror. It's pathetic to expect a relationship to be the answer to everything, but I'm still not all that into metamorphosing into *The Golden Girls*.

'Will you miss him?'

'Yeah, I will, I really will, but . . .' I'm ashamed to admit to a shard of relief. I realise I've been playing a bit of a role, shouting 'la la la' to avoid picking up my inner dialogue. 'He is truly talented, Milly, one of the greats. I think you should hang in there as an investor. You can keep an eye on him for me.'

Milly gets a faintly gooey look in her eye, and I refrain yet again from pointing out her blindingly obvious crush. But maybe it's not obvious to her, maybe the truth about human nature is that we're all so riddled with blind spots, it's a wonder we can even cross the road.

'The plain and simple truth is that I'm still too confused about Dom. About where his part started and mine ended.

And maybe it never would've worked out anyway, but I need to get to the point where that feels OK.'

'Isn't that just yet another impossible Amber Price high jump?'

'What do you mean?'

Milly pauses. 'It is sad, that's just the truth of it. Maybe it'll always be a little bit sad, but it will become bearably so. Like when someone dies.'

What if he does die? What if I have to stand at the back of the funeral like a leper while some gorgeous, busty Brazilian weeps and throws roses in his grave? It's such a ridiculous thought and yet it still sets me off again.

'Amber, what is it?' says Milly, putting her arms around me.

'He'll die ... one day he'll die.'

'OK, this is ridiculous. You need to talk to him.'

'There's nothing left to say. He's over it, I'm not. I need to get the divorce papers and start catching up. At least he'll be away,' I add.

'I'm not sure about your analysis. I watched him like a hawk on Friday night. Did you see his face when Marsha gave her speech?'

'Yes, I think he couldn't believe I'd been that good a friend when I'd been such a lousy wife.'

'Oh stop it! He was loving how much she loves you. He wasn't just watching her either. You kept missing him staring at you.' I look at her doubtfully. 'I mean it. Just talk to him.'

'I can't humiliate myself again.'

Milly groans with frustration. 'You're so fearless most of the time. I don't know what's got into you!'

'The only thing I need to do right now is get myself home.'

And so, like Dorothy returning to Kansas, I pack my bag and get myself on the first train north.

Chapter 16

Dad's fry-ups are legendary in our family. In fact, it's a miracle any of us have survived this long with our arteries intact, the amount of grease we hoovered up in our formative years. I arrived late last night, and collapsed into my teenage bed.

'One sausage or two?' he says, frying pan hovering over my plate.

'One. Oh sod it, two.'

'That's my girl.'

Mum looks over the top of *The Times*. 'You do look like you need a bit of feeding up. You're really quite pale.'

Normally it only takes a few hours of being around Mum for an unpleasant amalgamation of sadness and crossness to descend over me like a mushroom cloud, but today, today it's not feeling so chronic.

'Raggedy nails, darling,' says Mum.

'I've been pulling the innards out of rabbits! Nails weren't my first priority.'

'They're the first thing people see, Amber.' And breathe. 'How about I treat you to a manicure? You could come to

Howell's with me when I go for my blow-dry at one-thirty.'

I'm about to refuse, to sneer inwardly at the way she elevates her weekly blow-dry to a religious ritual, when I realise how teenage I'm being.

'Thanks, Mum. Will they be able to fit me in?'

'We can but try,' she says, going out to use the phone in the hall.

Dad casts a beatific smile in my direction, and I smile back.

'So, come on, darling, spill the beans. We hoped you might bring him home, but actually,' he looks at me fondly, 'I'm a bit chuffed we've got you all to ourselves.'

'The beans, the beans,' I say. I haven't quite got round to telling them I've hit the romantic skids, again. 'Well, he's an excellent cook ... though not better than you.'

Dad laughs.

'No, Dad, I mean it. I mean, of course he's more technically accomplished but ... you're a simple cook, but you're brilliant. I still think "what would Dad do?" when I'm stuck. Always.'

'Sounds like you'll be thinking "what would Oscar do?" soon.'

'No, Dad, I won't. I really won't. You're Yoda, not him.'

'Well, I'm honoured,' he says, doing a silly bow. 'Now stop swerving the question. Your dad needs details.' He looks at me expectantly, spatula hovering mid-air like a conductor's baton.

'Those eggs will be rock hard,' I say.

'Bugger!' he exclaims, scraping around in the pan and buying me some time.

'All booked,' says Mum, sailing back in.

'I'd better get unpacked,' I say hurriedly. 'We'll have to leave in twenty minutes.'

'Your eggs—' says Dad.

'Honestly, Dad, I'm stuffed to the gills with sausages,' I say.

'Come on, love, sit down. We were just getting to the good bit.'

'Let's talk about him tonight,' I say. 'I promise I'll tell you everything.'

It's actually rather fun having scarlet nails. I make them into claws and imagine I'm Alexis Colby. Mum and I are sitting in the café by now, where I've treated her to an enormous mug of cappuccino.

'Careful, you'll chip them,' she says, laughing at my silly roaring noises.

'I love them,' I say. 'I feel like a sex kitten.'

Mum and I never talk about sex, never ever. There's a pause.

'Your hair looks nice too,' I add. 'It's very sleek.'

'Thanks,' she says, patting it distractedly. 'Amber . . . I'm not very good at this kind of thing.'

'What kind of thing? The whole girly bonding over a cappuccino or . . .'

We aren't very good at this kind of thing, it's true. She's far more likely to do this with Beth than she ever is with me, a fact that's always infuriated me. But maybe it's not entirely her fault.

'Not just that. The whole talking thing. And I really do want to talk to you.'

I feel a rising panic, almost like someone's pushing a cushion over my face.

'About Oscar? About the divorce?'

'No, Amber, about what happened. I handled it so, so badly.' I feel a little bit frozen, even with my hands warmed through by the mug. I can't get any words out. 'We probably should've gone and talked to someone, as a family. And I never, ever should've asked you to lie for me.'

I'm crying now, defrosted, tears rolling down my cheeks. Mum dabs at them with a napkin before she hands it to me, and for a moment I feel about six. And oh, it's so lovely to feel about six, lovely to feel that there's nothing for me to worry about, no threat too big for my parents to defeat. Maybe that's why I've been so scared of motherhood, the knowledge that it's not true, that however much you pretend, however much you *have* to pretend to make a decent job of it, you can't really be invincible. But maybe, maybe that's OK. Maybe good enough really is good enough.

'I didn't know what to do,' I say, sobbing. 'I didn't know what the right thing to do was. I couldn't choose.'

'And I didn't mean to ask you to choose,' says Mum, compassion and regret etched into her face. She takes my hand. 'I wish I could make it up to you. I could, Amber, if I could take it away . . .'

'Why now, Mum, why are we talking about it now?'

'I've been watching you this last year, wheeling around, trying to make sense of everything.' I look up at her, struck by how true that sounds. Some of the time it's felt like there's a centrifugal force propelling me, like I'm no longer in charge of myself. 'It's made me feel so terrible that it's been,' she pauses, collects herself, 'an, an affair that's ended your marriage.'

'Why didn't you say that?' I say, aware of how shrill I sound. A couple behind us look round, taking in my snotty face.

'You weren't there for me to say it!' she says, emphatic. 'I didn't want to impose on you. I know you think I've been a terrible mum, and probably I have, so it's my own fault. But I didn't think you wanted me barging my way into your grief, and it's not the kind of thing you can say on the phone. That's why,' she's welling up now. I don't think I've seen her cry since that terrible day I confronted her about the affair. 'That's why I'm so glad you're home.'

Then we're both crying in earnest, like we're some kind of post-beauty-treatment support group. I think about wailing 'my nails, my beaoo-utiful nails' at the top of my voice (they are rather smudged), but I think better of it.

'This is ridiculous,' says Mum, pulling herself together. 'Let's get ourselves home.'

Dad's cooking some kind of seven-course feast that involves most of a game reserve, but he breaks off at the sight of us.

'Is he that bad?' he says.

'It's not Oscar,' I say. 'In fact, I've finished with him.'

'Blimey!' says Dad. 'I can't say I'm disappointed. Ralph said he was a flash so and so.'

'Well, he shouldn't . . .' I start, but then I peter out. He kind of is, but that's not all he is. I can't think about it now – my tiny, fevered brain will implode.

'I think we could all do with a nice cup of tea,' says Mum, sinking into a chair.

Tea soon becomes wine, the three of us sitting round the kitchen table until dusk descends. I don't think – scrub that – I know I've never talked to my parents the way I do today.

364

'The thing is,' says Dad, 'we totally buggered it up. We felt so guilty you'd been dragged into it that we tried to shelter you, but the damage had already been done. You were left second guessing what was going on.'

I look at Mum, my hostility a fragment of what it was. It's still live though, the charge not entirely gone. She looks back at me, holds my gaze.

'You're still wondering how I could've done it.'

I give a tiny nod. 'I just remember how depressed Dad was, how nothing made him laugh any more. I hated seeing you like that,' I say, reaching for his hand, a sob escaping.

'But that was the whole problem,' says Dad.

'What was?'

'My depression.'

I look back and forth between them. 'Of course you were depressed, anyone would be, finding that out.' Have I been depressed? Only for shards of time, I think. I've worked so hard to ward off the black dog, terrified it'll savage me. It's maybe been more exhausting than giving it a little bit of house room.

'No, darling, I was depressed before.'

'No you weren't!'

'Sweetheart, with respect, you were twelve. Me and your mum were having problems way before the affair. I was a miserable old sod when I wasn't trying to be dad of the year. And I was drinking too much. Talking of which . . .' he says, pouring himself a generous top up from the rather delicious Rioja he's found at the back of the cupboard. I look to see if Mum disapproves, but she's smiling.

'I shouldn't have done what I did,' she says, as Dad takes

her hand, 'but it didn't come from nowhere.' This is sounding horribly familiar.

'It needed to come to a head,' says Dad. 'I would've carried on feeling sorry for myself, ad infinitum. And of course it was tough, and it took a long time to really get past it, but I needed to stop managing the pub and take some time to think about *why* I'd been such a miserable sod.'

I look between them, watch Mum picking a strand of lint off Dad's cardigan, her ministrations so ingrained that they're almost unconscious.

'Who was he?' I ask, trying to remember what he looked like. That scene's burned on my brain, but he's a ghost. It's Mum I see.

She looks to Dad, and he gives a tiny nod.

'He was an American, would you believe, seconded to us for six months. It was ridiculous really. I was . . .' She looks at me. 'It's really hard to say all this to you. I suppose I was having a bit of a mid-life crisis – what a cliché! I was a few months shy of forty, three kids who weren't going to need me much longer and a marriage that was feeling a bit worn through. He flattered me.'

'Did you think about leaving?' I ask.

'I wasn't thinking. I felt desperately guilty, but I couldn't analyse any of it. I was just acting. Acting in every sense. It was like I was pretending to be someone else. Having a holiday.' She looks at Dad. 'It was extremely selfish and I'm extremely lucky that your father is the man he is, and forgave me.'

'I shouldn't have assumed I knew it all. I shouldn't have judged.'

366

'*Mea culpa*,' says Mum. 'Our fault entirely. You felt all that upset, and you needed to put it somewhere because we didn't tell you the truth. And then you were grown up and married, and stitched into your own little world. And now ...'

Then I really cry, cry for the end of my own little world. That's what I wanted, a perfect little microcosm that I could control where I could prove, once and for all, that marriage could be like a picture book. I was doomed.

'Sweetheart,' says one of them, I couldn't rightly say which. Both of them come and put their arms around me, embrace me like I'm a newborn. In a way I feel like I am, like I've finally understood what I needed to understand. I cry for ages, until my face looks like it's been flambéed with Jean-Paul's crème brûlée torch, but for once I let the tears come. I don't fight the familiar internal battle where I bark at myself fiercely to buck up. Mum and Dad sit there with me, stroke my hair, hand me tissues. The way they know exactly what I need – to just be held – makes me feel like they really can protect me from anything.

Once I have bucked up a bit, we have a much-needed break from the histrionics for a generous dose of Sunday-night telly. I sit between them on the sofa, dunking a bourbon in a cup of tea and we laugh at the explosion of Botox and sequins.

'Can I move home?' I ask at one point.

'Absolutely not!' says Dad. 'At least not until you bring back a Michelin star.'

'I'm not sure I want one like I used to.'

'And that's just fine,' says Mum.

But if I don't want a Michelin star, what do I want? Actually I do want one, but only if I can get it by running a gourmet tea shop that shuts at four o'clock every day and never opens on Sundays. A full-blown existential crisis is poised to enter stage left, but I keep it at bay with another Bourbon (biscuit).

'I feel I should warn you that's your fifth,' says Dad.

'Don't pester her!' says Mum.

It's funny how much of a choice there is to make about how I hear her. Yes, in one sense she is always telling him off, but it's maybe just their own funny Esperanto, the way they elect to communicate. Perhaps no one can ever translate a couple's language, even if they can hear the words. So much of the meaning is held beneath the surface, trapped in the silt. I miss Dom so much that I have to take a gulp of breath, swallow it down.

'Tell me it won't always feel this bad,' I say, gripping hold of Mum's hand. 'Tell me I'll pull myself together.' I'm crying *again*. Honestly, I should take out shares in Kleenex and have done with it.

'You're always so hard on yourself,' she says. 'It was a marriage, of course it takes time.'

'And I've seen him.' I tell them everything, right from his birthday up until now, the full gamut of hate to realising that love doesn't just conveniently disappear in a puff of smoke (unless the other person murders your children or something, but that could hardly be described as convenient).

'Oh, Amber,' says Mum.

'The stupid old divorce is going to come through any day now, and look at me.'

'You're feeling it,' she says, 'there's nothing wrong with that.' That's what I knew was coming, what I was dreading. 'And you two did have something special.'

'Why didn't you say that to me?' I snap. 'Why didn't you say, Amber, you need to work harder? Try and salvage it?'

'I did vaguely attempt to, and perhaps I should've tried harder, but I'm the last person you wanted to hear it from.' She's right. I remember verbally executing her at least twice. 'And anyway, only you and Dom could know. You're grown-ups.'

'Besides,' adds Dad hotly, 'I was absolutely bloody furious with him. All those shenanigans ...'

'But now he's going to end up with Maggie Hall or Ursula Andress or ...' They look at me quizzically but I can't be bothered to explain. 'No, he's making his own way now and so am I. I'll ... I'll meet someone else.'

Mum studies me for a moment. 'I shouldn't have read you *Sleeping Beauty* so much.'

'What do you mean?'

'Don't ... don't idealise you and Dom, for starters. It might've worked out if you'd given it more of a chance, but then again it might not. Just because we survived my affair doesn't mean you should have. No one's saying that.'

'We had kids,' adds Dad.

'Maybe you need to be on your own for a little while,' says Mum. I look up at her, pathetically terrified of being truly alone. I haven't really had time to consider what dumping Oscar means for my life. 'Have a bit of time out. You're exhausted. I know it won't be for long.'

'Are you sure you and Dom don't need to talk?' says Dad.

'I've already been humiliated enough. He shags someone else, and still I threw myself at him. Honestly, I'm taking the hint.'

'But—' ventures Dad.

'No buts, he can't *wait* to be divorced, he's biting my hand off for the papers. I'm not saying he doesn't love me, but I love our cousin Terry and he's covered in spots and deaf in one ear.'

I stare at them, all red and snotty, and then I start to laugh. It's such a relief to laugh. Soon we're all laughing, even though it's not that funny. Once the hysteria's subsided, I call a halt.

'Honestly, I can't talk about it any more. Can we do something pointless?'

'Boggle?' says Dad, giving the box a cheery rattle like it's a pair of maracas.

'Boggle!' I say, suffused with gratitude. And because Ralph's not there, I actually win.

The next couple of days are exactly what I need them to be. I'm sad, no question, but I'm also happy. It seems to be possible to feel both things at once and actually, happy plus sad doesn't turn out to equal grey. Rather than feeling gutted about the love I've lost, I try to enjoy the love I've rediscovered. That's a bit of an exaggeration, it's not like I didn't love my parents, but I hadn't experienced it as a living, breathing thing for ages. It's been too hypothetical – the odd phone call here and there, a hastily added x on the end of an email. Dad and I set ourselves culinary challenges and Mum ... I spend long enough with her for her to start annoying me again, which is kind of a relief. I was starting to worry I'd projected a whole waspish personality onto her when all the time she was Julie Andrews, skipping up a mountainside tra-la-laing about deer. She gives me a few lectures on long-term financial security, tries to give my jeans to Oxfam – is basically Mum.

It's really hard to leave. Both of them drive me to Stockport, put up with more waterworks. Dad buys me a Kit Kat like I'm nine-years-old, and I've run out of pocket money. He tucks it in my handbag, gives me a hug.

'Just call him,' he says. 'At least you'll know for sure.'

'But—'

'Honestly, Amber,' says Mum. 'You're so fearless about so many things. 'Summon up some of that grit.'

I think about her statement once I'm on the train. She's sort of right and sort of wrong. I'm fearless about some things, you have to be to survive in a kitchen, but when it comes to my heart, I think I've always been something of a coward. I haven't exposed myself the way I should, haven't wanted to hear too much in case it's more than I can handle. Maybe I do need to do this, even if it's just for me – even it's just so I know that being truly vulnerable won't bury me.

When I get home, I do a fingertip search of the flat, searching for the papers, but there's no still no sign. Honestly, much as I'm dreading their arrival, I'd rather know the axe had fallen. Am I still a wife, even in name?

I pick up my phone, every part of me shaking. Dom answers on the second ring, Radio 4 on in the background. At least he's not at work. The whole vulnerability thing doesn't start out so well.

'Are we divorced?' I bark. 'I just need to know.'

'Amber—'

'Because every day I expect the papers to plop through the letterbox and they don't.'

'What is this? Is this an especially nice way to tell me you're getting remarried?'

'Would you care if I was?'

'Of course I would care.'

There's a long pause while I try and listen to the resonance, detect what's held in the timbre of his voice. There's so much I want to say, but I can't. Maybe there's truth in silence.

'And no, we're not divorced. I only sent the papers back yesterday.'

'Yesterday?!'

'I'm sorry,' he says, 'you're obviously in a rush. I just – I found it hard to do.'

Tension rushes out of me like a water bomb. It's not just me being mad and stupid and stuck, he's in the quagmire with me. Maybe not in the same place, but his boots are definitely muddy.

'Can we meet?' I say, voice little more than a whisper. There's so much potential for more heartbreak, but I've got to jump.

'Lapaine?' he says. 'An hour?' And my heart lifts.

The funny thing is that I don't get dressed up, I stay in the very same jeans that Mum tried to send to Oxfam. I smear on a slick of lipstick, brush my hair to ensure I don't look too homeless, but I basically stay dressed down. Some part of me needs to keep this as simple as it possibly can be, without artifice. Lapaine is a little oasis of French chic in deepest Archway. You can forget the cars belching fumes as they career around the roundabout, ignore the sad battalion of drunks who hang round the off licence, and pretend you're in deepest Provence. I've missed this place. I kiss him hello on the cheek, feel the warmth of him, if only for a second or two.

'You look nice,' he says, smiling. He looks nervous, fidgety.

'Are you sure I don't look like him?' I say, subtly indicating

372

a tramp pulling the ring pull off a can of Thunderbird with his teeth.

'No, he's got much better teeth.'

'They do look very durable.'

'And multi-purpose.'

We look at each other for a minute.

'I'm sorry I've been dicking around with the papers.'

'Don't apologise,' I say. I really mean it, it's like a boulder's rolled off my chest. I take an involuntary gasp of air. 'I feel like I can breathe.'

'What do you mean?'

'It's been like waiting for an axe to fall.' I look at him, hoping my eyes say enough for me not to have to prostrate myself.

'But you've got Oscar now, you're a proper couple. That's what made me finally send the bastard things off, watching how kind you were to him. You're his now, not mine.' His face looks every bit as sad as Oscar's did when Lydia left, and I have to admit I'm gratified.

'I haven't ... I haven't been kind. I've told him I love him when I wasn't ready to love anyone. I was lonely and dazzled and out of control. I should've got a cat, not a boyfriend.'

'They make you sneeze,' says Dom, a smile creasing his face.

'Was that what you were trying to say at Marquess? That you hadn't sent them?'

'Yes, and you bit my head off!'

'I thought ... well, you know what I thought. Why didn't you text me?'

'I thought I'd try talking to you at Ghusto, but I saw you

with Oscar. What right did I have? I'd already fucked up your life once.'

I risk taking his hand, trace the familiar lumps and bumps and calluses. It feels like we sit like that for an eternity. Then I tell him about my trip home, and he listens intently to all of it, even my triumph at Boggle. Although the threat of penury looms large, it's such a relief not to rush, not to feel like I've got to squash every little bit of me into a tiny space between shifts.

'I don't mean to sound like some kind of dodgy TV psychic . . .'

'Don't knock Derek Acorah,' I say.

'I'd never knock Derek, but you do look like something's lifted. You look younger.'

I do feel lighter, it's true. It's like my filter on the world's changed, like I've taken off a huge pair of dark glasses and finally noticed the sun. It's no wonder all those fifties starlets kept topping themselves.

'Well, thank you!' I say, all silly and kittenish. Am I a fool? He may have felt weird about posting the papers, but he's still done it. He's still setting off for some far-flung swamp in less than a fortnight. I need to test this out.

'Why did you pull away when we kissed?' I ask.

'You pulled away!'

'No, I didn't.'

'Yes, you did. And you had a boyfriend. Well, a *man* friend.'

'Didn't you like him?'

Dom's face twists up like it might turn in on itself. 'No, but I was hardly going to, was I? And to be honest, Amber, I

374

wasn't sure what I felt then. I don't think either of us would benefit from going back to the relationship we had.' I must look stricken, because he cups my hands in his. 'Don't look at me like that.'

'Like what?'

'Like I just shot Bambi! I didn't mean that how it sounded. I meant me as well as you, not talking to you properly.'

'And the shagging of other people, let's not forget that.' I'm ashamed of myself as soon as it's out of my mouth. 'Sorry, sorry. I promise I won't let it poison everything. Oh God, have I presumed too much? And it wasn't just you, I really get that now. Tell me the truth, was I was the worst wife in human history?'

'I'm not having that,' says Dom, quick as a flash. 'What about that road-rage woman who stabbed her husband 124 times and then did a TV appeal?'

I smile at him, feel myself filling up with a joyous sort of toastiness. I love that he can be flippant and that I know he doesn't mean it flippantly: that's our Frankish.

'I want there to be an everything,' he says simply. 'I want everything. And I don't blame you for still being angry.'

'I'm not that angry any more, and I do totally get that it came from Gaia or whatever. It's more that I'm still hurt.' A sob wells up inside of me. 'I missed you so much, Dom. Sometimes, this will sound terrible, sometimes it felt like it'd have been simpler if you'd died. It would've been grief, straightforward horrible grief. And I would have got sympathy, not sympathy tinged with judgement. And I wouldn't have lost all those people as well as you.'

Dom looks away, chastened. 'Look, Amber, I behaved like

a total cunt,' he says, hands up. 'It's an ugly word, but I can't think of another one strong enough. But I will never, ever treat you like that again if you let me have the chance to not. Is that even grammar?'

I stare at him, feeling the residual hurt start to loosen. I'm not going to pretend that it will just go, that there won't be times an icy blast will hit me full in the face, but it certainly won't be the point. Dom says I look younger but a) I assume (I hope) he's trying to get his leg over, and b) I feel infinitely older. Older in a good way.

Dom suddenly scrambles out of his chair, drops to one knee. 'Will you do me the honour of un-divorcing me? I took the liberty of booking a totally radical honeymoon.'

'Oh my. That's the second most romantic proposal of my life,' I say, kissing him properly. This time it's definitely me who pulls away.

'Shit, if you sent the forms off, maybe we really are divorced? Maybe we're being divorced as we speak?'

And with a flurry of phone calls too farcical to recount, I restart my life as a wife. It's too good to resist.

Six Months Later

The taxi screeches down the M4, fearlessly weaving its way through the relentless stream of juggernauts and four-by-fours. England looks small to me now, the buildings like Monopoly pieces. This is no time for bad teenage poetry. I wonder how Marsha would feel about me offsetting my bridesmaid's dress with an eye patch, à la Long John Silver? It's a serious possibility: my mascara brush misses my eyeball by a hair's breadth, depositing a panda-like splodge of black across the left side of my face. Still, judging by the fuzzy photo she emailed me of my outfit, some form of disguise might be a blessing. Bo Bo the Chinese panda might be as good as any. I reckon I've put on enough weight from beach bar daiquiri drinking to pull it off.

'Shit, I can't believe I'm going to be late for this. She sulked for a month when I made us miss that Czechoslovakian war film at the NFT because I was bollocking the fish guy. If she can't go up the aisle because I'm not there . . .'

'She only had herself to blame,' says Dom reasonably. 'I'm surprised you turned up at all. Has no one told her *When*

Harry Met Sally makes you cry like Gwyneth at the Oscars every single time?'

'Are you implying I'm bird-brained?' I ask, feeling warm fingers wrapping their way around my heart at how well he knows me. It's still such a relief not to have to pretend or wonder. I got the most disgusting food poisoning known to man in Kerala and even that didn't repulse him. If it had been Oscar, I'd have been fixing a smile on my overly made-up face while I found five-minute excuses to go and violently hurl into my sun hat. Oscar. I do still think about him, slivers of guilt piercing my happiness at the thought of how unavailable I truly was. That said, I still believe that even if I had been primed and ready for marriage and 2.4 kids, what we had was all we were meant to have. The top layer of the cake was what he wanted and was all I had to give. I don't regret it, not for one minute, but I'm glad to be back where I belong. I'm not sure it'd feel so easy if I hadn't had my own moment of madness (exciting, consuming madness, but madness nevertheless). I slip my hand into Dom's.

'Could you call her?' I ask, wheedling. 'Or call Milly? Tell them how near we are? Neither of them have answered my texts.'

'Milly's probably having a tryst in the Slough Travelodge,' says Dom. 'She's forgotten the time entirely. Slough can really get a person in the mood,' he adds, leaning in to kiss me.

Milly's bringing a date, but she point blank refused to tell me who. It's hard to exert sufficient pressure by email, and I couldn't be running up south-east Asian phone bills on girly gossip. Besides, I didn't want to break the spell, not before I had to.

Dom's somehow managed to get through to Marsha. 'I promise you I'll deliver her with enough time to spare,' he says, voice soothing. 'No, don't worry, she won't need the make-up artist.' *The make-up artist?*

'No!' I mouth, waving my arms around like I'm drowning. I am not going down the aisle looking like Sue Barker.

'Her hair's fine,' continues Dom, 'lovely in fact,' he adds softly.

I clamp my hands over it, sun frazzled and split-ends-ridden, enjoying the sound of his voice. Like I said, so often it's not the words.

'We can't wait,' he says, 'we'll be there before you know it.' Marsha's voice has audibly dropped an octave, even from here. He hangs up, turns back to me.

'Are you sure you're done with maître d'ing?' I ask, deeply impressed by his Marsha wrangling. 'You're so good at it.'

'I'm done,' he says, resolved.

On the rare occasions we've had a decent internet connection, he's been researching journalism courses, determined to overhaul his life entirely (well, not entirely. I weave my fingers more tightly around his). And me, I'm going to try my hand at private catering. That way I can still do what I love without the blood, sweat and tears demanded by any restaurant worth its (hand-combed rock) salt. Mum and Dad are lending me some money to get me started, and we've also got a tiny amount left over from Oompa Loompa Towers. We're going to rent for now, somewhere completely new, take a step into the unknown. Turns out a bungee jump's nowhere near as scary when you've got a fellow jumpee strapped to your tummy.

*

Dom and the cab driver negotiate the map together, working out a back route through the country lanes to the nondescript hotel where Marsha's getting ready. As soon as I see her, I burst into tears, a highly risky move when her fiercesome, mannish make-up artist is standing to attention, brush held like a bayonet.

'No time for that,' says Marsha briskly, nodding to the clock. 'Obviously I'm thrilled you're home, but there'll be time for news once the vows are out of the way.' She really has missed her true vocation running the Hallmark Valentine division.

'You look . . .' Luckily I'm spared the need to finish my sentence by Hannah bustling in with my dress. Whose is worse? It's hard to call it. I have been truly punished for leaving the country at such a vital moment. I'm wearing a pale pink, shapeless, floor-length number with a white zigzag collar, reminiscent of a Snoopy nightie I begged to wear to school when I was six. Like I said, *I was six*! It's cut from some kind of slimy synthetic fabric, which is sure to hug every single daiquiri-induced love handle I've got. I sneak a look at the label. If it's flammable I might just cut my losses and turn myself into a human torch on the way to the church.

'Where's Lisa?' I ask suspiciously. If she's wriggled out of the ritual humiliation, I'm going to be murderous.

'Right here,' says Lisa, bursting in, a tiny baby clutched to her bosom. More tears, more menacing brush waving.

'He's so gorgeous!' I start, as Marsha thrusts the nylon shroud at me, temporarily unseating the strange fabric fascinator that's pinned to her bushy hair. It looks like it might be her knitting club end-of-term project. And as for the dress, what can I say, Lisa really should have made her continue the search. It's a yellowish off-white, the kind of colour Ford Fiestas came in twenty years ago, with an enormous inverted bell of a skirt. It's low cut, the mantelpiece of bosom adorned with a clunky lump of beads and silver, which she'll have bought at great expense from someone seeking asylum from a warzone. She must be wearing heels under there, as she's looming over us menacingly like an enormous crane. It's enough to make me skip the shower, running a flannel over my clammy pits and hurriedly pulling the nylon monstrosity over my head.

'Lovely!' says Marsha, beaming with sheer joy at the sight of us all. 'Come on, ladies. Wagons roll.'

As I follow Marsha up the aisle, my eyes frantically scan the church for Milly. I'm desperate to see her, and desperate to identify her mystery date. I hope he's worthy, I really do. Despite the lack of phone calls, I've missed her like crazy, only aware once we were parted of quite how much I leaned on her while Dom was absent without leave. If it hadn't been for the gentle intimacy I got from my time with her, I think I would've noticed far quicker how lacking it was from my relationship with Oscar. I feel a stab of shame at how wrapped up I was in my own grief (and then in my grief exterminating rebound). I hope I gave her something back, was more than a weepy, wine-guzzling energy vampire.

As we come to a stop in front of the vicar, all my questions are answered. There's Milly barrelling through the heavy oak doors, high heels beating out a tattoo on the mosaic floor. I can see how flustered she is, and it's not just down to her tardy timekeeping. Now I know why she was so uncharacteristically discreet: who should be sloping in after her, cool as a cucumber, but Oscar. I didn't see that one coming. I force myself to smile, though I'm not sure if she detects it, and rely on the vows to give me time to get my bearings.

So it turns out I'm far too unsaintly to make a worthy bridesmaid. I wish I could say I'm bubbling over with joy at the idea of Milly's new-found romantic happiness, but instead I'm mostly miffed. I know that our love didn't have time to get much deeper than a toddler's paddling pool, but I'm still annoyed that the proof is being flashed in my face as brashly as the neon lights of Las Vegas. And if Milly and I are that interchangeable, who's to say the next foxy supplier or minxy sommelier who passes in front of his carnivorous chops won't do just fine, thank you? I try my very best not to feel upset with her, to tell myself that once I'd walked away he became fair game, but it's hard not to feel she's somehow defied an unspoken rule of female friendship. As Marsha's booming vows reverberate around the church, I sneak a look at my own husband. His eyes are already on me, his smile telling me everything I need to know. Expecting perfection was partly what got me into this mess. Milly was lonely, she sought comfort – who am I to cast judgment from the safety of my feather bed?

She sheepishly approaches as the photographer herds us together for photos.

'Oh, sorry,' she says, awkwardly backing away. 'I'll come back.'

And I could revel in moral supremacy, play the ice queen before I graciously defrost some hours later, but I can't be bothered.

'Don't go,' I say, hugging her. 'It's weird, but it's fine.' I pull back, look at her. 'At least I hope it's fine.'

'If it's fine with you, then it's terribly fine,' says Milly, a sappy smile invading her face.

'So you're happy?'

'Well, it's hard to give in entirely because I've been tied up in knots about how you'd react.' She searches my expression and I force myself to stifle any residual annoyance. 'But yes, he's made me feel rather blissful.'

I think back to every complaint I ever uttered about him. Did I say anything fatally damaging? Lay any landmines that will ultimately erupt and blow her joy to smithereens? I can see Oscar now, puffing on a fag, disrespectfully close to a grave. Even the smoking would've ultimately driven me insane. I'd feel like shoving his handsome face right up to the headstone and giving him a lecture about lung cancer.

'That's great,' I say. 'But, I mean, how is it? You said in your email you're working in the restaurant full-time. Sounds pretty 24/7.' Oh my God, I can hardly criticise her for that! This is so odd, it's like she's slipped straight into my shoes: got to keep remembering I don't want the shoes, I put the damn shoes on eBay with no reserve price.

'It's utterly hectic. I've got a sort of general manager post, overseeing both sides of the house, and I'm on a major cost-cutting drive. I want to be turning a decent profit by the end of the year.' There's a steeliness in her tone, a focus that she was only starting to find when I left.

'But how about everything else? How's Tallulah taken it? Are he and Lydia still at each other's throats?'

'He hasn't actually . . .' Milly peters out.

'He hasn't *told* them? Jeez, you must be dreading it.'

Her face says yes, but she adopts a breezy insouciance. 'It just hasn't been the right time. Now it's Tallulah's AS-level year, I think he just wants to keep things on an even keel.'

She's so much better for him than I was, the way she loyally parrots back his explanations. I can imagine her effortlessly pouring oil over troubled waters, as soft and yielding as molasses. Given time, I would've been nothing but a thorn in his side.

'And is she behaving herself? Does he see much of her?'

'Oh, well, she comes in for lunch. He always makes sure they get table twelve.'

I wonder whether the tick tock of foreboding will start up for Milly in tandem with the pesky old biological tick tocking. Maybe I'm being too doomy. Unlike Lydia, she'll be a fabulous mum and maybe that'll compensate for Oscar's failings. After all, not everyone can have a dad as fab as mine.

Marsha's going into full sergeant major mode by now. 'Bridal party, I need you to gather,' she shouts. 'Amber, I'm afraid the chit-chat will have to wait.'

Milly rolls her eyes. 'She's furious with me.'

'Oh, I'm sure she's not,' I reassure her.

'It was just that Oscar's got a new sommelier, and he brought up completely the wrong wine for some guy from the *Observer*. I mean, he had to be told and he just got a bit carried away. He's still smarting about not getting a star, and I think it was a bit of a red rag to a bull.'

Let's face it, most things are. With Oscar, a white flag could be a red rag.

'I was really disappointed for you,' I say. It's not an idle

384

platitude, I Googled on the day and felt genuinely gutted. It's not like I stopped caring when I walked away, stopped wanting to be part of greatness, it's more that I had to accept that I couldn't have it all. I look across at Dom, allow the sight of him to soothe the pang of leaving behind the cut and thrust of it all. My eyes move onwards to Oscar, still resolutely looking into the horizon. I wonder what he's thinking.

I know what he'll be thinking at lunch: the chicken is as rubbery as a mongrel's chew toy; the wine is so bad it can only be ingested in mouse-sized sips.

'There's a pay bar isn't there?' whispers Dom. 'Shall we cut straight to gin and tonics?'

I nod surreptitiously, but as he starts to rise, Marsha's dad taps his glass. He slumps back, defeated, and I lean into him. Father of the bride speeches always make me blub, even this one – a staccato list of Marsha's achievements from birth to thirty.

'I didn't know she played hockey at county level,' whispers Dom.

'She did. And we haven't even got to her archaeology bursary.'

'I'm so excited I might be sick.'

The first dance is a smooch to 'Just the Way You Are'. From here, it looks like Marsha's leading, but that might come down to the way she's towering over Peter like a leaning skyscraper of taffeta. I force myself to stop with the mockery – gentle or not, it's inappropriate – and make myself focus on the sentiment, the way they're gazing at each other. It's very sweet to watch, very special to be a part of. The words are utterly true for them, and I hope they're finally true for me too. I could fill two sheets of A4 with mine and Dom's frailties and failings, but I hope that we can be kind enough to forgive each other for them, to air our feelings and know that they will be heard in the right spirit. Saddle up, Dalai Lama, there's a new spiritual guru in town. Orange is so my colour.

Dom and I have a tentative dance to 'Celebration' by Kool & the Gang (will wedding DJs still be doggedly spinning their *Super Hits of the 70s* album even when the icecaps are puddles and we're all living on an alternative planet?) but soon the pair of gin and tonics I've drunk start to weigh heavy my bladder, and I excuse myself for a loo break. I sit there a minute longer than necessary, jet lag kicking in, listening to the bass line of 'Don't Stop Me Now' pounding through the floor. Eventually I gather myself up, venture into the corridor, just in time to run slap bang into Oscar. Neither of us speak, then both of us speak across each other.

'If it isn't Fish Girl, back from her travels.'

'Oscar! How ... how are you?'

I feel oddly panicked, even though he has no power over me any more. I suppose I always felt he was in charge, right to the last, and the feeling still lingers. Both of us retreat back into silence, his gaze direct. Is that hurt I can see in his eyes or am I flattering myself?

'So, you and Milly—'

'She's a great girl.' There's a note of challenge in his voice, an underlying aggression.

'I know she is, she's my best friend.' I pause, then pull a cliché out of my tired old bag. 'I hope you'll be very happy together.'

'I'll be nice,' he says, a smile curling up like a smoke ring. 'I was nice,' he adds more quietly.

'You were,' I say, but before I have time to add anything else, he's moved on.

'And if you ever send me a begging letter, I might just find you something,' he says. 'After all, there are only so many onions Tomasz can peel on his own.'

He gives me that smile he always gave me, and I can't help smiling back, my insides giving a tiny shudder that won't quite die. After all, it's not like he's suddenly metamorphosed into Quasimodo. No, he's definitely still sexy, and I know he gave me something Dom doesn't, an old-fashioned macho charm that was fun to wrap around myself for a brief moment. Thank God I had the foresight to realise it wouldn't have kept me warm for ever.

The truth is, every relationship, however fabulous, is a compromise. When we commit, we're always saying goodbye to some perfect piece we'd promised ourselves Prince Charming would deliver when he finally turned up and kissed us back to life. Much as it pains me to admit it, Rachel must have given Dom something I didn't (and no, I don't mean herpes). But maybe it's the compromise, the acceptance of its imperfection, that ultimately makes it feel perfect. For one thing, it finally releases us from that fatal, soul destroying feminine curse of expecting perfection from ourselves. Talking of which, I really must get my legs waxed. Right now, I could give King Kong a run for his money.

'How very kind,' I tell Oscar. We look at each other and I can't help but feel a tiny bit sentimental. We did have our moment, however brief. 'We should get back out there,' I say.

'We should,' he agrees.

He strides ahead, pushing the door wide open for me. And as I step through it, back into the buzz and hustle of the moment, I know there's no earthly reason to look back.

Have Amber and Oscar
got your taste-buds
tingling?

Why not try out these
recipes, inspired by
Breakfast in Bed, from
the Kitchen Queen.

www.kitchenqueen.co.uk
Cooking lessons
in your home

Kitchen Queen

Roasted and Stuffed Butternut Squash with Spinach and Goat's Cheese

Serves 2 (or 1 very hungry person!)

Ingredients

 1 small-medium butternut squash, cut in half lengthways, seeds scooped out
   with a spoon
 4 tablespoons olive oil
 1 handful pine nuts
 1 handful pumpkin seeds
 6 spring onions, finely sliced
 1 small or ½ large red chilli, de-seeded and chopped finely
 2 large cloves garlic, crushed
 2 really big handfuls, or about 100g, fresh baby leaf spinach
 Juice of ½ lemon
 Freshly ground black pepper
 Salt
 100g Chevre Blanc goat's cheese, broken or cut into roughly 1cm cubes

Method

Preheat your oven to 190°C/fan180°C/Gas 5/350°F.

Lay the butternut squash on a baking tray and drizzle with two tablespoons of olive oil. Season with salt and pepper and then roast for 45 minutes to 1 hour, until you can easily cut the flesh with a knife. Remove from the oven and cool a little.

Using a spoon, scoop the flesh from the butternut squash, keeping the skin intact so that you can use this as a shell to stuff. Chop the flesh of the squash into 2cm cubes (it may well be quite soft, so don't worry if you can't cut neat cubes!).

In a large frying pan or wok, dry-fry the pine nuts and the pumpkin seeds until they begin to brown slightly, then remove from the pan and set aside.

Add 2 tablespoons of olive oil into the same pan and gently stir-fry the spring onions, chilli and garlic for a minute to just soften them and then add the pine nuts, pumpkin seeds, butternut squash and spinach to the pan. Squeeze over the lemon juice and season well with salt and pepper. Fold the contents of the pan until the spinach has just wilted and then taste, adding a little extra lemon, salt or pepper if required.

Fill the butternut squash skins with the squash and spinach mixture and place the stuffed squashes back onto a baking tray. Arrange pieces of goat's cheese over the top of each squash half, poking them into the filling slightly using your fingertips.

Pop the tray back into the oven for 15 minutes, or until the goat's cheese has browned a little. Serve with a wedge of lemon on the side and some salad. Enjoy!

Seared Scallops with Chilli, Lime and Coriander with an Avocado Puree and Coriander Yoghurt

Serves 2

Ingredients

For the scallops:

6-10 king scallops, *with or without roe*

Salt and freshly ground pepper

2 tablespoons olive oil

1 heaped teaspoon butter

2 spring onions, finely sliced

½ red chilli, de-seeded and finely diced *(use more or less chilli, to taste)*

1 large or 2 small cloves garlic, crushed

1 large ripe tomato, de-seeded and finely diced into ½ cm pieces

Zest and juice of 1 lime *(use a zester if possible, to obtain nice long, thin pieces of zest)*

1 heaped tablespoon fresh coriander, finely chopped

For the avocado puree:

1 small, ripe avocado, stoned and peeled

½ small red chilli, de-seeded and diced finely

1 small or ½ large clove garlic, crushed

1 heaped teaspoon fresh coriander, finely chopped

Juice of ½ lime

Pinch of salt and pepper, or to taste

For the coriander yoghurt:

2 tablespoons natural yoghurt

1 heaped teaspoon fresh coriander, finely chopped

Pinch of salt and pepper

Plus: *Bottle of balsamic glaze, to serve (optional)*

Method

For the avocado puree simply place all the ingredients into a blender or mini chopper and whizz until smooth. Taste and add further salt, pepper or lime juice to taste (or even a little extra chilli or garlic if you fancy an extra kick!).

For the coriander yoghurt, combine the ingredients together in a small bowl and leave to infuse for 10 minutes or longer before tasting and adjusting the seasoning if required.

Now you're ready to cook! Get 2 plates at the ready and your balsamic glaze if you have some, as these next steps will all happen quite quickly.

Place the scallops onto a plate and season on both sides with salt and black pepper.

Heat a non-stick frying pan and add 2 tablespoons of olive oil. When really hot, add the scallops to the pan and sear for about 1 minute, until browned (be careful as the scallops may spit and splutter).

Turn the scallops over and allow to cook for another minute before adding the butter to the middle of the pan.

Immediately scatter over the spring onions, chilli, garlic, diced tomato, lime zest and coriander. Squeeze over the juice of ½ the lime (or a whole lime if it isn't very juicy) and shake the pan so that all of the ingredients combine and flavour the butter and oil.

Cook for no longer than a minute, to ensure that your scallops do not over-cook, then immediately take the pan off the heat and serve, removing the scallops from the pan first of all to halt them cooking any further.

To serve: Squirt a little balsamic glaze around each plate and then, using a teaspoon, add 3 dollops of the avocado puree around the plate at even intervals. Using the tip of a teaspoon, create a crater in the top of each dollop and fill this with a little of the coriander yoghurt. Arrange the scallops in the centre of each plate, spooning over the remaining contents of the pan. Serve immediately with fresh bread to mop – Enjoy!

Mediterranean Beef Stew with Rosemary, Olives and Capers

Serves 6

Ingredients

> 1kg braising steak, cut into large 5cm x 5cm pieces (allow 2 pieces per person)
>
> 3 tablespoons plain flour
>
> ½ teaspoon salt
>
> ½ teaspoon freshly ground black pepper
>
> 3 tablespoons olive oil
>
> 3 medium onions, quartered
>
> 6 cloves garlic, crushed
>
> 6-8 sprigs fresh rosemary
>
> 3 bay leaves
>
> 1 teaspoon fennel seeds
>
> 400ml red wine
>
> 2 tins chopped tomatoes
>
> 150g pitted kalamata olives (or your favourite black olives)
>
> 2 handfuls or about 50g capers, rinsed well in water and drained
>
> 1 dessertspoon sugar, to taste

Method

Preheat your oven to 140°C/Gas 1/275°F.

Place the plain flour in a bowl and add the salt and pepper. Toss the cubes of beef in the flour, dusting off any excess. Set aside on a plate.

Heat the olive oil in a large flameproof casserole dish. In batches if necessary, fry the pieces of beef on all sides until browned, but not cooked through (just enough to seal the meat). Remove from the pan and set aside.

Add a little more olive oil to the same pan if necessary and add in the quartered onions. Stir-fry until the onions begin to soften and then add in the garlic, whole sprigs of rosemary, bay leaves and the fennel seeds. Continue to fry for a few more minutes.

Now add the beef back into the pan and then pour in the wine and chopped tomatoes. Also add in the olives, capers and sugar. Stir well and bring to a gentle simmer.

Once simmering, pop a lid on the casserole and transfer to the oven to slowly cook for 2 ½ hours, or until the meat is so tender it almost falls apart when prodded with a knife.

Remove the stew from the oven and taste, adding a little more salt, pepper or sugar to taste (add sugar if the stew has a slight coppery taste).

Serve the stew with cous cous or grilled polenta and fresh vegetables. Enjoy!

Acknowledgements

First and foremost I'd like to thank my beloved cousin Caitlin Plunkett for selflessly devoting Christmas to reading my manuscript and pointing out all the glaring errors! And researching what a Polish commis chef would be called in the real world.

Huge thanks are due to my wonderful agent, Sheila Crowley at Curtis Brown whose enthusiasm and energy made all the difference. I'd also like to thank Sarah Lewis for her exemplary support.

My next huge thank you is to Jo Dickinson for bringing me to Little, Brown and making it such a happy move: I couldn't have written this book without you. Thanks also to the rest of the team for their warm welcome.

For Soph, as always. The dustbin lives on eternal. Anne, too, for being both a brick and a thoroughly good egg.

For Kay, for being Kay and also for letting me borrow Frankish, a language pioneered by Frank Thorpe-Curram. I'm sure it's going to catch on.

Thanks are also due to Damian Barr for all the support, encouragement and general high jinks. And also for Cousin Mike.

I'd also like to thank Polly and Shaun and Barclay (my favourite dog in the world) for letting me write so much of this at Tilton House (www.tiltonhouse.co.uk). I can think of nowhere lovelier to hang out and try to feel the muse!

And Charisse and Kitty and Diana for all their kindness and brilliance.

Thanks also to Nicola Larder for another round of fabulous plot suggestions and input. I promised you would still fancy Oscar – I hope you do!

Thanks also to Sian Wyn Owen, head chef at The River Café, for giving me such great stories and suggestions. I'd also like to thank the rest of the team, particularly Joanna, for taking time out of their hectic kitchen lives to talk to me. And Siobhan Belton, the first chef I spoke to, who left me open-mouthed at how tough it really was.

And lastly I'd like to remember my uncle and godfather, Brendan Moran (1944-2010). You are very missed.

Coming in August 2012

THE REBECCA EFFECT*

Eleanor Moran

Have you ever felt like you were living someone else's life?
The stupid thing is how much I felt that way, even then.

Olivia Carter is convinced she's the last thirty-something single
woman left on the planet. But when she gets a phone call out of the
blue to tell her that her best friend from university has been killed
in a car crash in New York, her life is turned upside down
in ways she could never have predicted.

The girls had a devastating falling out, and Olivia's spent the
intervening decade running away from the reasons why. Now she
can no longer escape the past, not with Sally's widower William
so desperate for her to help him understand the truth about the
charismatic, unpredictable woman he's lost. And as she struggles
to extinguish her growing feelings for him, Olivia must also
try to unravel the mystery behind Sally's untimely death.

978-0-7515-4554-8

Read on for a short extract from **The Rebecca Effect.**

*working title

Chapter 1

Have you ever felt like you were living someone else's life? The stupid thing is how much I felt that way, even then.

I don't want to malign Tuesdays, but they really are the most deathly dull day of the week – comparing Tuesday to Friday is like comparing Slough with Buenos Aires if you ask me. I'm trying to liven up this particular one by cooking a lethally spicy Thai green curry for me and James. I've got Melancholic FM on full blast and I'm wailing along to The Carpenters like I'm on a charity edition of *The X Factor* for the musically 'special', so accomplished is my Karen-tastic falsetto that I don't even hear his key in the lock.

'Step away from the radio,' he says, turning the volume off.

I look over at it plaintively, but he's standing guard like an Alsatian. Well, sort of – if an Alsatian was topping six foot, with paws as big as dinner plates and the kind of blondy-ginger fur that cannot be tamed by any kind of styling product. I hope I'm not making James sound unattractive. He is emphatically not unattractive.

'Seriously, Livvy, I'm saving you from yourself,' he says, retuning the dial to Radio 4. 'Smooth Eight at Eight, is it?' I nod sheepishly. 'Why do they call it that? It's not like they were playing hard core house right up until 7.59, is it?'

He dives for the fridge, warbling 'My Heart Will Go On' like we're about to run slap-bang into an iceberg. Someone's dreary-sounding man is droning on about 'economic indicators' now, but before I have time to state my case, James is thrusting a glass of white into my hand. 'Cheers,' he says, peering into the pan. 'Ernie, you've surpassed yourself.'

We're *Burt* and Ernie, not Eric and Ernie, just to be clear. It's our stupid nickname for our eccentric living situation: much like Burt and Ernie from *Sesame Street*, we're best friends who share a home. They had a dustbin, we have a garden-flat in Kennington that can look worryingly similar to a dustbin when we've had a few too many late nights on the trot. Not that I have so many excuses for late nights these days – I'm thirty-four, and it's quite possible that, as a breed, I'm nearing extinction. The mid-thirties, single woman seems to be in sharp decline: I suspect we might be going the same way as the woolly mammoth. Perhaps I can get David Attenborough to sign up to the series. I can see it now: *'Observe the lesser-spotted singleton casting glancing looks at her prey while he, oblivious, ingests beer from his pint glass and surreptitiously scratches his distended gonads. Drinking dens such as this one are common sites for this kind of mating ritual, which has a worryingly low success rate. Please consider a monthly donation to the World Singleton Fund – every penny you donate goes straight to single women in chronic need.'*

Pretty much all of my friends from school and university are married or as good as, as are most of my colleagues – not all of them happily, far from it, but no one's in any hurry to roll the dice again, at least not yet. Statistically there's got to be a few divorces rolling down the track, but at the moment I feel a bit like I'm in a romantic-limbo land, stranded between the second-time-rounders and the wide-eyed innocents. It's not that I wish divorce on anyone, or that I'd ever pursue anyone else's husband, but it does feel quite lonely out here on the tundra.

'Shall I serve up?' says James.

'It could do with another ten minutes or so.'

'Come on, it's fine. It's not even fine, it's delicious,' he says, already heaping it onto our plates.

The thing about James is that he's a force of nature, and so there's very little point in arguing with him. And let's get one thing straight, this isn't one of those ridiculous books where I suddenly turn round in Chapter Ten and realise in a blinding flash that I'm madly in love with him and skip off into the sunset with a crown of daisies perched atop my curly locks. I've *always* been a little bit in love with James, in fact a lot in love with him for the first few years. He made his initial appearance in my A level Politics class, his timing impeccable. My parents were in the midst of their gruesome separation, and I was ripe for distraction. He'd been away at boarding school, but joined our sixth form when he came home, offering a mighty contrast to all those nose-picking Neanderthals I'd been learning alongside since we were eleven. I contrived some terrible conversational opener like asking to borrow his Tippex, and soon we started hanging out. It was that age and stage where boys and girls first peek over the barricades and try out being 'friends'. It's a funny old version of friendship, one where you can kiss at a party and think nothing of it the next day. I say that: James and I had a couple of those impromptu snogfests, and I did nothing but think about them for months, literally nothing except doodle his name with garish hearts round it and look longingly at him from under my mascara-sodden eyelashes, while he climbed merrily back onto the tonsil-tennis merry-go-round and continued to treat me like his long-lost sister. There was one more time, but now – now's not the moment to think about that.

I look at him shovelling the curry into his mouth like he's rescuing a very, very small casualty who's trapped under the rice.

'Livvy, this is gorgeous,' he says, looking up. 'Hot, though. I've drunk loads of the wine. Shall I go and get another bottle?'

It's seriously tempting.

'No, I've—'

'Shit, you've got a date, haven't you?! Get out the enigma machine so I can have a butchers.'

James is all about whizzy Apple gadgets that can simultaneously take your temperature, play your favourite song and mix you the perfect gin Martini, whereas I'm a bit of a technology refusnik. My computer is a bit monolithic and ancient, but frankly I'd rather spend my money going to Paris or bidding on first editions of Daphne Du Maurier novels on eBay. There's a distinct possibility I was born in the wrong century.

'Just wait a sec, I've barely started.'

I'm also deeply reluctant to engage with the idea of leaving the squidgy embrace of the sofa and venturing into the night to meet a shadowy stranger. The fact that I arranged it for a Tuesday says it all. I've been internet dating for six months and so far it's felt like being trapped in some kind of endless *Alice in Wonderland* job interview, where I don't know what the rules are or even what the job is. I'm not giving up though. I want it to work, I really do, it's most definitely time I met a male human to claim as my very own. Note to self: must be more positive. Addendum: you only get out what you put in.

James drops his fork on his empty plate with a clatter and emits a discreet burp. I wrinkle my nose at him.

'It was a goose!' he says. 'Go on, you tuck in and I'll go and get it. As long as my arms don't get wrenched out of their sockets.'

The thing is, in some ways James isn't much different from his compulsive and infuriating teenage incarnation. Sure, he's got a grown-up job – a senior role in an aid charity where he berates big governments for their indifference to the plight of the world's poor – but he's still skittish and hard to pin down when it comes to women. He's not exactly a bastard but he's not exactly *not* either. Take last month's victim (Anita? Angela? Something beginning with A anyway). I met her shaking the last of my granola into a bowl. When I futilely rattled the empty box she fashioned her mouth into a theatrical 'oh!' and promised to replace it. She was as good as her word, leaving a replacement on my bed the very next day with a sweet, flowery post-card saying how much she was looking forward to getting to know me better. No time: before I'd got so much as halfway through it, James had finished with her, spooked by the seven individually wrapped presents she'd lovingly bestowed for Valentine's day.

'How did she take it?' I asked, knowing from even those brief fragments of contact how gutted she'd be.

'It was like shooting a fawn,' he said, shoving his squash racket into a backpack, and I thanked my lucky stars for how it's played out between us.

It's not like I'm one of those weird masochists who marries serial killers and gaily drowns out the sound of their victim's screams with the Hoover: James as a friend is a million miles away from James as a boyfriend. He truly is my best friend, the only person I'm as close to is my sister Julia. Maybe it suits me that way. When it comes to girlfriends, I've had my fingers not so much burned as torched right off. Don't get me wrong, I'm not some kind of solitary *Rainman*-style autist. I've got a whole brace of girls on speed-dial, but I know that they only see as much of me as I'm prepared to reveal.

As for James, in contrast to the treatment he metes out to the temporary fixtures, he's never anything but unstintingly loyal and generous to me. When I got some kind of revolting gastric flu last winter, he told work it was him who was ill so he could stay home and tend to me and if a man treats me like anything less than a be-yoot-iful princess he's utterly outraged on my behalf. There's never a shred of comprehension that their behaviour is no worse than his own *modus operandi* ('but, Ernie, she was a dullard. She had the boxset of *Cranford*. And she called it a "boxed set!"').

We've been living together for a couple of years now, ever since I broke up with Marco, a man I'd moved in with far too speedily (merge kitchenware in haste, repent at leisure. With no bottle opener.). I did love him, but when I look back on it, there was certainly a degree of panic about the prospect of being left on the tundra playing out for me. Maybe I loved him but I wasn't in love with him – sometimes I find it so hard to take my own emotional temperature. We were fine when we dated, but living together threw up all the myriad ways in which we were incompatible. After six months of piffling arguments about whether the pepper pot should live on the table or in the condiment cupboard (let me be clear, he was the one who insisted on a condiment cupboard) it became apparent that if we got to the stage where the arguments were about things that actually mattered, we wouldn't survive. I felt bad, worried I'd forced the pace because Julia was getting married and I'd felt like a love dunce tortoise. I offered to move out (it was his flat and his condiment cupboard) and he agreed a little more readily than I would've liked. As I wept fat, salty tears on James's shoulder he came up with the brilliant idea of the dustbin, keen to escape the skanky, porn-ridden boy house he was occupying, and before I knew it he'd found us this place. I'm not sure how thrilled Marco was by it, but it was too late by then, and I was beyond grateful to be spared a one-bedroom rabbit hutch, with just me playing 'All by Myself' on loop and working out how many cocktails you can create with one bottle of Dubonnet. So here we are.

James drops the machine down on the table with an earth shattering crash.

'Be gentle,' I say, giving it a reassuring pat. He rolls his eyes and I reluctantly flip it open (I have to admit it creaks). I log on, turning the screen round so we can both see it. Member P459E, or Matthew as he prefers to be known, is 171 centimetres high, with brown hair (which could mean anything – the real point is how much), brown eyes (think we can safely assume two. I've been on multiple dates and none of them were actual Cyclops, though with a couple of them it would've radically improved our conversational options) and a GSOH (good sense of humour rather than gruesome short oily heterosexual). James is scanning his profile like a code breaker, eyes narrowed.

'Not much to go on, is there?'

'I think he sounds like he might be quite sweet,' I say. I look at it again, eyes alighting on body type. 'Although . . . well built.' I've been doing this long enough to know it's interweb code for 'gigantic fatty'.

'Dunno, he might really be well built,' says James. 'Look at his cheeks; they're not like full-on hamster with a face full of seeds. But what about the bit where he says he wants to find the right girl to have a family with?'

'What's wrong with that?'

'It's a bit needy, isn't it?'

'No, it isn't,' I say, aware I'm sounding defensive. Sometimes it seems so unfair that James doesn't have to submit himself to this indignity. Women just seem to appear in his life like fruit flies round a mango, while I meet decent single men about as frequently as I land on the moon, and I'm the one who's got to get a move on. Biology's a bitch. 'It's honest,' I continue. 'And I want someone honest, it's a page one requirement. If I wanted to date Hugh Hefner, I'd have a boob job and move to Malibu.'

'If you say so,' says James, hands up in surrender. 'Obviously I hope he's lovely. Besides, I can't see you and Hugh working out.'

'I'm too old for him for a start.'

'His balls must be like raisins.'

'Eurgh,' I say, snapping the lid down. 'I've really got to go. I promised I'd stop in on Jules on the way. She rang me when I was in a brainstorm meeting in a right old paddy.'

'What's up?'

'She said she couldn't tell me, she'd have to show me.'

'Weird,' says James. 'Maybe she's got a gross rash somewhere unmentionable.'

'On that charming note . . .' I say, grabbing my make-up bag and hoping my nice-ish cords are date-worthy.

*

My All-Time Favourite Love Stories
(some of which are slightly unromantic – sorry about that)

Rebecca by Daphne Du Maurier
I read this when I was fourteen and *loved* it (like hundreds of other hormonal, lovesick fourteen-year-olds before me). I was asked to speak about it last year, only to discover that Maxim de Winter is a million miles from the romantic, tragic hero I'd thought he was back then. He's furiously camp (see the scene where he files his nails and eats a tangerine while proposing) and also just plain furious, murdering his first wife to protect his house. No one seems to mind: it is Manderley after all. For all its flaws, I still adore it.

Sense and Sensibility by Jane Austen
My fave Jane Austen. The impoverished Dashwood sisters have wildly divergent philosophies on love; Marianne's a born romantic while Elinor's all about keeping her heart in check. Both of them have got a lot to learn . . .

Heartburn by Nora Ephron
Romantic might be the wrong word for this book, as it's a thinly veiled fictionalisation of Ephron's discovery that her husband was having an affair while she was heavily pregnant. She pulls off the incredible feat of staying funny while conveying the agony, all delivered in her uniquely acerbic style. You'll come away thinking she's your best friend and longing to go to New York. The woman's a genius (see also *When Harry Met Sally* for further evidence of said genius).

Wuthering Heights by Emily Brontë
Lots of the great romances have heroes who are total arses, and this one's no exception. Heathcliff's a world of trouble and Cathy's not

much better, but you'd have to have a heart of stone not to be transported by their torturous romance. No wonder Kate Bush thought it was ballad-worthy.

The Wonder Spot by Melissa Bank
I love Melissa Bank. This is a bit of an anti-romance too, in that it's as much about how often love turns us into self-deluding idiots as it is about its moments of unadulterated joy, but you can't fail to root for its loveable heroine Sophie and long for her to find someone as funny and endearing as she is.

The Time Traveler's Wife by Audrey Niffenegger
As romantic obstacles go, your boyfriend being trapped outside the space/time continuum has to rank pretty highly. This one's a total tear jerker but it's worth every sodden Kleenex.

Gone with the Wind by Margaret Mitchell
Love against the backdrop of the American Civil War. Scarlett O'Hara is every bit as infuriating as Heathcliff but it doesn't stop you willing her and Rhett Butler to stop fighting and abandon themselves to their grand passion. One of the most vivid, atmospheric books I can think of (though not madly politically correct, it has to be said).

After You'd Gone by Maggie O'Farrell
I love the immediacy of O'Farrell's writing, and the mystery that sits alongside the love story makes for a real page turner.

The Go-Between by L. P. Hartley
Forbidden love: an affair between an Edwardian lady and a tenant farmer, told from the point of view of the impressionable young boy they entrust with their *billets-doux*. Wildly transporting and atmospheric.